JAN'S PAPERBACKS
18095 SW TV HIGHWAY
ALOHA, OR 97006
503-649-3444

There is no other—
SHANNON DRAKE

"SHANNON DRAKE NEVER DISAPPOINTS
HER READERS . . . SHE DELIVERS HIGH
QUALITY HISTORICAL ROMANCE WITH
THREE-DIMENSIONAL CHARACTERS AND
A SIZZLING LOVE STORY THAT
TOUCHES THE HEART."
Romantic Times

"EXCELLENT!"
Rendezvous

"A WRITER OF INCREDIBLE TALENT"
Affaire de Coeur

"SHANNON DRAKE CONTINUES TO
PRODUCE ADDICTING ROMANCES."
Publishers Weekly

Other Avon Books by
Shannon Drake

BRANDED HEARTS
BRIDE OF THE WIND
DAMSEL IN DISTRESS
KNIGHT OF FIRE
NO OTHER MAN
NO OTHER WOMAN

Avon Books are available at special quantity discounts for bulk purchases for sales promotions, premiums, fund raising or educational use. Special books, or book excerpts, can also be created to fit specific needs.

For details write or telephone the office of the Director of Special Markets, Avon Books, Dept. FP, 1350 Avenue of the Americas, New York, New York 10019, 1-800-238-0658.

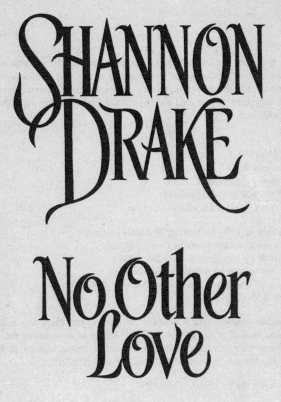

SHANNON DRAKE

No Other Love

AVON BOOKS ◆ NEW YORK

This is a work of fiction. Names, characters, places, and incidents either are the product of the author's imagination or are used fictitiously. Any resemblance to actual events, locales, organizations, or persons, living or dead, is entirely coincidental and beyond the intent of either the author or the publisher.

AVON BOOKS
A division of
The Hearst Corporation
1350 Avenue of the Americas
New York, New York 10019

Copyright © 1997 by Heather Graham Pozzessere
Inside cover author photo by Lewis Feldman
Published by arrangement with the author
Visit our website at **http://AvonBooks.com**
Library of Congress Catalog Card Number: 96-95491
ISBN: 0-380-78137-9

All rights reserved, which includes the right to reproduce this book or portions thereof in any form whatsoever except as provided by the U.S. Copyright Law. For information address Acton, Leone, Hanson, & Jaffe, Inc., 331 West 57th Street, New York, New York 10019.

First Avon Books Printing: July 1997

AVON TRADEMARK REG. U.S. PAT. OFF. AND IN OTHER COUNTRIES, MARCA REGISTRADA, HECHO EN U.S.A.

Printed in the U.S.A.

WCD 10 9 8 7 6 5 4 3 2 1

If you purchased this book without a cover, you should be aware that this book is stolen property. It was reported as "unsold and destroyed" to the publisher, and neither the author nor the publisher has received any payment for this "stripped book."

No Other Love

The Valley of the Little Bighorn
June 1876

*H*e came riding out of the golden haze of the late afternoon, a horseman silhouetted against the blinding brightness of the setting sun. He rode tall, one with the horse, and it seemed that he rode out from the center of the sun itself, defying the death of the day, and the death that lay on the field before him. For as night came, the fiery orb of the sun sank ever deeper into the horizon, and the rays streaking outward from it bathed the earth and sky in bloodred crimson.

Sabrina heard the deafening pop of bullets, the whistling of arrows, and still she stood transfixed.

Was he one of the enemy, immune to rifle fire, arrows, death itself?

Would he be the one to take her scalp as a trophy for his lance?

"Down!" shouted Sergeant Lally. "Mrs. Trelawny, down!"

Danger was far closer than she had realized, for another group of the Indians, four or five warriors, came riding close before them, their horses' hooves kicking up dust and dirt as they reined in.

An arrow sailed over Sabrina's head, landing in the tree

1

just behind her. She sucked in her breath, falling to the ground and lying flat against the earth.

Praying.

"Sergeant Lally! What's happening?" she cried.

Sergeant Lally did not reply. Sabrina carefully raised herself, then stood, looking over the small, rolling hill of earth and rock where Sergeant Lally had brought her to safety when the fur traders with whom she had ridden had become embroiled in a skirmish with Indians.

Sergeant Lally, her retired army escort, lay facedown, an arrow protruding from his back. Sabrina stared at him, fighting the scream of panic that rose in her throat. She rushed to him, falling to her knees by his side, gently lifting his face. She cried out, for his unseeing hazel eyes stared heavenward in death. She closed his eyes, yet even as she held the gentle man who had been her friend, an eerie feeling swept up her spine, and she knew she was being watched.

She looked up from the fallen man. A Sioux warrior, his naked chest decorated with vivid blue and white war paint, sat bareback atop an Appaloosa horse, staring at her. She thought at first that he must be the rider who had seemed to emerge from the flames of the setting sun, but beyond him, that rider was still coming. This brave had led the attack against her and her party. He was surrounded by three friends on horseback, but it seemed that he had been the leader of the battle. And the spoils of victory were to be his.

Sabrina returned his stare. She tried not to think about the traders who had been her escort—friends at one time with the Sioux!—who were lying dead now.

The Indian lifted his bow in his left hand and let out a high, chilling cry of victory, then threw his leg over his horse's haunches to jump to the earth with a barely audible thump of his feet upon the soft ground of the plain.

He stood very still, smiling as he surveyed Sabrina. He raised his bow into the air again, shaking it, letting out his terrible war cry. She felt his eyes, ink-dark, ripping into her with deadly menace.

She could not, *would not*, tremble before him, she determined.

She couldn't die. There was death all around her, she realized, but she couldn't die. Not now, when life had become so very precious.

Once upon a not-too-distant time, she'd had everything. But she hadn't known it, and she had lost what she'd had.

She had lost the baby that had brought them together, and she had lost Sloan, and perhaps her own soul.

Now she had the chance to get it all back.

She couldn't die. Not now.

Life. Always so very ironic.

She had never imagined that she might die out here. She'd found herself in dangerous predicaments before, but she didn't think that she'd ever faced death so certainly before. Now, too late, she realized what a fool she'd been to come here. The other women at the fort admired her for being strong and resilient; she knew now, far too late, that she wasn't strong at all, just foolish.

But she'd had to come. She had come to find Sloan.

Most ironically, to save Sloan.

And now she might die herself. And he'd never know that they'd had a chance again, that he might have had a son—that this time, their child might have lived.

The brave approached her, but she stood her ground. She had learned something about the Sioux during her time in the West.

And as Sloan's wife—for a very large part of Sloan was Sioux.

As was the child who had taken root within her.

If the brave intended to kill her, he would do so whether she stood strong or begged for mercy. He would probably enjoy killing her more if she were to scream and cry and tremble.

Yet he meant to play. Cat and mouse. He came to her, slamming a palm suddenly against her chest, causing her to stagger backward several feet as she desperately gasped for breath. The brave smiled, pleased with himself. He came at her again. She backed away instinctively, but this time, his hands shot out and he grabbed her by the upper arms, picking her up to slam her down to the ground.

Again, the breath was knocked from her. She turned her head and stared into the lifeless eyes of one of the young Sioux who had died in the skirmish. He couldn't have been more than sixteen, she thought. And tears suddenly sprang into her eyes. If she were to live to have her child, would the babe have its father's mahogany-dark eyes? Eyes that seemed to see into the soul at times; eyes that could be distant and hard. Eyes that were always steady and unblinking, set in a handsome bronzed face with fine high cheekbones and a decidedly strong jaw. What of this child might have been her, and what might have been Sloan?

She jerked her gaze from the dead boy, staring upward at the Indian who was about to straddle her. With a speed born of panic, she leapt to her feet, slamming his throat with her elbow when he started after her again.

He choked. Angry words erupted from him.

And he drew a knife from a sheath at his hip, smiling, placing it between his teeth, stretching out both arms, the better to render her helpless.

"Go to hell!" Sabrina cried to him, clenching her fingers into fists at her sides. He couldn't understand her, she thought. Oh, God! She wanted to live! Maybe she should let him see her fear, cry out, throw herself to his knees.

"Wait!" Sabrina tried, stretching out a hand, palm upward. "Wait; I need—"

No good. He moved swiftly, taking her by the arms, attempting to throw her down again. She struggled fiercely, clawing, hitting, kicking, using her nails, knees, the dirt, rocks, clumps of earth, anything she could clutch and throw or use as a hammer. She was suddenly released; she heard the brave uttering fierce, furious words and she realized she had caught him savagely in the groin with a knee. He held his knife in his left hand and came at her with the other open-palmed. He slapped her with a force that sent her reeling to her knees, tears stinging her eyes. Slowly, she looked up at him.

He didn't smile. He held the knife steady as he walked toward her.

The earth seemed to be pounding. Out of the corner of her eye, she saw the rider again. He was nearly upon them. He rode bareback. He was shirtless, but unpainted.

The brave paid no heed to the newcomer. He kept coming at Sabrina. She cast out her arms in self-defense, ready to ward him away.

But he never came for her. The rider had reached them at last. He reined in his horse in such a swift fashion that dust and dirt flew up all around him.

Then he pitted himself at the brave accosting Sabrina, taking the man down upon the ground in a deadly wrestling lock.

Stunned, Sabrina scrambled to her feet. She coughed and choked, unable to see what was going on. The brave's horse remained just feet away from her. Blindly, she hurried toward it, ready to leap up on it. She was confident that she could ride as well as any man—white or red.

"Sabrina!"

She heard her name shouted and froze, unable to believe she had heard his voice. She swung around. The dirt was beginning to settle, and now the rider walked out of the bloodred mist of dust and dirt and stood before her.

He was Sioux.

Coal-dark eyes assessed her. Sweat-slicked muscles in his arms, chest, and shoulders rippled and glistened a deep bronze in the crimson streaks of dying sunlight. Ink-black, straight hair fell collar-length against the strong lines of his face.

He was white as well.

His features were very cleanly cut, in a classical European manner. And though his chest was bare, he wore

dusty cavalry-issue breeches and high black cavalry boots.
Sloan.

"Oh, my God!" she breathed. "Sloan!"

She hurled herself at him, throwing her arms around
him, trembling. "Sloan—"

He firmly drew her from him, holding her at arm's
length. He arched a brow, studying her dusty face. "The
situation is almost worth the greeting," he murmured
dryly, then asked quickly, "Are you hurt?"

"No, Sloan, but all these men—"

"Are but a fraction of those who will die," he murmured softly.

"Sloan—" she began, then broke off.

They weren't alone. The brave who had attacked her
was still alive. As were his friends. All watching them.

Sabrina saw the brave Sloan had wrested from her, rising. Coming up behind Sloan.

The brave's friends were moving in around them as
well. Strategically.

"Sloan!" Sabrina gasped in warning, for the brave behind him was almost upon him. And there were three
more. Even if she had a weapon and known how to use
it, they would still have been outnumbered two to four.

Sloan, she realized, carried no weapons. Not even the
knife that was usually sheathed at his calf.

"I'll—I'll get the horse!" she cried.

"Sabrina, no!" he commanded, spinning around to face
the brave who had accosted her. He spoke loudly and
fiercely, gesturing as he did so. The brave returned his
angry words.

The brave's three friends stood stoically listening,
awaiting the outcome.

"Sloan! We have to get out of here!" She started for
the horse. She had nearly leapt upon it.

She could not do so. He caught her before she could
mount the horse. He held her in his arms, close against
his chest.

"Sloan, what are you doing?" she whispered desperately. "We have to get out of here!"

He shook his head, slowly, sadly.

"Sloan, we can run—"

"Sabrina, there are *thousands* of Sioux and Cheyenne just beyond that hill over there. Thousands upon thousands. More than I have witnessed together in all my life."

"Oh, God, Sloan, the more reason we have to run! Sloan, you've just saved me from that man, taken me from him. Let's escape—"

"Sabrina!" he murmured, shushing her. He smiled—ruefully, she thought. The old Sloan, the man who sometimes taunted himself as well as others with both his wit and charm. "I was allowed to save you from him."

"Allowed?" she repeated, her heart sinking. She'd known that he was no longer trusted by the Sioux. It seemed that her fears concerning him had been well-founded. And still, she fought the truth of their situation. "Allowed? Oh, God, Sloan, please, think, do something, dear God . . ."

Her voice trailed away as she stared at him. Were they doomed? Was her life over, just when she might have had the chance to begin it again? She moistened her lips. "I can't die now. Damn you, Sloan, put me down, I—"

"Sweet Jesu, Sabrina, don't you dare argue with me now!" he warned, his dark eyes blazing.

She hadn't come to argue with him. She was just suddenly so afraid.

"Sloan, set me down, I—"

"Indeed. Madam . . ." He turned in a sudden fury, setting her down. And she gasped aloud, staggering back against him, because more Indians on horseback had come. Dozens of them. Their bare chests were painted, and they were wearing various different headdresses.

Prepared for war. So many of them.

"Just a fraction of my friends and family," he murmured, drawing her close against him so that his chin was just above her forehead and his arms were around her waist in a both defensive and protective gesture.

One of the warriors broke away from the others, riding forward.

"Silver Knife, a lieutenant to Crazy Horse," Sloan informed her softly.

"Oh, God, Sloan, what exactly is going on?" she asked in sudden horror, nervously trying to writhe free from his grasp.

He pulled her back. "Sabrina, stop it!" he warned quietly. "The situation here is critical. I'm terribly sorry to disappoint you, for though I did my best to ride to your rescue like a knight in shining armor, I am, myself, a prisoner at this moment. It's only because one of Hawk's cousins saw that you were in the party Gray Heron rode to attack that I was allowed to ride after him. Of course," he continued with a bitter edge, "what in God's name you're doing out here is far more than I can fathom! If we weren't in such dire trouble, I'd be tempted to take you over my knee for being so foolish and headstrong."

She wanted to reply; she wanted to tell him so many things. Of course, as he could so easily do, he had managed to infuriate her. So she wanted to stamp on his foot, but more than that, she wanted just a few precious moments to talk.

She wasn't going to get those moments now.

The Indian Sloan had called Silver Knife began speaking with Sloan. Sloan nodded agreement, then lifted Sabrina atop the lathered horse he had raced across the plain to reach her. He quickly leapt up behind her.

They were instantly flanked by other Indians. "Where are we going?" Sabrina asked Sloan.

"Back to the camp."

It was just beyond the hill. The Indian encampment along a river seemed to stretch forever. Children played; women worked. Cooking fires burned, skins were stretched out for drying, and game hung from poles, ready to be skinned, cooked, and eaten.

But what alarmed her was the number of warriors she saw. Thousands of them, and all painted. All decked out for war.

They drew to a halt in the center of the camp, in front of a small tipi. Sloan leapt down from the horse and reached up for Sabrina. She set her hands on his shoulders and slid down before him. "You have to go in there," he told her.

"Alone?" she asked, and tried not to tremble.

"I'll be with you when the matter has been decided."

"What matter?" she asked.

He offered her a casual shrug. "Gray Heron is not one of our band. He thinks that I should have been killed instead of taken prisoner, and he insists that because he found you, he has a right to you."

Sabrina gasped, glad that he was with her then for her knees were giving out on her.

"Stand up straight. Trust in me for once, my love. Will you do that, please?"

She found her strength, met his eyes, and nodded. "Oh, God, how long—"

"Matters will be settled quickly," he assured her. "They know that Custer is out there somewhere, looking for them. They are looking for him as well. I'll be with you soon. Dammit, Sabrina, I've never seen you back down from anything in your life. You've sure as hell never backed down with me. Show those claws of yours. I'm well aware that you have them."

She pushed away from him and walked into the tipi.

There she collapsed. She fell to her knees upon a blanket in the rear of the tipi and buried her face in her hands. What had she done? What was happening now with Sloan? How had he been taken himself, and, oh, God, what would happen next?

Seconds seemed endless; minutes lasted forever. She managed to rise, and from there, she began to pace. Twilight faded to night, and she sat again in the darkness of the tipi, waiting. Outside, in the center of this grouping of tipis, a fire burned. Through the flap opening of the tipi, she stared out. The flickering flames rose in colors that resembled the evening's sunset. Yellows and golds crackled. Reds and crimsons blazed like the blood that soaked the landscape. And there would be so much more to come. So much more. Oh, God, she hadn't known there were so many Indians in all the world.

Fear took root within her again.

They had killed Sloan. They would kill her.

Then she saw him, shoulders bathed by the colors of the flame, muscles rippling. He walked as tall as he rode. He had bled for both Sioux and white men, but he had bowed down to neither.

He did not come alone, she saw. Two Indians dogged his trail. Yet when he slipped into the tipi, they waited outside.

She sprang to her feet, racing the few steps to him. Now he drew her to him very hard, and the savagery of his passionate kiss was tempered by a strange, wild sweetness. Protest now would not matter; she was his wife. He held her fiercely, hungrily, heedless of whatever anger might have lain between them before. She had so much to say; it seemed that he required no explanations. Her apologies, under such circumstances, would seem inane. Yet, oh, God, the way he held her, the feel of his arms, ruthless now in the urgency of his kiss. As if this might be the last . . .

"Sloan, dear God, what's happening?" she whispered when he released her at last.

He kissed her again, deeply, his fingertips playing over her face, his hands cupping her breasts.

"Sloan?"

"Would you fight me?" he queried softly. And even in the darkness, she felt his eyes, felt them burning into her, and she wondered what lay within his heart.

"What? No—"

"Ah, not here, not now! Not with all the Sioux Nation about to go to war."

"No, I would not fight you!" she cried in return.

"Pity, for we have no time!" he murmured dryly.

"No time? Sloan, please!"

He sighed. "This whole matter is quite an annoyance to the chiefs here, you see. The Sioux have been pushed very hard, and they are making a stand. Your party was attacked because the Sioux do not want their position betrayed before the fighting starts. Anyway, Gray Heron is adamant about having you, so it seems that I have to fight him for the privilege of keeping you as my wife."

"My God, Sloan, no!"

"Such faith!"

"He'll try to kill you—"

"Yes, well, that will be the point."

"Sloan, dear God, please, don't die, please, don't die!"

"I'll do my best," he promised lightly. "Listen to me, Sabrina. Whatever happens now, you're safe for the time being. Warriors don't—" he hesitated, then shrugged his shoulders. "They don't copulate before battle. God knows exactly when this battle will take place, but it will be terrible. Sioux braves believe that being with a woman will make them unpure for the fighting. In the event that something happens to me, you'll have time to get someone to take you to Crazy Horse. He'll be honor-bound to protect you because of our friendship in the past."

"Sloan, stop, dear God, please—"

His fingers tightened upon her shoulders. "What the hell are you doing out here anyway?" he demanded furiously. "I told you never to leave the fort without me again. I warned you—"

"I came to find you!" she protested desperately. "I came to find you because a Crow spy told a soldier at the fort that you were no longer safe from the Sioux, that they would kill you if they felt threatened. You weren't trusted going back and forth between two worlds. I had to find you—"

"Why?" he demanded bluntly.

She wanted to tell him. She had wanted to tell him so

badly! But she hadn't imagined it would be like this, both of them in such terrible danger, and Sloan so angry with her, his tone so hard and blunt.

"Why?" he repeated, and again she felt his eyes despite the darkness, felt the tension of his muscles, the heat and strength of his body. "We'd both know you were lying if you were to tell me there haven't been a good half-dozen times in the past year when you wouldn't have gladly seen me as a pincushion for Sioux arrows."

"Sloan, I was trying to tell you—"

He pulled away suddenly, and she realized that his escort had come for him. The two braves set to guard him were slipping into the tipi, coming to his side.

"It seems that I have to leave, my love. If I do return, I promise, I'll be expecting to hear a great deal from you."

If he returned. . . .

One of the braves took his arm, but he shook him off. He drew Sabrina to him one last time; the force of his kiss bruised her lips, yet infused her with warmth and longing.

She could hear drums beating in the night. A war cry sounded, then another.

Sloan released her at last. He took her hand, bowed over it, lightly breathed a kiss against her fingers. "Until we meet again, my love," he murmured.

And he turned and walked away.

"Sloan!" she cried, racing out after him. He turned, startled, then frowned as he saw the tears on her cheeks. She flung herself against his chest, breathing in his scent, trying to cherish the last of his warmth as she spoke quickly. "You can't die! Another reason why I came to find you is because I didn't expect you to be gone when I woke up the morning after . . . after . . . when I woke up that morning. I'd waited because I wanted to be really sure. I wanted to be past what the midwife told me was the dangerous time. I didn't want to disappoint you again after everything. I—"

His fingers moved her hair back from her forehead. He tilted her chin upward. His eyes seemed ebony in the firelight, and his touch was fraught with tension.

"What are you saying, Sabrina?"

"You can't die. We're expecting a child again, Sloan."

A high-pitched, keening war cry suddenly seemed to shatter the night. One of the braves came to Sloan, saying something, taking him by the arm. Sloan didn't protest; he didn't even seem to notice. He stared down at Sabrina. But the second brave came around her, pulling her away from Sloan.

Sloan said something sharply to the man in the Sioux language, and he released Sabrina. She started to run to Sloan again, refusing to accept the fact that he would be taken away.

The brave stopped her. He didn't hurt her; he just held her.

Sloan kept staring back at her.

"Really?" he queried softly, at last.

"Yes."

"You're quite certain."

She nodded. "That's why . . . I waited so long to tell you."

"When?"

"The baby will arrive in late November."

"Well," he murmured, "I should definitely be back by then. Go back to the tipi, Sabrina. For God's sake, keep yourself safe!" He shook off the brave who held him and turned away, walking toward the fire.

And going toward the blaze, he again became a black silhouette, now framed by the bloodred flames of the night rather than the crimson streaks of the setting sun.

"Sloan!" she cried.

He paused, then turned slowly.

"My love, I will be back," he vowed.

And when he moved again, it was around the flames, and it seemed that he had been swallowed by the fire.

"He will be back!" she whispered to herself. "He'll

be back!'' she told the brave who propelled her toward the tipi opening before leaving her.

She sat again, staring out at the night, at the fire, trying to still her thundering heart, trying to keep from screaming out her fear.

But crackling flames in the firelit night seemed to mock and taunt her. She stared at the flames, rising in their brilliant streaks of fire, and she found herself fiercely praying over and over again that Sloan would, indeed, be back. And she admitted to herself that she didn't think she could bear to live without him.

She was deeply, hopelessly in love with him.

Still staring at the flames, she began to wonder just when she had begun falling in love with him.

Perhaps the night at the fort when Lieutenant Jenkins had behaved so atrociously.

Perhaps when she had lost the baby.

It had begun even before that.

How odd it seemed now that she hadn't known how deeply she would come to love him when she had married him.

But that was long ago. Another lifetime, so it seemed. Yet perhaps the only lifetime they would have.

And so . . .

Left with only her fear as a companion, she traced the time back.

And remembered.

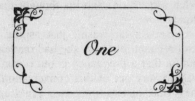

One

"*S*abrina! Sabrina, you're not paying the least bit of attention to me. How did this happen? How did you get . . ."

From the front of the stables, where she brushed down Aurora, one of the young Douglas mares, Sabrina could see the beauty of the Scottish landscape all around her, almost as if they were characters in a fairy-tale world. Far down the rolling hills, covered with mauve wildflowers, there was a silver mist over the water. The air was touched by the slightest breeze.

But she wasn't in a fairy tale. And her sister, arms crossed over her chest, had leaned stubbornly against the stone and wood wall of the stable. She was being incredibly persistent—even if it was taking her several moments to come out with the exact word she wanted.

"Pregnant?" Sabrina suggested softly. There had been a great deal of progress in the world since the end of the Civil War, but among proper society, "pregnant" remained a rather indelicate word.

But Skylar shrugged then, looking at her levelly. "How did you get pregnant? How did this all come about?"

15

How? What a question; Sabrina thought that her sister definitely knew *how*.

But of course, Skylar wasn't just asking about how she'd gotten pregnant, but how she had managed to be in such a situation that a pregnancy could occur.

There was no way out of this conversation. Naturally. Because they were sisters, only two years apart in age, and closer than most through the hard edge of the realities they had lived. Sabrina had managed to avoid the discussion for several days, but now the time had come to talk.

How . . . indeed?

Everything that had happened seemed incredibly distant—and of course, they were very far from the Dakota Territory where her fateful meeting with Sloan Trelawny had taken place. As Sabrina worked, industriously brushing the mare she had taken out for endless hours of walking hill and vale that day, she felt as if her heart and mind were equally as far from the Dakota Territory as the events that had happened in the past. The scenery here was exquisite, the silver water of the loch glittering beneath the powder blue of the sunny sky, the hills stretching away in shades of kelly green and mauve. Not that Scotland had been peaceful; they had come here because it was her brother-in-law Hawk Douglas's ancestral home, and because his half-brother, David, presumed dead for many years, was, in fact, alive. And in discovering the truth in the strange occurrences here, Sabrina had very nearly been killed herself.

She shivered suddenly, feeling a slight change in the breeze.

The tempest here was over. The day was glorious, the temperature surely warm for November in the Highlands. Nothing could be more peaceful than this moment, with the dew-damp air swirling around them, and the lush colors of the hills dotted with grazing cattle.

Yet it was here, just days ago, that she had followed a cry in the night and found herself drugged, bound, and locked in a mausoleum vault.

And it was in the hours that she lay so, as a helpless prisoner, that she realized how precious and dear life was to her . . .

And how much she wanted her child to live.

"Sabrina . . . ," Skylar pressed gently. "How?"

"How?" Sabrina repeated.

She'd entered the room and seen *him*. And she'd thought that she could manage herself, handle the situation, even once she had realized just who and what he had thought that she was. She had teased, and he had taken. Oh, God, it was horrible, how clearly and completely she could still remember his hands, dark against the ivory of her flesh, feel his force, the fire in his every supple twitch and movement. She could remember him drawing her into his arms, taking her down, holding her. She could remember his whisper, his eyes, the feel of his body . . .

Sabrina knew she owed her older sister some kind of explanation. Skylar was concerned. They had weathered a great deal together, including a most unusual life.

They had survived the Civil War as children, and, like many children of their generation, they had lost their father. But their father hadn't died in the war; he had been murdered by the apparently fine and extraordinary man who had quickly managed to take his place—their stepfather, Brad Dillman, who had become Senator Dillman, as time passed. Skylar had actually seen Dillman cleaning the murder weapon, but she had been a little girl at the time, and no one had believed that her accusations were anything more than a child's hysteria over the loss of a beloved father.

So they had grown up with Dillman. And they had both kept their peace, living in the elegant Baltimore townhouse, until their mother had died. Then there had been the night that had changed everything; the night that Skylar and Dillman had started fighting. And Sabrina had gone after Dillman, and the violence of the fight had escalated . . .

Until Dillman had fallen.

But he hadn't died.

Sabrina could still remember that night so clearly! She could shiver now, remembering how terrified she had been that Senator Brad Dillman would convince a magistrate that Skylar had been attempting to murder him. She had forced Skylar to flee, and then she had waited, tending to Dillman while he pretended to be a cripple.

Then Skylar had wired her the money to escape as well, along with directions to Mayfair, the home of Hawk Douglas, Skylar's new husband, near the Black Hills of the Dakota Territory. But the stagecoach had brought her to a place called Gold Town.

She hadn't planned her journey well. Dillman had followed her. She had been ready to settle down for the night at an inn before continuing on to Mayfair the following morning, but then she had heard Dillman's voice. And she'd tiptoed out of her room, unable to believe that it could be him. But it had been, and then . . .

Then she'd been trapped. She'd moved down the hall from her own room, and she'd heard him coming toward her, spouting his evil plans.

She'd almost been caught. She'd ducked into the first door she'd come upon.

And that was *how* it had happened.

She'd closed the door and closed her eyes. And when she'd opened them, *he* had been there. *Sloan* had been there.

She'd never seen anyone like him—so tall in the flickering firelight, so bronze. Ebony eyes, his face both handsome and harsh . . .

And Indian.

He'd worn a white shirt, opened almost to the waist, tight breeches, and high riding boots. His dark hair was long, down to his collar. His eyes had swept over her in a way that had set her on fire even as the corner of his mouth curled into a wicked smile, and he'd bid her come in. And she'd done so. She'd had to, but even so . . .

He'd been compellingly attractive. There was a marked sensual quality about him, drawing her even as the force of his dark mood had warned her away from him. Staring at him, she realized she had come upon a half-breed, a dangerous man. He was rough and brusque, totally impatient. Apparently he had wanted to spend his night in solitude. Even now, she had to admit, he'd tried to get her to leave. But she couldn't leave.

Dillman was in the hallway.

She couldn't leave, and she couldn't ask for help. Especially not from an angry, half-breed stranger, not against a United States senator.

And he had thought that she was a whore. And he had told her to either get in . . .

Or get out.

She had tried to rally her charms, accept a drink, keep him at a distance . . .

And keep from being thrown out into the hallway.

"Sabrina?" Skylar persisted.

Sabrina drew her brush energetically through Aurora's dark mane. She had to say something.

"I . . ."

"Oh, dear God. Did Sloan force you?" Skylar demanded, her voice shaking. "If he's to blame in such a wretched manner—"

"Skylar, no, I told you! I—I—" She broke off, gritting her teeth together because she wasn't going to cry. She was strong; life had made her very strong.

Then it had played cruel tricks upon her.

"I wish it had been rape," she said softly. "Then I could live with myself." She stared at Skylar, who looked at her with such sympathy that she gave herself a shake. "Your precious friend really wasn't to blame. No, it was Dillman's fault!"

"Dillman?"

"He was in the hallway at the inn. I tried to spy on him, and I was nearly caught, and so I slipped into a room. And there was a man in it—"

"Sloan? But he was a stranger then, right?"

"Right," Sabrina agreed.

"So you slept with a stranger to stay away from Dillman?" Skylar asked huskily.

It did sound absolutely terrible, the way that Skylar said it. And Skylar knew just how lethal Dillman had been.

"Sloan thought that I was a whore, sent over by Loralee from the Ten-Penny Saloon. I pretended I was exactly that. I would have done anything to stay away from Dillman."

"Oh, no. It was *my* fault," Skylar said. "I started the argument with Dillman that caused everything."

"It wasn't your fault, and that's why I didn't ever want you to know. It wasn't your fault!" Sabrina insisted.

It had been her own fault; she had found Sloan's room. And it had been his fault as well. The whiskey he'd given her had been his fault. The fact that he'd had the discourtesy to be in his room when she'd slipped into it had been his fault. His taking her for a two-bit saloon whore had been his fault. Her response to the way he'd touched her had been . . . her fault.

She had never, ever wanted to tell anyone what had happened between them, except that now it seemed she'd been left with no choice because . . .

She was expecting a child, and he had clearly stated that it was his child, and since it had been absolutely apparent to everyone that they abhorred one another . . .

Well, no one could understand the situation.

She gritted her teeth together.

"It definitely wasn't your fault," she assured Skylar.

"It just—happened."

"Something must be done."

"Nothing needs to be done!"

Skylar arched a brow, and Sabrina sighed with exasperation. "Please, Skylar, you can't take care of this for me, you—"

"No, of course not. This is between you and Sloan, isn't it?" Skylar inquired sweetly.

It was all so pathetic, and she absolutely despised her position now. She'd had terrible times in her life, but she'd always felt the power to fight before. Now it seemed that she was being beaten by sheer humiliation. The thought of what had happened still seemed to make her blood boil, and a pounding began anew in her temples. What in God's name was she going to do? Just when she had envisioned a life of freedom, it seemed that new chains had been cast around her. She tried so hard to pretend that it couldn't have happened, but it had. And he wasn't like anyone else. He played no games but spoke the truth bluntly, whether she liked it or not. He didn't bend, break, or bow, or give in . . . even an inch.

Once upon a time, despite everything wrong in her life, she had been coveted in society. Dillman had been a senator; she and Skylar had been window dressing, and she had been one of the elegantly gracious Connor girls, popular with Northerner and Southerner alike as the country healed its wounds. Men had flattered her wherever she went . . .

Until now.

Sloan didn't flatter or cajole. He moved straight forward, with single vision, demanding what he saw as right, accepting nothing less . . .

She shivered.

He was Indian, as well. Sioux. It was one thing to love Hawk as a brother. And quite another to realize that . . .

Sloan was one of the plains savages. His father's blood had made him so. His blood was that of the red-skinned warriors who had terrorized the whites migrating west, who had attacked without warning, with bloodcurdling cries, maiming, raping, slaughtering . . .

Sabrina turned from Skylar suddenly, brushing the mare again with a vengeance. She tried to remind herself that Sloan wasn't a savage. He was a United States Cavalry officer.

With just a little bit too much *savage* bred into him.

She glanced toward the castle, wondering if Sloan had decided to explain the situation, and if so . . .

Just what was he saying about her?

"Just how did this happen?"

"How?"

"How? Hell! This is, of course, rather difficult and damned awkward," Andrew—"Hawk"—Douglas said. He stood pouring brandy in his father's ancestral home, and it occurred to Sloan Trelawny that he and Hawk, two bronze men with their Sioux blood and straight black hair, must look peculiar sipping brandy in a castle in the Highlands.

Well, such was life, Sloan determined, standing by the mantel and accepting the snifter handed to him. Life certainly could be ironic.

"Nothing needs to be difficult," Sloan said, lifting his brandy snifter. "Cheers."

"Right, cheers! And since it's not difficult, I would appreciate it if you would explain. The young woman is my sister-in-law, in my care now. And still, it just seems so—so impossible. I mean, are you certain that you're the father—"

Sloan stared at him incredulously. "Am I certain? Of course I'm certain."

Hawk remained perplexed. Well, it was natural, certainly. They knew one another well. They knew the prejudices that could arise against half-breeds.

Hawk's father, a white man, had married his Indian love after the death of his first wife, but with or without that legal tie, Hawk would have been close with his elder brother, David, who had recently returned from the grave itself to take his rightful place as laird here. Blood ties had brought both Hawk and Sloan across an ocean—and far from the tempest between the U.S. government and the Sioux Nation, which they still couldn't escape—to discover the truth regarding certain evil and criminal events that had recently taken place here in the Highlands. Sloan was not actually related to David or Hawk, but in a different world, long ago, they had slashed their palms out on the plain and become blood brothers. There was more, of course, that had contributed to Sloan and Hawk's being friends: they shared the same dual heritage.

Sloan's mother had been a white captive raped by her Sioux captor. His father had fallen in love with his mother and made her his wife among the Sioux—his only wife. He had made her a promise as well. When he died, she and her son would be able to return to her people, the whites. So Sloan had spent his formative years on the plains, learning what boys needed to know in order to survive there and becoming a Sioux warrior.

Then his father died.

And he had suddenly found himself in his grandfather's house, and under the supervision of Lieutenant General Michael Trelawny, a Mexican War hero, a man powerful in both political and military circles. He had gone from being an Indian to a cowboy; a Sioux—to the cavalry. His grandfather's prestige had been enough to get him into West Point; his service in the Civil War had earned him the respect of his fellow cavalrymen. But nothing could buy him true legitimacy in the white man's world.

Nor could he have ever turned his back on what was becoming the annihilation of the Sioux people. He didn't believe that either the whites or the Indians owed him acceptance; he had been determined to win the respect of both peoples.

He had forged his own world, straddling a fence; the position was precarious. Hawk lived in that world, too. They understood one another, as few men could.

Which was why they were in the Highlands now, half a world away from the plains. They shared a strange, divided heritage. When one was in trouble, the other stood beside him. They shared a great deal.

Which was, of course, why Hawk was so baffled. His sister-in-law had just arrived in the West when he and Skylar had decided to bring her here to the Highlands with them. And now she was in the family way. And Sloan had claimed her child as his own.

Because it was.

Hawk swallowed his brandy in a long gulp, then looked at Sloan, lifting his hands. "This is truly bizarre. To the best of my knowledge, you met Sabrina in the midst of disaster, when her stepfather was trying to do away with us all. You didn't seem to like one another much at the time, and you have been even more antagonistic to each other each time you've met since then. I don't begin to understand how this could have happened—"

He broke off as Sloan arched a brow, then exhaled on a long breath. "No, no, I know how it happened, I just don't know how the hell it happened between the two of you." He was quiet for a moment. "Or why I knew nothing about it."

Sloan looked at Hawk evenly. "I didn't say anything to you or anyone else about what happened because I didn't feel that it was my place to do so. Sabrina most fervently wanted to forget what had taken place, and until now, I respected her decision."

Hawk arched a brow. "But—what the hell happened?"

What had happened? Despite the amount he had so purposely been drinking the night he had first met Sabrina Connor, Hawk's sister-in-law, he remembered everything about it in minute detail. And it hadn't been his state of desperately sought near-inebriation that had created confusion regarding her identity. Sabrina herself had brought that about.

Sloan set his snifter on the mantle, a wry, humorless smile curving his lip. "Well, it seems that I acquired Sabrina much the same way that you acquired your wife."

Hawk frowned. "If you'll remember, I discovered that I had a wife after the deed had been done by proxy."

"Brad Dillman," Sloan said quietly.

"Dillman?"

Sloan nodded. "Skylar was tricked into your father's proxy because she was so desperate to escape her stepfather—the man guilty of killing her father. Well, he was responsible for what happened between Sabrina and me as well."

"How? When?"

"It was after the disastrous meeting at the Red Cloud Reservation, when it became evident to all involved that some Sioux—poor deluded creatures who seem to believe they have a right to their own way of life—were going to fight. And the army was going to annihilate them. I went to stay at the Miner's Well and walked across to get a bottle of whiskey at the Ten-Penny Saloon. My mood was dire, to say the least, and I wanted nothing more than to drink myself into one night's oblivion. Our friendly Gold Town madam offered me her new girl—on the house. I declined. But shortly thereafter, a woman appeared in my room. Now I do admit to having been around a bit, but in all my life, I had never seen anyone like her—so perfect a female form, in so sensual a mode of dress, obviously a lady of the night, yet behaving so very strangely—"

Sloan broke off, gazing into the flames again.

How?

Actually, it had been damned easy.

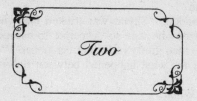

Two

The night had been strange, indeed. He was usually such a temperate drinker, but due to his very black mood, he had been sunken into a chair, halfway through his whiskey bottle, when his door suddenly opened and closed. Frowning, his fingers instantly resting upon the Colt sidearm he had placed on the occasional table next to the chair, he stared at his unbidden visitor.

It was night; he had lighted none of the lamps. The pleasant brocade drapes at the windows had been shut. The fire burning low in the hearth provided the only light, casting the room into a great deal of shadow. That there was very little light, however, only served to enhance the exquisite and stunning beauty of the woman who had come to him.

She leaned against the door, eyes closed. Her hair was glorious—dark, rich, waving down her back, over her shoulders. Her face, framed by the layers of thick tendrils, was an ivory oval, cheekbones high, mouth generous and defined, beautifully shaped. Her brows were arched, adding to the very regal perfection of her face.

Her lashes, thick and dark and as lustrous as the full fall of her dark hair, flicked open. She was alarmed. At the sight of him, he thought. Because he was Sioux. He thought that she must be Loralee's new "beauty," just in from the East. She was wearing an elegant white robe with chaste and virginal white lace at the collars and cuffs.

She hadn't quite tied the garment, though, and it hung open to reveal white hose, pantalettes, and corset. Even taking into consideration the effect of a corset, she had to be the most incredibly curved female he had ever seen, elegantly slim but endowed with voluptuous breasts and enticingly rounded hips. He had been drinking, but she was still exceptional. He'd been in a rotten mood; he'd been drinking with a purpose. But he was alive and breathing—and thus, aroused at the sight of her.

He'd never been quite so swiftly and completely affected by a woman. So he had told her to come in.

And, he admitted dryly to himself now, if he hadn't been drinking quite so much, he might have realized that her reluctance to do so was rather unusual for a whore. But he had been drinking, and so he had told her more harshly to come in—if she wanted to be there. And if not, he wanted her to get the hell out.

But she wouldn't leave. . . .

She'd been nervous, but he had assumed that to be natural, since she was new on the job.

He just didn't know how new.

And though he didn't feel that he carried any chips on his shoulders, he was damned aware of his blood. So he had asked her, "Do you have a problem with Indians?"

"Are you an Indian?" she'd queried in reply.

His brows shot up, and he stared at her incredulously. "Do I look Norwegian?" he asked slowly.

She extended a hand, indicating the cavalry jacket he had throw across the foot of the bed. "I—thought you were an officer."

"I wonder about that myself," he murmured. He stared at her again. "I ask you once more, do you have a problem with—"

He broke off. She wasn't listening to him. Again, she seemed to be paying attention to whatever was going on in the hallway.

The hell with it. War drums were pounding in his head, coursing through his body—loud, hammering, demanding. Sheer forgetfulness was at hand, appeasement for the thunder pulsing through him.

And that was how it had happened. He lost patience, and drew her into his arms, and kissed her. Brought his mouth down hard upon hers. Her lips were rich, provocative. He wanted more of them. He drove his tongue between her lips, drawing her hard against him. Her breasts rose lush and tempting against his chest, bared now as his shirt slipped farther open. Again he felt the rise of an almost overwhelming desire, stronger than anger, irritation, impatience, bitterness. The deeper he kissed her, the deeper his desire became.

Her hands were on his chest, pushing free. He groaned deeply, unwilling at first to let her go, his desire suddenly so strong that he was tempted to throw her down upon the bed with the brutal force firing its way into his being. He forced himself to free her. "Damn you, go!" he shouted, shoving her toward the door. She reached it; her fingers fumbled at the bolt. He thrust past her, opening the bolt.

He heard the voices again. A man was speaking. "If I can find the younger girl first—"

She refused to go. She asked for a drink, and then another. And another. And she began to sway, and he took the glass from her, determined that he wasn't going to let her pass out, not at that point. She was far too tempting, exquisite, and elegant. An incredible whore. He had never wanted a woman so badly. He pulled the satin ribbon on her corset. The garment fell loose. Another ribbon held her pantalettes. He tugged at it, then jerked the lacy garment down from her hips. The robe clung to her shoulders, but the rest of her lay naked beneath it. She was enough to rob him completely of breath.

No matter how beautiful, she was a whore. All the tempest, anger, and passion in him was now directed on one object—this girl.

She never screamed or cried out. Only her blue eyes betrayed her fury and her pain, when it was over. Yet he had been angry as well, totally irritated that she hadn't thought to mention to him just how new she was at her craft. And still, despite his very curt anger, she had refused again to leave—despite her apparent misery. And they had slept together through the night, and in the morning . . .

In the morning, he had awakened beside her, instantly made hungry by her nearness, her scent, the brush of her flesh against his own. And he'd determined to make her realize that her chosen profession could have its enjoyable moments, and so he had very slowly and sensually awakened her, arousing her from sleep, seducing her before she could fully come to her senses. And it had been damned good—amazing, actually . . .

Until she had a chance to talk, to tell him just what she thought of him—and storm out.

And he hadn't seen her again, until Dillman's men had been attacking her wagon when she had started out for Mayfair with Hawk's attorney.

"Sloan?"

Hawk's voice dragged him back to the present.

Sloan kept staring into the hearth, fascinated by the flames. "The strange thing is that I really did want her to leave when she behaved so strangely, but—I couldn't talk her into leaving," he told Hawk, then hesitated, realizing that he had wound his fingers around his brandy snifter with such force that he was about to snap the glass. He eased his hold and forced his gaze from the flames, focusing on Hawk's eyes. "Naturally, as it happened, the woman I assumed to be from Loralee's was in truth Sabrina, and she had run into my room to escape being discovered by her stepfather—who was talking with a few of his henchmen in the hallway of the Miner's Well. She might have just asked for help—but she didn't. She didn't know me, she didn't trust me, and she was terrified of discovery—which, of course, having had the pleasure of meeting her stepfather before his own demise in his attempt to murder us all, I do completely understand. But

she said nothing that night. Nothing. Not even after . . .
well, after. I was angry even then, still thinking, of course,
that she was a newcomer to the West, determined to make
her living indulging in the sins of the flesh—and that she
or Loralee should have told me that she was brand-new
at the game. But that night . . . she wouldn't leave, and
she didn't leave until the next morning when she ran out,
furiously spouting out her true opinion of me. So, you
see, the child she is carrying is very definitely mine.''

"She never said anything, anything at all, to Skylar or
me,'' Hawk said. He finished his brandy with a swallow,
went for the bottle, and poured more into their snifters.

Sloan lifted his glass, drank deeply, and set it down,
shaking his head with a twist of dry amusement. "When
I saw you again, Dillman's men were attacking, remember? If you'll recall, we stopped them from attacking the
wagon that was bringing Sabrina to your house. She kept
trying to tell you that I was one of the men attacking the
wagon, and I kept trying to tell you that she wasn't your
sister-in-law, she was a whore. Except that we both realized the truth before actually managing to say anything.
Then we all became embroiled in the showdown with
Dillman; he was killed, and it appeared that life might be
somewhat normal again. At that point, what was she going
to say? She wanted to pretend it never happened.''

"From what you said, it wasn't really your fault.''

"Maybe that's why she can't really forgive me,'' Sloan
said with a shrug. "Then, of course, there is the fact of
my tainted blood.''

"She has accepted me.''

"Circumstance sent her west; I don't believe she even
likes the plains, and I promise you, she sees you quite
differently. You are her brother-in-law, salvation in the
flesh. And until David so recently returned from the dead,
you were *Laird* Douglas. There is a difference when you
compare such respectability to a bastard half-breed.''

"I've never heard you sound so bitter before. Perhaps
there was no mention of a title to your name, but your

grandfather is an exceptional man who has—"

"I'm not bitter now; I'm telling you what I believe Sabrina feels and sees. She despised me when she left my room at the inn, and she didn't like me any better once she realized that I was a friend of yours—despite the fact that I did risk my life to help save hers. She would never have told me about the baby; I might never have known if your brother's new wife hadn't blurted out the truth, assuming that she and Sabrina were alone. I don't know if she knew about the baby and accompanied you and Skylar to Scotland in order to escape me, or if she only realized the truth herself once the three of you had already set out to come here. Still, as anyone around us might have noticed when we're together, Sabrina's loathing for me seems to erupt from her like volcanic fire."

Hawk didn't deny that. They'd never lied to one another. "You still want to marry her?" Hawk asked.

Sloan set his snifter down carefully on the mantel. "Come hell or high water, Hawk, I will do so." He hesitated, trying very hard to keep his temper in control.

When Sabrina had run out of his room calling him a bastard and arrogant oaf, he'd felt a fair surge of fury. And she'd done nothing but exasperate him since. Her refusal to marry him was not in the least flattering. She knew very little about the Sioux, and even if her outlook on his people as a whole might not be as negative as most, it was evident that she didn't like the idea of being touched by one herself. She cared deeply for Hawk, but then, her sister, not Sabrina, had married Hawk.

He lowered his eyes for a moment. He'd learned his lessons regarding white women a long time ago. When he'd very nearly married—until his blood had stood in the way. He'd been damned certain ever since that he'd never be vulnerable again.

Now, of course, Sabrina Connor wanted nothing to do with him. And he had to admit, Hawk was right—there was the old taste of bitterness in his mouth. Under normal circumstances, he could have turned away from such a

woman without a backward glance; the world was filled
with a fine variety of feminine forms.

But things were different this time. There was another
life at stake. He had been determined never to marry. And
he had thought that he was reconciled to life without children; in the Sioux camp, he could champion many young
men. But now . . .

He wanted his child. Fiercely. Since he had first heard
the rather astonishing news so inadvertantly blurted out,
he had felt the growing desire to have and hold his own
child, raise his child.

And yet he wondered . . .

Was that desire as fierce as his irritating desire to have
her, hold her again, touch her again, whether he wanted
to admit it or not?

Lust. Pure lust.

Could he allow his pride to admit even to that?

Perhaps lust could be enough to make a marriage. He
didn't know. Perhaps she just irritated him so much that
he had decided he was going to have his way. Whatever
his exact feelings on the matter, he was damned determined.

He replied to Hawk at last. "As you've said, there is a
responsibility here. Sabrina is expecting my child, Hawk.
That makes marriage the only solution. There is nothing
else that can be done. And quite frankly, of course, if this
weren't my position on the situation, wouldn't you be
required, as the lady's brother-in-law and closest male re-
lation, to bring me to the altar by way of a shotgun?"

"I'm sure that would be in order—if you weren't behaving so responsibly," Hawk admitted.

"Then?" Sloan arched a brow.

Hawk laughed. "Well, you're doing the right and noble
thing here, but there does seem to be a difficulty. Sabrina.
She keeps insisting she has no desire to marry you,"
Hawk pointed out.

"She needs to say yes only once. Perhaps you'll have

to bring *her* to the altar by way of a shotgun,'' Sloan said dryly.

"Right. And still . . .''

"Yes?''

"Well, then, there will be the simple matter of your both learning how not to despise one another,'' Hawk said with a pleasant smile. He lifted his snifter. "Cheers!'' He paused, shaking his head. "She never backs down. If she has set her mind on something, she will fight to the bitter end for what she wants. And as far as you go, Sloan . . . I'm afraid that whatever you insist, she will be all the more determined to do the opposite.''

Sloan studied Hawk for a moment, then laughed suddenly. "Indeed, my friend. You do have a point. This battle is surely like any other. It is the strategy that will count most.''

He turned from Hawk, determined to give Sabrina exactly what she claimed she wanted.

"Sabrina!''

Sabrina stood alone by the Druid Stones, her hands on the one piece of flat rock that had been used as an altar and was known as *the* Druid Stone. The Highlands could be very mystical. The wind rose in a keening sound, drifting about her with a sudden swift gust, heralding winter's arrival.

She had brushed the mare until the animal had been in danger of having all its hair fall out. And Skylar had at last left her in peace, probably to find Hawk—and see to it that her husband found some way to make things right.

Whether she wanted them "right'' or not.

"Sabrina!''

His voice again.

A shiver shot through her. It wasn't the wind; it was the sound of that voice.

"Sabrina!''

How odd that the mere sound of his voice could affect her so, when she had been through so much! It sometimes seemed to her that she had been fighting forever, since she had been a child, since her father had died. She didn't know how not to fight, and she did have courage, and she knew how to stand still and face almost anything at all, except . . .

Him.

She was suddenly tempted to run.

But she turned slowly, watching as he came, feeling the sensation of shivers tearing into her once again. How odd it was to see him here! A half-breed from the wretched wilds of the American frontier, striding across the emerald hills of Scotland with his customary ease and arrogance. As if he owned the world, and feared nothing. And would take whatever he wanted from the world, and defy God and the Heavens themselves to deny him.

Sloan was an exceptionally striking man, arresting in manner and looks. He stood at least six foot two, with the broad shoulders and honed physique of a man who had spent his life riding—and fighting—and working with weapons of war.

White men's weapons.

Red men's weapons.

His hair was very dark and thick, with a hint of his white blood just slightly curling the straight black length of it below his collar and adding just a touch of deepest red. His skin was bronzed by birth and sun, and his eyes . . .

Were black. Perhaps not black. Deep, dark brown, burning with a strange light that seemed to evoke the blazes of hell when he was angry.

As he so often was, when he looked at her.

He came to within five feet of where she stood. He was clad in riding boots, navy denim breeches, and a white shirt that was opened at the neckline, displaying a broad expanse of deeply bronzed skin. The expression in his dark eyes was unyielding, uncompromising.

And unmerciful.

She stared at him coolly in return, absolutely determined to keep her distance. How different the world seemed here, now. The two of them, alone upon this windswept cliff, a world away from the rugged western frontier of America! She hardly knew him, she thought. She hadn't known him at all when she had stumbled into his room, determined to escape her stepfather. And yet . . . the things that she could remember! Every inch of the hard bronze body, concealed now by his very *civilized* attire.

And it wasn't really true that she didn't know him. Sloan had traveled across half a continent and an ocean to be at Hawk's side when Hawk was in danger. His loyalty and courage were as fierce as his passion.

"Feeling sorry for yourself?" he queried, the tone of his voice amused.

"Don't be absurd," she responded quickly. Except, of course, she had been feeling sorry for herself. After everything, why had God decided to do this to her? Hadn't she fought hard enough, hadn't she deserved to have . . .

Freedom?

"So what have you decided?" he asked.

Now his tone was casual, as if it didn't make the least bit of difference to him. Since he'd first heard about her condition, he had been adamant that they marry. He'd once said that he'd make her *want* to marry him. Yet his question now was hardly a down-on-his-knees proposal.

She shook her head. "I can't marry you, Sloan."

"Why not?"

"There are so many reasons—"

He leaned back against the stone, crossing his arms over his chest. "Spell them out for me."

She inhaled deeply, trying to keep her eyes level with his without shivering. "I don't love you; you don't love me."

"That will be a fine explanation to our child. I am more than willing to tolerate you."

Tolerate her!

"Perhaps I'm not so willing to tolerate you," she said

as sweetly as she could, the slightest edge to her voice. She saw a pulse flickering against his throat, and she spoke quickly then. "Sloan, my stepfather was a murdering tyrant who dictated our lives for so long. I'm free of him at last—"

"And pregnant," Sloan said bluntly.

"I can make a life—"

He shook his head. "You can make a life for yourself without me, but not for my child. Let's hear your other reasons for refusing to marry me."

She stood stubbornly silent.

"Because I'm Sioux?" he inquired. "Could that be one of them?"

She spun on him, angry, passionate. "Fine—perhaps because you're Sioux! What kind of a life could a child have, on the fringes of society, not Indian, but always tainted with Indian blood—"

Sabrina broke off, horrified by her own words. She didn't really mean them; yet they were true. She'd learned in her lifetime that all men were equal—and equally flawed. Good men came in every color, race, and creed, just as bad men did. But the world was a brutal place; she had learned that as well.

"Sloan, please, I—"

She was barely aware that he had moved, yet he had. He was beside her, his hand grasping her wrist.

"The thing of it is, my dear, the child already exists!" he informed her heatedly. "And if I were to discover that you had intended murder against *my* seed—"

"Stop it, Sloan, stop!" she cried, frantically trying to free herself from his hold, to no avail. She gave up at last and stared at him furiously. "I've done nothing wrong. I have every intention of—of having this child." Oh, God, was it the truth? Hadn't she prayed that it might be her imagination, a sickness . . . that she might lose the babe?

"But I can go somewhere," she said quickly, "have the baby alone, survive on my own. Create a story, a life. And that way the child will be—"

"White?" Sloan suggested. The vise of his fingers around her wrist remained merciless. Looking into his eyes, she felt a strange trembling, and she knew that the fears she was voicing aloud were true; she didn't mean to be so wickedly prejudiced. It was the way of the world. And his people were slaughtering innocent whites all across the plains! But it was more than that. It was Sloan. The fire and electricity that were part of him, his force, his passion, his place in the world. He would never be told what to do; he would always choose his own path. He didn't know the meaning of compromise. And on top of all that . . .

If rumor held at all true, he had been the object of fascination to dozens of women. There was a sensual quality about him, in his eyes, in his smile. He could never be tied down to one woman.

"Yes," she said flatly. "I could raise the child white."

"What if he is born with red skin?"

"What if *she* is born light and blue-eyed?"

A slow smile curved his mouth, and he shook his head with amusement. "The world will know that you have given birth to an Indian child, Sabrina, because I refuse to allow you to deny me my child—or my child me, or even his Indian heritage. And if you think that you can pretend this child was an accident of rape, don't even begin to assume that I will be the gentleman to let such a lie stand."

Blood rushed to Sabrina's cheeks in such a wave that she felt that she might pass out cold with the fury of it. She tried to strike him with her free hand, but he was waiting for her impetuous wrath and easily caught her hand.

"Do you really hate me so much, Sabrina? Or just the truth?"

"Rest assured—I hate you!" she whispered, caught miserably now with both wrists in his grasp. Completely aware of how childish her words sounded, she was even more miserable. She had tried very hard to explain to him why she couldn't marry him. Her reasons were valid. But she couldn't explain why she felt so afraid of him because she didn't know herself. "Sloan, damn you—" she whispered.

But he suddenly released her.

"No, Sabrina, spare me. No more protestations. Ah, and don't feel that you must be gentle—or nice. You have convinced me that you really don't care for me, and have no intention to marry me. You have a right not to have me in your life, Sabrina," he said flatly. "But you don't have the right to keep the child, or live a lie and pretend that the child's father is dead. Whether you marry me is your choice. You say you don't want marriage. But don't try to run away and to hide the child—or the truth. Because I will find you. And I will have my child."

With that, he turned and walked away.

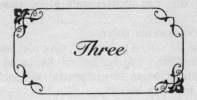

Three

That night at dinner, Sloan announced his intention to start his journey home.

Dinner, of course, was an interesting affair. Laird David Douglas sat at one end of the large table in the medieval hall; his wife, Shawna, sat at the other end.

Reunited after a great deal of danger and hardship, the couple were blissfully happy—nauseatingly happy, Sabrina thought at times. Then there was her sister, Skylar, and her brother-in-law, Hawk—still basically newlyweds themselves, and madly in love as well. Shawna's uncle and cousins dined with them as well, but they, at least, to the best of Sabrina's knowledge, knew nothing about her "delicate condition" as society was prone to call gestation. The residents of Craig Rock seemed content and at ease now that the danger and evil had been rooted out and the laird returned to the casle, so conversation tended to be light and pleasant. Nonetheless, Sabrina couldn't help noticing that the people who knew of her predicament were giving her strange looks.

Her brother-in-law, Hawk, looked baffled and a bit angry. He seemed to think that it was Sloan's half-breed status that kept her from marrying him.

His brother, David Douglas, the stalwart laird, didn't seem to understand at all her reluctance to marry Sloan.

Shawna, David's wife, stared just a bit guiltily, because she and Sabrina had become very good friends here, and it was she who had inadvertantly given away Sabrina's secret.

Then there was her sister.

Skylar. Who looked at her with pure hurt and reproach. Because she hadn't told her herself. Skylar adored Sloan, so she couldn't begin to understand Sabrina's determination not to marry him.

Sabrina was tempted to get up from the table and flee to her room; but, Shawna's family was being polite and courteous. Alistair, Shawna's very handsome and reputedly wayward cousin, was actually flirting with her. Sloan didn't even seem to notice. Sabrina, in turn, laughed pleasantly in response to Alistair until she discovered that Sloan was watching her with dispassionate interest. The slight curve of his lips seemed to imply that he wondered at just what stage of a relationship with the attractive young Scotsman she might divulge the information that she was carrying another man's child.

But he looked away, and then Shawna's older cousin, Aidan MacGinnis, asked Hawk and Sloan a question about the Sioux situation in the American West—truly not understanding how people couldn't find a way to live in peace on so very large a tract of land.

"It doesn't matter how much land there is," Sloan said. "Men will want more. To tell you the truth, the Sioux themselves have only recently migrated so far west— pressed by the white men who left the coast to claim the interior. Every year, the whites move farther and farther west. They came to the Black Hills because gold was discovered there. Gold is a dream that brings settlers by the thousands, and settlers bring more settlers . . . and in truth, it is difficult for two very different ways of life to coexist with one another. No matter how much land there is, Aidan, there will never be enough."

"There's plenty hereabouts in the Highlands," Gawain MacGinnis, Shawna's great-uncle, said gruffly. "Most of our young lads are lost—to the gold fields of America. There's plenty of fine land to be purchased here, and ye've plenty of friends among us, that's a fact.''

Sloan looked at his wine glass, smiling slowly and nodding his appreciation, but then looking back at Gawain. "I thank you for the invitation, but I have to go home. I have family.''

"White family—or Indian family?" Alistair asked.

"Both," Sloan told him.

"A lot of family?"

Sloan nodded, then said quietly, "Among the Sioux, the people in the same camp are something like what you call a clan or a sept here. I was glad to come here, but now I am anxious about what might be happening at home in my absence. I plan on starting the journey home tomorrow.''

To her horror, Sabrina was so startled that she clenched her fingers.

And shattered her delicate crystal wine glass.

All eyes turned to her. Skylar jumped out of her chair and ran to her sister's side. Shawna did likewise. "Oh, my God, it's bleeding!" Skylar cried, snatching Sabrina's hand.

"It's fine, honest to God!" Sabrina protested, wishing she didn't flush crimson so easily. "How clumsy of me! Excuse me; I'll rinse it off in my room. Please, continue with dinner. I'll be fine!''

She leapt up from her chair, a napkin wrapped around her hand.

Sloan was watching her politely. He didn't seem the least bit concerned about her hand. He didn't offer to help her. He stood courteously with the rest of the men as she fled the room.

In her bedchamber, she poured fresh water into her washbowl and cleaned her hand, muttering fiercely as the cut stung her. She wrapped it in a clean handkerchief and began pacing her room.

Sloan was leaving. It was what she wanted him to do. She had said that she wanted him out of her life, and he was going to get out of it. Of course, according to his warning, he'd be there when she had her child. Her illegitimate child.

She moaned softly, sinking down on the foot of the bed, clasping her injured hand with her other.

She had barely sat when she heard a tapping at her door. She rose, but before she could reach the door, it opened, and Skylar swept in, a look of pure reproach on her deceptively angelic features.

"Sabrina, just what do you think you're doing?" Skylar demanded.

"Tending to my minor cut."

"I'm not talking about that; I'm referring to Sloan."

"I'm not doing anything," Sabrina evaded. "Sloan apparently feels that he must return to the States."

"And you think that's fine."

"Naturally. It's his life."

"I see. This is what you want?"

"Yes, it is."

Skylar crossed her arms over her chest. "You want to have an illegitimate child, place a stigma on the babe, live with everyone pointing at you and talking and wondering—when there is no need for it?"

"Skylar, that isn't—"

"Oh, Sabrina, that *is* the way it will be! And by the way, I do know exactly what happened, even if you chose not to confide in me, after all we've been through together. I begged Hawk to speak with Sloan, and Sloan told him the truth—"

"His version of the truth."

"Would yours be different?"

"Oh, Skylar, I did tell you—"

"I managed to drag a few words out of you while Sloan explained exactly how you were caught in a desperate position because of our stepfather. He understands completely now that you felt you had no other choice but to play out a charade. He apparently feels that you must make your own choices, but he does intend to be responsible to the child."

"Well, there you have it."

"Ah, what a wonderful picture! My niece or nephew, growing up with a stigma cast upon him or her, because of your pride."

"What?" Sabrina gasped, staring indignantly at her sister. "It's not a matter of pride, it's a matter of—of—it's just ridiculous, that's all. Skylar, it was an accident, it was—"

"It's a life!" Skylar reminded her passionately.

Sabrina went very still, wishing she could explain her feelings to her sister, and wishing she could understand them herself. It seemed that so many thoughts were holding her back. She knew so little about the Sioux, and they were so much a part of Sloan's life. She was just as afraid of the unknown as anyone. And afraid of all that she *knew* to be savage as well. She wanted to be near Skylar, because Skylar was her sister and her best friend; but it was equally true that Dillman's death had left her free at last. She loved the East and wanted to live there. She wanted to go to parties and play games, and flirt and shop—and enjoy her life. She'd told herself a dozen times that she was being selfish. But she wanted more than what was on the surface. She wanted to be loved. She wanted some *acceptable* young man to fall head over heels in love with her.

And cherish her.

She didn't want to be married in order to be simply *tolerated*!

"Just think about it, Sabrina. Do you really want to refuse Sloan? What will you do? Do you want to cut Hawk and me out of your life? Because we'll have to go back to Mayfair; it's our home. And Sloan won't leave the cavalry—or the Dakota Territory—now. Too much is at stake; he's too involved. And if you try to go somewhere and pretend that you're a widow expecting a child, he'll only come after you eventually."

"Skylar—"

"Of course, it is your life. I'm so sorry. So very, very sorry." Skylar came across the room, hugging her tightly. "I'm sorry for you. And as for Sloan . . ." She pulled away, staring at Sabrina. "You're a fool if you don't marry him. There isn't another man like him in the world."

"Oh, I don't deny that."

"Because he's Sioux?"

"No. Not because he's part Sioux." It was only partly a lie. "I'm sure there are lots of half-breeds in the West," she said lightly.

"None like Sloan," Skylar told her. "But you do what you want. We'll always be there for you; you know that. Lifting your chin off the ground when respectable folks whisper behind your back and ostracize my poor little niece or nephew."

"Skylar!"

"Good night, Sabrina."

At some point during the night, Sabrina woke up realizing that she was being a complete idiot.

If Sloan were a different man, her life might go differently. Perhaps she could find a small town in California where she could go and pretend to be a widow and try to live out some form of respectable life. She had the means to live on her own now because at Dillman's death, she and Skylar had finally come into the inheritance that had actually belonged to them since their father had died.

But could she really leave her sister?

And it was true as well that her stepfather had been a senator, and the story of his murder of their father, his subsequent seizure of their property, and his attempts at murder had appeared in a number of newspapers in major cities across the country. People seemed to love stories about corruption in government. In several instances, sketches of her and Skylar—good sketches by talented artists—had even appeared in the papers. Sabrina felt that although she wasn't exactly well-known, she could never be sure that she might not be recognized as Dillman's stepdaughter.

It probably didn't matter anyway. No matter where she went, she thought uneasily, Sloan would find her.

And the truth of the matter was that Skylar was right. They lived in a harsh, unforgiving, uncompromising world. It wasn't fair in the least, but no matter where she ran, the truth would catch up to her. She would be an unwed mother with all the cruel stigma that was attached to such a position.

Worse. She could raise a child who would have to pay for her decisions as well.

She tossed in bed, burying her head under the pillow, fraught with fear, tension, and indecision.

At last, she came up from beneath the pillow. She needed to breathe.

Light was just beginning to come through her windows.

She leapt out of her bed in a sudden panic, realizing that morning had come.

She tore out of her room and down the second floor hallway to the room Sloan had taken. She tapped on the door but there was no response. She pushed the door open and looked quickly around the room.

He was already gone.

"Uh-humm."

At the sound of a throat being cleared, she nearly jumped. It was Myer, the astoundingly correct butler who served Castle Rock in the Highlands.

"I believe, Miss Connor, that Mr. Trelawny is still down at the stables. If you hurry . . ."

If she hurried. She wasn't even dressed. She was in a white eyelet nightgown and barefoot. But if she ran back to her room to dress . . .

"Thank you, Myer," Sabrina said, with what dignity she could muster. "I just wanted to say goodbye."

"Of course, Miss Connor," Myer said.

Sabrina smiled, then turned and hurried down the hallway and ran pell-mell down the stairs. She passed through

the great hall and out to the velvet green lawn that
stretched before the castle. The stables were placed outside the main wall that ringed the stone edifice, and Sabrina found herself wishing more and more fervently that
she'd at least had the sense to slip into a robe and shoes
before tearing after a man she had been eager to see leave.
Perhaps he had already ridden away; perhaps she would
be spared this conversation, and forced to manage on her
own . . .

No.

He stood outside the stables, his back to her. He was
just tightening the girth on the saddle of one of the Douglas horses. And he apparently heard her long before she
actually came to the point ten feet behind him where she
chose to stop, suddenly absolutely speechless. Could she
really do this? Pray God, he would make it easy.

Sloan wasn't going to make anything easy. Not for her.
Not ever.

"Well, Miss Connor?" he said after a moment, without
turning from his task.

Sabrina gritted her teeth together. Her feet hurt. And he
wouldn't even turn around.

"I've—" she began, but broke off. The words she
needed simply wouldn't come. She was gasping on pride,
she realized. She might just choke from it.

"You've what?" he demanded, turning around at last.

Caught in shadow against the rising sun, he might have
been any man.

A white man.

His tailored shirt was fashionably handsome, as were
his maroon frock coat, black riding breeches, and boots.
He wore a slouch hat pulled in a low angle over his forehead. She couldn't see his eyes for the shadow, and had
no idea of what he was thinking or feeling.

"I've been thinking."

"About what?"

"Damn you, Sloan—"

"About what?"

She clenched her hands into fists behind her back, trying to stand very tall and straight. "About your proposal."

"What proposal would that be?"

"Sloan, don't be so vicious—"

"Savage, isn't that what you mean?"

"Rude. Cruel. That's what I mean," she said heatedly.

He arched a brow, leaned against the horse, and crossed his arms over his chest. "I do apologize then. Let's begin anew. So you have been thinking about my proposal. And just what is it that you have thought?"

"Well, I suppose, I mean, it could be done . . . just for the sake of the child, of course."

"Just for the sake of the child—what does that mean?"

"Sloan, surely I don't need to be explicit—"

"Surely, you do. What exactly do you mean?"

"We can't possibly live together as man and wife."

"Why not?"

"Because—because—" she stuttered. He wasn't helping her at all. He just kept staring, demanding an answer. She threw up her hands. "We don't get along. We've both got wretched tempers; we can't agree on anything. So far, I don't like the West, and I'm—I'm afraid of people who mean a tremendous amount to you." His eyes narrowed at that, but he didn't comment. She inhaled again. "I would be a horrible wife to you—"

"I'd be the one taking that chance, wouldn't I?" he asked curtly. "And I'm willing to take it."

"For the sake of the child."

He shrugged.

"But, Sloan—"

"So what are you suggesting?"

"Well, we could marry but remain apart. A lot of people do it." She paused because he was laughing. "Sloan, damn you, people marry and can't live with one another, and so they live apart."

He shook his head. "Not me."

"Well, I can't see how it would disturb your lifestyle!" she snapped angrily. "To the best of my understanding, you have an Indian mistress on the plain, and a number of lady . . . friends in different settlements along the frontier. You could continue to live your life as you chose—"

"And what about you?" he queried pleasantly.

"What do you mean?"

"Do you intend to condemn yourself to a loveless life of chastity?"

"Well, I hadn't really thought—"

"Well, then, think about this," he interrupted softly. "I'd kill any man who touched my wife."

The shivering sensation he could evoke all too easily swept through her.

"Sloan—"

"No."

"No—what?"

"No marriage in name only."

He turned back to his horse, dismissing her, as if he had no further interest in her at all. She strode to him angrily. "Sloan, this isn't fair—"

He swung around. "Life isn't fair. I'd thought you'd learned that lesson."

He was just inches away. He smelled pleasantly of sandalwood soap, leather, coffee, and tobacco. He was very tall, wickedly muscled, and lean.

"Sloan—"

"What do you want, Sabrina?"

"You—you—asked—"

"I asked. You declined. It's your turn."

"What are you saying?"

"If you want me to marry you, Sabrina, it's your turn to ask."

"What?"

"You heard me."

She swung around furiously, ready to walk away. She stepped hard on a rock and cried out, hopping as she grabbed for her injured foot, nearly falling and hating herself all the more as he caught her when she would have fallen. She regained her balance, trying to wrench free from him. "I'm not asking you to marry me, Sloan Trelawny—"

"Good. I won't have to refuse you."

"Refuse me! You started this—"

"All right. I started it. Ask."

"Damn you, Sloan. I said I'd marry you!" she cried out, suddenly very afraid. She thought that she had wanted him to go away. But that wasn't true. She had wanted him to force the issue, but he was determined that she was going to have to enter into whatever bargain they made with her eyes opened.

"All right, I won't make you get down on your hands and knees."

"You bastard—"

"That's right, Sabrina. So let's keep the babe from being one, shall we?"

She hugged her arms around her chest. "So—we're both agreed. We will marry."

He nodded, a curious smile on his face. "But you accept my terms."

"Your terms—"

"When you marry me, Sabrina, you do so for better or worse. You don't run away from life, and you don't run away from me. You live with me, Sabrina, as my wife."

She stood very still, feeling the breeze lift her hair, feeling chills and then a wave of heat sweep through her.

"You accept what I am," he added softly.

"I . . ."

He turned back to his horse, adjusting the saddle once again. She felt a moment of pure panic. None of this really mattered to him. He'd been playing with her, and now he was just going to leave her.

"I—yes!" she hissed.

Then he was dead still for a minute, his back to her. And she realized that he wasn't leaving now—at least not yet. He lifted the saddle off his horse, setting it on a cross beam of the paddock fence. He turned back to her, his eyes raking up and down the length of her as he seemed to come to some conclusion she couldn't figure out. "Well, then, we need to plan a legal marriage, quickly. Bear this in mind: you have until the ceremony to be certain of your own decision in this. We'll be married as soon as we can arrange it. But I mean what I said. For better or worse. Marriage is until death do us part—and that isn't an invitation for you to hope that I might get myself killed soon."

She lowered her head quickly. "I don't hope that you'll get killed quickly."

"The hell you don't," he mused dryly.

"Well, then," she replied pleasantly, "I hope someone kills you slowly!"

He laughed. Then she gasped because his arm was suddenly around her waist, and she could feel the warmth and strength of his hand on her hip through the cotton of her gown. "You're freezing," he told her with a frown. "Let's get back inside the castle before you catch your death."

"Don't worry about me. I'm never ill, and I'm far stronger than you could ever imagine, Sloan Trelawny."

"That's to be seen, isn't it?" he inquired pleasantly enough.

He led her back toward the gray edifice, walking swiftly until he realized that she couldn't keep up because she was limping.

"No clothes, no shoes," he said irritably, sweeping her up in his arms.

"I can walk."

"Your foot is bleeding."

"But I can walk—"

He swore impatiently. "We'd best get this wedding arranged before you do any more bloody harm to yourself," he muttered.

They reached the castle and entered the great hall. Sloan started to set her down, then paused.

Hawk and Skylar and David and Shawna and their little boy all stood in the great hall.

All dressed.

All watching.

And waiting.

Sloan very slowly allowed Sabrina to slide to the floor in front of him, holding her steady there, which she greatly appreciated because her stomach was suddenly churning.

"Well, how convenient," he murmured dryly. "Since you're all here . . . Sabrina and I would like to invite you to our wedding. If you'd be kind enough to arrange it, of course, Laird Douglas," he added to David.

David bowed slightly, hiding his smile. "Of course. With the greatest pleasure."

Sabrina pressed against Sloan, feeling flushed and ill. "Sloan! I'm . . . going to be sick."

He released her. She fled for the stairs. Sloan shrugged to the others.

"She really loves me," he murmured dryly. "Will you excuse me?"

He followed her up the stairs then, bursting into her room behind her when she was seeking to be alone—to be sick! His arm was suddenly around her, and she was crying out, "I'm not sick because of you. I'm not afraid of you. It isn't the thought of you; it's—"

"The baby, I know," he said impatiently. "And I'm trying to help you. Stop, stand still, and breathe in deeply."

"What?"

"Do as I say."

"For God's sake, Sloan!" she cried with aggravation. "I'm trying not to be sick on you!"

"Breathe!" he insisted.

He held her shoulders, and to her amazement, when she breathed as he'd instructed her to do, her nausea ebbed away.

She stared at him, amazed, then heard a tapping at her

door. Skylar slipped her head in, then entered.

"David says he's sure he can arrange a license and get the reverend here by this afternoon. He thought you might like to be married quickly and quietly in the chapel here at the castle."

"That will be fine," Sloan said, his dark eyes on Sabrina.

The room spun.

She wasn't sick.

Silver mist appeared before her again. She was weightless, falling.

And to her deep distress, he was there again, to catch her as she fell into the blackness of oblivion.

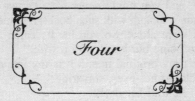

Four

He was never going to go away.

He was there when she opened her eyes, placing a cool, damp cloth on her forehead as she lay on her bed in the Douglas castle in a place that seemed a million miles from Indian territory—and the past life that had brought her to her present situation. She felt a strange warmth as she looked into his face. He was a very unusual man. Unique. For a moment, she was tempted to reach out and feel the texture of his cheek.

But even lying down, she felt slightly dizzy. She groaned softly.

"You did ask me to marry you," he reminded her, a smile curling his lips.

"Only because I had to," she said huskily.

His smile deepened. "Well, you do have until the moment of truth itself to make up your mind."

"So do you."

"My mind is made up."

She studied his striking features, admitting to herself that he had an exceptionally handsome smile, even when it was wry and so often mocking, as it could be, sometimes mocking himself. Yet she thought that it could be his very charm that disturbed her—as much as all the *savage* background. Still, she suddenly found herself smiling as well. "Your mind is made up! You didn't know a thing about having a child when you sailed the Atlantic to Scotland, and you might never have known if Shawna Douglas hadn't spoken with such concern to me when she thought we were alone. So you hardly came here determined to go home burdened with a wife.''

''It wasn't my original intent; it is my intent now.''

Sabrina closed her eyes, shivering.

''Sorry,'' he told her dryly.

Her eyes flew open again. ''You don't understand; maybe no one can understand. Living with Dillman was a travesty. All the years that my mother was alive, Skylar and I were always acting out a charade for her benefit. Then my mother died, and our entire lives became dedicated to getting away from him. When Dillman died, we were suddenly free to live our own lives.''

''And free to dream?''

''Of course.''

''And what were your dreams?'' he inquired.

She shook her head, her lashes lowering. ''The usual, I guess. To live each day as I saw fit—''

''Back East?''

''I—I don't know,'' she admitted, hesitating.

''Umm,'' he murmured. ''What you wanted was to live back East, in all the elegance and comfort to which your position in society has always allowed you. You wanted to dance the nights away with young swains rushing adoringly about you at all times, tripping over themselves for your slightest favor.''

Her eyes narrowed upon him. ''Sloan, don't you dare imagine that you've the right—''

''To an opinion?''

''To judge me.''

''You want freedom—and marriage is a shackle and chain,'' he murmured.

Again, she hesitated. His mood now seemed so mercurial. One minute, it seemed that she provided him the greatest amusement. The next minute, he seemed dark and dangerous.

''Well?'' he persisted.

"Shackles and chains—they are more or less what you're describing. You want so much from a wife," she murmured uneasily.

Sloan laughed. "I want so much? I think not. I expect my wife to live with me, sleep with me—raise my child with me. And accept what I am. I'm sorry about your losing what you thought was your first taste of freedom. I do understand your feelings. But there will be a child involved, and that changes everything, for everyone."

"Yes. But couldn't we just—"

"No."

"You don't know what I was going to say."

"I do. You want a marriage in name only, sharing responsibility for the child. You made such a suggestion earlier. Actually, marriage should be a far easier adjustment for you than many a bride."

"And why is that?"

The sudden twist of his smile was almost satyrical. "Because you know just what's expected of you."

"You're being horrible—"

"I'm being frank. And it wasn't horrible at all, and that's what irritates you most."

She snatched the cloth from his hand. "Sloan, I—"

"It will be repeated."

"You really are being completely wretched when I'm in this terrible condition—"

The sound of his laughter further irritated her and caused her to break off.

"I don't begin to understand what's so funny."

"Ah, well, do you think that your sister and Hawk are giving up their relations?"

"Why would they—" she began with a frown, then, meeting his eyes, queried, "My sister and Hawk are expecting a child?"

Sloan nodded. Sabrina was both amazed and annoyed to realize that he knew what she did not. Her sister hadn't said a word to her. But then, she hadn't said a word to Skylar.

"Skylar hasn't been sick," Sabrina said.

"And despite being such a wretched savage, I am aware that you really don't feel well. Any man accepts that his wife may be in a very delicate condition—just as long as it doesn't last eternally."

Sabrina allowed her lashes to fall over her cheeks. A reprieve!

"So you are more reconciled," Sloan said dryly.

"I am reconciled, and you can really quit being so sarcastic. You're telling me what marriage is. Well, Major Trelawny, I had a few dreams once upon a time regarding what a proposal should be."

"My proposal was less than eloquent?" he queried, amused.

"I was actually the one asking today."

"Only because you had so determinedly turned me down. I decided to leave you be until the child arrived. But if the lack of a proper proposal has disturbed you . . ." he murmured, his voice trailing as he shrugged. Then he dropped the cloth back into the bowl of cold water at her side, caught her fingers, and drew her up to a sitting position.

"Sloan . . ." she murmured, uneasy and wary. "You are making me very nervous."

But he ignored her and went down upon one knee before the bed, her hands in his, his head ever so slightly bowed. "Sabrina, on my knees, I ask you to be my wife."

"Sloan, stop this mockery—"

"No mockery."

"Get up!"

"Not until you reply."

"Sloan, you know that I've agreed! I came to you; you are mocking me—"

"No, I'm not. I'm most seriously going for a new beginning. I am asking you on bended knee to be my wife."

"But I've said that I agree we must—"

"Just say yes." His eyes were coal-dark fire, very intent on hers. She returned his stare, and a warmth seemed to suffuse her. He could be absolutely charming. Intense. Incredibly sensual, powerful in both personality and physique. If she had only met him under different circumstances . . .

"Sloan, stop it; do get up—"

"Just say yes."

"Yes! You know that it is yes—"

He rose, sitting at her side. "Did that help any?"

Sabrina had to smile. She gazed down to her lap where his hand still remained entwined with hers. "Yes," she admitted.

"It could have been worse."

"How is that?"

He shrugged, a very subtle smile playing upon his lips once again. "Well, you could have stumbled into the room of an old, balding, totally reprehensible *married* murderer or thief. Toothless, to boot."

"Well, if he'd been so old and decrepit," Sabrina said lightly, "he might have been incapable of . . . well, he might have been incapable."

"Of the act—or of reproduction?" Sloan demanded.

"Both," Sabrina assured him.

"How flattering—you'd have preferred to meet with a reprehensible, toothless, balding old coot rather than me."

"That isn't what I said. And you forgot the married part."

"Did I? Sorry. Close enough."

"Of course it could have been worse," Sabrina murmured.

To her surprise, his fingers tightened around hers, and he suddenly rose. She stared up at him and noted that his handsome features were tense.

"Indeed. You could have met up with a full-blooded Sioux. Such clientele is not uncommon in Gold Town. Until the wedding, my love," he said and turned away, striding toward the door.

It opened and closed.

And she shivered fiercely, hugging herself. For a few moments there . . .

She had almost felt warm.

He was well aware that his Sioux blood disturbed her—she had admitted it. *Things could have been worse for her, he had implied, because she might have run into a full-blooded Sioux instead of a half-breed.*

She groaned softly, burying her face in her hands. She wished that he could understand. She had spent just days of her life in the West. All that she knew about the Sioux came from the dreadful tales of their savagery that she had read about in the papers and heard from white travelers. *What* he was, did disturb her, but there was far more to it than he could understand.

She wasn't just afraid of Indians.

She was afraid of what might happen to Sloan himself, because of who he was. Part white, part Sioux. Straddling a fence . . .

That was about to crumble.

She starting shivering again, realizing to her dismay just how much it was all coming to mean to her.

There was never a single moment when Sloan questioned what he was doing. She wasn't just an innocent he had inadvertantly deflowered; she was the sister of his best friend's wife, carrying his child.

It seemed very strange to him to await his bride in the chapel of an ancient castle, Hawk and David Douglas by his side. They stood beneath an antique crucifix while a piper played. Yet as the unique music of the pipes filled the air, he felt himself tense up when she appeared. Shawna and Skylar preceded her down the narrow stone aisle to the altar where the Reverend Massey waited, smiling benignly. Shawna's family was in attendance along with some of the villagers, who provided a certain credibility and a festive air to the hastily arranged ceremony.

As Sloan had noted the first time he had seen her, Sabrina was uncommonly beautiful with her dark auburn hair, dazzling blue eyes, and classical features. She hadn't chosen a white wedding gown, but instead a gown with a sky-blue skirt and a royal-blue velvet bodice. The gown brought out the color in her eyes and contrasted with the auburn of her hair. As he watched her come to him— trembling though she was—he admitted to himself that morality and nobility weren't the only reasons he was so motivated to marry her.

Lust, he reminded himself.

It was that, and more.

She fascinated him.

Innocence, he thought, had faded from her eyes long before he had met her. There was skepticism in them, just as there was a certain wisdom etched into her beautiful features; she might have grown up with every luxury available to the stepdaughter of a wealthy senator, but she had spent years in hell. And he knew from what Skylar had told him that she had fought back all those years. She had raw courage and determination. She was accustomed to fighting; she had been doing so a long time. But if this marriage was going to be a fight between them for all eternity . . .

Well, he had been waging war one hell of a long time himself. It didn't matter. He wasn't marrying her simply to be noble. He was marrying her because he wanted her.

Yet, as she stood by his side, seeming to loathe every second of the ceremony, he sensed that revealing his true feelings to her would not serve him well. At least, not yet. She needed time to get used to him and the unusual life he'd forged for himself.

At this particular time, seeking to offer Sabrina the least affection seemed rather like trying to cherish a porcupine.

Sloan was amazed himself at how quickly and surely his vows came to his lips.

Hers could barely be heard. It seemed that she couldn't breathe. At one point, the reverend had to ask her to repeat herself. Yet the words she uttered were the right ones, and in a matter of minutes, Reverend Massey was pronouncing them man and wife—and instructing him to kiss his bride.

Sabrina's eyes were closed, her face was pale, and her body appeared tense, as if she were bracing herself for a passionate kiss from him. He briefly brushed his lips against hers, which were as cold as ice.

When she opened her eyes and looked at him, she appeared startled and even a bit grateful.

But she didn't look at him for long. Skylar rushed to her; Hawk was shaking his hand, David Douglas was clapping him upon the back, and David and Shawna's young son was tearing down the aisle to reach them. He'd just freed himself from the buxom cook, Anne-Marie, who was crying into her handkerchief.

"Weddings do make a body tearful!" she proclaimed, coming forward with her best wishes and the announcement that a light dinner would be served in the great hall.

Sloan turned then, offering his hand to Sabrina. "It's done, then. Shall we?"

She nodded, her lips and cheeks still pale. He drew his eyes from hers, disturbed. He knew that she hadn't wanted to marry him, but he hadn't known how much until now. Although she said nothing in protest and behaved with all propriety, she couldn't have appeared more distressed.

Sloan led her into the great hall and offered her a glass of champagne. She raised it to her lips as he raised his own. Hawk offered an eloquent toast, most of which Sloan missed because he was so distracted by his new wife, whose eyes glittered like sapphires against the paleness of her flesh.

She ate, she drank, she moved, she smiled; at one point, she even laughed at something Shawna Douglas said.

And yet . . .

She remained as pale as new-fallen snow.

Later in the evening, when she ascended the stairway with her sister and Shawna, the guests departed and the servants returned to their quarters. Sloan was alone with David and Hawk in the great hall, all of them before the fire, drinking brandy and staring into the flames.

"Well, the deed is done," Hawk murmured.

Sloan arched a brow at him. Hawk shrugged. "The deed is done? Hmm. Sounds as if we have successfully captured a band of renegade Rebs—or Crow."

"All right," Hawk agreed, grinning. "Major Trelawny, perhaps among the three of us, your marriage was the most normal—"

"Considering yours was by proxy and David's occurred only after he miraculously returned from the dead, I imagine that—among us—my marriage *is* the most normal. If such a thing can be said at all."

"Well, you and Sabrina are, at least, acquainted," Hawk pointed out. "Bear in mind, I discovered through my attorney that my father had acquired a wife for me just before his death."

"Ah, but she does seem to like you now," David teased his brother.

"There you have it!" Sloan said quietly.

"So you mean to say that you've done this—but you are sorry?" David queried.

Sloan hesitated. "No, I was quite determined to marry Sabrina . . . and yes, I suppose I am sorry in a way. Only because of who I am, what I am, and what we will be facing when we return home."

"There is the possibility of your not returning," David reminded him. "You've more than done your duty as a soldier; no man can be expected to fight his own kind. You know that you are welcome to stay here. And there is good land to be bought; you've a fair-sized inheritance from your mother."

"That is a tempting proposition," Sloan told him, glancing at Hawk. "There can be no good solution in the West, not with Sherman and Sheridan heading the armies. They're talented generals . . . but they're damned rigid men, with set ideas. We were at a social once, soon after Lincoln had been killed, and strangely enough I wound up spending half the evening with Mrs. Sherman. She was enthusiastic about the fact that, with the Homestead Act in full force and the war over, men would be looking westward again. So many soldiers suddenly without jobs—and Southerners with nothing but burned fields left! People would be hungering for new lives in the West. And she was so proud of her husband because, way back in the late thirties and early forties, when he'd spent time in Florida during the Seminole War, before they were even married, he'd written to tell her how glad he was of his duty in Florida because he was certain that the Indian would figure prominently as a key enemy to be fought in the years to come. Why Mrs. Sherman chose to tell me this—since it's obvious I've got Indian blood!—I don't know. Unless she was trying to be friendly and make sure I knew that she didn't consider me to be one of the savages with whom her husband was so determined to deal swiftly."

"And Sherman and Sheridan will deal with the Indian question," Hawk said. "We're both well aware of their policies. And, for that matter, we're both aware that they are usually fairly intelligent and just men."

Sloan nodded. "General Sherman loved the South, remember? He thought that some of the most beautiful land in the country lay in the South. But that didn't stop him from decimating everything in his path on his march through Georgia! And even if Sherman does understand a lot about the Sioux, and even admires some of the Sioux warriors, it isn't going to change his determination to carry out policy."

"Policy comes from Washington," David said.

"Interpretation of policy comes on the battlefield," Hawk pointed out. He shrugged. "Since I'm not cavalry anymore, I'm not as involved as Sloan. But we're both going home, and we know it."

"Like moths to a flame," Sloan said dryly. "I've got to go back; I've got to do what I can to keep communications open between the hostile Sioux and the white government, and pray that there will eventually be a peaceful—if damned sad!—settlement. Because there is no way out of the American 'Manifest Destiny'! Settlers will keep coming west, and Americans are going to claim Indian lands. By sheer force of numbers and superior weaponry, they will eventually win—even if the poor farmer in the path of Indian retaliation can't possibly see such a picture now. I'm sorry to drag a wife into this; that is all.''

But equally, he was sorry to cause Sabrina more distress. She hadn't lived an easy life thus far, which was why, perhaps, she was such an elegantly beautiful porcupine. Ever wary, ever careful, and ever defensive.

''Well,'' David murmured, lifting his brandy glass, ''to the best possible solution, the very least bloodshed.''

The three finished their brandies, and Sloan set his snifter on the large table in the great hall. ''David, my thanks for your hospitality and, naturally, for being the laird of the manor and so swiftly and smoothly arranging the marriage.''

''My pleasure,'' David told him. ''I can promise you, Major Trelawny—my brother in blood—that few lairds would have so good a friend as to cross the Atlantic to come to their aid when they had supposedly been buried for a good five years.''

''Well,'' Sloan replied quietly, smiling slightly, ''that, Laird Douglas, was my complete pleasure. Good night, then, gentlemen.''

He left Hawk and David in the hall and mounted the stairs to Sabrina's room on the second floor. She was alone, sitting at the dressing table, and though she had surely expected him, she jumped when he entered the room and closed the door behind him.

She looked very much like a typical bride; her lustrous auburn hair was loose, cascading down her back. She had been brushing it with such great industry that it shone almost as brightly as the fire that burned in the hearth. And though she had eschewed white for the wedding, her nightgown was an elegant white creation of cotton and lace and silk ribbons that covered her from throat to toe.

"Well," she murmured, meeting his eyes in the dressing table mirror, "the deed is done."

He nodded, frowning. The deed . . . something distasteful that needed doing.

He walked to the dressing table and stood behind her, aware that she watched him very nervously in the mirror. He touched the fall of her hair; the strands were as soft as skeins of silk. She lowered her lashes, and he felt her tension. She was dying for him to go away; to leave her alone. But she had just married him, fully aware of everything he expected from marriage.

She was going to be careful.

And play the role of delicate Southern belle to the hilt.

Her eyes met his in the mirror once again. "I—I swear to you, Sloan, I am not trying to be disagreeable to you, but I feel absolutely horrible."

"Sabrina, I don't think that you need to try to be disagreeable to me; you seem to manage to do it effortlessly. But you can relax. Remember, I told you this afternoon that I was aware of the fact you felt wretched. I've no intention of pressing a husband's rights upon you tonight."

Her sigh of relief was so great that he was tempted to change his mind, but he kept from doing so. Her lashes fell again, concealing the pleasure and triumph in her eyes, and she leapt up quickly, turning away from him. As pleased and happy as a little lark, she drew the cover back from the bed and plumped the pillows on it, setting them in the middle.

Sloan felt his temper smoldering, and he fought to control it. He walked past her, drawing one of the pillows back to the left side of the bed. "If you don't mind?" he queried with polite warning.

Her eyes widened as they met his. "But you said—"

"I said that I wasn't going to force myself on you," he interrupted bluntly. "But I've spent enough time sleeping on bare ground and floors. I will take half the bed, if you'll be so kind.''

She stared at him angrily, then swept out a hand. "I'm sorry," she said, her voice sweet with false innocence. "It was my belief that you grew up in a tipi and liked sleeping on the floor. I stand corrected."

He fought the urge to throttle her. "I did grow up in a tipi—and, come to think of it, I spent half the War of the Rebellion in a tent. Very similar, actually. I believe I have actually spent much more time sleeping on the ground as a white soldier than I did as a Sioux child. Ah, well, it's certainly no matter now, because, my love, I have discovered that I do like beds. I even like sharing beds—''

"So I've heard," she murmured.

"So you've witnessed," he said and smiled.

If possible, her pallor became greater.

He turned away from her, snuffing the candle on the bedside table. Shadows fell across the room as he began to discard his wedding apparel. She stood in darkness herself, not moving as she watched him disrobe; frock coat, boots, socks.

"You're free to go to bed," he told her politely.

She still stood rigidly. "You said that—"

"I said that I know you don't feel well, and that you needn't indulge in marital relations. I didn't say that I would sleep on the floor, or fully clothed." He dispatched his shirt and breeches, ignoring her, then crawled into bed and drew the covers comfortably about himself.

She still stared at him. "Fine. I'll take the floor.

"No, you won't."

She hesitated. "I'll take the chair by the fire—"

"No. You won't."

"Dammit, Sloan, I will do as I wish! You may order army privates about as you like, but not me." She grabbed a pillow off the bed and sailed regally over to the richly upholstered chair before the hearth.

He let her sit, then went after her, scooping her up into

his arms and meeting her eyes with a frown of pure warning.

She'd been about to scream, but the sound seemed to die in her throat. She grated her teeth together, pressing against his chest, then drawing her fingers back with alarm when she touched his bare flesh. "Sloan, you said—"

"Mrs. Trelawny, you married me," he reminded her, turning away from the fire and depositing her back on the bed. He truly had no intention of insisting on marital relations—a pity now, because his own nudity coupled with her touch and the silken caress of her hair against him were all but unbearably arousing. Yet, no matter what this torture to her—or himself!—he was convinced that the night would be a foretelling of the future, and he'd be damned if he'd be celibate now indefinitely.

Set back upon the bed, she looked up at him and let her eyes slip over the length of him.

When he heard her sharp intake of breath, he leaned over her, a streak of maliciousness within him. "I'm trying, my love. Honestly, I'm trying. Yet each time you move, each time I touch you . . . well, you can see what torments nature casts down upon me. And to think, you are my wife, and it is our wedding night . . ."

Her lashes remained lowered; she folded her arms across her chest in prayer like fashion, almost as if she were dead. "I'm going to sleep now. I hope you'll be very comfortable."

He smiled slowly and returned to his own side of the bed, slipping back beneath the covers. He reached for her, finding resistance at first, but forcing her gently into his embrace. He willed himself not to want her. That would never work. But he did want to touch her at the very least, draw her near as he did now, feel her hair tease his chest, chin, nose, scintillating with its delicate scent. He wondered ironically if she knew that it was the Sioux who had taught him self-control; in Sioux beliefs, relations with a woman weakened a warrior, and so all young Sioux men learned not to have all that they wanted.

After a moment, she eased against him, her cheek against his chest, her hand lightly resting upon it. She wasn't in a position to feel the extent of his arousal and so seemed peaceable enough after a number of minutes had reassuringly ticked away. "Sloan?" she said after a moment.

"Yes?"

"What are we going to do—now? That this is done. It was so sudden . . ."

She sounded desolate.

Again, he controlled his irritation that life with him, and a child of his, should be such a burden to her.

"It's not really so sudden, is it? We'll go home; the child will arrive in good time."

"Home—an army barracks," she murmured.

"You'll make an outstanding military wife!" he assured her dryly.

"How can a barracks be a home?" she whispered.

He thought of the many women he had met who had followed their husbands westward with nothing but hope.

And love.

And belief, of course. Women who had made homes out of blankets beneath wagons, in shanties in hastily built towns.

His fingers had been moving gently over her hair; they stopped midstroke. He struggled to keep from allowing them to tighten into the auburn mass. "Oddly enough, Sabrina, I do have a home—the kind you're talking about. It's an outstanding Federal manor in Georgetown, and should my aunt die without issue—which is likely, considering that she is nearly fifty now—it actually falls to me. Through the Trelawny side of my lineage, naturally. Most admittedly, my grandfather was deeply distressed by what had happened to my mother, and it was probably difficult for him to accept me at first. But for some reason, the old tyrant and I do get on rather well. He's blunt, honest, and fair, and it's a damned pity, actually, that he retired from the military."

"Then you could retire and live in Washington," she told him.

He hesitated. "Yes, I could."

"Perhaps that wouldn't be quite so bad," she murmured.

"I find my work with the military particularly important right now."

"But perhaps . . ."

"Perhaps what?"

"Perhaps we could have a home in Washington and—"

"Oh, I see. You could live in Washington, and I could ride off with the military."

"It's done all the time."

"You'd be happy as a little lark; it's the world you know and love. You'd be wonderful—the elegant young lady flirting happily away with besotted young congressmen, and possibly even influencing national policy!"

"You're being absolutely wretched."

"I'm not—you told me that you'd wanted your freedom to live in luxury back East."

"That's not exactly what I said—"

"Close enough—"

"Then you could retire."

"But I won't," he told her firmly. "And you will not live away from me. Besides, would you really want to be so far away from your sister?"

She didn't reply.

"We're going to go home," he said quietly.

"Fine, then. Let's go live where the Sioux slaughter the whites, and the whites are trying to decimate your friends and relations. It sounds like a wonderful life."

"It will be what we make it."

Once again, she didn't reply. She didn't move. She lay in silence for a very long time. He was certain that she wasn't sleeping at first, but in time he felt the even pattern of her breathing. He moved his hand over the softness of her hair.

A strange tremor shot through him. He willed himself not to want her so badly. He wondered what he had entered into; if he hadn't been the biggest fool of all time. He grew more obsessed daily. She had married him simply because it seemed that life had offered her no alternative.

Would it be like this, night after night, wanting her and lying awake at her side, tense as a grizzly, hungry as a caged wildcat?

No, she'd have the baby in due time.

And if he survived the torment of this marriage until then?

There would have to be a reckoning.

He closed his eyes and prayed for sleep.

He awoke several hours later.

She was moaning softly in her sleep, thrashing about. He sat up, concerned, placing a hand on her shoulder, shaking her slightly. Her eyes opened; he realized that she had actually been awake.

"Sabrina?"

"Sloan . . ."

She eased to her back, biting her lower lip. In the dim firelight, he could see tears of pain in her eyes.

"Shh, shh, I'm here. What is it?"

"It—hurts."

"What? Where?" he asked, smoothing back the tangle of her hair from the clammy dampness of her face.

"I don't know . . . my back, my lower back. I was queasy all day, but I've been sick so much lately that I didn't really think . . . Now it hurts!" she whispered.

"It will be all right," he heard himself assuring her. "I'm going to get James McGregor."

"James . . ."

"James McGregor. He is a doctor, Sabrina."

She nodded. James had been a convict for several years with David Douglas, but Sloan knew that if David had befriended the man, he had to be completely trustworthy.

He had also come to know the good doctor well himself, since it was James's arrival in America that had brought Sloan to Scotland.

He didn't think, though, that he needed James to explain to him what was happening to Sabrina.

He didn't know why he was so certain, yet he did know, with absolute certainty, at that very moment, that Sabrina had lost the baby.

Life.

It had its ironies.

Her fingers suddenly curled around his arm, so tightly that the nails dug into his flesh, drawing blood. She cried out—a sharp, swift, agonized cry.

Then she passed out, her fingers falling from his arm.

"Sabrina! Dear God, Sabrina!"

Indeed, he was certain that they'd lost the baby.

But he was suddenly praying with silent fervor and vehemence that he hadn't lost *her*.

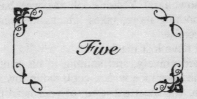

Five

$\mathcal{S}$he didn't feel pain again.

Not physically.

When she opened her eyes, James McGregor was with her. He was a small, ugly little man with the warmest eyes and kindest face imaginable. She knew that he had been a respected physician in Glasgow until a rich man had taken his mistress to his house, already dying from an abortion. She had perished under his care, and the rich man had maintained his own respectability by allowing James to be sent to prison.

Yet, oddly enough, James didn't seem a bitter man, and though he had been almost frightening in his gnomish ugliness when Sabrina had first met him, she knew that he had been instrumental in saving David Douglas's life.

He was by her side, bathing her forehead and her face. She wasn't wearing her elegant white nightgown anymore; she had been changed into a very simple blue cotton nightdress. She didn't hurt; she just felt exhausted. She wanted to speak, because he was smiling at her in a very kindly way, but when she opened her mouth, she felt tears welling in her eyes.

"I killed the baby!" she whispered. Oh, God, that hurt! She couldn't believe she had once thought that it would all be so simple if she merely lost the child. Now it was agony, and surely God had to be punishing her for being such a horrible person.

"Ach, now, lass! Y'didna kill the wee bairn. God's will, and nothing more, takes life, as it gives life," he said very gently.

"But—I have lost the baby."

He nodded gravely, still smiling in his gentle manner as he soothed her face with a cool, damp towel.

"Sabrina, you must get it out of your head that *you've* killed the child—"

"I didn't want it!" she whispered miserably, close to tears.

"There's many a doxie will assure you that not wanting a bairn does not make one go away! Lass, you were taken by those wretched criminal Satanists trying to do away with the Douglases one and all, and kept prisoner for two days in a tomb. Lass, none of that was your fault, though God alone knows if even such a thing took the bairn. . . . I was a good doctor, Sabrina, when I practiced. A very good doctor. And most of what I've seen is that God takes wee ones when there might have been some trouble with the babe—a heart too small, a mind not quite right . . . what matters, lass, is that you're going to be all right. And there can always be another bairn."

"Can there?" she murmured.

Oh, God, Sloan had accused her of not wanting the child, of even having considered attempting an abortion.

And now.

This.

On her wedding night.

She had been losing his child even as she promised to love, honor and cherish him. . . .

"Oh, James!" she whispered miserably.

She couldn't stop them. Tears trickled from beneath her lashes.

"Now, now, lass, you're going to be fine. And you're young as dawn; you'll have years and years ahead to have dozens of wee bairns if you choose."

"This baby mattered!" she whispered.

"All babes matter," James said kindly. "But there's

not a one of us who can undo the good Lord's will; all we can do now is accept it. Well, there are others quite anxious to see you, lass. Let me leave you be.''

"Wait," Sabrina said breathlessly as he rose to leave. "Wait, James—"

He squeezed her hand. "Lass, your husband has been up the night, and waiting down below since I told him he must do so. He's the one who must be with you now.''

"But—"

He released her hand. Before she could stop him, he had gone out the door. She bit into her lower lip, wishing she could disappear. The castle had dozens of secret passageways; she wished she could vanish into one of them forever.

She tried to sit up, wishing that she could rise, but a dizziness assailed her so that she lay back, closing her eyes, fighting the darkness that threatened to overwhelm her again. When she opened her eyes again, Sloan was there, seated beside her on the bed. He was dressed in breeches, boots, and a white shirt, the shirt only half-buttoned—in careless haste, she thought. His dark hair was queued back; the expression in his coal-dark eyes was very grave.

She fought the tears that threatened again; for neither his eyes nor the expression on his face gave away his thoughts. He surely thought her guilty of perpetrating some evil upon their unborn child, and he must hate the fact that he was now shackled to her when they were no longer expecting a child.

"Sloan," she whispered.

"It's all right. You're going to be all right," he said, a husky edge to his voice.

"Sloan, I didn't—"

"I forced too much on you, expected too much from you. Especially under the circumstances.''

"Wh-what?" she whispered.

"I'm sorry, Sabrina. I'm truly sorry."

"Sloan . . . Sloan, you think that it was your fault?" she whispered.

"God alone knows," he murmured, brushing his knuckles over her cheeks. For a moment, his eyes seemed to burn with a strange fire. "For a time there, I thought we might lose you as well. James, however, says that you'll be fine."

She lowered her lashes and nodded. "I feel fine. Just—" She hesitated. "Sloan, I know you believe that I wanted to lose this child. Your child. Perhaps, in a few minutes of pure panic when I first realized the situation . . . I did. But I swear to you that I did nothing—"

"Sabrina," he said with a tired sigh, "I know that you wouldn't endure the distress of marrying me, and then seek to lose the child. If anyone is at fault, it is I, for rather mercilessly insisting on a hasty marriage."

A very bitter huskiness seemed to remain in his voice. She felt painfully distant, as if they had never been greater strangers than they were at this moment, though why, she didn't know. She had fallen asleep in his arms. She had awakened last night in pain, yet still in his arms. Held, secure. She suddenly felt very much alone. He had insisted on the marriage, yes. Because of the child. And now, the child was gone.

"You . . ." she breathed. "You could probably get the marriage quickly annulled, if you wished."

He arched a brow, and the corner of his mouth curved into a dry smile. "An annulment?"

"If you wished," she murmured, feeling again the power of his eyes as he looked at her. She couldn't face him; she was going to start to cry again. She let her lashes fall. "I've lost the child, Sloan—"

"When we agreed to the marriage, Sabrina, we determined that it was going to be a real marriage. No matter what."

"Yes, but this is entirely different. You were doing the noble, honorable thing, giving up your freedom. I can't hold you now—"

"No, my love, you were the one who spoke about wanting freedom. But I'm sorry, Sabrina. I can't give you that freedom. I won't give you that freedom."

"Sloan—"

"No," he stated flatly.

"But—"

He stood abruptly. "Don't worry," he said curtly. "I know you need time to heal. Maybe we both do. I've got to go home; you should really take some time to regain your strength before you undertake a long ocean voyage."

"You're going to leave me—here."

"Yes, I intend to leave you here. With your sister and Hawk. They'll be returning to America next month, and by then you'll be fit to travel. I come and go frequently from my army barracks, but should you arrive when I'm away, any of the soldiers will help you move into my quarters."

She stared at him blankly, wondering why it hurt so much to lose a baby when she couldn't really feel any physical pain. Then wondering why it hurt so much that . . .

He was leaving her. She hadn't wanted him to come here, and she hadn't wanted to marry him, and now . . .

He was leaving her. It should be what she wanted. Time away from him, to think, to plan.

And plan what? Her life? He wasn't giving her life back to her. He didn't want a divorce, but she served him no real purpose.

"What—what if I don't return to America?" she whispered.

He smiled grimly, brushing her cheek with his knuckles once again. "You'll come home, because you'll promise to do so."

"And why should I do that?" she whispered rather breathlessly.

He leaned toward her. "Because if I have to, I'll cross the ocean again to come back for you. And should I do that, my love, you might find yourself ruing the day you decided not to keep a promise to me.'' He straightened, then looked down at her again. ''For the love of God, Sabrina, don't play games with my patience now. I'm trying my best to be decent under the circumstances. And honest as well. I'll give you time. No more—I warned you from the outset that neither of us would walk away from our marriage, no matter what.''

''No matter what!'' she repeated.

''No matter what. So the bargain is this. I give you time. I leave you here. But you come home with your sister and Hawk, and we set up house within the next three months.'' He stood suddenly. ''Are we agreed?''

''Sloan—''

''Sabrina, are we agreed?''

''Yes, yes! I'll go back with my sister and Hawk.''

''I'll take a promise on that.''

''Is a promise good—when it's been threatened out of someone?'' she asked him.

''Your promise, Sabrina.''

''I promise,'' she cried with exasperation. Oh, God, this couldn't go on. She had never felt such a torment and confusion. Wanting him to go.

Wanting him to stay.

He stood abruptly, exhaling on a long breath. ''I'm sorry, I'm not trying to argue with you. James says you could use more sleep. Get some rest. I'll see you again before I leave.''

''No, Sloan, wait . . . please!'' she said, startling herself as she reached out to him.

Puzzled, he hesitated. He took her hand and sat again at the side of the bed. She lowered her lashes quickly, amazed by the strange sense of security she felt from his touch.

''What?''

''I'll go back west; I've promised to do so. But Sloan, I can't begin to understand why . . . .'' Her voice faded as she looked up and found him watching her.

"What is so difficult to understand? We are a married couple."

"But you married me because you had to. What kind of a life can we possibly have—"

"It's my most sincere belief that life is what we make of it. Why are you so unwilling to give life a chance?"

"You are so dead-set determined to live in the West among the S—"

"Savages?" he inquired tightly.

"Sioux."

"That's right. And you wanted the luxury of the East!" She shook her head. "I'd like the luxury of safety. I'm going to be a horrible wife, you know. I'm not familiar in any way with the frontier, with army life—"

"You'll manage fine."

"But Sloan! You didn't want this!"

He rose then, studying her eyes as he stroked her face. "From what I've seen, my love, you can wage war under any circumstance. Someone should probably warn the Sioux that you are coming. You're an incredible challenge."

"You want to stay married—because I'm a challenge?"

He smiled. "I want to stay married because there is an incredibly beautiful and passionate woman within you, and I'm going to find her again."

With that, he left her.

Sloan stood by the fire. Hawk came and set a hand upon his shoulders.

"I'm sorry."

Sloan nodded. "Thanks."

"James says, though—"

"Sabrina will be fine. And God, yes, I have to admit, I prayed until dawn that she wouldn't bleed to death! And God knows I didn't help the situation—"

"Sloan, you had nothing to do with Sabrina's miscarrying. You must know that. James says that such events occur even among young and healthy women, and that they happen under the best of circumstances. Sabrina had a bad time here, which had nothing in world to do with you—"

"Ah, but then I did arrive and learn she was expecting my child—and naturally I did think the worst. I probably accused her of the worst and bullied her into marriage."

"Sloan, you aren't to blame. You've years ahead of you; you'll have more children."

"Will we?" he murmured politely. "She has already asked for an annulment."

Hawk inhaled sharply. "And?" he inquired carefully.

Sloan shook his head. "Well, I do admit, I am torn with guilt, but I'll be damned if I'll give her so easy an out. I'm leaving; I can accomplish nothing more by being here, and I do need to go back. I may well resign my commission soon, but when I do, no matter what my arguments with the government, I intend to leave with a decent record. I'll start home tomorrow—Leave here and arrange transportation out of Glasgow. But I've asked Sabrina to promise that she'll go with you when you return, assuming that it will be soon."

Hawk nodded. "I plan to stay only a few weeks more. The situation at home disturbs me too much."

"It disturbs me, too," Sloan said.

"Don't go getting yourself killed."

"By the Indians—or the soldiers?"

"Either—and keep in mind, you do take a chance with both!" Hawk warned.

Sloan shrugged. "I'll take care. I intend to stop and see my family in Washington, but still, I'll report back to regimental headquarters by the end of January. The going can get damned rough in winter, but I imagine you'll be back by the end of February as well?"

"God—and the weather—willing," Hawk assured him.

* * *

To Sloan's amazement, Sabrina descended the stairs in the great hall of Castle Rock just as the household was sitting down to dinner that evening.

She was elegantly dressed; her hair was beautifully upswept. Her auburn hair and blue eyes were brilliant against her still-far-too-pale features.

He had just been about to sit when he saw her coming toward the table. Without volition, he discovered that he was moving toward her. He was dimly aware that a condemning frown knit his brow as he halted her at the foot of the stairs, a good twenty feet from the table.

"What in God's name are you doing down here?" he asked, taking her arm.

She offered him a smile that encompassed the great hall, for from the large table, everyone was staring at her: David and Shawna, Hawk and Skylar, the MacGinnises and even the good Doctor McGregor. "I'm really quite well."

"But Sabrina—" Skylar protested.

Sabrina interrupted her quickly in reply. "I'm fine, honestly. And I've read stories in which indentured servants and slaves and other working women have had babies and gone right back to doing the laundry or picking cotton the same day. I'm glad that I don't have to pick cotton, but I am feeling well enough to have dinner."

"Sabrina," Sloan reminded her firmly, "you never worked in a cotton field."

"But I'm fine, honestly, and I'd like to be among friends."

Sloan quickly turned to McGregor, who shrugged a little guiltily. He had surely been the one to tell her just how quickly she could mend.

"I would imagine the lass could manage dinner quite nicely," James murmured.

"Sabrina, you're not a field hand," Skylar told her.

"Skylar!" Sabrina offered her sister a rueful half-smile. "We're Americans. All created equal—and we just fought a war to see that people were set free because we are all human beings, God's creatures, very much alike,'' Sabrina said firmly.

''We're all alike as human beings,'' Skylar agreed, ''but your constitution is quite different from that of a laborer!''

Sloan found himself arching a brow at Sabrina in absolute disbelief.

So all men were equal . . .

Except for the Plains Indians.

''I would, however, love to have a chair and sit,'' Sabrina murmured sweetly, looking at Sloan.

He stared back at her, still convinced that she should be in bed.

She lowered her voice for his ears alone. ''Please, Sloan, I can't stand being alone another minute.''

''You can injure yourself,'' he said irritably, further irritated with himself. She'd been so damned pale all day yesterday; he should have realized that something was very wrong. Something even more serious than her aversion to him.

''Sloan, I can't sit up there any longer just thinking,'' she insisted.

He led her to the table, seating her next to him. Myer quickly came to fill her wine glass, hesitating only a moment to look at McGregor, who nodded imperceptibly. Meat, bread, and Anne-Marie's fall harvest of vegetables made it around the table with the only murmurs of conversation being ''Will you pass the bread, please'' and ''Thank you so much.''

Sabrina moved her food about on her plate and took a few bites. She sipped her wine. To Sloan's relief, she seemed to gain color from it. Yet as she drank, she smiled awkwardly, suddenly aware that everyone was silent and watching her worriedly.

''Please!'' she murmured uneasily. ''I'd not have come down had I thought I'd ruin the evening for everyone!''

''You haven't ruined the evening,'' Shawna assured her quickly. ''We're just concerned, naturally . . .'' Her voice trailed away. She cleared her throat. "Sloan, will it really be safe to travel at this time of year?" she asked politely.

"With a sound ship and a good captain, a voyage now might be rough, but quite safe. And I didn't resign from the military; I took a leave of absence."

"Can't you extend your leave?" Skylar asked.

"Skylar, Sloan knows what he must do," Hawk said. "The army frowns upon you when you don't come back. They call you a deserter, and they have been known to shoot deserters upon occasion."

"Yes, but—" Sabrina interrupted, then went still.

"But what?" Sloan persisted.

Sabrina looked down at her plate. "Nothing."

He didn't know why he didn't just leave it alone.

"What were you about to say, my love?" he demanded.

She looked up at him. "Your army shoots deserters, as Hawk said. But then again, your army shoots Indians, right? I mean . . . well, in the West, killing Indians is a main occupation of the army. One day, someone could get confused."

He sat back in his chair. The room had fallen silent. Well, he had forced her to speak. And maybe she had a right to wonder just where his heart really lay.

Especially when he didn't really know himself.

He was beginning to know Sabrina. When she was pressed to a wall, she fought back. It was one of the things he'd admired about her. She was capable of being a tigress.

And right now, if he pressed, she was going to be a little tigress who had just miscarried, who should be upstairs in bed, who still looked as pallid as a ghost.

God help him; he would control his temper.

Maybe.

He smiled at her.

"Please, explain what you're getting at more fully."

"What I said was very simple."

"No, you meant to say more. Please do so."

She stared at him, her blue eyes wide and beautiful, her tone soft. "I would think it's very difficult to be in your position," she said. "For Hawk, it has to be just terrible. But for you, Sloan . . . my God! Imagine, you've remained in the cavalry; working alongside the very people most of the Indians claim have decimated their own. It must be an amazing dilemma. Now, Sloan, you talk. You talk to the whites, and you talk to the Sioux. And they both listen to you, and you try to explain what each side is really saying to the other. But what happens when the talking is over? When it comes to war, just what do you do? What happens? Does everyone embrace you as a friend in the midst of battle—or do they all shoot at you?"

Sloan set his fork down with great care and rose with even more precision, aware that a deadly silence had settled over the table once again. Even Skylar and Hawk seemed pained—and at a loss for words.

He made a point of smiling as he rose.

"Excuse us," he said. "I don't think that Sabrina is as strong as she believes she is; it seems she isn't quite ready for the stress of company," he continued pleasantly.

"I think my concerns are valid," Sabrina said.

He slipped behind Sabrina, speaking softly. "My love, perhaps they are valid; I still think that these are matters we should discuss in private, don't you?"

"Sloan, these are our friends and relations—your blood brothers!" she said, talking very quickly. "And everyone here is concerned with the coming Sioux wars. I'm sure that, realizing the danger of your situation, they might persuade you that the Dakota Territory is not a good place for you to be. Nor is it a good place for you—to bring a wife."

Though he struggled fiercely for control, he drew her to her feet far less gently than he had intended.

Control, he reminded himself. His temper was blazing.

"My poor, poor dear!" he murmured and placed his hand against her forehead. He sighed deeply and swept her up, despite the pressure of her hands against him and the cry of alarm that escaped her lips. "She just isn't feeling well."

" 'Tis a hard thing, losing a wee bairn," Gawain MacGinnis said with sincere sympathy.

" 'Tis sure that it will take healing," James McGregor added softly.

"I'm well enough—" Sabrina started to say, but he quickly hushed her.

"My love, you shouldn't fret about the Sioux situation at a time like this! You need rest," he said firmly. He forced a smile and looked at the others who sat at the table in tense silence. "Our pardon; please do go on. Enjoy your dinner," he said and then led Sabrina up the stairs, holding her so tightly that surely no one could see that she struggled within his arms.

He kicked open the door to her room and put her on the bed. When she would have risen, he straddled her, keeping his weight from her but pinning her to the bed.

"What in God's name was that all about?" he demanded.

She closed her eyes, ceasing to struggle.

"You persisted, if you'll recall. I said 'nothing' several times, I believe."

"You said 'nothing'—but meant to goad me."

"That's not true! Sloan, I don't feel well—"

"How convenient. How damned convenient. But I'm sorry: it won't work, not after your performance tonight. Open your eyes; talk to me."

She opened her eyes, staring at him.

She was pale again, amazingly pale, and her eyes were very beautiful. In the firelight, they dazzled, and he found himself staring deeply into them. She seemed very much the delicate Southern belle suddenly, casting herself on the mercy of a man who would behave as a gentleman.

"Now tell me—what the hell was that all about?"

She shook her head. "You explain it to me!" she cried suddenly. "You explain to me *why* you have to go back to Sioux lands, why you have to fight a war with your-self."

"Damn it, Sabrina, I'm not fighting a war with my-self!"

"You are!"

He leaned back, crossing his arms over his chest. "Sa-brina—"

"What if I insisted that I had to be somewhere—"

"Where?"

"I don't know; anywhere. What—"

"Sabrina, times may change, but wives follow their husbands. Where and when they say. That's the way it is."

"Sloan, times may change, but whites are at war with the Sioux! They kill Sioux, and Sioux slaughter whites. That is the way that it is!"

If she had struck him, she could not have caught him more thoroughly off guard with her vehement—and not at all foundationless—attack.

He felt his every muscle grow rigid. "Is it? Maybe you just don't understand all the intricacies of what is going on. No, Sabrina, whites don't automatically shoot down the Sioux, and even among the so-called hostiles, there are many men who refuse to slaughter white women and children, despite the many times Indian women and babes have been slaughtered in army attacks."

"Are you all able to stop in the midst of an attack and ask who is noble in their methods of warfare and who is not?"

"You certainly seem to be feeling better!" Sloan in-formed her. "Well enough to fight me."

She shook her head, looking down at her hands. "I'm just trying to make you see that . . . that . . ."

"That you want an annulment."

"That you wish to live a very strange life and—and I'm not what you want at all."

He stood, not trusting himself any longer. "You're mistaken, my love. You are precisely what I want. You're my wife.''

''A cavalry wife—to an Indian!'' she said, feeling a rise of hysteria.

''A cavalry wife—to a half-breed,'' he corrected her matter-of-factly. ''A rather good role for you, now that I think about it. I honestly believe that you'll do amazingly well.''

''But Sloan—'' she began, rising as well and coming to him, placing her hand upon his chest as she tried earnestly to press her point. ''Sloan, you don't see—''

''You'd be amazed at what I see. I married you, I want you, and I will have you.''

''You'll have nothing if you're dead.''

''Why are you so damned convinced I'm going to be killed?''

''Because someone—white or red—will kill you because you haven't chosen a side in this conflict.''

He arched a brow suddenly. ''Would you care?''

''I—I don't want to be a party to it—''

''You'd have your freedom.''

''Don't! Damn you, don't do that to me. I've seen enough bloodshed, and I wouldn't want freedom at such a price!'' she cried. She shook her head. ''Sloan! It's true, and I'm sorry; I don't want a rugged life. I don't want to be afraid of the Indians. I don't know a thing about army life. And—and—''

''And you don't want a half-breed,'' he murmured.

She looked downward quickly. He caught her chin, bringing her eyes to his.

''I can make you want me,'' he promised very softly.

She shook her head.

She was so close to him, touching him. And though he knew he had to forcibly dampen all thoughts of making love . . .

He couldn't quite keep from touching her. Not the way she was looking at him now, with the passion and the vehemence that was so much a part of her. Her eyes were brilliantly ablaze. Blood had rushed to her cheeks; her lips were as tempting as wine. Drawing her suddenly and forcefully into his arms, he tasted her mouth with all the savage persuasion burning in his blood. He ravaged the sweetness of her mouth with the thrust of his tongue, caressing and teasing and kissing her until she was pliant in his arms . . .

No longer fighting.

Indeed . . .

But it seemed that his blood was rushing through his veins like hot lava, and he was the one falling. He longed to hold her so closely. Longed to . . .

His arms still around her, he broke the kiss at last and stared down into her shimmering eyes. "Sabrina, if I were a full-blooded Sioux, there would be no question about your coming home to me now. You made me a promise; don't break it. Don't make me come back for you, Sabrina, I warn you."

"Sloan—" she whispered, shaking.

"No, Sabrina, no protests, no arguments. I'm leaving, so we can't argue, so that I can't want to either throttle you or—or just want you. But I warn you again: don't break your promise."

He swept her up again despite her startled cry of protest, deposited her gently back in bed, and left the room.

He left the castle that night as well, riding across the beautiful, rugged terrain of the Highlands by moonlight.

He spent the next day in Glasgow. Luckily, he managed to book passage out the following day.

As he sailed away from the Scottish shore, he couldn't help but brood. He wondered if she would follow him home, as she had promised.

He wondered if he would ever see her again.

He would.

Because he would come for her if she didn't come to

him. Hell or high water—or Indian wars—he would come for her.

With that determination in mind, he turned his face toward the wind.

Westward.

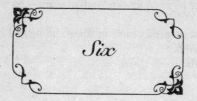

Six

$\mathcal{E}$verything that Doctor James McGregor had said held true. Sabrina was young and strong, and within a few days she felt fine, as if she'd never lost the child. As if she'd never been carrying the child.

Yet, oddly enough, it actually seemed painful *not* to be sick. She longed for the queasiness that had been a part of expecting the baby. It was an absolutely miserable feeling of loss, which she couldn't quite explain since she'd never actually had the child, of course. But though she was well and healthy and felt as if she could run a million miles, she felt as well an incredible, painful void. And strangely enough, she felt terribly alone.

The world, she had realized while coming to Scotland, was immense.

But he had to go back to the Dakota Territory.

She sighed, leaning her cheek on her knee.

"Sabrina."

She turned around and saw that David Douglas, kilted in his clan colors, had come to stand behind her. "You need to come back to the castle, lass. The wind is growing sharper; there will be some fierce cold here soon enough."

She smiled at him, shaking her head. "I'm not cold. I love to watch the colors of the land and the water."

He came around, taking a seat in the grass beside her, drawing a blade of it to chew on as he, too, stared out over the loch. "It's beautiful land. Much like the land my

88

father fell in love with when he went to America, exploring the West.''

She rocked slightly where she sat; the wind was growing colder, yet she liked the way it felt, and she smiled as she looked up at David Douglas. He and Hawk resembled one another, and yet Hawk had definite Indian features as well. How strange. Yet the brothers were approximately the same height; they had the same striking green eyes. And somehow, with a world between them, they had maintained a strong relationship.

''So, lass, will you miss this country when you've gone home?''

She smiled. ''My home is in Maryland.''

He shook his head. ''Land can be much alike. My father fell in love with land in the West because it was rugged, like his Highlands. Home is where the heart and soul long to be.'' He looked at her. ''Where your husband awaits you.''

She looked back toward the loch.

''The Sioux are not all wild slaughterers,'' he told her.

She shrugged, then looked at him again. ''David, is it so strange that I should be afraid—and prejudiced? There have been awful attacks—''

''Both ways.''

''But I'm white, and naturally I see the destruction of a wagon train and the slaughter of women and children as savagery.''

David shook his head, gnawing upon his blade of grass. ''I'm sure you've heard of the Sand Creek Massacre. Soldiers rode into a Cheyenne village, killing infants, old men, and women . . .''

''Yes,'' Sabrina murmured defensively, ''but then I'm sure you've heard of the Fetterman Massacre, when an entire company of men was slaughtered—''

''Soldiers, out to do slaughter themselves,'' David reminded her. ''All right, aside from the fact that there are hostile Lakota Sioux who might well want to scalp you, are you worried about being accepted in society?''

She looked at David, smiling dryly. "I've admitted to the fact that I prefer the luxuries of the East, but I can honestly say that I don't give a damn about society. I grew up with the bastard who murdered my own father and yet managed to create a niche for himself in public life! The opinions of society have very little sway with me."

"Bravo," David told her simply. He lifted his hands. "Well, then, I can honestly say as well that I wish you all happiness with Sloan. He is my blood brother. I do agree with you that he wages war within himself, but then most men do so at some point during their lives. James McGregor went to America at my bidding to find Hawk and reached Sloan instead, and Sloan came here—to help in whatever way he could. He has managed to straddle the fence between the Sioux world and the white world quite well. There was no more diligent a soldier in the Civil War than Sloan. And there is no better friend to the Lakota Sioux than Sloan—he doesn't say what they want to hear; he tells the truth. And they know it. His position is not quite as precarious as you think." He hesitated briefly. "Perhaps you should be forewarned, though, that . . ."

"That? Please, David!"

David shrugged. "Well, Sloan's rank and position are quite unusual. He's considered a liaison, and he doesn't actually have to answer to anyone other than General Sherman, who is the head of the entire military. He somehow manages to get along with Phil Sheridan—who *does* believe that all Indians look for the first opportunity to rape, rob, and murder. They probably despise one another personally, but they respect one another professionally, and Sheridan is a military man who goes by orders rather than his personal opinions.

"Even though Sloan keeps quarters at Fort Abraham Lincoln, he doesn't get along at all well with George Custer, who is head of the Seventh Cavalry there. Fortunately, Custer is not always in residence at the fort. Sloan and Custer rode together in the Civil War; they were both very young—hotheads who could ride circles around a lot of other men. Anyway, Custer ordered some of Mosby's guerillas to be hanged, but Sloan happened to be the officer in charge of the prisoners and he managed not to carry out the orders. He considers Custer to be vain and pompous, though he does like Custer's wife, Libbie, very much. Custer considers Sloan to be stubborn, volatile, and determined. They manage—lots of military men who can't really abide one another manage. But if you encounter some tension once you arrive at the fort, maybe now you'll understand it a bit.''

Looking at him, Sabrina nodded.

David patted her knee. ''Good. My brother says that you're heading home tomorrow!''

David rose.

''Home? Tomorrow?''

It hadn't been much more than two weeks since Sloan himself had left.

They wouldn't be at all far behind.

''So Hawk has said,'' David informed her. ''He's been worried about you, but James says that you're really quite healthy, and sea air will do you good. You'll take an easy carriage ride down to Glasgow, spend a day there, and then start your voyage home on the *Lady Luck*, due out the next morning.''

Home.

Home now meant Sloan. A new life on the edges of the wilderness, in a land where people braved the elements—and the *savages*—to find adventure, or simply to make a better life for themselves and their families. Far away from the society of the East. She closed her eyes. She could remember the majesty of the Black Hills, rising in the distance, ''black'' because of the heavy growth of pine upon them. Staggeringly high at some points, they were far more than hills, and sometimes, when dew settled on the ground, it seemed that horses rode on air. The land was wild, but exquisite.

She touched her lips with her fingertips and felt the

strange sweet fire of Sloan's last kiss sweeping through her again, and she realized that to her amazement . . .

She didn't know what the future held. She didn't know her own place within it. She had made a promise to Sloan that she would return to the Dakota Territory. And she would keep her promise. Yet by then . . .

Would he still be so determined on their marriage? Maybe, back where he belonged, busy with his life, he wouldn't be so determined on keeping their marriage intact. He might have discovered that he didn't want her. And she could remain in the West with Skylar until her sister's baby was born, and then head back east. Where there were no Indian attacks. Where there were no powerful, compelling, half-breed Sioux to both infuriate her and . . .

And seduce her. Into a life of danger and fear.

She wanted him to release her. Certainly. Didn't she?

She didn't know anymore. Because, despite herself, she wanted to see him again.

Sloan reached Georgetown on a cold day in January. Myra answered the bell and enthusiastically asked after his welfare as she took his overcoat. With iron-gray eyes and hair and a handsome face, she looked like the perfect austere housekeeper, except that she had been with the family since she had emigrated to America from Ireland nearly forty years ago and had become a part of it, and she wasn't austere in the least. "Ah, you're looking fine, lad, and that's a fact!" she told him, then added in a whisper, "and 'the dictator' in there is well and good, just the same, healthy as a horse—even if he is getting on in years! Sloan, he has been anxiously awaiting your arrival for weeks now, since you wrote saying that you were leaving the country and would stop here on your way back home."

"I'm anxious to see Grandfather as well," Sloan told Myra, plagued with a sense of guilt. "I'm afraid I don't get east very often."

"No, you don't, and you should be ashamed," Myra agreed sternly, but then she took him by the upper arms and smiled and kissed his cheek, looking him over from head to toe. "Sloan, you have grown into an impressive man; we're all quite proud. And certainly, you leave the ladies breathless. One would think, however, that by this time, you'd have had enough of them casting themselves down at your handsome feet—and chosen a wife from among them."

"Now, Myra, behave. I've not really played so hard and fast, my good woman, because you are forgetting the circumstances of my birth—which my handsome *bronze* feet never allow me to do. Some young ladies might have been intrigued, but they didn't dare face the wrath of their papas. But—"

"General Michael Trelawny is in fine health, young man, but he's not getting any younger! You need to marry, Sloan. Settle down. Give him grandchildren."

Sloan winced inwardly but kept a smile on his face. "Myra, you'll be quite pleased then. I've married."

Her jaw fell and she stared at him, amazed.

"What's this?" boomed a gruff voice.

Sloan turned to see that his grandfather had come into the foyer. He was a tall, thin man with a military bearing. His eyes were a flashing hazel, his thick hair, silver. His face was clean-shaven, with classical contours and angles that made him an arrestingly handsome man, even at the age of seventy-three. Sloan was strangely aware then, facing his grandfather, that he had inherited his grandfather's physique and facial features, even if his coloring was all his father's.

All Sioux.

He smiled, for though General Michael Trelawny could be a fierce-looking man, he was a good, fair one as well—who loved his grandson, regardless of the circumstances of his birth. Sloan strode across the foyer, embracing his grandfather, glad to feel the fierce strength behind the embrace he received in return. Then Michael drew away, looking him up and down, much as Myra had done. "You look fine, son. You look fine. Now what's this about marriage?"

A slow, wry smile curved Sloan's lips. He thought it a pity now that his sense of guilt had caused him to let Sabrina return with Hawk and Skylar, at her leisure.

"It's true, General. I've married."

"Myra! Champagne. It's a miracle!" Michael Trelawny said dryly. "Come, son, tell me about it."

"Make it Grandfather's best Tennessee bourbon, Myra," Sloan advised.

"Make it bourbon," Michael agreed.

He set an arm around Sloan's shoulder and led him into his library, an expansive room to the left of the foyer, rich with mahogany bookshelves and fine leather furniture, along with an excellent display of maps on the far wall. He seated Sloan in one of the thickly upholstered chairs in front of the fire, perching on his desk himself and staring at his grandson with amusement and pleasure. "A wife! I will be damned. You warned me time and again you had no intent of marrying. Who is the young woman?"

Sloan smiled. "Hawk's sister-in-law, Grandfather. Her name is Sabrina."

"A white woman?" Michael was careful to keep the relief from his voice.

"She is a white woman, Grandfather, yes."

Michael sighed, looking down at his hands. "I'm not judging, Sloan. Whomever you might have chosen to marry, I'd have found it in my old heart to be glad for you. And I'd have loved your children—as I came to love you. But Sloan, even in your absence, the picture here has grown blacker. Have you heard any news regarding the situation in your homeland?"

Sloan shook his head, frowning. "I came right here, as quickly as transportation would allow."

"Well, then—" Michael began, but broke off. "Where is this wife you've acquired?"

"I—I have to report back to duty, sir. Sabrina had suffered . . . a minor illness. She'll be coming back quite soon with Hawk and her sister."

"Ah," Michael said, staring at him. "I understand."

Sloan hoped that he didn't. If there was anyone in the world he didn't want to hurt, it was Michael Trelawny.

"So . . ."

Michael threw up his hands. "Where is Myra with that bourbon?"

As if on cue, Myra appeared, silver tray in hand, with glasses and a decanter on top of it.

"The thickest steaks in the country are on the menu for dinner, Sloan. Cook is so delighted, and wait until Georgia hears that you are here; she will swoon!"

"Oh, I don't think so, Myra. Aunt Georgia is actually a touchy old bird."

"Sloan!" Myra said.

"If given half the opportunity, Georgia could have outled half the commanders in the Civil War—including the intelligent and talented men we lost to the South!" the general said. "Now leave that bourbon and go elsewhere to prattle on, Myra. We've business here."

"Yessir, General!" Myra said, winking at Sloan and departing the room with a swish of her skirts.

Sloan, staring down at the bourbon she'd poured for him, had to smile.

"Now, mind you, I don't think that Grant is such a bad man," Michael Trelawny said. "I never faulted him for lack of courage, and that's a fine fact. He was a cunning general; I'm afraid he's not so good a president. He is giving key military positions to old friends, regardless of whether they're corrupt or inept. There's all kind of cries about graft going on, and often the worst of it is in the War Department."

Michael rose, walking to one of the maps on the wall. Sloan narrowed his eyes, studying the map his grandfather was pointing at. It was a map that showed the three army administrative regions presently in operation.

Michael slammed a palm against the map. "Grant is president; Sherman becomes the head of the United States Army—under Secretary of War William W. Belknap. Sherman despises Belknap, and not without good reason. All right; bear with me—you're giving me that look that obviously means you know these things, but follow me and I'll get to my point.

"Three sections, three generals right under Sherman. You've got 'Little Phil' Sheridan in the Division of the Missouri—encompassing Sioux lands. You fought with both men, and you know them. Hard fighters, determined men—they follow their orders. And yes, I grant you, Sherman has often said that any Indian killed this year won't have to be killed next year—not because he has a personal hatred for the Indians, but because he *knows*. He knows that gold has been found in the Black Hills, and he knows that the whites are just going to keep going west, and that eventually they'll completely outnumber the Plains Indians . . . he knows that there has to be a solution to the conflict between the Indians and the whites."

"I *am* in the military, Grandfather."

But Michael only nodded. "Living here in the East after I fought so long in the West, I'm still amazed at times how little the people here understand. They think that all Indians are the same. They have no knowledge of the tribal wars that have gone on for more than a century. If a Pawnee kills a settler, they think you might as well kill a Sioux for revenge. If a Sioux attacks a wagon train, you should round up and slaughter the Nez Perce. They don't begin to understand what's going on, so they pressure the politicians to order the military to kill the Indians. And, ironically, there are many men in the army who know and respect the Indians, and have friends among them. But I tell you, son, so far the military remains damned legitimate in this upheaval—despite the fact that Belknap is a master of corruption!

"But the truth of the matter is that much of the trouble has come from the fact that Grant put the Department of

Indian Affairs under the jurisdiction of all sorts of moral dictators—religious zealots and fools who don't begin to understand that in their concept of 'civilizing' the Indian, they're asking the Indian not to be an Indian! They're asking him to grow food crops on land where weeds won't grow. It's a sorry state, and the latest news is that the government has issued an ultimatum that all Indians must report to their agencies by January thirty-first. Any Indians who haven't reported in and are straying from their contractual lands are to be considered hostile. Sherman is hoping for a quick war; to be honest, I think the generals are praying that the Sioux hotheads *don't* report to their agencies, because they want an excuse to go in and fight, and get it over with.''

His grandfather's prize bourbon seemed to burn in Sloan's stomach. Michael Trelawny had it pegged right for damned certain; the only way the whites would abide the Indians was if the Indians became white.

How could you ask a man like Crazy Horse—a fierce warrior who nonetheless was just, fair, conscientious, and spiritual—to cease to ride the plains, to hunt, to fight for his freedom and his rights?

How could you ask such a man to become an *agency* Indian? The government had supposedly bought land for the allotments that were then given to the Indians. But that's where the corruption was at its zenith: government contractors took enormous kickbacks. If the Indians received grain, it was rat-infested. If they received meat, it was of the poorest quality. The whiskey that came their way was sheer rotgut.

And even if conditions at the agencies had been far better, most whites still couldn't grasp the fact that each warrior was an individual. The white army was organized; Plains warriors fought for individual pride and honor. They were not obliged to follow the dictates of one chief.

Red Cloud had been a great warrior, Sloan reminded himself, but he had seen that the future lay in dealing with the whites, and he led on a peace platform. Still, many braves were leaving the reservations just when the army was preparing to exterminate all hostiles—because Sitting Bull and Crazy Horse were leaders who still saw that there was open land, far from the whites, and there could be no peace between peoples who led such different ways of life. To the Indians, the land belonged to all men. To the whites, the land was something to be claimed and owned.

Michael walked back to Sloan, setting a hand on his shoulder. "You know, Sloan, I hated the Sioux. When your mother was taken, I hated the Sioux with a vengeance. I would have killed every man I could lay my hands on, without remorse. But in trying to get my daughter back, I found myself spending months living among the Sioux and their Cheyenne allies. And I learned that the Plains Indians were not the incredibly noble tribesmen of some of the eighteenth-century adventures, nor were they the filthy, violent savages seen by some of our contemporary writers. They are people. Indian children defy their parents and get in trouble. Young men and women fall in love. They must survive, they must eat, laugh and cry, live and die. They are people. When your father died, his wishes that his wife and child be returned to me were respectfully adhered to. I've been back to Sioux villages with you—and I can honestly say, son, that I'm sorry for it, but the warriors of the plains will soon be brought to heel, and there will be little help for it. I'm glad you've married a white woman. It will help bring you a personal peace."

Sloan set his hand on his grandfather's, where it remained on his shoulder.

"Perhaps."

"Sloan—"

"You know that I have to be a part of this war, Grandfather. You wouldn't advise me to do anything less, would you?"

"No, Sloan. I wouldn't. But I do beg you to be careful."

"That I will be, sir. I promise."

"I wish I could meet your wife."

"You will meet her, sir."

"Hawk Douglas's sister-in-law! Well, I am pleased. Especially since your letters from Scotland informed me that David was, in truth, alive and well. With David alive, Hawk will not feel obligated to the Scottish Douglas holdings. You and Hawk have always been such close friends; with sisters for wives, you'll have strong family ties."

"Yes, sir, I imagine so."

"Have you a picture of your bride?"

Sloan arched a brow and shook his head ruefully. "It was all really rather sudden. I never thought to seek out a photographer, or even ask Sabrina if she had a likeness of herself for me to carry. The marriage occurred at the very last moment."

Michael Trelawny grunted. "I should hope so, grandson—for you wrote me regarding the good news about David, yet failed to mention marriage in your letters."

Sloan shrugged. "Well, for awhile there, sir, we were all rather busy staying alive when I first arrived. Then, when the criminal matter at Craig Rock was settled, I had to turn my attention to getting the young lady to say yes to my marriage proposal."

Michael hesitated. "Well, I wish that she were with you now. When a man rides to a war such as this one . . . well, dammit, Sloan, what will I do if I lose you, when you've left no little ones behind you? Unless, of course, she might be expecting already?"

"No, sir, I'm afraid not."

"Sabrina . . ." His grandfather stroked his chin, musing. "A pretty name—unusual, and yet oddly familiar. What is her maiden name?"

"Connor, sir."

Michael's brow shot high as he surveyed his grandson. "Stepdaughter of Brad Dillman?"

Sloan frowned, startled that his grandfather recognized the name so quickly. But then, Michael had lived in Washington for many years now; he spoke frequently before boards of inquiry and was still active in both military and political circles—not to mention the fact that Dillman's death might well have been front-page news in Washington.

"Yes. Sabrina and her sister, Skylar, were his step-daughters."

He was startled to see his grandfather smile suddenly.

"What is it, General?"

"Naturally, I read the articles about Dillman's death after his attempt to kill the girls . . . you were mentioned in those articles, by the way, in a most flattering light. But I have already met your wife upon a few occasions."

"Oh?" Sloan said, startled and curious.

"Indeed."

"She . . . never mentioned that she met you."

"Well, she met me briefly a few years ago at a dinner in honor of several soldiers, and again at a soiree given by a Washington hostess. Both were large social events, and she was young; I doubt that she or her sister remembers every old codger she was introduced to. Or perhaps she would remember having met me, but wouldn't think to associate my name with you, since . . ."

"Since I do look like an Indian?"

"I'm quite proud of the fact that you also resemble me, Sloan."

Sloan smiled. "Well, sir, I'm proud of that fact as well. So tell me: what was your impression of my wife?"

"Beautiful name, beautiful girl. Spellbindingly beautiful. Exquisite! Captivating."

"Umm. Really."

"Surely you also find her so."

"Yes, of course. I'm well aware of her appearance, but what was your impression . . . other than that?"

Michael was aware that his grandson was impatiently awaiting more, and he took his time. "Mind you, I could have told the American people a decade ago that Brad Dillman was a name synonymous with corruption! But he had a way of speaking; he could sway crowds. He was able to appear to be an absolute pillar of society! Anyway, my heart went out to both those girls the moment I met them. They both doted upon their mother, who appeared very frail. Yet I'll never forget seeing Dillman touch your Sabrina on the arm, and the way that she stiffened in response. The way she looked at him. She behaved so perfectly . . . she was absolutely charming to everyone there. But every time she had a moment's freedom—dancing with a handsome young officer, perhaps—Dillman would approach her, whisper something to her, and have her back talking with some constituent of his, trying to smooth out some troubled waters. I'll never forget the look in her eyes when he touched her or spoke to her. It seemed that she'd created something of a wall of defense against him. Can you imagine living, year after year, with the man who had killed your father?''

''Well, sir, where I grew up, a lad had the right to challenge and kill his father's murderer.''

''Precisely! Those girls had no such rights! Frankly, after their years with Dillman, I'm surprised either of those girls chose to marry.''

''Well . . . Sabrina did marry me,'' Sloan murmured.

''No pictures, eh?''

Michael reached into his desk suddenly, lifting a gold chain from a small silver jewelry box there. He brought the chain to Sloan. ''Take this.''

Frowning, Sloan opened his hand to accept the delicate gold chain. A teardrop locket set with diamond chips dangled from it.

''Remember this?'' Michael asked softly.

Sloan nodded. ''My mother used to wear it.''

''Open it.''

Sloan did so. His own likeness—a photograph taken by the famed Brady at the end of the war—had been fitted into the left side of the locket, while a small lock of his hair was in the right.

''I never knew what was in it!'' Sloan murmured softly.

''You meant the world to your mother. I've always

cherished this, but I think it would be a fitting gift from me to my new granddaughter-in-law. Give it to her for me.''

Sloan hesitated. It was probably the last gift Sabrina desired. But he managed to smile for his grandfather as he pocketed the locket. ''As you wish, sir.''

Michael clapped Sloan on the shoulder. ''I wish you both well. I'm a God-fearing man, but God will surely forgive me for saying that I was delighted to hear that Dillman was dead. Are you quite sure that I'm not about to become a great-grandfather?''

''I'm afraid not, Grandfather,'' Sloan murmured. ''For the time being, sir, you're going to have to trust in me not to get myself killed.''

Michael sighed. ''I trust in your abilities; after all, you learned your military prowess from some of the finest army men as well as from your father and his warrior societies. I trust in your abilities—and then, of course, I also do a lot of praying, down on these old knees. I don't see nearly enough of you. Let's enjoy the time we have. Ah, well, I hope to see your wife again soon enough. For now, I imagine that Cook's got dinner just about ready by now, and your tough-as-nails aunt is surely on her way down to see you.''

''Sloan!''

He heard the trill of his Aunt Georgia's voice, and he winced and smiled simultaneously.

It was good to be here.

Family—Sioux or white—was much the same. And it was good.

He felt a sudden twinge of pain and a keen sense of loss.

He had once been so content living as a loner.

And now . . .

Well, he had a wife.

And James McGregor had assured him that Sabrina was capable of having a family.

And he was suddenly damned determined that, come what may, they would have a family.

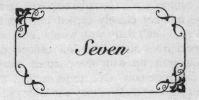

Seven

$\mathscr{G}$eneral Sherman, who despised Secretary of War Belknap, had moved his headquarters from Washington to Missouri, and so Sloan traveled first to St. Louis to report back to duty, managing to reach Sherman's headquarters well ahead of schedule. He arrived in the middle of January, despite the rigors of traveling during a rough winter.

Sherman was a harsh man, but down-to-earth and brutally honest. His battle tactics were merciless, and his vision was damned focused; but Sloan knew him well from the war, and the two men respected each other. Sherman was a great believer in the nation as a whole, and he would fight to preserve it, whether the enemy was rioters in the North, Southern defectors—or Indians.

There had been a time during Sherman's conquest of the south when Sloan had been assigned to him as an aide-de-camp. His service then had stood him well in the years to come; since the war, Sherman had listened to what he had to say, and he knew how to make use of Sloan in the arena of "hostile" communications.

The general greeted him, offering him brandy and one of his best cigars. They sat in the general's office, and Sherman explained the latest movements of the army. "I'm glad you're back; if there's a voice of sanity around here, it's you. You somehow manage to deal with your fellow officers, even when they are complete, arrogant oafs and asses. God knows, I've had enough of those, though of course . . ." The plain-spoken general—his years in the military cleanly etched into his features— paused. "Well, I can't dally with words. You've managed to gain respect from all your fellow officers despite the fact that you grew up with the damned hostiles we're seeking to confront now. Odd thing is, half the men— even the braggarts who claim they can wipe out the Sioux population with one swift stroke—think more highly of the renegade Indians than they do of the 'loafers,' as they call the agency Indians. And hell, half of them can't tell an Indian we're supposedly still at peace with from the Lakota we're chasing."

"But there are no more peace games going on with the Lakota?"

Sherman shook his head. "Let's see, you went on leave in the fall . . . well, you know what happened at the council when we tried to buy the Black Hills."

"You always knew they wouldn't want to sell."

Sherman shrugged. "I'm not the government. Since you've been gone, a number of miners have been killed. That's been seen as a justification for us to claim that any Indians not properly within the boundaries of their reservations are 'hostiles.' That includes the Indians on the so-called 'unceded' lands. On December sixth, Indian Commissioner Smith directed the agents at the Nebraska and Dakota agencies to warn Sitting Bull, Crazy Horse, and any other hostiles that the government is requiring them to be within the bounds of the reservations by January thirty-first."

"Not a lot of time."

"No."

"So . . . the army doesn't really expect—or want—the hostiles to comply, and is intending to hunt down certain bands and wage full-scale war?" Sloan queried.

"Crazy Horse and Sitting Bull are the trouble-causers, I'm afraid. Their bands are the ones I want. I know we're talking about some of your friends—and family, Sloan. If you can talk to them, talk. I take no pleasure in death, except on the battlefield, when death becomes numbers. A thousand dead—a thousand less to fight, a thousand less to kill my men.''

"Regardless of whether treaties are being broken,'' Sloan murmured. He knew that different tribes of Indians had been given different—and specific—lands as reservations, but huge areas of the West were "unceded'' lands: not reservation land, but not land that the Indians had agreed to as being "white,'' either.

"No white person or persons shall be permitted to settle on or occupy any portion of the unceded land without the consent of the Indians,'' Sloan said, paraphrasing the contents of the Fort Laramie Treaty. "And those unceded lands include the Black Hills.''

"Hell, I know that, Major, but I'm not so sure God Almighty could keep miners, prospectors, and adventurers out of the Black Hills right now. There is gold in the Black Hills. Whites are coming, like a tidal wave. Like I said, the game of war always disintegrates into politics, and that's what this is.''

"I'd heard,'' Sloan said. "You're planning on attempting a pincer-movement war against the hostiles.''

Sherman arched a brow. "You've heard—about my plans?''

"I've been at my grandfather's.''

Sherman snorted. "That old war horse would serve me better in the field than half the young fools I've acquired since the war's end. So he sits in Georgetown plucking apart my military operations!''

Sloan shrugged. "Sir, there is no such thing as a secret; the press keeps every bit of news in the papers.''

"We haven't settled on the particulars of the expedition yet, but yes, I see the best way of settling this conflict as striking quickly: a winter war. A pincer movement would press the hostiles between large, prepared forces. So tell me, what will happen with my plan?''

"You have your commanders moving from various forts, and you plan on crushing the hostiles between them somewhere along the rivers west of the Black Hills—the Powder, the Tongue—in that area.''

"Yes. Well?"

Sloan hesitated. "What have your generals reported?"

"Crook is in a hurry, certainly."

Sloan smiled, looking down at his hands. "General, I'm warning you, you can't imagine what winter will be like. You're talking about an area where it can be thirty degrees one day and sixty below the next. Winds, snow, hail—all will have an effect on what's happening. I think you should take great care, sir, if you're really trying to reduce the hostiles to a peaceful situation, that some of those fools and oafs you're talking about don't go attacking the wrong camps, or you'll have Indians who consider themselves friends of the American government joining up with your hostiles and creating one great tribe that will be a huge and formidable enemy to the military."

Sherman scratched his jaw, shaking his head. "Each minor chief makes his own decisions; we both know that."

"Yes, but look at the ardent followers both Crazy Horse and Sitting Bull have drawn."

Sloan saw that Sherman weighed his words, but the general recognized, as many men didn't, how many different tribes of Indians traveled the same hunting grounds at times. "Under the circumstances, Sloan, I'd say that you came home just in time to do your damned best to get the word out regarding the time limit we've imposed. You know damned well that some of the agents who've been ordered to spread the word will make little effort. And even if agency Indians, deserting the agencies to follow Crazy Horse or Sitting Bull, tell other Indians about the ultimatum, they may not be believed. Take your message to the Hills. You may be trusted."

"I can almost guarantee you it won't matter. Crazy Horse isn't an insane warrior; the 'Crazy' didn't come from any foolish or rash actions on his part. His name was his father's, and it came to him when he reached adulthood. He's a thoughtful, serious man who has watched what has happened to his people throughout the years. He doesn't believe a white is capable of telling the truth, and to the best of my knowledge, there isn't a white man alive that he trusts.''

''He trusts you.''

''I'm not white.''

Sherman smiled. ''Whiter than you think. You've got your orders, Major Trelawny. Damned strange ones. You go out there and do your best to make sure that both Sitting Bull and Crazy Horse understand that their Great Father in Washington wants to settle the problems between us, and if it means annihilation of those Sioux who refuse to report to their agencies . . . well, Major Trelawny, I hope they don't decide to shoot the messenger. I expect you to keep in close communication with my generals in the field.''

Sloan nodded. ''Right. I'm afraid, sir, that communications may be all that we have for a time; I'll find *our* troops bogged down in snow, and no more. And may I suggest that we haven't given the hostiles time to comply with these wishes, if they chose to do so?''

''You may suggest as you please, Major. But the question of a Great Sioux War against these hostiles is out of my hands,'' Sherman said. He tapped his fingers on his desk. ''I know well that my friend General Sheridan is not one of your favorites—''

''Well, sir, every time he looks at me, I know he's thinking he ought to be hiding his wife and children.''

Sherman inclined his head with a slight smile, not arguing the fact. ''We've all come in from our various battles with different visions,'' he said dryly. ''I'm not expecting General Sheridan to be in the field, but the division here remains in his hands, and he is your superior officer. I expect you to keep that in mind.''

''I have remained in the military, sir,'' Sloan reminded him, ''and I am aware that he is my superior officer.''

''As to field communication, General Ord is out; General Crook will be leading troops. I know that you have great sympathy for the hostiles, but try not to let our men be taken by surprise or perish while walking around lost in the snow.''

"I won't, sir.''

Sherman nodded. "I'll expect to hear from you personally within the month. Telegram any communications you have for me, and you'll receive further orders. I know that you've often used Fort Abraham Lincoln as your base. General Terry may well be riding from there—''

"Terry? Terry hasn't taken a field command in years, sir. Custer usually leads his men—''

"Custer is now on extended leave in the East. Certainly, he'll hope to lead his men, but . . . well, you know Brevet General Custer. President Grant is hemming and hawing about him right now. George can be a flamboyant braggart, and I know you've disagreed with many of his tactics, but I think that even you would stand by him now, Major Trelawny. He's mouthed off about the graft and corruption going on at the Indian agencies; he's made accusations against Belknap—and he's gone so far as to implicate President Grant's brother. He may be in for a different kind of battle than what he's become accustomed to fighting.''

"Custer is not wholly rational at times, in my opinion, sir,'' Sloan said. "I grant you, Custer isn't exactly my favorite officer, either, but beneath Terry, he is head of the Seventh Cavalry, and I've spent a great deal of time with the Seventh. It is my command. In fact, sir—I intend to make more of a home at Fort Abraham Lincoln. I've recently married.''

"Well, congratulations, Major Trelawny.'' Sherman puffed on his cigar. "You may have more good news coming your way soon. Colonel Perry has apparently expired of a heart attack in Texas.''

"Sir, I'm afraid that I'm not sure how Colonel Perry's expiration is good news,'' Sloan murmured.

Sherman grinned. "Perry was a good old soldier; he

went quickly. His death has left a vacancy in the ranks.
You're up for promotion. Naturally, I'll be the first to let
you know if your promotion is approved.''

Sloan nodded slowly. He hadn't seriously sought promotion; he was pleased with his direct assignment as a
communications officer aide to Sherman—and the freedom it gave him. He hadn't been permanently attached to
any one regiment, and he'd been damned glad of it.

"Sir, my status—"

"Major—you report to me. And naturally, of course,
owe your respect to the ranking field officers you come
across in the line of your work. You're damned lucky,
Major. You have to be one of the only men who has
managed to retain for himself a hint of freedom in the
military. If you're hoping to have a chance to persuade
any hostiles into the agencies, you'd best get a move on.
To the best of my knowledge, the trains are still running
through to Bismarck.''

Sloan quickly rose, shaking Sherman's hand, and
started out.

Even if the trains were running, he still had a rough
trip ahead of him.

And he realized with a sinking feeling that time was
running out.

There was no reason why Sabrina couldn't take her
belongings and set up housekeeping at Fort Abraham Lincoln. Hawk and Skylar would escort her, and her brother-
in-law would see to it that the move was handled
smoothly for her.

But they learned in Chicago that Sloan was riding the
river country west of the Black Hills, and in the winter
weather, there was no telling exactly when he would return.

And then again, it *was* winter.

In all good conscience, she could hardly ask people to
go running about for her in such wretched weather.

Then, of course, the truth of the matter was that she

had now been apart from Sloan for over two months. There were times when she felt incredibly anxious to see him—when she felt tremors, hot flashes, reminding her of what had been. At those times, she felt like a moth drawn to a flame, and she reminded herself sternly that moths drawn to flames burned up. There were other times when she could keep all of her memories of him in the back of her mind and pretend that none of it had ever happened. She knew she wasn't cut out for the West. She was glad to be with Skylar during her pregnancy and wanted to help her with the baby, but more and more often she wondered if perhaps Sloan had changed his mind about remaining married to her now that time had passed, and if she could convince him that an annulment would be the best course for them to follow. She had promised him— in a moment of weakness—that she would come to the Dakota Territory with Hawk and Skylar, and she had honored that promise.

For the time being, she remained quite happily at Mayfair as the days and then weeks passed. It was fun to help her sister plan for the arrival of her baby. Occasionally, though, a fierce stabbing seemed to pierce her straight through the heart; she and Skylar should have been giving birth at almost the same time. It had hurt her to lose the baby, in a way she had never imagined. She had never felt life, but she had known it was there. She didn't begrudge Skylar her happiness in the least; she was delighted for her sister. It was best to forget. And now that they were home, Scotland and her wedding seemed very long ago.

Her initial meeting with Sloan in Gold Town might have taken place during another lifetime altogether, except that sometimes, when the strange hot tremors swept through her, she could remember too much, in agonizing detail. It was best to forget, and go on about life.

She was really managing to do so quite nicely.

Except that now and then . . .

She couldn't help but wonder where he was. And what he was doing.

Despite the winter weather, or perhaps because of it, Hawk and Skylar decided to throw an impromptu party. Anyone and everyone in the vicinity who could make it was invited—of course, in the vast Dakota Territory, neighbors who lived a few days' ride away were considered to be in the near vicinity. A number of soldiers were invited, along with businessmen from Gold Town, their families and wives, miners, scouts—and even the household servants. They were to take turns serving and enjoying the festivities.

The night of the party was beautiful. Getting ready for the party had been fun as well. She and Skylar had chosen what to wear together, and they laughed and joked about how fashionable they were dressing. Skylar had talked her into wearing a gown of royal-blue velvet—a dignified color, Skylar had assured her, yet a gown cut perfectly to the female form. Skylar had chosen hunter green. They both opted to wear their hair down.

Stepping out onto the porch with Hawk and Skylar as the guests arrived, Sabrina breathed in the clean air and felt strangely rejuvenated. It was one of those very rare winter evenings when the temperature had climbed remarkably, hovering very near fifty degrees. Tomorrow, of course, it could plunge far below zero, but for now . . . it was exquisite. A fluffy, new-fallen snow lay on the ground, and the sky was a clear, dark cobalt, streaked with the golden glow of the moon. Henry Pierpont, her friend and Hawk's attorney, arrived, and she greeted him warmly. Hawk's cousin, Willow, a Sioux, came with his pretty white wife, Lily. Soldiers arrived with their wives, and some of the matrons of Gold Town arrived with their young marriageable daughters—eager to introduce them to the handsome young officers who were in attendance.

By early evening, the house was filled, and Sabrina found herself enjoying Hawk and Skylar's eclectic group of guests. The cavalry officers were wonderfully attentive, and she felt young and alive as she hadn't felt in a very long time. It felt good to flirt, to laugh, to feel the warmth of men's admiration.

She danced with several lieutenants, all of whom were absolutely charming but well aware that she was Sloan's wife.

"Ma'am, you are easily the most beautiful woman here," said Lieutenant Blake, a tall young man with an earnest face, as they danced about the room.

"Lieutenant! You are an incredible flatterer. There are many lovely young women here."

The lieutenant sighed. "Perhaps a few. Still, it seems that the really special women are always the married ones!" He smiled again good-naturedly. "But, I grant you, you've married a good man."

"Thank you."

"Major Trelawny is quite amazing, actually. When he sets out alone, he can cover in two days the same ground that it might take a company of men a week to travel. He knows this land better than any man I know. The major has a nose for an ambush, and it seems that no matter how fierce the weather becomes, he knows where he's going. He can keep men safe in the most severe storm. There's no man with whom I'd rather ride."

Sabrina arched a brow, wondering if the man might not be up for some kind of a promotion—one in which Sloan might have a say. "Yet Major Trelawny is half Sioux," Sabrina reminded Lieutenant Blake, wondering why her teeth were grating beneath her forced smile.

Lieutenant Blake offered her a puzzled frown. "Ma'am—you're in Sioux country. Out here you'll find lots of men who are Sioux or part Sioux. And Cheyenne," he added, then shrugged. "Lots more. We use Crow scouts, often enough. And Rees, though of course the Crow and Rees are traditional enemies of the Sioux. We all manage to get along in the military. Personally, I like the Cheyenne. 'Human Beings,' as they call themselves. They tend to have high principles of living, but then . . .''

He shrugged. "You have to live among them to see their principles, right?"

Sabrina laughed, realizing that she liked the lieutenant, and perhaps he wasn't up for a promotion.

"I imagine. And not many white folks want to do that, right?"

"Right."

"But you're cavalry. You'll have to fight them."

He shrugged. "I'm a West Point graduate, Mrs. Trelawny. I follow orders."

She frowned as they spun around the room. "I admit, I've talked to a lot of people who do agree that the only good Indian is a dead Indian, but a lot of the soldiers I've come across have friends among the Indians. It just seems like a rough way to wage war."

Blake shrugged. "Not so hard as the War of the Rebellion, ma'am, though I wasn't quite of fighting age back then. Lots of men came up against their old classmates, commanding officers, teachers. That must have been hell!"

"I'm sure it was."

"Except that . . ."

"Yes?"

"Well, ma'am, soldiers like glory—and they like medals. Why, take Custer!" He flushed and lowered his voice. "Lowest marks ever by a cadet at West Point, demerits enough to fill a dozen books—but he meets old Winfield Scott at the start of the war, ends up with the Second Cavalry, one of the damned few Union heros at the first battle of Bull Run! Why? The man is a soldier—and he'll fight. Oh, my, yes, he does love a fight!"

Sabrina felt a strange little chill go up and down her spine, even though the speed of their dancing had made her warm. "So," she murmured, "war is for glory?"

Blake shrugged again. "Well, military men do need to excel, but actually, this war is going to be for gold—and greed, but begging your pardon, don't say that I said so! Major Trelawny would tell you the same. There was no great rush to push the Sioux to sell the Black Hills until gold was discovered. Truthfully, the Indians often helped the first settlers who headed out west. They were intrigued by them. And it seemed at first that there was plenty of land—except that, of course, there will never be enough land when cultures clash so thoroughly.''

The musicians brought their reel to a rousing halt. She and the lieutenant ceased dancing and clapped for the fiddlers with the others. Lieutenant Blake then offered to get her a cup of punch.

''That would be lovely, Lieutenant. I'll wait by the door; it really is a beautiful night.''

Blake smiled and made his way to the buffet table. Sabrina wandered over to one of the French doorways at the rear of the house. It was open; with so many visitors, the rooms were very warm, and someone else had apparently already felt the need for the cool night air.

She wandered out onto the porch, hugging her knit shawl about her shoulders. She was surprised to realize that it felt very good to be out here. It was beautiful country, and in the night, with the Black Hills etched far to her west as dark leviathans against the moonlit sky, it reminded her oddly of Scotland. She could easily see why a Scotsman like Hawk Douglas's father had found this land so enchanting.

She leaned against one of the porch columns. She started when she heard voices but then saw that a couple of women were seated in rockers at the other end of the porch. They were sipping punch, apparently getting a breath of fresh air as well. One was a young woman with a headful of carefully arranged blond ringlets and a pretty round face. The other woman was slightly older and gave the impression of being an old-maid schoolteacher: she had a long horsey face and dark hair, and was bone-thin. She sipped slowly and deliberately from her mug, rocking all the while and talking.

About her! Sabrina quickly discovered.

''Mind you now, Norah,'' the horsey-faced one was

saying, "it's not as if I actually *know* that there was something strange about the wedding, but I have been with my father at his assigned posts out here for a very long time! And I tell you, Major Trelawny was not a man who set out from here with marriage on his mind! There had to have been something going on, and I can't imagine that it was very ladylike on *her* part!"

The pretty blonde, Norah, sighed. "It's just the most intriguing mystery, isn't it, Louella? She must have something pretty special."

Louella snorted loudly.

Not at all in a ladylike manner, Sabrina thought resentfully. She shouldn't be listening to the women. It was rude.

But why not? She figured they were being rude, talking about her.

"You know what I think?"

"No, what?"

"I think she's really a little opportunist, and that she threw herself at Major Trelawny, and got herself . . . well, in the family way."

"Louella, she has a waist as slim as a reed."

"Maybe she lied to him, made him think that she was in the family way."

"Oh, Louella, remember, his best friend is married to her sister—"

"All the more reason. She plays foul with Major Trelawny, and what choice does he have? He wouldn't want to cause friction between himself and Hawk Douglas! And I have it on very good authority that he certainly hadn't intended to bring a wife back to the fort. All of this happened after he went to Scotland."

"Really?"

"Definitely. There's a man named Raleigh who takes care of Sloan Trelawny's quarters, and Raleigh told me the first he ever heard about a wife was when the major returned from Scotland. He told Raleigh a woman would be coming, and to assist her, naturally, but not to make any special preparations because she was going to be a cavalry wife and she'd have to learn the cavalry way. No beds of roses.''

"Well," Norah murmured thoughtfully. She glanced quickly around. "But he did marry! And he said he'd never marry. He said so to Ally Reeve."

"Ally Reeve!"

"Oh, yes!" Norah said excitedly. It was her turn to impart some deliciously juicy gossip. "You didn't know? Why, I thought the entire world had been aware that after Jim died . . . well, they were scarcely even decent about it; it was nearly scandalous! Ally said he was built like an Adonis in *every* way! She claimed that she didn't want to marry again, but I think that she would have married him in a flash if he'd asked, which is why his returning with a wife seems so peculiar to me! I mean, I think that he did care about Ally, even though she knew about his Cheyenne woman."

"Indeed," Louella said regally. "I *had* heard that there was an Indian . . . wife, mistress—whatever one would call her! Heathen, of course, but the soldiers say that she's a Delilah, wickedly tempting. Voluptuous." She straightened her own slim body disapprovingly.

"I'd have married him, happily," Norah said with a little sigh.

"Your father never would have approved, Norah Leighton. Why, you had family among the first colonists in Massachusetts, and he is . . . half-heathen!"

"Umm, half-heathen. Delectably . . . savage, I do imagine!" Norah replied with a little shiver.

"Norah! As I said, your father—"

Norah laughed delightedly. "Oh, my father would have approved. He admires Major Trelawny." She paused, then said, "I had heard that once, very long ago, he had been about to marry—" She broke off.

"Who?" Louella demanded indignantly.

"A woman. A white woman. A cavalryman's daughter."

"Who?" Louella pleaded.

Norah shook her head. "I can't say; you just wouldn't believe it. She's such a hussy, yet she is society and old money all the way!" Norah laughed delightedly. "Anyway, you can guess, if you like. She married a man with very old English roots in America as well, and he's gone bald as an eagle and round as a house! I imagine she's quite sorry, the way things happened, now."

Louella sniffed, loudly and self-righteously. "There are bloodlines to be considered! Right and wrong, and proper behavior."

Norah smiled. "I'd have married him."

"I'd never do so."

"Oh, Louella, you poor thing, you are just drying up! You'd have married him in a second flat, and you know it!"

"I would not. How can you say such totally improper things—"

"Speaking of proper behavior, have you seen her tonight?" Norah asked. "His wife. It's disgusting, the way the men flock around her. Oh, that's it! Pure lust—I mean, she's a real Jezebel, don't you think? And she flirts with the vigor of a true harlot. Oh! Did you know, she and the major had met here, when there was all that scandal about the Connor girls' stepfather, and Senator Dillman was killed. And I had heard that they couldn't abide one another!"

"Maybe it isn't a real marriage."

"Not a real marriage? Then what?"

"Who knows? I still think that she wickedly seduced him, cried foul to her sister, and forced him into it!" Louella announced, flushed. "Or worse: she pretended she was in the family way!"

Leaning against the pillar, Sabrina longed to step forward and slap them both.

She might well have done so.

Except that Lieutenant Blake chose that moment to reach the French doors and paused there, calling her name. "Mrs. Trelawny? Mrs. Trelawny, are you here?"

The two women in the rockers went dead still, turning a dozen different shades of red. Louella leapt up; Norah did the same.

"You're looking for—Mrs. Trelawny?" Louella asked. "Was she coming out here?"

Sabrina slipped around the column in a manner that suggested she might have just come up the stairway—or might have been there all along.

"Ladies," she said pleasantly, inclining her head and wondering if her eyes were blazing, she was so angry. "Lieutenant Blake, thank you so much for the punch!" She drained her glass quickly, setting it upon the railing, and spun around to face the two women. "Louella, I assure you, I didn't seduce Major Trelawny—he seduced me. And Norah, my husband's past love life is hardly your concern, now, is it? Lieutenant, I think I hear the fiddlers warming up again. Shall we, if you don't mind?"

Somewhat stunned, Lieutenant Blake nevertheless rallied quickly.

"Indeed, Mrs. Trelawny, of course!" They slipped back in and instantly began moving to the music. Still smarting from the vicious conversation she'd overheard, Sabrina moved with him enthusiastically to the music, smiling, chatting, laughing. The lieutenant was a talented dancer, and she felt as if she sailed gracefully around the room.

Damn the harpies! she thought. Good God, she should just ignore them!

"Of course, I'm not quite sure what happened or what was said," Lieutenant Blake told her, "but you do have to take Louella Lane with a grain of salt. She was to marry a young soldier who was killed the last year of the war. She's never gotten over it, and . . ."

"And?"

He shrugged sheepishly. "Well, she's never found another man. And, of course, she and Norah Leighton are both jealous."

"Why?"

"Well, I did tell you before. You're the most beautiful woman here."

He was very kind. Sabrina smiled, feeling a very real warmth and affection for Lieutenant Blake.

"Thank you; thank you very much," she said, looking up into his eyes.

He smiled back down at her.

She spun in his arms.

The music ended; the dancing stopped. The dancers applauded.

Sabrina noticed that a number of people had gathered near the front door to greet a new arrival to the party.

She didn't need to wonder where Sloan was any longer; he was there in the doorway, in full dress uniform, except for the hat. He looked very tall, imposing. He held a cup of Skylar's punch casually in his hands as both men and women clustered around him, anxiously asking questions.

A fierce, jagged chill struck like lightning down to the base of Sabrina's spine.

He nodded, smiled, and talked to the people near him.

But he was watching her.

And she had to wonder then, just how long had he been there?

And how long had he been watching her?

Eight

$\mathcal{S}$loan had known, from the moment he had first seen her, that Sabrina was probably *the* most beautiful woman who had ever walked into his life.

That assessment had probably been far easier for him to make when he had assumed she was a two-bit Gold Town opportunist.

Tonight . . .

It was irritating. It was more than irritating.

She was dressed in royal-blue velvet, a simple full-skirted gown with a single row of ivory lace to line the rim of the bodice and the long sleeves. She wore her hair in a sheer fall of sunset-touched sable down her back, somehow erotic, and somehow sweet, indicative of youth and innocence. She'd managed to regain both her vibrant coloring and a few pounds since they had parted, and it seemed to him, at that moment, that all the weight she'd gained, as well as whatever had been there before, was spilling out of her bodice. She was beautiful, elegant, sensual. And when he first walked in, she was all those things while happily dancing in the arms of another man.

Of course, he knew and liked Lieutenant Blake, who was, however, a puppy—all but fresh out of West Point. A young, handsome fellow. Actually, very young. Closer to Sabrina's age than he was himself. He and Hawk had managed to do their West Point years directly before the opening battles of the Civil War—and had learned on the battlefield what they hadn't been able to acquire from books and drills.

He was astonished to realize that he was jealous of a man—simply because he was dancing with his wife. There was no reason Lieutenant Blake shouldn't have been dancing with her. The party had been under way for some time when he arrived. She had probably danced with lots of men. *But he had never heard her laugh that way when she was with him; he'd never seen her eyes dazzle so!*

Of course, it didn't help that he might have arrived at Mayfair much earlier himself—in fact, he might have arrived two days earlier—if he hadn't expected to go home and find his wife settled into his barracks, as he had instructed her. But he'd given her time. Plenty of time. And he had thought that if she'd truly reconciled herself to the marriage, she would have been there. Waiting.

But no . . .

Here she was. Dancing with the greatest pleasure, laughing, flirting, teasing . . .

And, of course, staring at him now. Appalled. Horrified. Some of the lovely rose flush that had colored her cheeks fading away as she stared at him.

He lifted his punch glass to her.

He willed her to come to him.

She didn't.

So much for the power of his will.

And so much for hoping that she might be glad to see him.

She turned quickly, as if she hadn't noticed that he had arrived, and hurried off toward the French doors leading to the rear of the house—without even excusing herself to her dance partner. No matter. Blake followed right after her, a puppy dog indeed. He might as well have been wearing a leash.

"I can't begin to imagine how you move so quickly through such horrid weather, Major Trelawny!" someone was saying to him.

Mrs. Postwaite. Her husband, who owned a millinery shop in town, was at her side, smiling, nodding; they had a daughter of about eighteen.

"It's a matter of practice," he said politely, "and traveling lightly."

His eyes met Skylar's. She smiled, looking a little flushed, and gave him a quick hug again. "Sabrina is just dying to see you, of course. . . ."

He gazed at her hard, arching a very skeptical brow.

"Naturally!" Skylar said firmly, and he remembered that they were surrounded by guests, all of whom adored gossip—especially in the winter, when there was often so little to do except endure being cooped up in one place. "We're all so happy that you're back; it's just going to be so hard to let my sister go! I know that you'd mentioned something about her settling into your quarters when we arrived, but honestly, I needed to have her here for a while. I just couldn't seem to get myself to allow her . . . to . . . to leave. . . ." Skylar's voice drifted away as she stared at his face. She tried to smile.

"Well, now, I can imagine that it might be difficult for a young woman, unaccustomed to the West, to pick herself up and move into a roughshod fort all by her lonesome!" Josh Postwaite said, an arm around his plump wife, a hopeful smile on his white-bearded and mustached face.

"Well, now, women from the high society of the East Coast do sometimes find it hard on the plains," drawled Cissy Davis, a young captain's sister. She smiled very sweetly at Sloan. "Well, we are rugged and rough in comparison!"

Sloan considered Cissy a walking headache. At that moment, it didn't matter. He smiled at her.

"Well, Miss Davis, since I'm missing my wife and it seems that I've ridden miles through sleet and snow to hear such fine music, perhaps you'll dance with me?"

"Oh, Major!" Cissy said, giggling.

He offered his punch to Skylar and led Cissy out to the

floor. She knew how to dance, and she was a very pretty young woman. She kept up a barrage of conversation, talking with great excitement about the fashion magazines she had just received from New York. He smiled and nodded, at, he hoped, the appropriate times. He carefully searched the room and at last saw Sabrina again, standing just outside the back doors, which remained open. She was surrounded by a flock of military men.

The dance came to a halt. He thanked Cissy, thinking he would have been better off to have asked Mrs. Post-waite to dance. She was a good bit grayer and heavier, but she didn't chatter, and she wouldn't cling to Sloan's arm the way Cissy did now. "Oh, Major Trelawny, indeed, it is so wonderful to have you back with us. There are so many times when you ride away that we girls worry about you, just praying that you won't get yourself into trouble and—"

"Major! Major Trelawny!" a voice interrupted.

Someone was tapping on his back.

He turned around. "Welcome home. Dear sir, we are naturally delighted to see you, hale and hearty—and Major! I must compliment you on your wife."

He groaned inwardly. It was Louella Lane, a prim and proper schoolteacher, who stood before him now. He took her hand, bowing over it. "Thank you, Louella. You are looking exceptionally lovely yourself."

Louella flushed. "We didn't expect to see you tonight."

"Well, I'm back this side of the Black Hills for a few weeks, at least."

"We're delighted. Did you come straight here—for your wife? It's just so amazing—I mean, we had heard at the fort from Raleigh that you had married . . . but *you*, Major Trelawny! We just can't believe it!"

"Well, it is true. I am married. And no, I didn't come straight here; I went to the fort first. I must have missed those riding here by no more than a few hours."

"What a pity. We would have enjoyed your company."

"Thank you."

"You are certainly welcome to ride back with us to-morrow. The Douglases are putting us up here for the night so that we can start back in daylight."

"It will be so much nicer if you do ride with us!" Cissy said. Inevitably, she giggled.

"Well, again, thank you; I will take that into consideration. Excuse me, ladies—" he began.

Louella slipped in front of him. "Major Trelawny, we are all just . . . just stunned by your wife. When did you decide to marry? She is such a lovely creature, of course . . . but so many of us are at such a loss. Did you elope?"

"Elope? Ah—no, it wasn't an elopement."

"But—it's real? You're really married? I mean, even the majority of the men at the fort can't quite believe that you're married!"

"Louella, dear, don't be so rude," Cissy said.

"It's all right," Sloan said. "I am really married."

"Oh, well, we are disbelieving, and deeply jealous, of course!" Cissy said, wide-eyed.

Sloan's head was beginning to pound. Nights spent alone on the hard-packed snow beneath wind and weather were beginning to seem like heaven. Still, he gave Cissy a smile.

"My dear, you're as lovely as can be, and I can't imagine your being jealous of anyone. And Louella . . ." To his own horror, he skipped a beat, but quickly recovered. "Louella, you are completely unique among women! God knows, maybe it was the air in Scotland—and maybe it was my wife's sheer beauty—I don't know! It was rather sudden, I do admit."

"We were so convinced that you'd never marry, that you'd remain a dark, mysterious, half-bre—er, loner, all your life! And anyone would have thought that if you were to marry, it would be to a woman more familiar with the frontier. With Indian ways," Cissy said.

"Ah," Sloan murmured, wondering just which of the women in Cissy's acquaintaince was really familiar with

Indian ways. "Well, maybe opposites attract. Sabrina is from the East, and she'll learn about frontier and Indian ways. If you don't mind, I've not seen my wife since departing Scotland. If you'll excuse me?"

With that, he firmly slipped past Louella and strode toward the rear doors.

The group of military men surrounding Sabrina broke apart instantly, allowing him a path as he approached. Men saluted and called out greetings, which he returned. Sabrina stood alone, as if at the end of a strange honor guard, like a queen holding court.

"Why, Major Trelawny!" Jimmy Blake said with pleasure, saluting and smiling. "Sir, it's good to see you— well, other than the fact that I've enjoyed dancing with your wife, and I'll surely have to give that up now. . . ."

"If you don't mind," Sloan said lightly.

"Major!" Captain Tim Beakins, a dark fellow who probably had some Indian blood somewhere in his distant past, shook his hand firmly. "Sir, the lady is exquisite, but still, have you two really tied the knot?"

"We have," he assured Tim. And his eyes were for Sabrina then, who stared at him as if suddenly at a loss.

"My dear!" he greeted her, taking her hands.

"Sloan!" she murmured, coming to life. "You're— here. How—wonderful. I—I didn't see that you had arrived."

It was on the tip of his lips to call her a wretched liar, yet he realized there was a better way to cut off her insincerity.

"Yes, I'm here," he said very softly.

Then he drew her against him. Hard. Pressed his lips against hers with raw demand and passion. The latter wasn't hard to come by; just seeing her had sent a surge of desire through his body. She was beautiful. Neverbending fire. He had always wanted her, would always want her.

His right arm remained around her back, holding her tightly against him, no quarter given. He cupped her cheek with his left hand. She was very stiff, struggling against the intimacy of his public embrace. How intriguing. He was certain that she'd been prepared for a kiss—just not one as lusty as this kiss.

Maybe he was far more savage a man than he had ever realized—one with the wolves, because it suddenly became very important to him that she, and everyone around them, know that she was his wife. And it was important that these men see them greet one another with the enthusiasm of newlyweds long parted. Of course, she was trying very hard to keep her lips and teeth closed against him. He wouldn't allow it. This evening, it seemed, his passion was going to have to be enough for both of them. One way or another, he was determined to make it appear as if she'd been eagerly awaiting him.

The rise of her breasts pressed against his chest, tempting him to take far more than her lips. Her anger was like a blaze; the pounding of her heart was rampant. The scent of her perfume was intoxicating, evocative, arousing.

Even more so than he had remembered. . . .

His lips broke from hers. He stared into blue eyes that rebelled against his with sheer fury and venom.

"Indeed, it's good to see you, my love," he murmured and released her.

She had been struggling against him so she staggered back, yet he caught her again, steadying her.

"Sabrina, my dear, dear, Sabrina!" he said, smiling at the officers around them. "It's a marvel to come in from the cold and into the arms of a loving wife. Were you anywhere near as anxious to see me, my love?"

She was anxious . . . anxious to hit him, he thought. But she smiled. A huge, sweet—false smile.

"Anxious? Oh, sir! That doesn't begin to describe my feelings!" she informed him, gingerly touching her ever-so-slightly-swollen lips.

"Dance with me," he said. "Gentlemen? . . ."

The men cleared a pathway for them, and Sloan led Sabrina back into the house, where the musicians were playing a waltz. She moved as easily and lightly as if she floated; she had been trained well in all the social graces. Sloan realized that it was the first time they had ever danced together.

"You're very good," he commented. "I can see why Jimmy Blake is sorry that I've returned."

She delicately arched a brow. "The lieutenant has been a complete *gentleman*, charming in every way."

"You mean he is a gentleman, whereas I am not. And surely, he is charming, whereas I am not."

"Oh, I understand that you can be very charming," she informed him sweetly.

"And what led you to that conclusion?"

"Why, the various women in your muddied past who so freely discuss your anatomy."

His brow shot up in surprise. He swept her around the room, seeking someone in it with whom he might have once had a liaison.

"I can assure you: there's only one person here tonight who could describe me in the natural state with any degree of accuracy."

"Only one?" she queried.

"Umm . . . ," he thought a moment. "Well, two. You would be one."

"And the other?"

"Hawk."

"Hawk!" she gasped.

He nodded somberly. "Small children among the Sioux often run around naked when they splash in the streams."

She didn't smile; she wasn't amused.

"What do you want me do, Sabrina?" he asked impatiently. "Pretend I have no past? Obviously, my pretense would do little good. You will hear things. Some of them true; most of them exaggerated."

"Where have you been?" she asked curtly.

He frowned. "On duty—why?"

"On duty where?"

"Looking for Crazy Horse and Sitting Bull."

"Did you find them?"

"Why?"

Her lashes fell in a sweep over her cheeks. "I'm curious as to the state of affairs. The men I've met all seem quite excited about some big maneuver that's about to happen."

He nodded, watching her.

"And you're concerned?"

"Naturally. I'm living out here now, close to sacred ground. A number of miners have been killed recently."

"I see."

"Well?"

"Well, what?"

"Were—you able to spend any time with Crazy Horse?"

"Very little time."

"How much time?"

He frowned. "How strangely persistent you are regarding a soldier's time in the field. I think it's my turn. How long have you been here?"

"Not very long," she said.

"How long."

"A—bit."

He smiled. "Amazing. Hawk told me that you'd actually been back at Mayfair for more than three weeks."

She shrugged. "Has it been that long? Perhaps."

"You were supposed to set up housekeeping at the fort."

"I intended to."

"When?"

"When the time was right." She let out a long breath. Her voice changed ever so slightly, and he could tell that she was well aware that, although she'd arrived in the Dakota Territory as promised, she hadn't completely kept her word, since she had promised to move into his quarters at the fort as well. "Skylar is really not feeling at all well, you know. She needed help settling back in."

"Umm. She has Meggie and Sandra, and a host of servants to be called upon if she's in need."

"It's not like having your sister."

"I'm sure it's not. You told me you'd go to the fort."

"It seemed a rather silly thing to do—since you weren't there."

"But I did go there, expecting to find you."

"I'm sorry."

"Are you, my dear?"

"Sloan, you needn't be so rude."

Again he arched a brow. "I'm just curious about what is really going on in your mind. And if you're capable of really keeping your word."

"I always keep my word—"

"But you didn't."

"I would have. What difference does it make?" she demanded, her eyes flashing a brilliant blue. "You're a soldier; you'll come and go as you please, and I'll sit there in misery time and time again with people I've never met!"

"Once you move into the fort, you'll meet people there, and surely you'll find friends among them."

She hesitated, looking down, shaking her dark head. "In truth, Sloan, I hesitated because . . ."

"Because?" he demanded.

The music came to a halt. Around them, people applauded as they laughed and talked.

"Look at me, Sabrina."

She looked up slowly. "The last time we met, we were both under a fair amount of emotional strain," Sabrina began in a soft voice. "You've been home awhile now. And I've been at Mayfair for a few weeks. Naturally, it's no great hardship to be at Mayfair, especially since my sister is expecting her baby, and I do want to be with her when the baby is born. But I had thought that maybe . . ." Her voice trailed as she looked at him; she faltered, then continued. "I thought that maybe you'd had a chance to rethink our relationship."

Sloan led her away from the crowded dance floor to a quiet corner of the large room, where they wouldn't be overheard. Then he crossed his arms over his chest. "Rethink it how?" he asked her politely.

"Well, think and realize that there really isn't much of a relationship. I'm simply not cut out to be the wife you want. I like the East. I don't like . . ."

"Indians?"

"I don't like being afraid all the time."

"I see," he said slowly, carefully, studying her beautiful features.

"No, you don't see!" she exclaimed, spinning around—headed where, he didn't know. He caught her arm, drawing her back.

"Don't walk away from me."

She looked at him a moment; then her lashes fell. Her cheeks were flushed. She looked very young, very elegant, and very lovely.

"I don't think I can live at your fort!" she whispered.

"There are good men in the service, and many of them have good wives, sisters, and children."

She stared at him. "Malicious gossips, from my experience. But it's not that; I—I really think that getting an annulment is the only rational thing to do."

"No," he said softly.

"All right, maybe you need some more time to think. But, Sloan, with all the excitement going on around here now . . . I should just stay here. I mean, Hawk is your friend, right? My sister is going to have a baby; she needs me. I should stay—right now, at least. And obviously I'd be safe in Hawk's care."

"You think that you should stay here?" he repeated. The pounding in his head suddenly seemed to come from a kettledrum.

"While we both think this out. It would be a good idea, right?" she said anxiously. "We can keep up the pretense of a real marriage if you wish; it will certainly be easy enough tonight. I'll have to share my room with a number of the women staying at Mayfair because Skylar and Hawk are putting up so many people. Many of the men will be sleeping on the floor down here as well, I imagine! Thankfully, soldiers are accustomed to making do with few comforts.''

"Thankfully," Sloan said dryly. He felt stunned. He hadn't known exactly what to expect when he was re-united with Sabrina, but he certainly hadn't expected to discover that while he'd been planning his family, she was considering herself a free woman once again.

"Sloan!"

His attention was diverted by Hawk's cousin, Willow, who was setting a hand upon his shoulder.

"Willow! It's good to see you," Sloan told him. He realized that Willow was looking at him with grave concern, wanting to ask him what he'd learned about the Crazy Horse people; his brothers and family were among them.

"Excuse me; I'll let you two talk," said Sabrina, never one to miss an opportunity. She offered Willow her most charming smile—to which he naturally responded—and then she slipped away.

It didn't matter, Sloan determined. There was really no-where for her to go.

Yet.

"How are my people?" Willow demanded.

"Well, they're far across the hills, heading farther north and massing in very large numbers."

Willow nodded. "My brothers? Sisters? Nephews, nieces?"

"All are well now and send their greetings. Blue Heron has died since I was there last, but he was very old and died in his sleep.''

"He was old when we were children," Willow said. "His death is a natural one. But I'm very glad to hear that all my family are well, though I do fear for the future. Do my people still understand why Lily and I have chosen to live among the whites? Am I resented?''

Sloan shook his head. "Each man follows his own quest. Crazy Horse believes deeply in his visions, and he saw in one of them that you were meant to live among the whites, teaching them that all people are human beings—as his allies, the Cheyenne, say."

"Does he resent you?"

Sloan shook his head. "Not yet, anyway. He had already heard about the government order for all Indians to report to their agencies and reservations. He says he has no reservation, that he's never taken government handouts and isn't answerable to the United States government."

"Did you think that he will change his mind?"

Sloan shook his head again. "No. I sincerely doubt that he would do so."

"He will never surrender." Willow nodded his head very slowly. "As Crazy Horse saw in his vision, I have chosen my way. I have opted for peace—though in my heart, I envy some of my brothers the fight they will wage. What about you, *Cougar-in-the-Night*?" he asked, switching to Sioux and using Sloan's Indian name. "When the bullets start flying, where will you shoot?"

"I can hardly shoot my own people," Sloan said quietly.

Willow grinned. "It remains as I have asked: when the bullets start flying, where will you shoot?"

"It is a fight in which I cannot be in the middle."

"You will wind up forced into the middle."

Sloan shook his head. "I will not be forced."

"What if the white men seeking their battle send you out to find the Crazy Horse people?"

"Crazy Horse has already moved since I have seen him—northward, to take his people to camp with Sitting Bull and the Hunkpapas."

"If you were to choose to track Crazy Horse, you would find him."

"Maybe not. It's big country. Very big country."

"So that is the way the wind blows!" Willow said quietly, then laughed.

"It seems that we must pray a lot."

"Pray a lot, die a lot. Live hard in between," Willow said. He gazed across the room, then glanced at Sloan, a sly smile curling his lip. "So . . . you married Hawk's sister-in-law."

"So . . . yes, I did."

"Hmm."

"What does that mean?" Sloan demanded.

Willow shook his head. "Beautiful woman. All eyes turn when she walks into a room."

Sloan followed Willow's gaze. Sabrina was surrounded by soldiers again—all of them keeping a respectful distance, of course.

Yet all of them . . .

Looking like puppy dogs, ready to trip on their own damned tongues. And she was being charming, talking to each man, laughing, smiling. She had a way, it appeared, of making each man think that he was special, and that what he was saying was either very important or very funny.

Yet she must have sensed him watching her. She looked across the room at him.

She smiled.

Naturally.

She was quite safe. Or so she would assume—here, tonight, in Hawk's house.

With all this company. And all the women sleeping in certain rooms, and all the men sleeping in other rooms.

"She has the right spirit," Willow murmured.

"Pardon?" Sloan asked him, realizing that while he had been watching Sabrina, he'd been thinking and planning, and not listening to Willow.

Willow smiled. "She is very strong. Like a little cat, lost in the woods, well aware that predators exist, and ready to face them head-on. She'll do very well, I think. Very well indeed."

Sloan gazed at him skeptically, and Willow laughed, clapping him on the shoulder. "She hasn't realized that you aren't a predator. Just a *Cougar*—a bigger cat. Maybe that's best at first. I like your wife. Very much. Not just to look at. One day, you will like her, too."

"Naturally, I like my wife," he told Willow. It was his wife who did not like him.

"No, my friend. You lust after her. And maybe you're falling in love. You haven't really taken the time to like her yet. That will come."

"Well, thank you very much for straightening my life out for me, Willow."

"Someone needs to do it," Willow said. He smiled, listening to the musicians. "Another waltz. I must find Lily and help prove that we Sioux are trainable," he said dryly. "And there, ahead of us, is your lovely wife. I didn't intend to interrupt your dancing."

"That's fine—and see, she's about to dance with—ah, young Harris, I believe."

"You can cut in."

"Not this time. I have a few things to do. Go dance, and thank you for the advice."

Willow nodded. "Keep your head low, Cougar," he warned.

Sloan nodded and smiled as Willow left him. Then he hurried through the throng of guests as quickly as he could, briefly greeting those who stopped him, until he reached the kitchen and found Meggie, Hawk's housekeeper.

Ten minutes later, he returned to the room. The musicians were still playing.

Sabrina was dancing with Jimmy Blake again. He smiled as he watched her, and went so far as to ask Mrs. Postwaite to dance, since Mr. Postwaite seemed quite winded.

When the dance ended, he escorted Mrs. Postwaite to the punch table, where Sabrina stood with Jimmy.

"Ah, there's your husband!" Jimmy told Sabrina. "We were looking for you," he told Sloan.

"Oh?" he arched a brow at Sabrina.

She smiled. Charmingly. As if she meant it. She was still keeping up the charade while she tried to convince him that he wanted an annulment.

"I lost sight of you. Where did you go?" she asked.

"Ah, well, I had a bit of business to attend to. Those fiddlers are really quite good, aren't they? Lieutenant, if you don't mind, I will dance with my wife now."

"I'm a poor stand-in, sir."

"You're an excellent stand-in, Lieutenant," he assured Blake, his hand on Sabrina's waist.

In minutes, they were sweeping around the room. They danced well together. He was aware that they were being watched.

"You've been absolutely charming to all the men," he told Sabrina. "They seem quite smitten."

"Well, as I said, I didn't know your feelings on a number of matters, and I've tried very hard to appear to be the perfect cavalry wife until we decide what to do."

"Oh, indeed."

"And where were you? Seeing to the entertainment of all the sisters, daughters, and female cousins of the cavalry, Major Trelawny?" she asked very sweetly.

He smiled down at her, shaking his head.

"I am concerned with only one cavalry family at the moment, my love. My own."

"So . . . if you're concerned with me," she queried, perhaps just a little worriedly, "why on earth did you leave the party for so very long?"

"Was I gone long?"

"Rather."

"And you noticed, with all that attention being lavished on you! I am flattered."

"Umm. And you're not answering me."

"Well, I had to see to the packing, of course."

"What packing?" she asked, a definite edge of concern to her voice now.

His smile deepened. "Your things."

She stopped dead, and they missed a beat. He swept her back into the rhythm of the music.

"We're not leaving yet, and I can tend to my own things, so you—"

"We are leaving."

"But not now—"

"Not this minute, no, my love. But we are leaving tonight."

She faltered completely. They were near the French doors, which were still open. He led her outside. She backed away from him, staring at him as if he'd lost his mind. "Sloan, I thought that we'd agreed to think—"

"I didn't agree to anything."

"I'm trying very hard to be completely reasonable and rational—"

"I made my intentions very clear before we married," he informed her flatly.

She moistened her lips. "Sloan, even if we were to go through with this charade, we—we can't leave tonight."

"Why not?"

"Why not?" she repeated. "Snow! There's snow everywhere. And darkness—"

"There's snow by day or night, Sabrina. And for those of us accustomed to living here, this isn't just a beautiful winter's night; it's damned near a miracle to have weather this good. It won't last."

"But there will be a large party going back to the fort tomorrow. We could travel with the others. We'd be safe—"

"You'll be safe. With me."

He knew from the way her eyes widened that it was he from whom she thought she needed protection.

"Sloan, I am not going. You're insane!"

Maybe his decision to leave tonight wasn't completely rational. If he hadn't been so irritated. . . .

Damn, but she had a way of getting beneath his skin.

"Tell me, Sabrina. Have I really been so horrible to you?"

"I . . ." She paused, inhaling, shaking her head. "No, but you don't understand—"

"Have I ever hurt you intentionally?"

"Truly, how can I know your intentions—"

"Have I?" he insisted.

"No, but—"

"Last question. Can you honestly say that you felt nothing at all when we were together?"

Her cheeks flamed crimson. "You don't understand—"

"Can you say that there was nothing between us, that you could really walk away from me feeling nothing at all?"

"Sloan, please, don't force this from me—"

"You married me, Sabrina."

"I'm trying to tell you that you don't understand—"

"*You* don't understand. There will be no annulment; our marriage is real."

"Why?" she whispered.

"Because you are my wife," he told her. "And I want you."

She seemed stunned, taken completely off guard. Yet it seemed that she was determined to fight a different battle then and buy herself time. "Sloan, please think. Truly!" she whispered. "We can't leave tonight!"

"We can," he assured her. He smiled pleasantly. "The moonlight will allow for some really beautiful riding. We'll leave in an hour, Sabrina."

The flush in her cheeks was gone. She was very pale. He wondered if he wasn't the world's greatest fool, determined to keep her when she was so desperate to be free. Why was he so obsessed?

He drew her to him suddenly. "Once upon a time, Sabrina, I touched pure fire within you. I will find it again. And we will leave tonight."

"I won't—"

"Trust me, my love. You will," he told her, and he turned around, reentering the house before she could argue further.

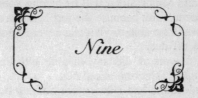

Nine

Sabrina stared after Sloan incredulously as he strode back into the house. He couldn't mean it. He was teasing her, tormenting her because she hadn't jumped to follow his orders. He couldn't mean that he wanted to leave in the middle of the night.

She stepped back into the house, suddenly sorry that she had been quite so sweet to quite so many soldiers— it was difficult slipping through the main room to the foyer because she was stopped every few steps to meet another soldier, a wife of someone, a cousin, a daughter, a great-aunt once removed. Finally, though, she reached the stairs and ran up them so swiftly that she was breathless by the time she reached the doorway to her own room.

Meggie, Hawk's very kind and matronly housekeeper, was humming away as she carefully folded a delicate chemise to pack into a saddle roll. Sabrina paused, staring at her in disbelief.

"Ah, Sabrina!" Meggie said, shaking her head, her eyes damp. "I was so accustomed to you bein' here. It's a joy. But then, that's the way of the world, isn't it? A husband says it's time to move on, and so . . . it's time to move on. Well, I knew I couldn't keep you forever, lass. Your sister is going to miss you frightfully, too, you girls having been through so much together and all. But Skylar's wee babe will be along soon enough, and after that, well, you and Major Sloan will be having your own family. You needn't fret because the fort is not at all far from Mayfair; you'll be able to visit whenever Major Sloan has a few days off duty.''

''So . . . the major did say that he intended to leave here—*tonight*?'' Sabrina asked her.

''Oh, indeed, he and Hawk were both up here, and the major was saying how there would be more room in the house for the guests if you left tonight, and what a beautiful night it was for traveling. Hawk agreed, of course. You've seen how blindingly bad the weather can be! A night like tonight is a sheer gift from God; it's just so stunningly clear. And no wind! But, ah, lass! I will miss you!''

Meggie wiped a large tear from her cheek, and Sabrina went to her. ''Meggie, how sweet, how wonderful of you. As you said, I won't be far. I can come back.'' She didn't know if she was trying to reassure Meggie or herself. ''And before the baby comes at the end of June, I'll be back, and you will all be so busy here!''

She was losing her mind, babbling. She'd been so torn over her feelings for Sloan, and then in such a panic when she had first seen him downstairs and realized the strength of both his presence and his will. She wasn't sure if she had immediately brought up the issue of an annulment because it was what she really wanted—or because she would rather end the marriage than live with him when he had virtually been forced into it.

It didn't matter. It had seemed that she had forever to contemplate the future.

But her ''future'' was about to begin tonight.

And she was suddenly afraid.

She wondered if she couldn't feign an illness that would force Sloan to stay here through the night. It was the coward's way out, she told herself.

Well, she had already decided that she was a coward.

''I'm acting like an old fool!'' Meggie sniffed, patting Sabrina's shoulder. ''This is all quite right, the way it should be. And how wonderful, really, Skylar and Hawk, you and the major! Those men have always been best friends—blood brothers, if you will—and now their children will be cousins.''

''It's just—wonderful,'' Sabrina said dryly.

''Now, I think that I've packed you well for the next few days . . . Willow will be going to the fort with the remainder of your things very soon. There's your good, warm, wool coat, the one with the hood, ready for you to ride in—oh, dear, perhaps you should change your clothing; you've got on that lovely party dress . . . oh, here I am going on and on and your husband has come for you at last! And you'll have a wonderfully romantic ride in the moonlight—you must be so very excited.''

''She's just beside herself,'' Sabrina heard Sloan say.

She swung around. He was leaning against the doorframe, his arms casually crossed over his chest.

''Well, Major Sloan! As you requested, your bride is all set to go. How lovely for you both; it will be like a second honeymoon.''

''Well, not quite,'' Sabrina murmured.

''What was that, dear?'' Meggie said.

Sloan strode into the room, his arms encircling Sabrina's waist. ''She means that we never had a first honeymoon, so this will be true ecstasy.''

Sabrina curled her fingers around his arms where they encircled her waist, trying to break their hold. ''True ecstasy—riding into the snow, in the middle of the night. I can't wait.''

''Well, there is no need to wait, if you're packed,'' Sloan said pleasantly.

Meggie smiled. ''I am delighted for you young people!'' she assured them.

''I haven't said good-bye to my sister,'' Sabrina said, struggling to break his hold with renewed energy. ''If you'll just excuse me . . .''

He released her. She fled from her room and down the stairs, wondering at her sense of panic. Well, she had

deluded herself into believing that she could bring Sloan
around to her way of thinking. She should have known
this was coming. She had married him. She had married
him despite his threats and warnings—and promises that
it would be a real marriage. But that had been in Scotland,
before she had lost the baby. And now . . .

Now they were in territory where the tensions escalated
daily, where she had agreed to live among strangers with
a man who remained an elusive stranger himself in many
ways.

The fort! She wasn't going to be able to bear it, living
among those women who gossiped about her . . . about
him! What was the fort like? How harsh were the living
conditions? Every day would be a far more rugged experience than she was accustomed to, and every day might
offer new dangers as well.

Sabrina walked back into the parlor, where the musicians continued to play. Nothing had changed. The guests
were still dancing, laughing, and drinking punch.

She looked around but saw neither her sister nor her
brother-in-law.

Louella and Norah stood by the punch table. Norah was
flirting with a young soldier. Louella was returning Sabrina's stare.

Sabrina smiled, grating her teeth. She was going to
have a wonderful time at the fort. Indeed.

She walked on through the room, looking for Skylar.
A handsome young man with long gold curls and light
blue eyes stepped into her pathway, excusing himself.

"Mrs. Trelawny, I'm Lieutenant Nathan Greenway. I
ride with your husband upon occasion. I've been trying
to meet you all night, but you've been incredibly busy.
Perhaps you'll give me this dance?"

"I—certainly," Sabrina said, and with Greenway, she
found herself whirling around the floor once again.

"Frankly," Greenway told her, smiling, "I didn't believe that Major Trelawny had really married—not until
I saw you. Now, of course, I know why he did."

No, Greenway didn't know, but Sabrina decided not to enlighten him.

"Thank you," she said simply.

"I'm grateful that you'll be with him now, Mrs. Trelawny. These are difficult times for the major."

"So I understand."

Greenway nodded gravely.

"Personally, I think that the generals are daft, but please, don't go repeating that."

Sabrina smiled, shaking her head. "No, Lieutenant, I certainly wouldn't do that. But why are they so daft?"

He shrugged. "It's a beautiful night tonight. But the weather here is fickle and brutal. A winter campaign is sheer folly. Sloan knows that. I'm sure he's voiced his opinion. Then, of course, he recently went in search of Crazy Horse, and while he was gone, apparently, the springs of action wound into motion. There are a few honest Indian agents out there, men who knew that the Indians hadn't really been given time to comply with the government order. Didn't matter—no one gave a quarter of an inch to allow more time. Not that Crazy Horse was coming in, nor Sitting Bull, for that matter. Those two advocate living completely away from white influence. Can't say that I don't admire them. Still, since the time limit has expired, I think we've already taken steps toward a really terrible war."

"It was my belief that the generals intended war."

"Not the war they're going to get. Some of the fellows in the field wouldn't know a Sioux from a Chinaman, if you'll pardon me, ma'am. Not to mention a peaceful Sioux from a hostile one."

"Aren't the peaceful Sioux on the reservations?"

"My point, ma'am. Some who might want to be peaceful haven't had time to reach their agencies—some of the big reservations have several agencies, and you know what paperwork can be—and it's hard to imagine just how big this country can be! Beautiful country, though. Some of the prettiest in the world!"

"And most hostile—and I don't mean just the Sioux," Sabrina murmured.

"Your pardon?"

"The weather, Lieutenant. You've told me that it's vicious."

"Well, yes, that at times, I do admit. The snows can last through to June. But, oh, you should see the rivers in the spring, the wildflowers . . . it's all quite glorious. And yet, for now . . ." His voice trailed away, and he looked at her unhappily. "Sioux attacked the men at a post established by traders, called Fort Pease. General Terry ordered a Major Brisbin to relieve the post, which Brisbin did. The Sioux had escaped, but—"

"They know that it was a Sioux party attacking? How?"

"They found the Sioux war lodges. Anyway, the Indians, it seems, are playing right into the hands of those who want to annihilate them. That's why I'm glad you're here." He grinned. "There isn't a traitorous bone in your husband's body, but I'm sure that some of the events that occur must infuriate him—they make me angry, and I haven't a drop of Sioux in me. I think your presence will be good for Sloan. You can help him through a very difficult time."

Greenway frowned suddenly, halting though the music continued to play. He turned around, and his frown faded. Sabrina saw that Sloan stood behind him.

"Major!" Greenway said with pleasure.

"Lieutenant," Sloan said. "May I?"

"Of course, sir!" Greenway said, allowing Sloan to cut in on the dance.

Swept into her husband's arms again, Sabrina searched his eyes. "He was just telling me about a Sioux attack."

"Anyone can tell you about a Sioux attack," he responded, and she was surprised because he sounded bitter, and he so seldom did.

"A place called—"

"Fort Pease."

"Yes. Sloan, if you've just been with the Indians who instigated such an attack, isn't it your responsibility to make sure the army knows exactly where they are?"

"Sabrina, I wasn't with the Indians who attacked Fort Pease. I did see Crazy Horse, but that was weeks ago, and in truth, I don't know where he is now, though I imagine he has gone farther north. I delivered the government order to him, as I was instructed."

"And he ignored it," she said.

"Actually, Sabrina, you would like Curly."

"What—who?"

"Curly—Crazy Horse. He's light for an Indian—much lighter than I am, actually. And he's careful and thoughtful and considerate."

"When he isn't scalping people."

"You do know, my love, that from the time the Europeans first came to this country, white men have scalped the Indians to prove how many they had killed, in order to receive the bounty on their deaths."

"That doesn't happen anymore."

"Don't fool yourself."

"But Sloan—"

"Sabrina, I am a major in the United States Cavalry, and I don't forget that fact. Enough said?"

She swallowed, wishing that it was.

"Wonderful. Old Curly will put a bullet right through your heart one day! And since you insist on straddling this fence between two worlds, he's going to have every right to do so. Just like General Sherman will have the right to shoot you!"

"Well, if it happens, you can applaud from the fort, my love. Have you said good-bye to your sister? There's a point I want to reach before dawn."

"Before dawn!" Sabrina whispered. She'd forgotten for a moment that she was leaving. She missed a step. He steadied her.

"Are you all right?" he queried.

"Of cou—I—no! Oh, Sloan, I'm not feeling at all well—" she began.

But his quick laughter cut her off.

"What's so funny?"

"You."

"I'm glad I'm so entertaining."

"Oh, I intend for you to be much more entertaining!" he assured her.

She was tempted to kick him.

"Sloan, really—"

"Sabrina, our horses are outside, their packs are secure, Meggie has filled the saddlebags with good things to eat—and it's time to go."

"You're a wretched man."

"You'll have to get accustomed to that fact."

"I'd rather get used to it while starting out in daylight!"

He smiled. "But if I were kind and gentle and allowed you to lead me around by the nose, I'd no longer be such a wretched man—just a pathetic cuckold. We're leaving tonight, Sabrina. Buck up. You knew you had to face me. Or were you, perhaps, hoping I'd get killed *before* coming for you?"

"Don't be absurd. I've no desire for you to be killed; I had simply thought you might have come to your senses and allowed for an annulment, or if not an annulment, at least enough time to consider an annulment!" she told him hopefully.

"Tell your sister good-bye, and let's go now, Sabrina."

"The party is still underway—"

"I'll carry you out," he warned.

"Oh?" she lifted her chin. "In front of all your men, and the good people from the town and the fort?"

He smiled, his dark eyes smoldering strangely. "Is that a dare, my love?"

"A dare? Sloan, you'd be a fool—"

She broke off with a gasp, because he had easily

whisked her up into his arms and begun striding from the room.

"Sloan!" she gasped, her palms pressing against his chest.

He swung around at the open doors that led to the foyer, "Excuse us, ladies, gentlemen, fellow officers!" he called out pleasantly. "As you all know, my wife and I are newlyweds!"

Sabrina was still struggling against him as those in the room broke into applause and laughter.

"Being that I'm a military man," Sloan continued, "I take what time I can for privacy. Thank you all for your good wishes; we'll see you at the fort!"

He spun around. Sabrina felt herself flush crimson. Laughter was rising again, along with ribald shouts from the men—and a few of the women.

"Sloan, put me down!" Sabrina urged.

"Not on your life. Not until we're out of here!" he informed her.

"But my sister, my cloak! I can't ride like this—I'll ruin this dress—"

But they had reached the front door and were out of it, onto the porch. She saw that Willow stood just beyond it with two horses: Sloan's black military gelding, Thomas, and Ginger, the pinto she had ridden since she'd come to Mayfair. The roll of clothing Meggie had packed for her was tied behind Ginger's saddle, while Sloan's horse carried saddlebags that looked as if they were about to burst.

"Sloan, put me—"

She didn't finish her sentence. He had set her upon the porch and turned her around. Hawk and Skylar had come out to say good-bye. Her brother-in-law held Sloan's overcoat and her hooded cloak.

Her stomach seemed to do a cartwheel.

"Skylar!" Sabrina said, suddenly feeling at a total loss. More than ever, she didn't want to leave. She didn't want to leave her sister.

"Sabrina! This is so sudden; I really wasn't prepared,"

Skylar told her as she embraced her warmly.

Sabrina hugged her back.

Clung to her.

"Incredibly sudden. And I'm not prepared."

Skylar drew away from her slightly, staring at her intently.

"Perhaps Sloan could be dissuaded? . . ." she whispered, since Sloan stood close by, talking to Hawk.

"I've tried. You talk to him. He likes you."

"Sabrina!" Skylar exclaimed. "Sabrina, you married him—"

"It was all your fault!" Sabrina hissed to her suddenly.

"What?" Skylar gasped.

"Shh!" Sabrina said.

"I cannot shush! What did you mean—"

"I didn't mean anything—really, I didn't! I'm sorry, I'm just . . . afraid. He wants to ride into the night! To live with those awful people!"

"What awful people?" Skylar demanded. "Sabrina, Sloan has quarters at the fort. Officers' quarters. Very pleasant. You don't have to live in a barracks with dozens of men. You know that."

"The men are fine. It's the women."

Skylar stared at her a long moment, then said, "Sabrina, Sloan is married now. He never married before. Naturally, you're going to hear tales. And most of the biddies are just talking because they're jealous, and half of what you're going to hear is going to be highly exaggerated."

Sabrina sighed softly. "I'm sorry, Skylar . . . I just . . . I've been taken by surprise, that's all." She gave her sister another fierce hug. "We won't be far away."

"Not far at all."

"Take care of yourself and the baby. And we'll be back, of course. Definitely, before the baby is born. I want to be with you."

"I want you here—if possible. We're really going to be close. And you, Sabrina, take care of yourself."

"Sabrina?"

She felt hands on her shoulders. Sloan's hands.

It was time to go.

She hugged Skylar again, then felt herself warmly enveloped by her brother-in-law. Then, once again, she felt Sloan's touch. He set her cloak around her shoulders and took her by the hand, leading her to her horse. Despite her elegant blue dress, he picked her up and set her down astride her mount.

He mounted his own horse and lifted a hand to Hawk and Skylar, and then started off into the night.

Sabrina turned around, waving to her sister.

She waved and waved. Then she saw Skylar shiver, and Hawk slipped his arms around her. Then they turned toward the house, and went back in.

The house became smaller. The lights eventually dimmed.

Her head was smacked by a low-dipping branch, and Sabrina turned around at last, touching her stinging cheek and looking forward. Ahead of them, it seemed that the snow-covered ground stretched endlessly. There was nothing, nothing at all except endless snow and endless sky—and the moonlight.

Sloan rode ahead, apparently heedless of any difficulty she might be having.

"This is insane!" she called out to him.

He didn't reply.

"You are a cruel tyrant!" she informed him next.

He still kept riding.

"I'll never forgive you for this!"

He stopped, turning around.

"Were you ever going to forgive me anyway?" he inquired.

"I don't know what you're talking about," she informed him, suddenly not liking the way he was looking at her, as if he could see clear through her.

"Yes, you do."

"I really don't."

"What you can't forgive, my love, is Gold Town."

Her cheeks colored, and she suddenly nudged her horse, moving ahead. He caught up with her, catching her horse's reins so that she was forced to stop and look at him.

"You simply can't forgive what happened the night we first met—"

"Don't be absurd. Just because I was horrified to see you again didn't mean that I blamed you."

"You're not angry with me—you're angry with yourself."

"With myself! I was trying to save my sister's life, my own life—"

"And if that had been it, you wouldn't have hated me half so much."

"I don't understand—"

"It had nothing to do with the night—and everything to do with the morning. You were willing to make a sacrifice; you just couldn't handle it when sharing my bed wasn't such a damned sacrifice."

"You're wrong!"

"Am I? Of course, there could be more."

"Oh, really?"

His horse edged very close to hers. "There is the savage Sioux blood—and the fact that I straddle those fences!"

"Let go. You wanted to ride tonight; let's ride."

"And it seems you always want to fight. Let's have at it, then!"

"I am not going to sit out here in the middle of the night in the snow and argue with you!"

"Excuse me! I think I was leading the way in silence when you decided it was important to inform me that I was a tyrant."

"You are a tyrant. May we go, Major Trelawny?"

He studied her for several long moments; then he nodded. "Yes, let's go."

He kneed his horse, moving away from hers. Thomas

broke into a lope. Her mare followed instantly. She was glad that she was a competent rider; otherwise she'd have been thrown into the snow.

They rode hard for at least fifteen minutes; then he slowed their gait. She knew that he would never abuse the horses. When she looked around herself, though, she felt a fierce chill, for now there were dark pine forests to their left and, still, the endless white snow stretching ahead.

They continued on in silence for another hour.

Her limbs grew cold and stiff.

Sloan kept riding.

And riding.

She realized that he was accustomed to these long hours of riding without a break. He could probably go on throughout the night. She could barely move her legs or wiggle her toes. She'd never taken the time to change. She wasn't even wearing proper riding boots, just lace-up shoes with small heels.

Her fingers . . .

Even with the woolen gloves she had taken from the pocket of her cloak, they were freezing. And everyone had kept insisting that the night was so warm! She had been comfortable herself, near the heat of the house, on the porch. But out here . . .

In the never-ending white snow . . .

It was absolutely freezing.

She grated her teeth. She wanted to scream and shout at Sloan, but she forced herself not to do so. She wasn't going to let out a cry for mercy. She'd be stronger than he was, and she'd never falter. Never.

They kept riding . . .

The pines seemed to have a life of their own. They swayed in the darkness—huge, looming shadows. She heard rustling noises from the trees, and she searched through them nervously. Miners had been killed near Gold Town. Sioux had attacked Fort Pease. The Indians weren't fools, and many of them were like Sloan, able to travel great distances at high speeds when they were alone or in small war parties.

There was a cracking sound in the pines . . .

As if someone had stepped on a branch.

She couldn't feel her fingers.

She was frozen . . . from the cold—and from her fear.

Finally, despite her determination, she snapped. She reined in and started shouting. "You arrogant, vicious fool! It is freezing out here. I am going to die from exposure, if I'm not fricaseed by one of the Indians following us in the trees. I'm not riding any farther, I'm not, I'm not, I—"

She broke off. If she didn't ride, what was she going to do?

He reined in and swung around, staring at her with narrowed eyes.

"Are you cold?" he queried politely, as if he hadn't begun to feel the least chill. "You should have said something."

"I did say something. I said that I didn't want to leave tonight, that I wanted to ride back with the others in the daylight."

"Ah, but we're newlyweds, remember? And this is so much more romantic."

"Romantic! Major Trelawny, the woman you married is an iceberg—of your own making!"

He shrugged, amused. "Umm. I wonder. There's a lodge just ahead."

"A lodge?"

"Sioux lodge."

"No . . . wait, no—I don't want to stop at a Sioux lodge, Sloan—"

But he was loping over the snow once again, and she had no choice but to follow.

Somehow, within what looked like a solid mass of dark-green shadow, he found a path. She kneed her horse to follow him closely along the path.

They came to a clearing, bathed by the moonlight. She

could hear the trickle of a creek nearby. In the center of the clearing was a large, wind-weathered, ramshackle tipi.

"Don't worry—it was abandoned months ago," Sloan said, dismounting from his horse.

She still sat her mount, staring at the tipi. She'd never seen one close-up before. In the moonlight she could see that the outsides of the skins had once been painted, but wind and weather had taken their toll upon the patterns. They seemed to run together, yet as she continued to look, she saw that someone had very artistically painted a buffalo hunt: red buffalo ran in mass with a field of warriors racing behind on ponies, and behind them, women and children ran along on foot to take part in the kill.

"Come down."

She drew her gaze from the tipi. Sloan stood by her, reaching up.

"I can get down myself."

He shrugged and went back to his horse, unlacing his saddlebags.

She tried to dismount. Her limbs were frozen. They wouldn't work.

Her foot caught in the stirrup. She started to fall, and for a moment she was terrified that her mare would panic and run, and drag her through the pines until her head was crushed.

But Sloan was there, lifting her, disengaging her foot.

"You know, I could probably stand dead center between Sherman and Crazy Horse and have less chance of injury than you seem eternally determined to inflict upon yourself!" he informed her.

"I can walk," she told him.

He let her go. She started to fall despite her words, her limbs refusing to work. That time, he swept her up.

"Really, please, do allow me the honor," he murmured lightly and entered the tipi.

He set her down on the ground, and she realized that there was a flooring of rough hide as well.

It was dark, yet there was a small opening to the sky

in the center of the tipi, which let in some moonlight. Sabrina could vaguely see Sloan moving about; then she heard the flare of a match, and in a minute he had a fire going.

"That was quick," she murmured.

"It was set; I stopped here on my way to Hawk's."

She was shivering wildly then, unable to feel her feet. Sloan stood and went to her, towering over her. He hunched down in front of her, taking her hands. She tried to snatch them back; he pulled off her gloves and let out an irritated oath.

"Why didn't you tell me how cold you were?"

"You didn't ask."

"You could have said—"

"You wouldn't have believed me."

"When you tell the truth," he informed her, "I believe you. When you pull stunts like tonight, when you suddenly decided to tell me that you were sick, I know damned well that you're lying."

He rubbed her hands vigorously between his own. Warmth began to return to them.

"Give me your feet."

"My feet!"

"Your feet."

"I'm all right—"

He caught her knees, drawing her legs out before her. He made quick work out of the laces of her delicate dance shoes. "This is incredibly stupid footwear for riding—"

"Indeed it is, but then, I didn't know that I was riding tonight."

"I gave you fair warning. You had time to change."

"Fair warning!" she exclaimed, then winced and let out a startled gasp. He had taken off her shoe; then his fingers had moved swiftly up her calf to her thigh and her garter, and her stocking was pulled free.

She froze.

But he warmed her foot between his hands, as he had done with her fingers and hands. He seemed to sense exactly when feeling returned to her, for he started on her second shoe—and stocking—then. He warmed her, but she still shook.

"Your cloak is damp," he said, taking it from her shoulders. "You need to be closer to the fire."

She didn't fight him as he picked her up bodily and moved her toward the fire, setting her down close to the flames. She hugged her arms around her chest, still shivering but delighting in the warmth of the blaze.

Then he left her.

He had been gone several minutes before she swung around, searching for him in the dark shadows outside the tipi. She might be furious with him, but she didn't want him leaving her out here in the middle of nowhere!

But just when she might have stood up and called out his name in sheer panic, he returned, carrying a prepared coffeepot. He set the coffee on the fire, then departed again, returning with his saddlebags and their bedrolls, which he dropped on the floor. He glanced at her then and frowned.

"You're still cold."

"I'm thawing," she assured him dryly. But he sat down at her side and drew her against him, ignoring the fact that she instinctively stiffened. He started to rub her arms and her shoulders, then let out an impatient oath. "You're still damp. How did you get so soaked?"

"How in God's name do I know? It was cold, the air was damp, icicles formed on my nose and then melted—how do I know?"

He pressed her forward, squaring her shoulders, then began working on the elaborate lace ties and buttons that closed her dress. She felt his fingers, and a tremor shot down the length of her spine. "Don't—don't, please, I'm freezing, I'm—"

"Because you're wearing cold, wet clothing, Sabrina. Don't worry. I've told you what I expect from a wife, but I haven't brought you here to force you into anything—well, into anything you don't want to do."

"I don't want to do anything, except warm up," she assured him quickly. "Meggie sent some of my things. Something warm, dry."

"She did. But you've got to get out of the wet before you get into the dry."

She went still, biting her lip. She felt her gown loosen, then felt his hands as he pulled it over her head. She was left in chemise, corset, pantalettes, and petticoat. She kept shivering as he laid the dress out some distance from them, and she was surprised to see that he seemed to be taking care of the garment. She was clenched into a tighter ball, shivering away, when he returned to her. He started to reach for her, and she twitched—involuntarily.

His hand fell. He turned away from her, pulling a blanket from the bedroll and throwing it atop her. "Get the rest of your things off and put that around you."

The blanket landed on her head. She came to life, ripping it off, staring at him furiously.

"You are a dictator—" she began heatedly, but it was the wrong accusation at the wrong time, and she cried out suddenly as she found herself being dragged to her feet and spun around. His hands were on the ties to her corset, wrenching it free.

"I'm a damned dictator, and you, Sabrina, are a spoiled brat with a chip on your shoulder like a two-ton brick—"

"Me?" she inquired incredulously, trying to spin free. "I don't need your help!" she told him.

"My dear wife! I'd not dream of letting you struggle alone!" he said, jerking on the ties to her corset, sending her spinning back around. Then the garment was free and falling off her, and she was blinded and stumbling as he pulled her soft cotton chemise over her head. She reached to retrieve it but missed, for he suddenly caught her by the knees, and she wound up down on the hide flooring, her bare flesh now warmed from the heat of the fire. She gasped for breath as he caught the drawstring to her petticoat, then that of her pantalettes, and each garment was ripped free even as she stuttered out that certainly she could manage on her own.

Naked, she grabbed wildly for the blanket he had given her, wrapping it around herself, and coming before the fire on her knees. "You accuse me of having a chip on my shoulder! How dare you!—"

"My love, you must be warmer. And I haven't even heard a word of thanks. Never mind—I live to serve," he assured her, his tone light.

"Don't taunt me. Just because I'm trying to be calm and rational. This can never really work—"

"You had your choices, Sabrina," he said, and the lightness left his voice. "I remember them well, even if you don't. I didn't drag you to the altar."

"Yes, but—"

"Yes, but what?"

"I just don't think that I can do this! I'm an Easterner, Sloan. I haven't an adventurous bone in my body."

"You made a vow. To me. I won't let you break it. You can do anything you set your mind to. You can be absolutely charming when you want to. I watched you in action tonight."

"You watched me in action!"

"You're an incredible flirt."

She inhaled sharply. "You're missing the point! Sloan, you didn't intend to marry! I've heard that from everyone." She hesitated only a second, her eyes narrowing. "And you call *me* a flirt! I spent the evening learning about a few of your conquests."

"My conquests!" he returned, and seemed startled. "You're talking about the past, my love, while I'm referring to the present. This evening, my love, I arrived to find you flirting outrageously—"

"Flirting!" She was on her feet and almost forgot the blanket. She managed to grab it before it slid down her body. "Flirting! Major Trelawny, you are wrong about so much! You are simply an impossible basta—" She broke off, dismayed, not wanting to call him a bastard because he literally was one. "An impossible wretch!"

She startled even herself with the force of her voice as she shouted at him.

But all he did was slowly cross his arms over his chest. "Am I indeed?" he asked.

"I think that you expect far too much, and I can't begin to see what you want—"

"Well, then, maybe we should discuss what I expect and what I want. Here, now—this very moment."

Quite suddenly, she didn't want to fight. She didn't want to solve anything that night. She wanted to sleep, and gather her strength and wits together.

"Wait, Sloan!" she protested. "It's very late. I'm tired—" she began, then broke off warily as he strode toward her.

"Sloan—"

"Here and now!" he assured her, reaching out. She flinched from his touch, but he simply snatched the blanket cleanly away from her.

He was dead still for a moment, as stunned as she was. They stared at one another; then his eyes slowly swept up and down the length of her as she felt her blood rushing to her face.

"Here—and now," he repeated with a deadly quiet. "Let's assess our situation."

"That's not fair at all!" she whispered.

"Why not?"

"You have the advantage!" she gasped out.

"Shall I take off my clothes, too?"

"No!"

"I wouldn't dream of denying you—me."

"Sloan, damn you—"

"Fine! Then I shall assess the situation. As I see it."

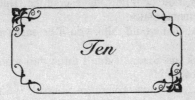

Ten

Sabrina swore at him, reaching for her blanket, but he held it beyond her grasp and tossed it behind him. When she tried to rush past him to retrieve it, he waylaid her with a hand on her arm.

"Let's see . . ." he drawled. Then, releasing her, he walked around her. She started to lunge for the blanket, but he drew her back again. "Stand still. Let me make me make my assessment. Sabrina Connor, a spoiled young lady indeed, out from the East—"

"How dare you say that?" she demanded. "You know that I grew up with a murderer—"

"Yes, the man who murdered your father—Senator Brad Dillman. So you hated Dillman, but you had your mother and Skylar—and Dillman was determined to create the perfect family, so naturally you were educated in the proper manner, dressed in the best clothing, pampered—and you traveled in the best social circles, where the young men fawned over you."

"You don't know anything about my past—"

"But I do."

"How could you—"

"You're not stupid, so you know that you're beautiful. And you know how to flirt and charm—and manipulate. You've got courage—I'll grant you that. It certainly took a will of steel to stand up to Dillman when Skylar fled out here, and to wait for her to send you the funds to

159

follow her. You definitely have courage. But you are a flirt and a manipulator.''

''Indeed. One would think you'd be eager to get rid of me.''

He shook his head. ''I don't think you really want me to get rid of you.''

''Major, your high opinion of yourself is showing.''

Amazingly, she didn't feel cold anymore. She was hot with anger because she was on display.

He stood, his arms crossed over his chest, continuing to study her, assessing every inch.

She folded her own arms over her chest, staring at him in return.

''There's nothing new here,'' she informed him casually.

He smiled. ''Well, you know, the memory isn't perfect. It's been some time.''

''May I have the blanket back? Are you through finding fault?''

''There is no fault, is there, Sabrina? Not a fault anywhere on your perfectly formed little body!'' He turned away from her with such violent speed that she nearly cried out, but all he was doing was grabbing the blanket and tossing it back to her.

She retreated slightly even as she rewrapped herself in the blanket because two long strides had brought him right back to her, and his hands were on her shoulders. ''You are perfect in every way, perfectly desirable, a wife any man would envy. But it doesn't mean a damned thing. No amount of beauty means anything, Sabrina, when there is no heart to go with it.''

''Why are you doing this, then? Making me keep my vows?'' she demanded in a pained whisper.

''I told you. Once, I touched fire. And I don't believe that you didn't feel it. And I'm going to find it again.'' He paused, grating his teeth, then shrugged. ''Besides, I do find you incredibly—damnably!—desirable. You are beautiful, and it would take a saint not to want you.''

He released her abruptly, turning from her. He hunkered down by the fire, took tin camp cups from his saddlebags, and poured out the coffee.

She stood dead still, shivering and angry.

And more hurt than he might ever have imagined.

He wanted her. No emotion involved. He wanted the girl whom he had thought had been sent to him from the Ten-Penny Saloon.

Oh, God. If only she had not gotten so tipsy and let him take her to bed . . .

She wouldn't be caught in this terrible situation. Discovering that she did admire him, that she was compelled by him. Fascinated. And very afraid that if she reached for what was tempting her, she would find herself terribly hurt. . . .

She lowered her head. Maybe she had been just a bit offensive herself, immediately trying to talk him into an annulment. If only . . .

Oddly enough, she realized both suddenly and painfully, she did want to be with him. But on her terms. With him, at Mayfair. No military, and no Sioux involved. And no tales from other women to make her feel such a strange piercing of jealousy . . .

"Coffee's ready," he said.

Coffee's ready, just like that. All those things he had said, and then . . . coffee's ready.

"No, thank you," she said smoothly.

Walking away from him, she found her own bedroll. She laid it out on the ground, then lay down to sleep, curled in her blanket, her back to him.

Sloan said nothing more. A tense silence filled the tipi.

Minutes later, she heard him moving about, then stretching out on the other side of the fire.

She was exhausted, but she was too cold to fall asleep. She had settled down too far from the fire.

Still, she didn't want him to realize that she hadn't fallen instantly to sleep, so she didn't want to move. She started to shiver again.

More time passed, and she heard a clicking sound. She realized it was her teeth, chattering. Still, she didn't move. By that time, she wasn't quite sure she could have done so if she had tried.

Then she nearly jumped sky-high, because Sloan so suddenly and loudly swore at her. "Damn you, Sabrina, you haven't the sense of a buffalo!" She felt his strong arms lifting her not at all tenderly. He moved her closer to the fire—and against his warm body.

She realized dimly that when she had heard him moving about earlier, he had been undressing. He was wrapped in a blanket as well, nothing more, and stretched out on his bedroll.

She stared blankly at the tongues of light and shadow cast upon the tipi walls by the flickering firelight. She felt his arm, wrapped around her waist. And she felt his warmth. The fire was good, the blanket was comforting, but it was the heat from his body that warmed her through and at last allowed her to sleep.

When she awoke, daylight was filtering into the tipi. The fire was down to embers, but the sun had come up and was shining brightly.

Sloan had kicked his blanket off in his sleep.

Sabrina noticed that hers had fallen to her waist. She quickly drew it up around her chest. She lay very still for a long time, hoping that he wouldn't move, wondering if she dared leap up and try to dress quickly before he awoke. Yet as she lay there, barely breathing, she found herself . . .

Studying him.

His back was to her. The color of his flesh was a perfect bronze except in those many places where scars marred his back. She frowned at the scars, then wondered again at the slight difference in the color of his flesh above and below the waist, and then she realized that in warmer weather, he probably rode without a shirt some of the time.

Did he do so with the cavalry—or the Sioux?

He was really quite incredibly . . . well-formed, she decided. His shoulders were very broad, handsomely muscled. His back then narrowed to the lean line of his waist, while beneath that . . .

His buttocks were tightly muscled as well. As were his thighs.

She dragged her eyes upward, to the back of his head. His hair was dark, thick, and glossy . . . she was tempted to touch it, feel its texture.

Her eyes slipped downward again.

And as they did so . . .

He suddenly rolled over, facing her, one brow slightly arched, a curious smile curving his lips.

Leaning on an elbow, he observed her gravely in return. Her gaze jerked quickly to his.

"Good morning," he told her.

She felt a flood of color washing over her, and she drew the blanket closer to her breasts, her lashes fluttering low over her eyes.

"Good morning."

"Did you sleep well?"

"Yes, thank you," she said primly.

His smile deepened.

"But you've been awake awhile."

"Not really. I—"

"Long enough to take your turn and assess me?"

She met his dark gaze, ready to protest. She smiled sweetly instead and informed him, "I'm just trying to see what all the excitement is about."

"Oh? Well?" he asked, and smiled. "Nothing has changed since you saw it before."

"You're covered with scars."

"None of them is new."

She hesitantly touched one of the thin white lines on his chest. "What's that from? It looks very old."

He nodded. "It is. I was a boy. I was told to watch the ponies when I went with a number of older boys to raid a Crow camp—stealing back horses they had stolen from us.''

''And?''

He shrugged. ''I wanted honor and glory. I wanted to count coup—touch and mock my enemy, and ride away.''

''But?''

''A big Crow with a big knife touched me when I touched him. Amazing how humbling fear can be.''

''Fighting the Crows taught you to be afraid. So you became a soldier.''

''You should have seen the Crow.''

She was surprised to find herself smiling. ''I thought that—I thought that the scars in your chest might have come from a Sioux ceremony I've heard about,'' she said somewhat hesitantly, shuddering slightly as she continued. ''Where they hang a man by skewers through his chest.''

Sloan shook his head. ''Ah—the Sun Dance. My father died before I was quite ready to take part in that ceremony, and they didn't practice it in Georgetown.''

''Georgetown?''

''My white grandfather's home.''

''Oh,'' Sabrina murmured.

She had known that Sloan had lived in the white world, but she was surprised to learn that he had spent part of his youth in the East, and very close to her own home.

''You did tell me once that some of your relatives had a large home in Georgetown, but I didn't realize that you grew up there.''

''I didn't exactly grow up there, but I spent time there. As a matter of fact, my grandfather has met you.''

She arched a brow at him, then realized that she had heard the name Trelawny before. Then she remembered the gentleman and gasped softly. ''Of course—Colonel Trelawny. Colonel Michael Trelawny. An older man, very tall and dignified, but kind. He rescued me once!'' she blurted out, staring at Sloan. ''But I'm afraid I'd never have made the association—'' she began, then broke off with a wince.

"I know—I haven't exactly got his coloring," Sloan mused with a trace of dry humor. "How did he rescue you?"

She shrugged. "Dillman was being odious at some social event, and Colonel Trelawny, who is certainly powerful in political circles—Dillman even respected him— came along and insisted on my taking him out onto the porch to tell him about the flowers in the boxed gardens." She smiled suddenly, wrinkling her nose. "I didn't have to see Dillman again the entire afternoon."

Sloan smiled. "Well, I'm glad to hear that my grandfather was of service. By the way, he's a general now and he sent you a gift."

"He sent me a gift?"

"As my new wife. Shall I get it now?"

If he got the gift, he'd have to stand up naked. "That was very kind of him, but I'm sure it can wait for a more convenient time."

His eyes sparkled, as if he knew exactly why she wanted to wait, but he didn't argue.

"My grandfather's service in the military is why I exist—why my mother happened to be on the plains when she was abducted by the Sioux."

"She must have been terrified. She must have hated them."

He shook his head, then shrugged. "Maybe, at first. But she adored my father. She brought me home when he died, and we lived some of the time in Georgetown—or else with her father at his various posts. She served on committees, went to parties, rejoined society—but she never married again."

"Is she . . . ?"

"She passed away about five years ago."

"I'm sorry."

"So am I. She was a great lady."

"You must remember her better than you remember your father."

Sloan shrugged. "Naturally, she lived a lot longer." He

hesitated a moment, then shrugged. "There's a misconception regarding the Plains Indians in the East. They aren't constantly on the lookout to kill, rape, and plunder. In all honesty, many of the Indians were intrigued by the whites and were ready to lend them a helping hand on the way west. My father was Sioux, his brothers were Sioux; they were a large family. Those who are still living have gone their separate ways. Two of my uncles live near the Red Cloud Agency; two of my cousins ride with Crazy Horse, and an old uncle of mine has been following Sitting Bull for many years. My maternal grandfather was also very good friends with Hawk's father, so any tour of duty out here included time spent at Mayfair, and for Hawk and me—and David, when he was in the States, as well—it meant riding out to find our Sioux family, wherever they might be hunting. Actually," he murmured softly, his dark eyes strangely tender for a moment, "I imagine my upbringing was a bit more normal than yours."

Startled at the change in the conversation, Sabrina shrugged, wondering why she felt so quickly on the defensive. "Oh, it was normal enough."

"Your stepfather killed your father. And nothing you and Skylar could do would convince anyone else of that truth. That had to be very hard."

"We hated Dillman but learned to live around that fact."

"Do you hate me? And will you learn to live around that fact?" he inquired.

"I don't hate you," she told him.

"Careful," he teased, "I may take such generous words far too seriously."

She ignored him and quickly touched another scar, a thin white slash on his shoulder.

"Where did that one come from?"

"The War between the States. A Marylander with Lee's Army of Northern Virginia. I should learn to be careful of folks from Baltimore, hmm?"

Sabrina shrugged. "Maybe. I haven't given you any scars."

"Yes, you have."

"Where?" she challenged.

He smiled, rolling a shoulder toward her. There were a few tiny white scars on his back. They did look newer than the others, as if they still might heal.

She looked at him skeptically. "And when did I give you those scars?" she demanded.

He smiled. "The first night we met. In Gold Town. When I thought that you had come to the Miner's Well as one of Loralee's girls from the Ten-Penny Saloon."

"Oh!" she murmured and flushed. "I think you're making that up just to goad me."

He shook his head. "I don't think that you marred me intentionally."

"I was . . . startled, to say the least."

"Umm. I might say that I was stunned by your behavior."

"But I didn't come into your room seeking to claw you—"

"Oh, the scars were well worth the evening," he said, his voice so husky and taunting that despite herself, she felt her temper flare.

And she very nearly struck him.

Except that he was prepared, and caught her wrist. She lost the modesty of her blanket in the bargain.

She bit into her lower lip, fighting to remain silent. Her lashes shading her eyes.

"I'm really sorry. But I did think you were a whore, and you didn't inform me otherwise," he reminded her.

She kept her lashes lowered. "Would it have made things any different?"

"You know that it would have."

"And you know that I didn't dare trust you!" she whispered.

He was silent, and she raised her lashes at last, startled by the way he looked at her. He brushed his knuckles lightly against her cheek, a feathery caress, and she felt her breath catching. His eyes were steady on hers, intent, probing.

"I'm sorry that you didn't dare trust me," he whispered softly.

She felt a subtle tightening within him, and her gaze slipped again, and she felt a new sensation of panic as she realized how aroused he had become. A trembling started to rake through her. A warmth. There was something very pleasant about his nearness. And something more. Something that teased, tempted . . . seduced.

She raised her eyes to his.

"We should probably get dressed and start riding," she said. Oh, God, her voice was just a whisper.

He smiled. "Should we?" he queried softly.

She nodded strenuously, trying to forget that her breasts were bare, and to ignore the way he was leaning against her, so that her nipples were brushing his chest. She could feel him . . . where he wasn't even quite touching her. Heat suffused her. Color flooded her cheeks. She was incredibly aware of every inch of his body, aware of his eyes, the beating of his heart.

The quickening of his breath.

The hardening of his . . . body.

Their position was all but unbearably intimate.

Then he spoke. Softly, almost tenderly. "Do you really think that you can deny the inevitable, Sabrina?"

"I . . ."

Deny the inevitable . . .

She had been trying to do so.

"And it's really rather like falling off a horse," he said, a flicker of amusement in his dark eyes.

"I beg your pardon? *It*? . . ."

"Making love."

"Oh, my God. You're comparing—" She couldn't quite manage to say the words.

"Making love," he supplied.

"With riding horses?"

"Well, you were hurt once. So it's like being thrown. If you don't get right back on, it will be more and more difficult with every day that passes."

She stared at him incredulously, wondering whether to laugh or scream.

"I'm willing to take my chances!" she assured him.

"I'm not so sure that I am," he whispered very softly in return. And then he had her wrists, his fingers wound around them, and he raised them over her head as he leaned over her, his eyes intently upon hers as he came closer and closer. His mouth moved over hers, hot, open, and persuasive. She felt his tongue, thrusting in a sweet, seductive invasion. And she felt the force of his muscled body against her own, his sex so hard against her thigh. . . .

Hot streaks of sunlight seemed to ripple and cascade into her. She wanted to close into herself and escape, but she couldn't possibly do so. It was frightening to be so quickly tempted, to feel the questing, the wanting . . . the seeking. It was frightening . . . to want to be touched, to want to touch him.

Oh, Lord, she wanted to protest, but she couldn't quite do that, either.

She wanted to deny that she felt . . . a sweet, shimmering stirring of fire deep inside of her, but that was there, too, inevitably.

His mouth was alternately light . . . and forceful, teasing and then demanding, until she realized she was returning his kiss . . . seeking it. But then his lips left her, and his body hiked low against her own, and his tongue teased her navel, and his caress nuzzled the soft flesh of her abdomen until he shifted again.

Her hands were free, she realized. And her fingers were in his hair, and she was touching the dark length and texture of it. . . .

His hand curved around the fullness of her breast, cupping it as his thumb grazed her nipple to a hardened peak just before his mouth closed around it. He teased with his tongue . . . sucked, laved. . . .

Heat, like the pure blaze of the sun, swept through her. She shuddered, her fingers winding into his hair. She clenched her eyes, remembering the ecstasy of the feeling . . .

And the humiliation. He had thought he'd been taking a common whore.

She twisted within his embrace, suddenly determined that she'd not be seduced again so easily . . . despite the fact that he was her husband. Because he was her husband! Because he was a practiced lover . . . and this all came so very easily to him. He'd known so many women. He was good. Always good. Just as he had been with her that night. He seduced but gave nothing of himself.

She risked so much with him. Perhaps, in some ways, she had been spoiled, just as, in other ways, she had lived the most bitter life. She had always been confident in her poise and independence; she had learned to keep her own counsel and to trust only in her sister. But she had learned to flirt and tease and manipulate, in the manner of the very best of Southern womanhood. She was the one who charmed, not the one who was so easily seduced. . . .

"Sloan," she murmured. "I . . . no . . . I—" she broke off with a gasp. His hand was between her thighs, his fingers stroking and thrusting. Her words gave way to the vivid sensation. She twisted to escape, and managed only to feel his touch with greater force. Flames seemed to explode within her . . . where he touched, warming her, stirring her. . . .

She tossed her head restlessly, trying to remember her protest, determined . . . on . . .

"No, Sloan, no, I'm not ready for this—"

Her eyes were closed, but she heard his whisper, husky and wry, against her earlobe. "My love, trust me. You're ready."

His hands were on her knees; her thighs were pushed apart. And she shrieked and dug her nails into his shoul-

ders as he rose above her, impaling her with his sex. There
was the slightest pain . . . almost as if it were the first time
again. But it had been so long. So long . . . and yet . . .

God, that fire could burn so hotly, so brightly, so wildly
. . . and feel so sweet. She didn't want to feel so completely, to want, to ache . . . to feel the growing hunger.

She sobbed slightly, clinging to his shoulders, knowing
that she couldn't stop the wave engulfing him, engulfing
her. She held herself rigid, bracing against him, fighting
the very honeyed sweetness that his every thrust, coming
deeper and deeper into her, seemed to bring. Her breath
came in gasps. He sealed his lips over hers, stealing what
little she had left. Then his mouth formed over her breast
again as he moved against her, and jagged shafts of lightning seemed to tear into her. She tossed her head, straining against him.

She was scarcely aware of his muscles tensing at first.
Then the hardness of his body was suddenly such a stiff
constriction that she gasped against its raging force as he
pressed into her and held . . . once, then again, and
again . . .

And despite herself, she felt as if something shattered.
Something hot, sweepingly liquid and yet crystalline,
sending tiny slivers of exquisite sensation throughout her
limbs, from the throbbing at the juncture of her thighs, to
her extremities . . .

He fell against her for a moment, then eased himself
from her, and to her side. She lay stunned and, somehow,
furious with herself.

He could seduce her so easily, draw so very much from
her with so little effort!

Oh, God, it was so easy for him!

His hand lay upon her rib cage. His fingers moved, just
idly, underneath her breast. She suddenly couldn't bear it.
She clasped his hand and moved it away. ''Must you?
Even now?'' she demanded, alarmed to realize that she
was close to tears.

''What?''

"I—I—did what wives are supposed to do. Isn't it enough, for now?"

She couldn't look at him. She felt him staring at her, and she felt his confusion . . . and then his anger.

"Fine," he said impatiently, after a moment. "Get angry at me every time you enjoy an—" He broke off and was silent for a moment, then leaned against her and whispered, "Excuse me. Surely, you took no willing part in this; you've been nothing but dutiful. But dutiful is certainly enough—for now."

She winced, closing her eyes and pulling the blanket around her, wishing she could explain what she didn't quite understand herself. Why was she so defensive?

She remained on the ground, the blanket around her, curled into a ball against the dying embers of the night's warm fire. The sun, coming though the vent, was dazzling.

She heard Sloan rise and don his clothing. She still didn't move. He left the tipi, and she still lay huddled on the ground.

He returned and then she heard a match strike, and she smelled the smoke and the delicious scent of coffee as the fire bounced back to life and the coffee heated.

Then her blanket was suddenly and rudely wrenched from her. "Get up. Get dressed," he told her curtly. "Not the blue dress—something more appropriate for hard riding."

She lay where she'd been, suddenly bereft of all cover. She closed her eyes tightly and remained there, shivering.

She opened her eyes. He still stood there, looking down at her now with a touch of amusement.

"Must I dress you as well?"

"No!"

She leapt to her feet, dismayed to realize that he was watching her. She fumbled with her stockings and pantalettes as she stepped back into them, then quickly snatched up her chemise. Half-clad then, she looked through the clothing Meggie had packed for her, finding a gray riding habit with a snug jacket and a heavy, voluminous skirt. She sat to put on her shoes, and when she was done, she realized that Sloan was still watching her. Much to her annoyance, he still seemed entertained.

"I was afraid you were going to topple into the fire . . . burn to death—rather than ask for help."

"I didn't need help—"

"No, not at all."

"All right, so perhaps I needed help. Perhaps I shall always need help. I'll be an inept cavalry wife because I really belong back East!"

"You belong with me, dear wife. Enduring any discomfort for the sake of your wedding vows! The coffee is hot," he added.

She noted that he hadn't poured her any.

She rose and poured her own coffee. Her hands were shaking, and she dropped the pot. She quickly leaned down to pick up the pot before all of the coffee spilled out; he did the same. Their heads crashed together, and she stumbled back dizzily.

"Perhaps I should pour," he commented, rubbing his temple.

"I'm not going to be good at this at all."

He handed her a cup of coffee. "You needn't fret, my love. You're proving to be good at all that really matters!"

"Oh!" she cried out, clenching her fists at her sides.

"I meant it as a compliment."

"And it would have been a fine compliment—if I were, in truth, one of Loralee's whores!"

He let out an oath of impatience. "All right, you're only so-so. Is that better?"

She wanted to take a swing at him again, but he wasn't going to allow it. He caught her, drawing her against him so that her arms were pinned.

She stared at him furiously. He smiled suddenly, and she flushed as she realized that he was growing aroused once again. She began to struggle against his hold.

"Stop! Be very still."

"Sloan—"

"Shh!" he warned. "If you move away quickly once I let go, we'll probably get out of here without working at improving our intimate relationship!" he murmured.

"Damn you, Sloan—"

"There are probably biscuits and jerky in the package Meggie packed in the saddlebags. Why don't you see?"

She swallowed hard. "Yes, indeed, Major, sir!" she responded without moving.

"Ah, that's what I like! A cheerful coworker. An amiable, charming mate with whom I can go through life! Considering how damned independent you like to be, you will surely want to pull a little of the weight around here!"

"I'm not at all good at pulling weight."

"We'll have to see that you become so—through practice."

He suddenly released her, slapping her lightly on the derriere.

"To work, cavalry wife."

"Squaw!" she muttered.

"As you like it!"

She crossed her arms over her chest, staring at him. But a flicker of guilt arose within her. He had made the fire last night and this morning, carried in the bedding and the saddlebags. He'd made the coffee.

Perhaps she could contribute.

But then again, she could also have spent the night in a comfortable bed . . .

With an army wife snoring beside her.

It didn't matter. She didn't owe him a thing. He had dragged her out quite rudely in the middle of the night. She wasn't going to budge.

But she did.

She had to.

Because Sloan had solved the dilemma for her, getting the saddlebag himself, finding the package of food, then tossing it to her.

She caught it, reflexively.

She stared at him, simmering with anger, but then took out the linen bundle of food, untying the knot and indeed finding Meggie's biscuits, chunks of cheese, and strips of jerky.

She kept the food on her lap and daintily tasted a bit of cheese.

"Do you mind?" he inquired.

"Pardon?" she asked innocently.

"Sharing, my love. Hand it over!"

"Oh, do excuse me."

She passed the food to him, and they ate in silence. He rose in a smooth movement then and began to repack with the speed and organization of a man long accustomed to camping out on the trail. He started out of the tipi with the saddlebags, but then paused.

"Douse the fire," he said.

"Is that another order?" she demanded.

"If you wish."

She flushed, her eyes falling. "As you say, Major!"

"I'm up for promotion, my love. It may get worse quite soon," he said, laughing and leaving her behind.

Sabrina watched him go, then turned, carefully doused the fire, and collected the coffeepot and cups. She came outside, feeling somewhat contrite.

"Where should I wash these?"

"There's a brook right back there," he said, pointing toward it. "It's high now with melted snow. Be careful."

She nodded and walked toward the water.

It was frigid.

She rinsed the pot and the cups, then shivered as she scrubbed her face. She dried her hands and face on her skirt, then turned for their eating utensils. To her dismay, she realized that she hadn't set them far enough from the water. Somehow, as she had vigorously washed, she had pushed their cups back into the water.

And they were drifting far downstream.

Yet even as she watched the cups, she heard Sloan

swearing. She jumped up, turned back, and saw that the tipi was on fire.

She came rushing back just as he snuffed out the last of it with one of the blankets.

He stared at her, arching a brow. She knew that he was wondering if she had caused the fire on purpose.

"I asked you to put out the flames—not to fan them."

"I really thought that I had. Honestly."

"Umm," he grunted. "Are the cups clean?"

She shrugged. "Well, they are clean."

He groaned aloud. "And where are they?"

"Just a bit downstream."

She bit into her lower lip, trying not to flinch as he went striding past her. She opened her eyes and breathed more easily when she saw that he had gone after their belongings and wasn't going to touch her.

He returned with the cups. His expression was darkly forbidding as he packed the last of their gear.

"I'm really sorry," Sabrina offered somewhat nervously. "But I told you that I'd be horrible at this."

"And I told you—you're doing just fine at what really matters," he said politely, controlling his temper. Then he lost control and shouted, "Dammit! Just get on your horse."

At that particular moment, she didn't have the inclination to argue.

She hurried toward Ginger. He came to her, ready to help her mount.

"It's all right; I can manage."

"Can you?"

"Yes."

He lifted her atop Ginger despite her assertion. "Can't take a chance of having you injured," he said sharply, against her gasp of protest.

"Injured—"

"Broken. In any way. I mean, I need you functioning at what you're so very good at!"

She stared down at him, an angry retort on her lips. He

returned her stare, his eyes dark and fathomless, and she wasn't sure if he was taunting her or if he was serious.

"You—you know that I can ride," she said primly.

He smiled suddenly.

"Umm. At least that has been proven."

He wasn't talking about the horses. And she suddenly found herself losing control of her own temper once again. "I wish you would quit taunting me!"

His smile faded, and his eyes seemed to pierce right through her. "What you wish, Sabrina, is that you had never married me. I can't begin to understand you—or your argument against me. You don't want to be married to me, but you are. And I am the man I am, and that's not going to change. I don't know what new pranks you're planning—"

"Pranks!"

"The fire, the dishes."

"Those were accidents!"

"Perhaps. But I warn you, keep trying to prove what a poor wife you'll make, and you will regret taunting me!"

"Oh, how dare you—"

"I dare because we are man and wife. And because you are going to get used to being married, and to all that being married to me means."

"Would you get on your horse so that we can ride?" she demanded in return.

"Indeed; let's ride."

He mounted his horse. Sabrina nudged Ginger, breaking out in front of him. "Let's ride. Indeed, he likes to ride! Where he's been riding is surely in question, but—"

"I beg your pardon, my love?"

To her dismay, Sloan was right by her side. And he'd heard her words.

He arched a brow to her as he drew his horse right next to hers. He was amused. He smiled and reached for her, pulling her against himself even as the horses plodded through the snow. He placed a lingering kiss on her lips even as her heart thudded and she attempted to press him away, afraid that at any moment he was going to drag her from her mount, down into the snow.

But she didn't fall, and she wasn't dragged down. He broke away from her, steadying her as he did so.

"My love, trust me," he told her with mock gravity, "it's good to be back in the saddle again."

"You and your double entendres! I'm going to hit you," she informed him. "Right in the jaw. And I don't care what you do in retaliation!"

But she never managed to carry out her threat. He laughed, and the minute she moved to swing, he caught her wrist—and balanced her back upon Ginger when she would have fallen due to the force of her own movement.

"Careful—that striking out is a bad—and dangerous!— habit. And hardly compatible with your promise to love, honor, and obey!"

"Major, you can take your promise and—"

"Can't hear you out here, my love! The wind!" he said apologetically. Then he quickly nudged Thomas's flanks. The horse reared slightly, then broke into a canter.

Ginger immediately broke into a lope behind him.

And despite herself, she discovered that—just like a good cavalry wife—she was racing along behind her husband.

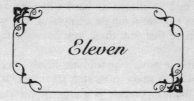

Eleven

They rode hard throughout the remainder of the morning. Sabrina remained determined not to say anything, no matter how hard he chose to ride. She was glad she had been riding Ginger around Mayfair since she'd been back, because otherwise, she was quite certain, she would have been screaming in agony by now.

The day was quite beautiful, the sky a gorgeous blue, and the temperature unseasonably warm. Thanks to natural conditions, Sabrina was able to pretend that she wasn't tired, wasn't aching, and was certainly, at the least, a *capable* woman.

In the midafternoon, Sloan paused at last, following a trail through a grove of pines to a picturesque, clear-running stream. Sabrina dismounted with pleasure at the sight, praying that her legs wouldn't give out on her.

The water was icy and delicious. She drank deeply and splashed her face, grateful for the sun that quickly warmed and dried her skin. When she rose, brushing off her clothing, she discovered Sloan's dark gaze hard upon her, but he turned away from her and dug into the saddlebags for the food.

''When the horses are watered, we'll start out again.''

''We've just stopped.''

''The wind has changed.''

''The wind has changed?'' she demanded, her hands on her hips. ''Do you know, Major, I have done what you've

179

asked of me. I've ridden as hard and long as a soldier, and I haven't made a single complaint, but you are just trying to prove that you think you have the right to be a tyrant—''

''We can ride now,'' he told her firmly, ''or start looking for shelter to make it though the night. It's going to snow, and the temperature is going to plummet.''

''Is it?'' Sabrina demanded skeptically. She looked up at the sun, which was still shining brilliantly.

Sloan shook his head. ''Sabrina, I've spent most of my life in this territory. I'm not trying to hurt you, wound you, or irritate you. The wind has changed, and the weather is more fickle than any woman I've ever met. May we please ride?''

She swallowed hard, suddenly feeling like a fool. ''Certainly,'' she told him. She turned quickly, hurrying back down to the stream to catch Ginger's reins and lead her horse back to the trail. Sloan had taken out some of the jerky, and he handed her a piece.

''Sloan, won't the other guests from Mayfair be along the trail somewhere, riding back to the fort as well?''

''Yes, they will be.''

''Won't they get caught in the bad weather?''

He hesitated. ''Yes, they might. But they're riding with far more supplies, canvas shelters, and a few wagons for the women. They're better prepared to face a snowstorm than we are.''

''Oh.''

''Come on, I'll help you back up.''

''I'm perfectly capable,'' she informed him.

But she wasn't. Her muscles were so sore, she had difficulty putting her foot in the stirrup. She wasn't sure she could swing her own weight over the horse.

But he had come up silently behind her, and he lifted her.

''Thank you,'' she said stiffly.

''Not at all,'' he told her and, mounting Thomas, led the way once again.

She kept watching the sky. For a long time, it remained beautiful.

Then she began to see the changes, so subtle at first! The blue became grayer . . . and grayer. The wind began to strengthen and the temperature fell. She hadn't been wearing her gloves; she put them back on. Despite her hooded cloak, she felt the wind and cold shearing viciously against her. The horses were moving more slowly, their heads bowed against the wind.

And then the snow began.

Hours had blended into hours. She had no idea of how long she had been riding upon the horse.

"Are you all right?" Sloan called to her.

She tried to nod. She was not at all sure that she managed to do so.

Night was coming; a darkness deeper than the gray clouds would soon be falling around them.

Sloan suddenly dismounted. She couldn't see what he was doing at first because the wind picked up the snow, tossing it around, but then he was at her side, reaching up to press a blanket around her. "Get this all the way around your head and shoulders. It will help," he told her.

She nodded. The blanket did help. Yet as they moved on, she realized that she was afraid they'd soon be freezing to death.

"Ahead!" he called to her.

Ahead . . .

There was snow.

No, there was a fort! She could see it. Though the snow had drifted around the wooden structures, she could see that there were a number of buildings. Thomas broke into a trot; Ginger followed, and Sabrina nearly fell right off of her. Sloan called out to the guard, and they were greeted by welcoming shouts.

And she rode into her new home.

Despite the now-blinding snow, a number of soldiers hurried out to welcome them. One of them helped Sabrina down from her horse and quickly led her into a log build-

ing, where it was warm. A heating stove in the center of
the office offered wonderful comfort, and coffee brewed
atop it as well. The room was typically military, sparsely
furnished with wooden desks, tables, and chairs. But it
felt good to be inside.

"Welcome, Mrs. Trelawny!" said the enthusiastic
brown-haired young man who had escorted her inside.
"Some weather, eh?"

"Thank you—yes, the weather is something indeed,"
she agreed. Sloan entered behind her then, along with an
eager young private. The door closed behind them, caught
by a strong gust of wind.

"My dear, Captain Tom Custer—" Sloan began by
way of an introduction.

"Custer?" Sabrina interrupted, startled. She bit her
lower lip, realizing just how rude her interruption had
been, but then, Custer was a name she had heard frequently; the man had been a war hero, and now, good or
bad, his exploits were constantly in the newspapers.

"I'm Tom," the brown-haired man said, smiling. "My
brother is the colonel you've heard so much about."

"Oh! I'm sorry—" Sabrina said.

"My brother was on leave in the East but is due back
here any day, and yet . . . oh, never mind, here I am talking away. Private Smith!"

"Sir!"

"See to it that Mrs. Trelawny's belongings are taken
to the major's quarters. Major, I understand that congratulations are in order."

"Are they?"

"Rumor has it that your promotion has been approved." He grinned a bit wickedly, and Sabrina thought
again that he was a pleasant and handsome young man.
"Well, *I* don't have the official papers, of course, but it's
my understanding that General Terry will be informing
you when you next meet."

"Really? Well, thank you; that's good to hear."

Tom winked at Sabrina. "Not that it means anything

to an old scout like Sloan. What's that official title that lets you come and go like the wind—liaison? He's never taken orders from anyone, anyway. He's the only man I know in the military who managed to spend a decade doing just about whatever the hell he felt like doing. Not that Autie—my brother, Colonel George—doesn't try, that is! But Autie seems to get himself in trouble more often than Sloan.''

"Oh?" Sabrina inquired, glancing at Sloan. But his facial expression gave away none of his thoughts, and she wondered about his relationships with many of this band of Indian-fighters.

"Well, I imagine that it's been a hard ride, Mrs. Trelawny, and you must think that you've been consigned to live at the most frigid ends of the earth, but we are not without our amenities here! We've seen to it that your quarters are ready, Major and Mrs. Trelawny, and we hope that you'll enjoy our efforts to make you feel welcome!"

"Thank you. I'm certain that whatever arrangements have been made will be fine," Sabrina told him.

"You've only to brave the cold a minute longer!" Tom Custer assured her. "You won't be lonely. We've a number of wives and family members here at the fort."

"I'm sure I shall manage just fine."

Sloan had her by an elbow, leading her back out of the office. The cold was like a slap in the face when the door opened, but Sloan quickly had his arm around her, leading her along. She had to close her eyes against the stinging snow, and she wasn't even sure in which direction they walked. She still hadn't managed to look up and was only dimly aware that they had come to a long, single-storied, wooden structure, when Sloan pushed open a door and quickly ushered her inside again.

"Welcome, sir, ma'am!"

It was the young private, Smith, who had met them when they had first reached the fort. He stood by another man who was bewhiskered and older.

"Sergeant Dawson, ma'am. Welcome. Excuse us; make yourselves at home. We hope you'll be happy here. Sir!" he snapped suddenly, saluting Sloan.

"At ease, Sergeant, and my thanks."

Dawson nodded and quickly stepped back out into the cold, appearing to be oblivious to it. Smith started out right behind him.

"Private Smith!" Sloan said.

"Yes, sir!" Smith answered.

"Above and beyond the call of duty. Is that a bathtub there, with steam issuing from it?"

"It is, sir!" Smith said, his young cheeks coloring.

"For me—or my wife?"

"Well, sir . . . of course, you're welcome, but the lady, coming through the hardships of the snow . . ."

"Above and beyond the call of duty, indeed, Private! Our thanks, indeed."

Smith, still flushing, smiled, aware that he had been teased. He quickly followed Dawson out. The door closed.

Sloan's quarters consisted of a suite of rooms; there was an archway between a bedroom and an office, and though a fire burned briskly from a hearth in the bedroom, there was plenty of delicious heat provided by a handsome, tiled Dutch oven that sat beneath the archway. Cupboards lined the archway walls on either side of the oven, and a small dining table was set in front of the oven, creating a small kitchen out of the area.

The bathtub Sloan had mentioned was made of wood and copper, but appeared much larger than the more elegant tubs she was used to. Steam was rising from it. The private and sergeant had taken pains to see to it that she had plenty of hot water.

"You should get into that right away," Sloan told her. "They went through a lot of trouble to prepare it for you."

She nodded uneasily, stepping into the room, realizing that this was the first place that they would live as man and wife. She was slightly unnerved, aware that he was watching her, and aware that she would be a tremendous curiosity to every man, woman, and child at the fort.

"Don't you . . . have to report to duty or something?" she inquired.

He laughed, coming in, taking off his coat, and hanging it on one of the hooks by the door. "I just came in from weeks in the field, my love. No, I do not have to report to duty—or something."

"Oh."

"I'll take your cloak."

He did so, then walked past her. The small outer area held a mahogany secretary that was loaded down with newspapers and correspondence, and it was to the desk that Sloan went then, giving his attention to the top memorandum.

Sabrina gave a silent sigh of relief that he seemed to be so occupied, and stepped further in.

There were two upholstered chairs that flanked the Dutch oven, and beyond that was the bedroom area with a large wardrobe and two cherrywood dressers. She was surprised to see that a number of pictures hung on the walls; somehow, she hadn't thought of Sloan as being the sentimental type, and yet even here, in his army quarters, she was surprised to see the merging of his two cultures. A very handsome war bonnet was displayed above the bed, while on the opposite wall was a picture of an extremely dignified man in full dress Union uniform. Sloan's maternal grandfather, she recognized.

Above the mantel was a painting of a young warrior, long black hair flowing in the breeze, his face turned toward the sky, arms outstretched. It was a stirring painting, capturing all that the whites saw as noble in the Indian; it was a painting of a free, strong man, one who might well fight forever for love of his freedom and his life.

"My father," Sabrina heard Sloan say, and she spun around, startled that he had come so silently upon her. He added, "Hunting Bear."

Sabrina nodded. "He was a handsome man."

He smiled slightly. "I'm sorry to interrupt your inspection of your new home, but your bath is growing cold."

"Wait. Is the other man—"

"My grandfather. General Trelawny." He walked across the room, showing her a smaller portrait, framed beautifully and set on his dresser.

"I do remember him," Sabrina mused, smiling.

"Well, I'm glad that he meets with your approval, and that you have an affection for at least one Trelawny." He wasn't expecting a response; he showed her another picture from his dresser. "More of my white half. My mother."

The woman had been beautiful. In the portrait, she was young—twenty, perhaps. Whereas Sloan was so very dark, she was fair-skinned and fair-haired, but he had inherited her high cheekbones and clean, arched brows. Sabrina could easily see why Sloan had turned out to be such a striking man.

"She was very, very lovely."

"I'm glad you approve."

"It must have broken your grandfather's heart, losing her."

Sloan had started back to the other room. "You'll have to ask him sometime," he called back to her.

She followed him out. "So . . . I will most probably get to see him sometime soon?"

He was distracted, already going through papers on his desk, and he didn't look up as he spoke. "I'm not sure how soon—and don't go getting too hopeful. I'm not sending you to Georgetown to live with my grandfather."

"You probably should spend more time with him. He's old."

"Old and hale and hearty, and busy writing editorials and telling the Washington politicians just what he thinks of them," Sloan assured her. "He might well outlive us all." He sat down at his desk, his eyes narrowing at one of the papers that lay on it.

"Your grandfather is still old, and you should spend more time with him."

He paused, looking at her. "Sabrina, I'm not going east any time soon, and you're not going anywhere. You're not buying time. Time is something I suddenly feel that I cannot waste anymore."

She hesitated slightly, wondering if she was trying to fight a battle she was afraid she might win. "Sloan, I still think that it would be so much better if we put both time and distance between us and gave serious consideration to my suggestion of ending this marriage—"

"You are stubborn."

"I can't understand why you're so insistent!"

He watched her, his dark eyes brooding for a long moment. "We're not ending the marriage. I hadn't realized until circumstances cast us together that I do want a family. Badly. Such a goal would be quite difficult to achieve if I sent you east."

She bit into her lower lip to keep from gasping in dismay. The miscarriage she had suffered had been more devastating than she might ever have imagined. But now she wasn't at all ready to hope for another child. Not out here, on this frontier where danger threatened constantly.

"Maybe I can't have children."

"James said that there was no reason you shouldn't have a dozen children, if you so desired."

"He might be wrong."

"And the moon might collide with the earth. Sabrina, I do have some correspondence I have to deal with, and your bath, which did cause the men some extra effort, is growing cold."

Still, she hesitated. "I've gotten the impression that there are a number of women who would most happily bear your children."

He set his papers down and gave her his full attention. "But I'm not married to them. Shall I help you into the bath?"

"No," she snapped irritably and walked back into the

bedroom, looking at the steam that wafted above the tub.
The men had gone to a great deal of trouble for her, but
the idea of just casually disrobing around Sloan still
seemed so strange to her.

But Sloan remained in the other room. She heard him
rifling through his papers.

Towels and a bar of soap had been left on the bed, and
after a moment, she suddenly went into double time, doffing her shoes and stockings and then the rest of her clothing, doing so with such speed that she nearly tore the
ribbons off her corset. She plunged instantly into the water
and just barely kept herself from screeching out loud—it
was still so incredibly hot.

But then, as she sank into the water, it felt wonderful.

The tub was big and deep—it had been made for army
men, she thought with a slight smile. Big men. Which
made it just delightful for a medium-sized woman. She
sank all the way under, soaking her hair; then she started
to scrub her body. In a few minutes, she had forgotten
everything other than the sensual feel of the warm water
and the deliciously clean smell of the soap. She leaned
against the wooden rim, closing her eyes, luxuriating in
the heat as it seeped through her.

She opened her eyes and screamed with surprise, then
clapped her hand over her mouth, wondering just how
loud she had been. She hadn't heard Sloan move! But
now he stood at the foot of the tub, watching her, a ce-
ramic mug in his hand.

"Private Smith was very thorough," he told her, his
tone dry as he ignored the scream. "He left warmed wine.
I brought you some."

She reached for the cup he handed her. "Thank you.
I—I didn't mean to scream. You startled me."

He nodded, a brow slightly arched, and turned away.
He left her again, going back to his desk, sitting in the
swivel chair. Sabrina sipped the wine. It was good and as
much a luxury as the steaming bath after the fierce cold
and brittle stiffness she had endured while riding.

But as she sipped it, she realized that Sloan had returned once again. He leaned against the archway, not really watching her, and she thought that there had been something in the correspondence he'd received that had disturbed him.

She swallowed her wine very quickly, set down the mug, and grabbed a towel, quickly wrapping it around her as she stepped from the tub. "It's still warm," she said as his eyes met hers.

"Is it?"

She scampered away as he approached it, threading her fingers through her hair to untangle it. She went through the roll of clothing Meggie had prepared for her, found a robe and her brush, slipped quickly into the former, and started working with the latter—trying to pretend that she wasn't vividly aware of Sloan pulling off his boots and stripping down to the buff. In a moment, he had sunk into the tub, and she heard his sigh of comfort and contentment.

A moment later, he spoke. "You know, if you come closer to the fire, you can brush your hair and dry it. Ah, but then again, *I'm* close to the fire. Hmm . . . this is wonderfully like a honeymoon, isn't it? We're married and living together. Our first home."

"This is a military barracks, not really a home," she pointed out nervously.

"There's a chair by the fire," he said, his dark hair drenched and straight to his shoulders, an expression of amusement in his eyes.

"I'm fine—"

"You've very long hair. You'd better dry it—you wouldn't want to catch cold, would you?"

With a sigh of irritation, Sabrina brought her brush and towel to the chair by the fire.

"There's more wine."

"Can I get you some?" she asked politely.

"I just thought you might like more," he told her, still seeming to be amused.

Maybe she did want more wine. She picked up her
mug, then found his. The warmed wine was in a carafe
on a warmer on the Dutch oven. She brought him his,
trying not to look into the water. She took her wine with
her, setting it by her feet while she brushed her hair before
the fire, aware that he sipped and watched her.

"This is strange."

"What?"

"I never imagined such domestic bliss."

"Don't you dare torment me—"

"Madam, I spoke with complete honesty," he assured
her.

Sabrina looked away from him, startled that just the
look in his eyes could cause such a rush of sensation
within her. Yet even as the warmth of the wine and his
gaze enfolded her, the front door was suddenly flung
open, then slammed again against the wind.

"Hello! Sloan? Sloan, are you here? I'd heard you had
returned . . ."

To Sabrina's amazement, a woman came walking into
Sloan's quarters, sweeping off her cloak and spraying
snowflakes about as she did so.

She was startlingly beautiful. Her hair was nearly black,
her skin was a perfect ivory, and her eyes were sheer
emerald green. She was elegantly slim, but her breasts
looked as if they might spill out of her bodice. Sabrina
realized that the woman was older than herself by perhaps
ten years, yet those years had done nothing to dim her
elegance and beauty.

From the outer room, the woman had apparently noticed Sloan in the tub, but she had not seen Sabrina. Not
yet.

"Sloan, I'm so grateful that you've returned. I worry
myself sick every time you go out, and naturally I've
missed you so . . . oh!"

She came to a dead halt in the archway, staring from
Sloan in the tub to Sabrina where she, too, had come to
a dead halt, her brush halfway through her hair.

"I—I—" The woman stared at Sloan, then at Sabrina; then her eyes were riveted back on Sloan. "My God, then it's true—you are married!" she exclaimed. Then she quickly seemed to recover herself. "I am sorry. Do excuse me, my dear," she said, addressing Sabrina. "I—I must confess, I didn't believe what I'd heard. But then . . . she's a charming chi—girl, Sloan, absolutely charming. Do excuse me, both of you."

Sabrina was simply too stunned to move. Sloan wasn't. He dragged his towel into the tub, heedless that he soaked it as he wrapped it around himself while he rose from the water.

"Hello, Marlene. This is unexpected."

"It is? Oh!" She glanced at Sabrina. "Of course."

"I have married. This is my wife, Sabrina. Sabrina, Marlene Howard is the daughter of a colonel I served with during the war, and the widow of Congressman Howard of Delaware, who passed away a few months ago. She is also the sister of Captain Jones of the Seventh."

"How do you do," Marlene said graciously. "What a pleasure, what a rare pleasure indeed. Well, excuse me. Sabrina, lovely to meet you. You will enjoy the Seventh. Sloan, it's so good to see you—alive and well."

She turned elegantly about, resetting her cape around her shoulders. A minute later, she was gone; the door closed in her wake.

"I can't imagine why I didn't think to bolt the damned door," Sloan muttered.

"I can't imagine why anyone who wasn't welcome at all times would just come in without knocking," Sabrina said angrily.

Sloan stared at her; she could hear the grate of his teeth.

"She seemed so surprised that you were surprised. Was she *unexpected*?" she demanded sweetly.

"Don't be an idiot, Sabrina—"

"Let's see—she just walks into your private quarters without being asked, and I'm the idiot."

"I have a past, Sabrina. That's been established from the beginning."

She didn't know why she was so hurt, but it was making her feel completely unreasonable. The woman who had just walked in was trouble—most evidently.

"A very recent past," she commented.

"Well, now, I wasn't married until I went to Scotland, was I?"

"But you've been back here—"

"I made arrangements with Raleigh to see that my quarters were prepared for a wife; I had to ride out almost immediately. And I won't sit here making explanations for events in my life that occurred before I was married."

"This woman—"

"If Marlene didn't know that I had married and was bringing back a wife, she's the only damned person in the fort who wasn't aware of the situation."

"But she must be a very good—friend."

"She isn't a friend at all."

"Oh?"

"She's an old acquaintance."

"An old *acquaintance*?"

"You're going to argue about this tonight?" he demanded, stepping from the tub. Dripping water, he knotted the towel and stood in front of her before the fire.

"I'm not arguing; I'm stating the facts as I see them. I'm pointing out these facts so that you can see yourself that our marriage is ridiculous and makes no sense whatsoever," she told him, wrenching her brush through her hair with a vengeance. She tried not to look at him. She was at eye level with his stomach, watching muscles ripple with his anger. She wished she didn't feel tempted to touch him.

"Well, as I see the situation, the marriage took place, and that's that, and you keep creating arguments out of nothing."

"Out of nothing?"

She stood, managing not to touch him, not even to

brush his body, and turned away. "I've no intention of arguing," she informed him coolly. "I'd just as soon be left alone for the time, however. Surely, you were missed. Perhaps you could go spend the evening with friends."

She started walking smoothly from the bedroom area, her gait not too slow, not too swift, just . . . regal.

She made it to the archway before he was behind her, catching her upper arm, spinning her around. "I have a past. But I'll be damned if I'll let you use it against the future."

"Let go of me, Sloan. Don't you dare act like this."

"I married you. And I want a wife, *and* a family."

"Not tonight."

"Yes, tonight. Most importantly, tonight!" he told her firmly.

"Sloan, you've decided you want a family; perhaps I haven't come to the same decision. Let me remind you once again—which does appear so obvious now!—that there do seem to be other women who would far more willingly take on the role of mate in your life!"

He stared hard at her, smiling slowly. His eyes glittered, but she wasn't at all sure whether he was incredibly amused or incredibly angry.

"I don't want other women. I want you."

"But only because you married me."

"Well, you are my wife."

"But—"

"Still, I want you for the gentle words you so endlessly rain down upon me. For each tender touch you brush upon me."

"Sloan, quit mocking me—"

She broke off with a gasp because she was swept off her feet, and the breath was knocked out of her as she landed on the mattress. He was down with her, with his weight seeming to bear her deeper into the softness, and she was powerless to rise. He braced his arms on either side of her, staring down into her eyes.

"We are married. And I want you for the fire that burns

so sweetly within you, even though you try to fight me whenever I go about setting that fire. I want you because you are an obsession, and I will not let you go.''

"Have you been so passionate with all your mistresses?'' she whispered, dismayed to feel such a depth of jealousy.

"I have never been so passionate. And I have never had a mistress in this bed, you may rest assured.''

She closed her eyes, suddenly wishing that she could believe him, and dismayed and angered by the force of the emotions she was feeling. She was as angry with herself as she was with him, because she was surprised to realize that she really did want to be here, sleep here, feel him with her.

He didn't touch her lips.

She felt his mouth pressing against the pulse at her throat, felt his hands parting her robe. She lay perfectly still, swallowing, trying very hard not to want . . .

His towel slid away from his lower body. She felt the rough texture of his legs, the pressure of his hips, his groin. His lips teased, caressing her flesh.

She didn't dare breathe.

His fingers brushed over her body, across her breasts, along her hips, against her thighs. She kept her eyes closed, so very determined to remain still. He'd admitted to his past. And now his past was making itself felt in their present, and she couldn't pretend that she wasn't angry—or hurt. Nor could she dare believe in a man who had married her only because she had been expecting his child.

His tongue slipped around her breast, teased the nipple. His mouth fastened there while his fingers slowly stroked down the length of her body. His kisses teased at her pulse, her breast, down into her navel. She bit her lip and remained still, her eyes tightly closed. His palm pressed lower against her abdomen, his hand slipped between her legs. His weight pressed them apart, and she braced herself, but . . .

His kiss fell against her kneecap, her calf, her ankle. The softest stroke of his fingers flew over her limbs, along her inner thigh. His lips followed. She tensed, feeling a burning at her center long before the hot fire of his caress fell intimately against her, and no strength of will on her part could keep her from crying out.

Protesting . . . raking her fingers through his hair, over his shoulders, until she was breathless, until no words would come to her, until she was writhing with wild desperation, wanting him . . .

Having him. Then his mouth seized hers, plundering with a strange, sweet violence that matched the taut rhythm of his body. Her fingers fell upon his shoulders, stroked down his back, curled around his arms . . .

Pushing him . . .

Holding him . . .

Clinging to him.

She wanted to stop the wild flames lapping so voraciously through her . . . and yet she wanted to feel them more and more; she wanted to reach that pinnacle, the overwhelming sweetness that could be savored at the very peak, oh, God, if she just didn't know how good it could feel . . .

She cried out despite herself, shaken violently with the force of her climax. Her erratic trembling seemed to precipitate a fierce, ragged explosion within his taut body that seemed to spill liquid sunshine into her.

He ran his fingers through her hair, smoothing it from her face. His eyes were on hers. His lips brushed hers, and there was tenderness along with the dark, sensual laughter in his eyes. She expected some gentle words, some promise or assurance.

"You are incredibly stubborn," he told her. "But I do thank God . . . fire does burn beneath your ice."

She frowned instantly, causing his amusement to become outright laughter. His laughter, when she felt so very shaken, infuriated her. She slammed her hands against his chest in raw fury, which only entertained him more.

"You're offended?" he mocked.

"Indeed, I am offended to be such a source of amusement for you, you bastard!" she charged him, pummeling against him. She caught his jaw, and for a moment she was frightened of retaliation, and she went very still.

He merely rubbed it, as if surprised by the power of her punch—and taught a lesson by it.

His amusement faded. "I am that," he told her very seriously. "I am that!"

He rose, heedless of his abandoned towel—and, so it seemed, of her. Without looking back, he pulled a blue woolen robe from a hook by the bed, slipping into it and starting through the archway.

"Sloan!"

She startled herself, calling his name. But he turned back to her. "I'm sorry."

"For hitting me?"

"No, you deserved that. I'm sorry for what I said."

He smiled slightly, but then inclined his head.

"I'm sorry, too," he murmured gravely.

She sat up in bed, gnawing into her lower lip, feeling the strangest sense of desolation. He was sorry. For what? That he was a bastard? That they had made love? Or that their entire relationship had come about?

She lay down, and, to her amazement, tears stung her eyes. She didn't know what she wanted at all anymore.

Except . . .

His warmth.

It seemed that she had once had it—and pushed it away. And there were others who might well want it, too.

She reminded herself that she wanted an annulment; she wanted to live in the East. She wanted to laugh and dance and be carefree, to attend parties, to come and go as she pleased. She didn't want to live in the midst of warfare and bloodshed. Afraid . . .

For Sloan.

She closed her eyes and stayed in bed. Pride wouldn't allow her to rise or to go to him.

Sitting out at his desk, Sloan folded his hands as if he were about to pray and tapped his fingers against his chin.

He should let her go.

He couldn't.

He could touch her; he could reach her.

Or could he? he mocked himself. Maybe she would always crave her freedom. And maybe, every time he made love to her, he would, in a way, be forcing her.

He ran his fingers through his hair, suddenly bone-weary.

Not yet! He couldn't let her go. Not yet!

He pushed his resolve to the back of his mind, and he turned his attention to the correspondence that had disturbed him so deeply when he had first read it.

Twelve

$\mathscr{F}$eeling more confused than ever about her marriage to Sloan, Sabrina spent the following day moving Sloan's belongings into one set of the dresser drawers and unpacking the few things that Meggie had sent along for her. She found a soft aqua dress with an underskirt of linen and an overskirt of wool and chose it as a serviceable gown for the day. When she had dressed, she combed and pinned up her hair, opting for dignity—since she knew that sooner or later she was going to meet up with the gossips who had been discussing her.

Around sunset, there was a knock on her door. When she opened the door, she saw that it had stopped snowing.

The evening was very cold, and her visitor's breath fogged before her. "Hello, Mrs. Trelawny. I'm Cissy. I met you at your sister's house the other night."

"Of course," Sabrina said. Cissy. The giggler. But she smiled sweetly enough now. "Come in, please."

"Oh, no, I've come for you. A number of the menfolk are busy playing soldier with their maps and plans, and we thought—well, we were hoping that you'd join us. Maggie Calhoun, Tom's and Colonel Custer's sister, has planned a nice supper . . . we'll have sherry and talk, and hopefully the men will be along before the roast pheasants turn into stones!"

"Why, that's very kind, but—"

"Oh, do come!" Cissy encouraged her. "Please? We

might all have been terrible gossips the other night, but we do form some tight bonds out here. I mean—we never do know if our men really will come back or not each time they ride out. It's not easy being army women. We're not half so bad as we may have seemed. Honestly.'' She grinned suddenly. ''Besides, if you join us, we can't talk about you behind your back, right?''

''You've a point.''

Sabrina found herself smiling, and she remembered that she wasn't accustomed to spending time feeling sorry for herself. She moved forward and lived life, no matter what obstacles arose.

Besides, if she had enemies among the women at the fort, she wanted to know exactly who they were.

''Thank you. Thank you very much for the invitation. Just let me get my cloak. Perhaps I should leave a note for Major Trelawny—''

''Don't worry. He'll know where to find you.''

As she walked with Cissy, the other girl pointed out the different buildings at the fort and explained what they were used for. ''Officers, of course, get very nice quarters. Well, perhaps they get nicer quarters in the East, and this may all appear a bit rustic, but . . .''

''Sloan's quarters seem fine,'' Sabrina said.

''Oh, I'm glad,'' Cissy told her. ''I do hope you'll be happy here.''

''Well, I do admit, it's a different life from what I'm accustomed to,'' Sabrina murmured. She added dryly, ''I've already met such interesting people.''

''Well, I'm not quite sure whom you've met as yet, but I suppose that circumstances do make us *interesting* people, at the least. Please don't judge us too harshly,'' Cissy said. ''We do live a strange life,'' she added, then gave Sabrina a searching glance. When she saw that Sabrina was watching her in turn, she flushed. ''He must have simply fallen head over heels in love with you,'' she said with a soft sigh.

''I beg your pardon?''

"Major Trelawny. Oh, I am sorry, we're all just so startled that he married. He's come and gone as he has chosen for so very long . . . he can be so devastatingly charming, yet dry and distant. I confess, we've all rather had a few fantasies about him. Oh, what an awful thing to say. You must think I'm terrible. I'm sorry, I'm babbling again. Forgive me. We're happy to have you here, and happy for the major. Ah, here we are; follow me." She ran up two short wooden steps to the porch of one of the residence buildings, tapped quickly on a door, and opened it. Sabrina followed her in. A gust of wind blew the door shut behind them.

"I've brought Mrs. Trelawny," Cissy said happily.

Sabrina quickly surveyed the women in the room as Cissy led her to a tall, solid, but attractive woman whom she introduced as Margaret Calhoun, known to her friends as Maggie, the sister of George and Tom Custer and the wife of Lieutenant James Calhoun, acting commander of Company L, of the Seventh. Cissy then went on to introduce her to Sarah, the minister's wife, and Jean, the very shy wife of a captain—and then Cissy brought her to two ladies she had already met, Norah and Louella. To Sabrina's surprise, Louella came to her quickly, in a no-nonsense manner, taking her hand.

"I'm afraid that I must apologize. Living on the frontier makes us far too blunt at times, and far too quick to gossip."

"It's all right; it's surely natural that you might speculate about the welfare of an associate," Sabrina assured her, ready to attempt to make peace between them.

Cissy seemed to exchange a glance with Louella, as if Sabrina were a bright young student who had managed to give the right answer.

"Good! Now that's all settled, and we're all great friends," Norah said, setting down her knitting so she could take Sabrina's hands and lead her to a love seat in front of a central stove. "Mrs. Trelawny, if you're sure you don't mind, please do tell us what happened with Senator Dillman.''

Sabrina was startled, but her stepfather's death had been big news, and it had created a scandal. She realized suddenly that it might have been a very damaging scandal to her. Although she and Skylar had inherited a great deal of money, they might have become off-limits to ''nice'' families, despite their own innocence. Scandal and prejudice were such that a man or a woman might have to pay regardless of whether he or she was guilty.

To many men, she might not have been marriageable material at all.

These women were being blunt, but she found that she was able to smile. She was glad for their straightforwardness. She didn't mind being asked about something; she minded when people talked behind her back.

''I'm afraid it's a rather sad story,'' she said, sitting.

Maggie Calhoun approached her with a cup of tea, which she accepted with quick thanks.

''Please, we'd like to hear a long story,'' Louella urged.

''Well, when I was very young, Brad Dillman and my father were best friends,'' Sabrina told them. ''We trusted him completely. Then my father's brother was in trouble and needed to get back into Virginia. My father was trying to help him and . . . well, the story came back to us through Dillman that the Confederates who were supposed to take my uncle turned around and viciously murdered my father. But my sister reached my father before he died, and he tried to give her a warning, and then, later, she saw Brad Dillman cleaning his knife—''

''The very knife that had slain your poor father!'' Tom's wife said, her hand against her heart.

''The very knife,'' Sabrina said.

''How sad!'' Jean echoed.

''How terrible! Naturally, your sister told you—''

''She told everyone, but no one believed her, you see. My mother was devastated, and Dillman was being kind and handling everything for her, and he was the most

incredible actor you could imagine.'' She lifted her hands.
''My mother thought that Skylar and I were being cruel
to Brad Dillman because we simply couldn't accept our
father's death, and she tried to be patient with us, but
strong as well. Eventually, she married Brad Dillman.''

''Oh, how awful!'' Sarah said. ''But sometimes God
will have his say in the end! And that's what happened,
isn't it?''

Sabrina smiled. Sarah was very young and wore her
sandy hair in pigtails, but she seemed to be strong in her
convictions. How strange. Some of these women had been
talking about her so viciously before—and now they
seemed completely eager to make amends. Maybe she did
have a great deal to learn about living on the frontier. And
maybe it was important to reach out and accept friendship
when it was offered.

Especially when it seemed that she might so badly need
to have a few friends here.

But the door suddenly swung open again, and with a
burst of wind and motion, Marlene Howard came into the
room, sweeping off her cloak and stamping her feet together for warmth. ''What a bitter, bitter winter!'' she
announced. ''Norah, dear, grab me a sherry, will you—
something against this terrible chill! We should be like
the men, swilling whiskey against it, lighting up cigars
and such just to keep some fire near us!''

''Here's sherry,'' Norah announced.

''Do come in and sit, Marlene—Mrs. Trelawny is telling us a most fantastic story.''

''Ah, Mrs. Trelawny!'' Marlene Howard saw Sabrina
and walked over to her, her arms extended. Sabrina rose
while the other woman took her hands, smiling at her.
''Welcome into our fold!'' she said, her beautiful eyes
flashing with amusement. ''And a most fantastic story—
how wonderful. We will all await this story most anxiously.''

''About Senator Dillman!'' Sarah warned.

''Oh, of course!'' Marlene said. She sipped her sherry

and sat elegantly across from Sabrina. "My late husband was a congressman, you know. I had occasion to meet the senator. He seemed a most charming man, intelligent . . . I'm quite afraid that half the world must still believe you and your sister to be ungrateful stepchildren!"

The woman said the words very sadly, as if she was so sorry people could be so misguided, yet Sabrina sensed that she meant to injure with every inflection of her voice.

Sabrina forced a smile. "Thank God there were witnesses to what the man did!"

"But you didn't tell us the rest!" Sarah pointed out, and Sabrina glanced quickly at her, her smile deepening. Sarah was such a wonderful minister's wife, so it appeared. But she did love a good, scandalous story.

"We lived a fairly normal life, while my mother was alive," Sabrina told her. "But then my mother passed away."

"Poor child!" Marlene drawled sweetly.

Sabrina lowered her lashes for a moment, trying to control her temper and carefully weighing her next words. She didn't mind telling these women the truth of a bad situation, but she didn't want to bring her sister's life into her own confessions.

"Well, it's quite simple. Dillman had an accident; he blamed Skylar. She met and married Hawk and left the area, and I looked after Dillman until Skylar was settled and sent for me." She stared straight at Marlene. "Dillman wanted me back—I was the younger of his stepdaughters, and he wanted control of my family's money. He also wanted to kill Skylar for the trouble she had caused him—and perhaps because she knew he had murdered my father. He first tried to hire Crows to kill Skylar, but when that failed, we had a showdown on the plains, and . . ." Her voice trailed away for a moment.

Cissy suddenly clapped her hands in delight. "But Hawk and Sloan went after Dillman, wasn't that it? How romantic! That's when you met Sloan, of course! He rode to the rescue, like a knight on a white charger—"

"A Sioux on a black gelding called Thomas," Marlene interjected dryly.

But Cissy hadn't heard her. She was inventing her own story. "Naturally, Sloan was with Hawk. So he swept you away from the danger."

"He took one look at you," Sarah contributed, clasping her hands over her heart, "and he fell deeply, madly in love."

"Yes, yes!" Cissy agreed. "The dashing loner rode to the rescue, saw the damsel in distress, and fell instantly, irrevocably in love!"

"Does that really sound like our dear Sloan to you?" Marlene queried gently. "What did happen, Mrs. Trelawny?"

Sabrina stared at her. "Well . . ." she began, then paused and smiled very sweetly. "Sloan did ride to the rescue. And he was absolutely wonderful, a white knight slaying a dragon, if you will!" she offered to Cissy and Sarah. "My sister and Hawk had to go to Scotland; I went with them. Sloan decided to come over and help Hawk—"

"Oh, dear girl! He was following you!" Sarah supplied.

Hardly, Sabrina thought, but she wasn't about to say so with Marlene sitting in front of her.

"Well . . ." she murmured slowly, lowering her lashes and smiling somewhat secretively. "Well, in Scotland, we decided to marry. It was sudden, but a decision we felt we just had to make."

"Hmm . . . but then the adoring bridegroom came home alone, leaving you in Scotland! How intriguing!" Marlene said.

"Well, you do know Sloan," Sabrina said. "He felt compelled to return to duty because of this Sioux situation, which is naturally very painful for him."

"He has family and friends among the good reservation Indians," Marlene said impatiently. "We're at war with the hostiles, a situation he must accept. He's been in the military a long time, and if he isn't careful, men will start accusing him of failing to make proper reports on enemy strength and numbers. And if he keeps siding with those hostiles, sympathizing with their position, he'll find himself court-martialed!''

"He would never do anything dishonorable," Sabrina said angrily, startled by the woman's attack.

"There's the pity, my dear. You're just far too new to all this, you're from the East, and you don't understand what is happening—and you'll endanger your husband's life if you don't get a solid grasp on the situation!" Marlene informed her. "Norah, dear, pour me more sherry. And do go on, Mrs. Trelawny. You married in Scotland because of this instant burst of love, and then your husband returned home . . . and then he found you—where, dear?"

Sabrina was only slightly aware of a thumping sound on the porch, Marlene had so thoroughly commanded her attention. But before she could answer, Cissy did so for her.

"Well, at her sister's house, of course, Marlene!"

"Excuse me; I'll see what's going on," Norah said, leaping up and going to the door.

Marlene's eyes didn't stray from Sabrina's. She smiled. "Ah . . . I see. You came home from Scotland but avoided coming 'home' to his army life as long as you could! For shame, Mrs. Trelawny."

Sabrina felt her forced smile beginning to crack. "I waited for Sloan," she said softly. "And it didn't matter where. Home is where my husband is, and nowhere is home without him."

"How . . . charming, dear!" Marlene drawled.

"Yes, indeed!" a pleasant tenor suddenly boomed. Sabrina looked up and saw a young man with spectacles, sandy hair, and a broad smile. He came forward, pausing to place his fingers in an affectionate, ruffling motion on Sarah's head, then introducing himself to Sabrina with a firm handshake. "David Anderson, Sarah's husband," he

said. "Welcome, Mrs. Trelawny. We've had the pleasure
of meeting your sister. You're just as lovely—in a very
different way, of course."

"Thank you," Sabrina said.

"Oh, she's wonderful!" Sarah cried with enthusiasm,
leaping up to stand by her husband's side. She clasped
his hand. "It's so delightfully romantic. Sabrina has been
telling us about how Sloan rode to her rescue, and how
they fell madly in love and couldn't wait to marry!" Sarah
explained.

"Did you hear that, Sloan?" David said, grinning.
"Would that my wife were so enthusiastic when she
spoke of me!"

"Oh, you are terrible!" Sarah charged. "I never say
anything but that you were heaven sent, my love!"

Sabrina was barely aware of the exchange between the
Andersons because she'd turned toward the door when
David Anderson had said her husband's name.

And Sloan had indeed come.

Dark and handsome—and silent, he stood just ten feet
away, a very slight smile curving his lips. He came to the
love seat where she had been sitting, but by that time,
surprise and unease had brought her to her feet. Despite
the fact that she was aware Marlene Howard had to be
watching her every move, she was flushing.

Sloan reached for her hand, a wicked gleam of amusement still playing in his eyes. "So you've told them all
how we fell madly, wildly in love?" he queried, drawing
her against him and kissing her.

It wasn't a decadent kiss; it was a perfect kiss for the
company present—quick, but just-so-slightly lingering,
very tender.

"Actually, I'm not sure exactly how I explained it all,"
she murmured in response. He hadn't even glanced at
Marlene yet, and still the woman seemed determined to
drag some kind of truth from her, as if she actually knew
that Sloan couldn't possibly be in love with Sabrina.

She felt oddly grateful that Sloan was behaving as a

dutiful husband in front of the other wives. The smile he gave her then, certainly for the benefit of the others, was amused, wickedly charming, and sensual. His laughter was soft and husky, and she found herself discovering why her sister had always found Sloan so charismatic and such a good friend, and why he was apparently so intriguing to other women. He had an elusive quality. He had a strength that blended with a quick intelligence, a will of steel, a charm that quickly acknowledged the truth of a situation. And, of course, physically . . . he was compelling, and it might even have been the mixture of races in his blood that made him so very . . . sexually attractive as well.

She wanted to pull away from him because she suddenly felt very afraid of the depth of what she had begun to feel for him.

Sloan turned toward the others in the room. "I don't know what she told you, but since I am continually being haunted with your questions as well . . . well, then, I suppose we'll have to tell you what did happen. Initially, it was quite a strange meeting. Nearly violent. I quite literally forced the poor girl into my arms." He grinned at Sabrina again, a look of pure wickedness in his eyes. Her stomach twisted. Oh, God, was he about to tell them all the truth?

"Do tell your side of it, Sloan!" Marlene drawled.

Sloan sat on the love seat, drawing Sabrina down beside him. She nervously awaited his words.

Their stories certainly *could* be quite different.

"When she first entered my life . . ." Sloan began, staring at her, then shrugging. "Well, you see, she was on a runaway wagon, under attack by Senator Dillman's supposed Indians, and when I tried to ride to the rescue, I was with Hawk. So, naturally, between the two of us, it appeared that she was being attacked by more Indians. I was in uniform . . . but then, I might have been a Sioux who had slain a cavalryman to steal his uniform. So I did quite literally have to force her into being rescued. And then there was more, of course. A happy ending to the horror of the Dillman situation, but when things should have been far more open and honest between Sabrina and myself, she was suddenly off to Scotland with Hawk and Skylar, leaving me with no choice at all but to follow.''

"Oh, how lovely!" Cissy cried.

"Indeed," Marlene said dryly.

Sabrina stared down at her skirt.

"Here, here!" cried Tom Custer, who had come in as well. "A great story! Let's toast the newlyweds, shall we?"

Sloan's smile deepened; he accepted a glass of whiskey from Tom, and the room rose in a toast. By then, more of the men had come in, and Sabrina found herself in the kitchen with the other women, helping to put food out on the table.

The men were soon in the seats the women had vacated, and, listening to them in bits and pieces, Sabrina suspected again that something had happened in Sloan's absence that hadn't pleased him. She heard him arguing about the winter's campaign against the Sioux with one of the men. She believed it was Captain Jenkins, the very shy woman Jean's husband.

"Face it, Sloan," Jenkins was saying, "you don't like the entire campaign in any way, shape or form. You've been excusing every atrocity the Indians have committed against the whites!"

Sabrina, setting a large bowl of soup on the table, knew that the man was angering Sloan, and she also knew that Sloan would control his temper. She was surprised to glance at her husband's face and realize just how hard it was for him to keep control of it now, though.

"I don't excuse atrocities, no matter who commits them," Sloan said. "But the fact of it is that, to most whites, the treaties we make mean nothing—no Sioux is really entitled to anything that a white man wants."

"You're forgetting the massacres—"

"During the Washita Campaign in 1868, the soldiers

were ordered to kill or hang every warrior in the Cheyenne camp, destroy the homes, make prisoners of the women and children. By white newspaper accounts, one hundred and three warriors were killed. According to the Cheyenne accounts, eleven warriors died—and the rest were women, children, and old folk.''

"According to the *Cheyenne* accounts!'' Jenkins grated.

Sloan ignored him. "According to the last treaty the government signed with the Sioux, the Black Hills belong to the Indians. You can say what you want. When the cavalry has ridden in to fight the Indians, you know as well as I do that innocent men, women, and children have been slaughtered, so how you can say—''

"When the Indians attack, they kill everything that moves!'' Jenkins interrupted. "Remember the Fetterman Massacre!''

"Fetterman taught us a lesson we should have learned. His commanding officer knew that he hadn't enough men to fight a real battle, and Fetterman was ordered not to pursue the Indians. He was a braggart who claimed that his superiors were fools and that he could clean out the hostiles with eighty men. Oddly enough, exactly eighty men were slaughtered with him. Apparently, he died for a good cause. The whites back East demanded that the government take action against the hostiles—slaughter them all. It's been happening ever since.''

"There you go defending the Sioux and their warriors!''

Sloan threw up his hands. "Well, sir, there is no one more reknowned for going to battle against the Indians than our own George Armstrong Custer—and I have heard him say that he can well understand how a Sioux man would prefer to be a hostile than to accept the bug-laden, rotting allotments handed out by the government.''

"Damn you; you are one with them—''

Sloan took a deep breath, then leaned forward. "If I were one with them, I'd be living on the plains. God knows, what I've tried to do is bring peace when it's possible and save captives when I can! No one fought harder than Red Cloud in his day, yet he went to Washington, and he saw what I have described, that the whites will never stop coming West. This conflict between the whites and the Indians is going to end; it's damned evident that it's going to end. Thousands of homesteaders, miners, adventurers, settlers, emigrants, and more will keep coming west, and eventually all the Indian tribes, all the *Sioux*, will be forced to cede the open plains and retire to *government* reservations. Will it be right? No. Will it be a complete injustice? Who's to say? The Rees and Crows are always damned willing to take the side of the cavalry against the Sioux, because they feel that the Sioux forced them off their hunting grounds. It's numbers, Jenkins, sheer numbers. More and more whites forced the Sioux west. There were more Sioux than Crow, so the Crow were forced west. Eventually, it will end—for much of the same reason that the North won the Civil War. We could keep sending men and arms; the South could not."

"Major, sir!" Jenkins exploded. "Now you're siding with the damned Johnny Rebs?"

"Now this is becoming absurd. You know that I fought for the Union, Jenkins—but I'll be damned if I'll take any pleasure in having killed my Southern friends, teachers, and classmates. And I'll be damned now if I'll take pleasure in the death of a people, and a way of life."

"You are speaking like a complete traitor to the whites, Major Trelawny!" Jenkins said.

"Lloyd!" Jean Jenkins murmured, slipping to her husband's side and taking his arm in warning.

"Stay out of it, Jean!" he said curtly, shaking his wife's touch off with a violence that surprised and frightened Sabrina.

"Captain!" Marlene remonstrated, stepping into the argument smoothly. "We all know that there isn't a traitorous speck in the major's body!"

Sabrina didn't know why she was suddenly quite so

furious to hear Marlene defending her husband. It stirred a sense of fight and possessiveness within her own heart, and she stepped forward quickly. "Captain Jenkins, I do admit to being terrified by the many tales I have heard regarding Sioux attacks. And though I've little firsthand experience, of course, my sister has spent time among the Sioux camps, and there are two ways to view any situation of conflict! It will, of course, be sad to think that a way of life must be ended!"

"Ladies, ladies," Sloan murmured, irritated. "I thank you both for your thoughts, but I am quite capable of defending my own loyalty and honor. Excuse me, though, if you all will be so kind. I think I will leave you all to your dinner."

"Major!" Jenkins said, swallowing hard. "Sir, I beg pardon for my bad manners, especially in this social situation. Stay, sir, if you wish, and I will leave."

Sloan shook his head, bowing it slightly, the curve of a very dry smile about his lips. "Captain Jenkins, your apology is accepted. I'm feeling restless and would enjoy a walk."

He strode toward the door, taking his overcoat from a hook and throwing it around his shoulders. Sabrina took a step forward, certain that she should accompany him.

But he stopped her when she would have reached for her cloak, taking her hands. "Stay, enjoy dinner, my dear. I'm sure Reverend Anderson will escort you back to my quarters. There's no need for you to miss your meal because I feel restless." He brushed her lips briefly with a kiss. His behavior was perfectly polite. He didn't want her with him; others couldn't see it, but she knew it perfectly well.

He stepped out and closed the door behind him.

"Jenkins!" Tom Custer said irritably when Sloan had gone. He looked sheepishly at Sabrina.

"All right, I'm sorry, and I said that I was sorry," Jenkins said. "But white is white. And I'm white, and the damned Sioux kill whites! This war against them is necessary. Crook is already in the field—killing Indians. That's what's got the major's goat tonight. He came back in and received letters from Sherman, Sheridan, and Terry, all telling him that any information he manages to gather now on the hostiles must be reported immediately; there will be no more negotiation. I'm sorry if I offended Major Trelawny. I'd rather the Sioux die than the whites. Well, it can't be helped.'' He swung around quite stiffly to Sabrina. ''I'm sorry, Mrs. Trelawny. I was especially out of line, because you are with us tonight.''

''There are plenty of soldiers who feel that the politicians have dealt dreadfully with the Sioux,'' Marlene said before Sabrina could reply. ''But soldiers follow orders and fight where they're told—even when they know the fight might be wrong. And face it, gentlemen, every single one of you wants the glory associated with a rousing Indian kill!''

Jenkins clenched his teeth, then responded to her. ''Maybe we do seek glory. Maybe it's damned true. Most men are anxious for the confrontation. A hostile is a hostile, and war is the only way that we will ever stop those hostiles from killing us!''

''Well, sir, take heart—you have been ordered to war,'' Marlene said cheerfully. Then she rose, yawning. ''I think I'll skip dinner as well tonight . . . it's gotten so very late. Good evening to you all.''

''Oh, dear, oh dear, such a great effort!'' Sarah said unhappily. ''And now no one wants dinner!''

''I would absolutely love dinner,'' Sabrina heard herself say. It wasn't true; she was upset herself, but she didn't want to walk out on the fine meal poor Maggie had worked so hard to prepare. ''Everything smells delicious. I would very much like to start dinner now, with anyone who chooses to join me!'' She swirled around, going back into the kitchen area for a platter of meat. Jean sprang quickly to her side; then Louella joined them.

Marlene, slipping back into her cloak, offered Sabrina a strange smile before departing.

As if she were—just perhaps—going after Sloan. And as if—just perhaps—Sloan would welcome her presence when he would not welcome that of his wife.

But Sabrina was going to ignore her despite all of her misgivings about her marriage.

And, if nothing else, she was damned determined to present a united front with Sloan to their neighbors at the fort.

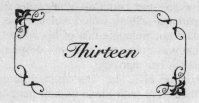

Thirteen

The remaining company sat around the table.

Conversation became much lighter than it had been, as if everyone was determined to be polite—and careful. Captain Jenkins talked about some of the pranks played at West Point, and David Anderson kept them all laughing about mishaps that had occurred on the way west. Sabrina made a point of paying close attention to all that was being said, as if she were perfectly comfortable and not worried in the least.

But, she noted, no matter what stories he told, Jenkins was still tense himself. It was visible only when his wife came near him. He all but barked at her once when she put more potatoes on his plate, and the glance he gave her was chilling.

Sabrina told herself that she was reading greater rudeness and hostility into his character than was truly there because she was angry about the fight he had picked with Sloan. Still, she didn't like him, even though she did think that Jean was as gentle and sweet as a shy little dove.

Eventually, the remaining guests finished eating, and the dishes were cleared, washed, and put away.

The young Reverend Anderson and his pigtailed wife escorted Sabrina back to Sloan's quarters, and she discovered that she liked the two of them very much.

"You stay here, David," Sarah said as they approached

Sloan's quarters. "I'll walk Mrs. Trelawny to the door and be right back with you."

"Gossip!" David sighed.

His wife frowned.

"Go on now. I'll be waiting right here."

Sarah let out a *Hmmph!* and slipped an arm through Sabrina's. She walked up the two porch steps with Sabrina and warned her in a whisper, "Do not let that woman bother you."

"I beg your pardon?" Sabrina said.

Sarah smiled. "Ah, there, now! That's the spirit!"

"I don't know—"

"Yes, you do, but don't you worry. You're very beautiful, young, sweet, and strong."

"I don't know about the 'sweet,' " Sabrina murmured.

"Well, if you're going to make it out here, you can't be a reed, getting flattened by any wind that blows your way. But you do know exactly what I'm talking about, and your husband apparently wants you very much, so just don't let her get to you!"

"But—"

Sarah gave her a quick kiss on the cheek and went running back to her husband. Sabrina pushed open the door to Sloan's quarters.

As she entered, she worried that he wouldn't be there. But he was.

He sat at his desk, apparently absorbed by his work. Thanks to the dinner conversation, she now knew why he had been distressed by what he had read when he'd returned to the fort.

She closed the door behind her, knowing he was well aware that she had come back. He always heard the slightest sound. He turned, acknowledging her with a nod.

"Was dinner nice?" he queried.

"Very good. You shouldn't have left."

"It wouldn't have been so nice had I stayed. Jenkins and I do not get along."

"Many men feel the same way he does about the Indians."

"There is more to the difficulties between Jenkins and myself than our fundamental differences regarding the Sioux," he said simply.

"But still—"

"Let it suffice that I needed to leave."

Sabrina nodded, walking on into the room. "All right."

"And though I do appreciate the way you chose to defend the Indian way of life, I don't appreciate anyone fighting my battles for me."

Sabrina hesitated a moment, keeping her tone measured. "I wasn't the only one attempting to wage battles for you."

He stared at her a long moment.

"Ah. You're referring to Marlene. Well, I don't appreciate her misconceived conceptions of defense, either. As I said, I can fight my battles alone," he told her. He turned away from her. "You should go to bed, Sabrina. You must be tired."

He was dismissing her, she thought, and she felt bad. She couldn't blame him; she'd been antagonistic enough.

"Sloan, Jenkins is a fool. He had no right to attack you."

He turned around, studying her curiously. He smiled then. "Well, thank you for that vote of confidence."

She nodded. "Sloan, when you left dinner . . ."

"Yes?"

Again Sabrina hesitated. She didn't want to appear to be petty or absurdly jealous. "Marlene followed behind you."

He smiled. "I didn't suggest that she follow me."

"I wasn't saying that you did."

"Well, she might have followed, but she didn't catch up with me. Is that what you wanted to know?"

"No, no, not really—"

"Yes, really," he said. A quick flash of amusement touched his eyes. "You musn't let her disturb you, or you'll be giving her what she wants. Marlene has a flair for trouble, and I have told you she is nothing more than an old acquaintance, and there's nothing between us now. I do appreciate your support. But please, go on to bed. I'm in a wretched state of mind and not in the mood for company.''

Sabrina nodded, surprised to realize that she felt strangely hurt.

She hesitated, then murmured. ''I'm tired; I am going to bed. But Sloan, you told me in the tipi that your grandfather had a present for me. If it's not too inconvenient, may I see what it is?''

''Oh,'' he murmured. ''I'm afraid it's not that exciting.'' He stood and reached into his pocket, drawing out a locket on a gold chain. He walked over to her. ''It's a picture of me. Grandfather was aghast that I didn't have your likeness with me. Anyway, the picture may just be a reminder of the man you don't want to be married to, but the locket is a family heirloom. My mother wore it throughout the war.''

Sabrina studied the little locket. It was exquisitely crafted, and the picture of Sloan within it was very handsome. He looked younger in it. There were fewer lines about his eyes, and yet . . . she liked the lines now etched into his features. They spoke of tremendous character.

''It's a very nice present. I'll write to him tomorrow, thanking him.''

''I'm sure he will greatly appreciate it.''

He stared at her a long moment but then turned away, heading back to his desk. Once again, she felt his need to be alone. Considering her hostility regarding their marriage, she couldn't blame him.

She turned around, leaving him alone.

She had told herself for so long that she wanted her freedom. Yet now, it felt so very odd to have him push her away. She had already been growing accustomed to his demanding her company.

She disrobed, slipped into a nightgown, and carefully folded her clothing.

She lay in bed, listening. She heard the fire crackle in the hearth by the bed, and she drew the covers about her.

She closed her eyes, willing herself to get some sleep. Indeed, it was odd; it had seemed that she was always fighting him. And now, when she didn't feel like fighting . . .

He was nowhere near her.

Still, she eventually drifted to sleep.

She awoke to a luxurious feeling of warmth.

Sloan . . .

He was with her, and she was both warm and lulled. His hands were upon her, stroking her, drawing up the length of her gown. She thought that he had probably been arousing her while she'd been sleeping for quite some time. He was behind her, his lips searing slow, provocative kisses through the cotton of her gown at her back. She felt his hands over her hips, between her thighs, seeking. Then she felt him, suddenly thrusting, strong within her, and it seemed that a swiftly churning, molten heat began a wild sweep within her. . . .

He made love hard and fast, and was quickly explosive. She had no chance either to protest or to give in return, and she wondered if he had decided that she was never going to admit to wanting him, and therefore he no longer felt compelled to prove just how easily she could be seduced.

At that particular moment, she wasn't certain that she cared. His arms were around her, she was pressed against his body, and she quickly drifted in a sea of warmth and security.

And slept.

George Armstrong Custer, anxious to return to his men of the Seventh, had left departmental headquarters in Chicago by train to return to the fort and prepare for his part in the three-pronged attack upon the hostile Sioux.

But his train was cut off by the snowdrifts, and he telegraphed his brother for help.

Sloan discovered the situation in the morning when a tapping sounded at his door. He rose, careful not to wake Sabrina. He was somewhat surprised by the pleasure it gave him just to see her sleep; her dark hair was splayed out over her nightgown, pillow and sheets, her lips curved into a charming half-smile. He paused, halfway into his trousers, watching her and experiencing a strange tremor. He liked marriage; he'd never imagined it possible, but he did like sleeping beside Sabrina, holding her, making love to her . . . waking beside her. Watching her sleep. Even if she wasn't quite ready to leap into his arms at any given moment, neither did it appear that she'd rather slit her throat than be with him.

Slipping into his jacket, he touched a length of her hair, wondering how it might have been if they hadn't lost the child. They could still have children, of course. The children he had determined that he wanted. A family. Yet he realized, oddly enough, that she was what mattered. He had wanted his wife, but he hadn't realized just how much strength and fire lay within her, and he was beginning to realize that he was becoming involved with her in a way that went beyond mere desire. And it seemed that she was at least becoming resigned to their marriage. And last night . . .

She'd actually defended him.

He sighed, hearing the soft tapping at his door again. He buckled on his scabbard and slid his cavalry hat onto his head.

He pulled his hat low over his eye, glancing at her perfect profile and trying to warn himself that she might have felt it a wife's duty to defend her husband—especially against a man like Jenkins. He needed to guard both his heart and soul against her . . . even if she had accepted the locket with far greater pleasure than he had imagined she would. She had been entirely honest with him—she didn't want him or the marriage. She was resigned; he was obsessed. He needed to take the gravest care.

Still . . .

He paused, touching a tendril of her hair one more time before moving to answer the tapping on his door that was becoming more and more insistent.

He opened his door, only to discover Colonel George Custer's problems, and the fact that Tom was ready to ride out in a mule wagon with a few of the men to bring back George, his wife, Libbie—and their hounds.

Sloan knew that he probably would have gone out with Tom one way or another; Custer was, after all, a superior officer. But though he frankly didn't care if Custer was caught in the snow, he was extremely fond of Libbie and was happy to be of any service to her. She was small and incredibly vivacious—her husband's greatest supporter. Her smile was warm and earnest, and she attracted attention wherever she went.

When the mule wagon reached the stranded train after a brutal day's ride and a night in the severe cold, she greeted Sloan with a hug, and he hugged her in return and then shook Custer's hand. Though he found Custer an arrogant and irritating man, they were seldom in a position to have difficulties with one another; Sloan was officially assigned as a communications officer attached to Sherman. He wasn't "officially assigned" to the Seventh Cavalry, but he considered his quarters there his home, despite the amount of traveling he constantly did.

Libbie chatted—nervously, Sloan thought, telling him about other family members.

Custer talked about the three-pronged attack against the hostiles with great enthusiasm, and then launched into a description of his testimony against the Indian agents and Secretary of War Belknap. The scandal had forced Belknap to resign, and Sherman had moved his headquarters back to Washington. Custer naturally seemed pleased that Belknap was gone.

Libbie, a trooper in the harsh conditions of the wagon ride back to the fort, still seemed nervous and upset, despite the cheerful front she was trying to maintain.

Sloan thought it odd that he should have formed a friendship with Libbie—especially when Custer had said often enough that he'd rather see Libbie dead than taken alive by the Indians. Although Sloan was cavalry and the grandson of a reknowned general, he was half Sioux, and any man need only look at him to remember it. Apparently, in Custer's mind, there was a difference between a half-breed and a full-blooded Sioux living on the plains.

The weather remained severe, the wind against them as they journeyed, but eventually they reached the fort.

Once there, Sloan started back to his own quarters, hoping that he might come in and discover Sabrina there with coffee perking or soup on the stove. He'd been gone more than two days, and he was cold to the bone and tired.

Nothing was on the stove, and Sabrina was nowhere to be seen.

Raleigh, a civilian servant who worked for a number of the men, arrived just as he realized he was alone. Raleigh brought him water for a bath. Sloan washed, dressed, and stretched out on the bed, reflecting on the orders he had received—and how they had been stressed by his successive correspondences with both Sheridan and Terry, neither of whom seemed to trust him.

He closed his eyes, wishing he could sleep. But he had just begun to drift when there was a tapping on his door. His eyes flew open, and he went out to discover that Tom Custer had come for him again.

"Autie wants you, Sloan; do you mind?" Tom asked. Tom was a friendly fellow, an extremely competent officer. Sloan often thought that Tom should have been the brother with the higher rank, but "Autie," as his friends and family called him, had been the one to ride hell-bent into glory, risking his own life and the lives of those around him every time he went into battle. In the Civil War, results had mattered.

In the plains wars against the Indians, results—dead

Indians—also mattered. And Autie could ride hell-bent into battle.

"Well, he is Colonel Custer," Sloan said, buttoning his jacket and accompanying Tom.

Tom didn't remain with him when he entered the headquarters room.

Sloan saluted.

George saluted in return.

"I hear you're about to receive your promotion," George said, tossing his hat onto his desk and easing back into his chair. His light eyes raked over Sloan. He smiled suddenly. "Congratulations. It's been a long time coming. It's hard for the government to recognize a Sioux to such an extent, I imagine."

"Maybe," Sloan said.

"I won't outrank you anymore," Custer said with a grin.

"No."

"Not that it matters—you've always been Sherman's pet."

"Sherman's pet? I might point out that although I do have a working relationship with both Sherman and Sheridan, they are both of a mind that war with my father's people is absolutely necessary, and that hostiles must be exterminated."

"Your father has been dead a long time, and your grandfather still has a great deal of weight in Washington—he has the power to sway public opinion."

"He can't quite compete with gold in the Black Hills, I'm afraid."

"You're still Sherman's pet; would that I could say the same."

"I could point out that both Sherman and Sheridan have helped you out on a number of different occasions."

"Because I can fight, and half the fellows we put in a uniform won't take a step forward. But you . . ."

"I have a different place in this, and I've had different assignments," Sloan reminded him.

Custer sighed suddenly. "Dammit, Sloan, I've really no desire to argue with you. I need help. You do know that. And you know as well that it's because I tell the truth like I see it."

Sloan shrugged; he could well acknowledge what Custer was saying.

George was a unique man. He could be arrogant to a fault, he loved to play pranks, and more than anything, he loved to be victorious on the battlefield while playing at war by all his own rules. There had been times when Sloan had felt an absolute contempt for Custer; he'd been involved in military actions in which innocent Indians of several different tribes—women, children, infants, and old folk—had been slaughtered.

George Custer had been breveted a general early on in the War between the States. After the war, like many officers, he lost his brevet and accepted an appointment as lieutenant colonel of the newly formed Seventh Cavalry. His first Indian fighting had been in 1867, a badly managed campaign known as Hancock's War, in which friendly Indians wound up alienated. Custer was suspended from rank and pay for a year, and he was under sentence of court-martial. General Philip Sheridan, eager to have Custer with him for an expedition against the Kiowas and the Southern Cheyenne, had had his sentence lifted. Custer was then part of the Battle of the Washita River, in which Black Kettle's people were all but annihilated.

Sloan had disliked Custer heartily for his tactics against the Cheyenne, but Custer had gained enemies as well for his lack of concern regarding his own men. A major named Joel Elliott and his detachment had gone after some of the fleeing Indians when the main fighting was over. Custer was informed that he hadn't returned but didn't take the situation seriously. It was later learned that Elliott's detachment had been slaughtered just a few miles away. Custer might easily have saved the men's lives. Ever since that time, there had been a serious split in the

Seventh Cavalry. Custer's family and friends supported him; many other men turned to Captain Frederick Benteen, the senior captain among the Seventh, who heartily hated Custer from that day forward for his disregard for a fellow officer.

And there were men in the Seventh Cavalry who had never forgiven him for what had happened. Thankfully, most of the time, the Seventh was split up—spread across the vast spaces and the many army posts of the West. And although Custer had acquired many enemies, his enemies were commanding certain companies of the Seventh at other posts, and trouble was thus frequently avoided.

Sloan respected the fact, however, that Custer knew his enemy. He was exceptionally fond of his scout Bloody Knife, the half Ree–half Sioux who served him with pride and loyalty. Bloody Knife and Sloan kept their distance from one another, and so no trouble erupted between them. Custer knew the differences between the Plains Indians, and he understood a great deal about Indian ways. And he was actually in trouble now for defending both his fellow soldiers and the Indians.

"They expect us to do our jobs, while they sit like yellow-bellies in their comfortable armchairs and put us in impossible positions!" Custer said angrily. "Damn it, Sloan! On the eve of my troops' taking to the field to seek out and destroy the hostiles forever, I'm being summoned back to Washington!"

"You've just arrived *back* from Washington," Sloan said, startled.

Custer nodded, deeply upset. "Politicians! My military service is beginning to consist of traveling back and forth between their hearings in the East and my troops out here! It seems that they don't care what is going on out here, if they can just get the right results from us. Damnation!" Sloan arched a brow; Custer so seldom swore. He seemed incredibly shaken. "They are a pack of hypocrites. Kill the Indians—just don't get any blood on us! Befriend the Indians—just don't let it cost us anything. I told them the truth!'' he said. ''I told them about the graft and the corruption, and I told them that President Grant's fat, pompous brother was getting rich on government contracts—and because I spoke the truth, I'm being summoned to Washington when my troops will face danger without me!''

Sloan lifted a hand, then hesitated. Custer had a habit of mixing truth and rumor, and not realizing the difference between the two himself.

Though Custer had taken a permanent army position after the war without the benefit of his ''brevet'' rank, it was still deemed appropriate and courteous to refer to the man as ''general.'' Despite the fact that Custer irritated him nearly to death upon most occasions, Sloan thought now that the one decent thing Custer was attempting to do here was going to hurt him. ''General, you have a habit of telling me government policy and then, when I ask you for a sane and rational explanation, you say, 'That's the way it is!' Well, Autie, listen to me: this is the way that it is. Our old General Grant is President Grant now, and that's the way it is. His brother is corrupt, and I'm damned sure that he's admitted it, but that isn't going to make you a popular man. You've been summoned. You've got to go back. Answer the questions you're ordered to answer, and do your damned best to be both honest—and diplomatic.''

Custer stared at him, shaking his head again. ''How the hell have you done it, all these years? You've said what you think; you've defied Phil Sheridan—who does think you're capable of scalping him, by the way—and they've never hanged you.''

''I never took on the president's brother,'' Sloan said.

Custer sighed, looking at his hands. ''The whole damn thing is a mockery!'' He shoved a letter toward Sloan. ''Will you look at this!'' He thumped the letter with his forefinger. ''I started this argument because Belknap was forcing soldiers to buy their goods from his corrupt contractors. I argued that the management of the agencies should be in the hands of the military instead of with those inept robbers in the Bureau of Indian Affairs. Emergency rations were requested for a number of the agencies; our 'good' Indians were starving to death because their government subsidies had met with the highway thievery of the government contractors, so now hundreds—perhaps thousands!—of those peaceful Indians have left places like the Red Cloud Agency to go and join with the damned hostiles, wherever the hell they may be! The government cries out that we do not punish our enemies, but each time we take to the field, the government causes us to face more and more of our enemies!''

Sloan quickly scanned the letter. He'd seen the situation; he'd expected no less.

"All those Indians leaving the agencies are going straight to the hostiles, aren't they, Major?"

"I would imagine," Sloan said. "What would you do under the circumstances?"

Custer swore. He stood, pacing the room. "I know that you're aware of Sheridan's planned three-pronged attack. Hell, everyone who can read ten sentences in a row knows Sheridan's plan; surely the Sioux know it, too. General Crook has already ridden out of Fort Fetterman, heading north, on the Bighorn Expeditions. He's supposedly an 'observer,' and Joe Reynolds is supposed to be field commander, but I know Crook, and he'll be commanding. He's the first of Sheridan's columns to take to the field. And I'm on my way back to Washington.''

"Apparently, you have no choice. And you are aware, as is General Terry, that we are still in the midst of winter, and that winter can be treacherous. General Crook and his troops could be bogged down for months.''

"But he is still in the field!" Custer said wistfully. He cleared his throat. "We disagree often enough, Trelawny, but in this instance, I'm requesting that you do something for me.''

"At this moment, you still outrank me," Sloan reminded him.

"I don't want to give you an order; I want your help in something that means more to you than it does to me. If you write letters to Sherman, Sheridan, and Grant, you will help my cause." He shrugged. "I believe that the generals will stand with me, support me, but your opinion on matters regarding the Sioux, hostile and not, is respected, and if you were to write regarding the corruption and graft at the agencies . . ."

"In this matter, you know that you have my support."

Custer nodded gravely, looking down at his hands. They were trembling. He clenched them tightly together. He appeared a very grave man indeed. He had shorn the long curly blond locks that he had worn on his reckless rides to glory during the Civil War. He appeared older now, and far more solemn than Sloan had ever seen him. Sloan saluted him before turning to leave the office.

On the wooden porch walkway just outside the building, he paused. He would support Custer because the cause was just. But it was ironic. Custer would come back and viciously lead his troops against Sloan's own blood. And they had reached a point in the conflict where there wasn't a damned thing he could do about it. Crazy Horse was determined on war; Sitting Bull, who had drawn the respect of so many of the Lakota Sioux from all the tribes—Miniconjou, Brulé, Oglala, Hunkpapa, and the rest—intended to make a stand.

Sloan thought wearily that he should have stayed the hell out of the damned cavalry.

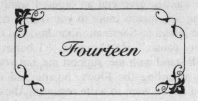

Fourteen

Sloan had left the fort without a word to her.

One of the young men in the Seventh had come by the morning he had left to tell her that he had gone with Tom Custer to retrieve Libbie and George. When he didn't return that night, she was startled to realize how much she missed him. She found herself frequently playing with the locket his grandfather had given her.

She knew that in the cavalry, men rode away. She simply hadn't expected them to do so without so much as a word.

She had always read the newspaper, eager to know what was going on in the country. On her first morning alone at the fort, a strange little bone-thin Englishman named Raleigh, who had wispy gray hair and the energy of a hummingbird, brought her the newspaper and assured her that he could help her with all domestic tasks; he had worked for a number of the officers at the fort for a very long time. She thanked him for the newspaper and told him in return that she would certainly be pleased to call upon him for assistance when she needed it.

She was amazed to see how much army business made it into the papers. There were certainly very few secrets that might be kept. Likewise, the papers screamed with headlines regarding corruption in high office. Everyone had been glad to see Secretary of War Belknap go. The president himself was under attack.

And Brevet General George Armstrong Custer was therefore under attack by President Grant.

With Sloan gone, Sabrina found herself invited to join the women once again. She spent two days with prim little Sarah, shy Jean, and her former enemies, Norah and Louella. They worked on quilts together. Of course, the other ladies being much better at quilting than she, she usually read to them while they worked. They loved to hear and discuss the news. Most of the women were intelligent and aware of what was happening, even when their husbands tried to hide both their excitement regarding the campaign, and the danger it might involve.

As it happened, Sabrina was with Maggie Calhoun when she met Libbie Custer, and like most people, she was immediately charmed by the small, energetic woman who offered her such a warm and sincere welcome. Libbie, however, was distressed. The general had barely arrived, it seemed, before he had found himself ordered to leave the fort to return to Washington to face an investigative committee. Still, she said that they must come visit, enjoy a drink and one another's company, and bolster dear Autie before he had to go face down dragons.

When Sabrina left the women to dress and change for the social that evening, she was dismayed to find that Sloan wasn't in their quarters. She dressed and left without seeing him, admitting to herself that she was growing somewhat anxious. She wondered if she should wait for him; then she told herself impatiently that she might very well wait for hours.

When he was ready, he could come find her, she told herself firmly.

So it was that when Sloan did find her, she was sipping sherry in the company of numerous young men and women, laughing, poised, betraying not the least bit of anxiety.

"Well, when we must wait and cool our heels, we do sometimes manage to create our own diversions," Lieutenant Jenkins was saying.

"There is no reason that living on the frontier should keep us from the joys of civilization, even if we must create those joys ourselves," Norah agreed, smiling.

"I say a picnic, a day trip, is in order," Louella declared, smiling at the young captain at her side.

"A picnic!" Sarah said delightedly. "Oh, what a very good idea. A ride out—on one of those days when the temperature climbs!—sun, good company—indeed, it sounds lovely."

"And naturally, Mrs. Trelawny, we will be delighted to show you what is breathtaking about our surroundings!" Louella's young captain assured her.

"Well, thank you," she murmured. Then, at last, she saw Sloan.

"Ah, my dear!" he said, approaching her with a smile for those around her.

He took her hand, kissed it. She offered her cheek, and he kissed it as well. "I missed you in our quarters," he murmured.

"Well, sir, it seems that I missed you there as well," she replied coolly.

"There's music; shall we dance?"

"As you wish."

"Ladies, gentlemen?" Sloan said, excusing them to those around them. He sounded polite, his voice even, as if he were in a decent humor. But as they reached the floor, Sloan questioned her. "So, where were you, my love?"

She arched a brow. "Where was *I*?"

"That was the question."

"How strange. Where were you?"

"I'm sure you were informed that I left the camp."

"Oh, yes."

"Then—"

"I was informed, but not by you."

"You were sleeping when I left."

"There have been other times when I slept that it did not deter you from disturbing me." Despite herself, she flushed slightly. She cast her head back. "And how intriguing! I met Mrs. Custer, I saw Tom . . . but not you, and when all of you had arrived here at the same time!"

"Well, my love, I returned seeking no more than a little warmth—to find cold ashes in the fire."

"Your return must have been brief."

He hesitated just slightly. "It was."

"Ah. You had other business."

"I did."

"Well, sir, you have said that I should be a good cavalry wife. I am making friends."

"With every man in the cavalry?" he asked pleasantly enough.

"I do try my best," she said sweetly. "Since, of course, you are so very good at befriending the women."

"Ah," he murmured, swirling her around.

"We should all have friends," she said pleasantly.

"What will you do when the force here rides out?" he queried, his tone still light.

"Do you ride with them?"

"I imagine that I will be summoned out again before the columns are ready to ride from here."

"Ah, yes, and with any luck, you might even inform me that you are leaving. And then, of course, I will have to be tremendously grateful that I do have my friends, and that they are interested in seeing to it that I can occupy my time."

His dark eyes fell on hers. "You do enjoy testing my temper."

"You do enjoy testing mine."

He smiled. "You're not to leave this post without me, do you understand?"

"I beg your pardon—"

"Don't beg anything. But don't leave this fort without me. Whether you find my behavior courteous or not, you will not join your friends on any expeditions out of here."

"Sloan, I am not a child—"

"No, you're my wife," he said. And there might have

been more, but a young captain tapped him on the shoulder, nervously asking if he might cut in. Sloan obliged.

They danced. When Sabrina saw Sloan again, he was circling the floor with Libbie Custer. He was laughing at something Libbie was saying, and the amusement in his face was sincere. He smiled at Libbie then, and his features were striking and sensual, and she felt a strange stirring of jealousy in her heart, even though she knew that Libbie adored her Autie.

Since there was a shortage of women compared to the number of men, Sabrina found herself dancing most of the evening.

At one point, she saw Sloan with Marlene Howard, and she was deeply distressed by the feeling that assailed her. It was like having a knife twisted in her stomach.

As always, Marlene looked elegant and gay. She laughed with Sloan; he smiled; they chatted. Together, they were an incredibly handsome couple. The worst of all was that Sabrina hated the way Marlene looked at her husband. Devouring him with her eyes . . .

As if she knew what she might touch, what sleek muscle lay beneath his uniform jacket. . . .

She found herself standing with Norah and Louella while a young captain went to get her a glass of punch.

"How do you tolerate that?" Louella said to her suddenly.

"Pardon?"

"She's something, that one!" Norah agreed.

"Who?"

"Your husband's old flame, dear Mrs. Howard!" Louella supplied.

"She's really quite despicable," Norah said.

Sabrina forced herself to shrug. "Well, she's so recently a widow. Perhaps she's lonely."

Louella let out a disdainful sniff. "Hardly. She cuckolded that poor man she married for years."

With Sloan? Sabrina longed to demand. Yet she didn't. She felt the knife twisting into her, deeper and deeper.

"And from what I hear, she's regretted her decision all her life to marry Howard, when she claims she had the opportunity to marry Sloan."

That was a statement Sabrina couldn't ignore. "Excuse me?"

"Oh, it was supposedly quite some time ago. Colonel Warren, Marlene's father, was on duty at a post in Missouri right after the war, and Sloan had been assigned there. It was a good place for him; he wasn't fighting Indians, just outlaws—some of those awful men who had done such terrible murder under Quantrill. Anyway, rumor had it that he and Marlene were quite an item—I mean one of those things that was hotter than a July day, if you know what I mean—but then . . ."

Norah paused for dramatic effect.

"But then?" Sabrina pressed.

Louella picked up the story for her. "Oh, well, there was a problem with her father, apparently. Sloan was a half-breed, just not acceptable to some papas. And Mr. Howard already had this budding political career—"

"Not to mention tons and tons of money made in the fur trade," Norah said.

"So she married Mr. Howard, and she created a buzz in Washington, but . . ." Louella drawled.

"But!" Norah said. "She continued to visit her father and brother at their various posts . . . you see, Howard had been a fairly attractive man, but as the years went by—"

"He grew squat and bald," Louella murmured with a knowing nod.

"And you've only to look at Sloan—," Norah said.

"Or any number of soldiers!" Louella added hastily.

"Well, anyway, she's been known to frequent military posts for quite some time," Norah ended. She smiled suddenly. "Actually, it's quite wonderful that he has you—as a wife. It does put her right in her place, don't you think? I mean, surely there's no hope for her at this point, but . . . I think that she might really be ready for marriage now. I mean, after all, she married Howard, as her father wanted, and gained incredible prestige and a great deal of money. Now, she's free to marry for . . . well, to marry whomever she chooses.''

They went on to argue the outrageousness of Louella's mode of speech. Sabrina felt as if the knife in her stomach was twisting ever deeper and deeper . . .

Hitting an artery.

The musicians were still playing later and she was talking with young Emma Reed when she felt a hand land firmly upon her arm. Turning about, she found Sloan, his dark eyes hard on her. ''Miss Reed,'' he said politely, acknowledging Emma. ''My love,'' he said to Sabrina, ''if you don't mind, I think I'd like to retire for the evening.''

''Of course, I don't mind. Retire, sir, whenever you please,'' Sabrina told him.

Sloan arched a brow.

Emma laughed softly. ''I think your husband wants to retire with you, Sabrina. Army men get so little time with their wives! I quite understand—good night!'' she said quickly, smiling at Sloan and hurrying away to join another group of friends.

''Shall we?'' Sloan suggested.

''Shall we what?''

''Retire.''

''I told you; you are free to do so.''

''And I have told you, I'd like you to accompany me.''

''But I'm not ready to leave.''

''Sabrina—''

''Sir, you have chosen to leave a gathering without me before. Please feel free to do so now.''

She saw a dark flicker of dangerous anger in his eyes. ''Sabrina, I'll carry you out of here,'' he warned.

And he would.

And actually, she was ready to tell him that he could sink right into hell with his *ex*-mistress and one-time-almost-wife any time he chose.

Sabrina swung around. She stood very stiffly and let him set her cloak upon her shoulders and escort her from the Custer home to their quarters.

Once outside, she walked quickly, trying to keep ahead of him. He followed easily enough with his long strides. When they were inside his quarters, she was already walking away from him as he took her cloak from her shoulders.

"All right, what in God's name is the matter with you now?" he demanded irritably.

She spun around. "An old acquaintance?"

He frowned. "I don't know—"

"The delightful widow Howard."

He sighed with irritation. "What about Marlene Howard? I am weary of this."

"*You* are weary of it!"

"I don't know what you're talking about."

"She's far more than an acquaintance; you were going to marry her."

Sabrina held her breath, watching his face as she threw out the accusation.

It was the truth; she knew it even before he thundered out, "So?"

She inhaled sharply, dismayed that she could feel so stricken and devastated. She wouldn't allow him to do this to her, make her feel so very hurt!

"You could have told me!"

"What difference does it make?" he demanded impatiently.

"What difference does it make?" she repeated. He really didn't seem to understand at all how awkward the situation was for her. Maybe he didn't really care. He had insisted on keeping their marriage vows because he was stubborn and wanted a family. He had never claimed any deep devotion to her.

"I'm in a horrible mood, Sloan. I should really be left alone," she said regally. She moved away from him but soon found herself backed against a wall, confronting him.

"Sabrina—" he began, his hands flat against the wall on either side of her head. "Sabrina, I won't—"

"You wanted to be left alone the last evening we were together; now it's my turn." She bit into her lower lip, trying to turn her head, her lashes falling. "Please, go away, Sloan. You're so good at leaving. Please, leave now."

"No, Sabrina. I was upset about a situation that had just occurred, while you're upset about something that happened years ago."

"But you didn't—you didn't even tell me!"

"Because it has nothing to do with the present."

"Were you lovers?"

"What difference does it make?"

"I want to know."

His features were tense, his eyes very dark as he stared at her. "Yes," he said flatly.

"Oh."

"Don't say 'oh' in that tone of voice."

"What tone?"

"It's over, Sabrina; it's been over for years and years. So don't let her cause trouble!"

She stood silently, staring at him, wanting to rage against him because she couldn't help but feel so insecure, and yet wishing that . . .

He suddenly let out an exasperated oath and catapulted into motion. She gave a startled cry as she found herself swept up into his arms and cast down on their bed. As she gasped for breath, he was on top of her.

"Sloan!" she protested, pressing against his chest, struggling beneath him.

He held dead still above her. "I've been gone, and I've missed you incredibly," he told her huskily.

I've missed you . . .

The words were on the tip of her tongue, and yet she was still too uncertain to utter them.

He stared into her eyes, seeking something. His jawline

hardened somewhat, and he eased back—about to leave the bed, she was certain.

Except that he didn't. "I've missed you incredibly," he repeated, rolling her over and struggling with the buttons of her dress. He was determined and impatient. She heard the buttons pop, felt him tugging against her clothing.

"Well, you could help!" he said, exasperated.

She rolled over, meeting his gaze. "I don't think that I'm required to help when you're shredding my clothing."

"I wouldn't be shredding your clothing if you weren't being so damned stubborn."

"I'm not stubborn, I'm—"

"Jealous."

"Oh, don't be absurd!" she cried, praying her flush wouldn't give her away. To hide her face, she did help, pulling the yards of fabric of her party dress over her head and casting the gown to the floor by her side.

He arched a brow, a slow smile forming on his lips as he studied her angry face.

"Thanks!" he murmured softly, with amusement. His eyes continued to meet hers as he found the tie to her corset, his fingers brushing the bare flesh of her breasts as they spilled above the bones of the corset. Heat flashed instantly through her at that touch. She'd already had difficulty breathing; now it seemed that she was gasping to draw each breath, and yet she couldn't take her eyes from his or evade the sheer feeling that rocked her from the simple brush of his fingers. . . .

He was fast, perhaps seeking the advantage of her stunned compliance. She quickly found herself stripped naked, lying on the bed, waiting.

He rose and doused the lamps. She heard him disrobing and remained where she lay, still but shaking. Waiting.

A moment later, she felt his weight as he lay down beside her.

She felt his hands, his arousal against her bare flesh. She felt as if she were on fire, she wanted him so much.

She bit into her lip, somewhat ashamed of herself and still in such a state of gnawing hunger that it was nearly torment. His body eased against hers, and she felt the rough pressure of his chest against her breasts, the force of his groin against her abdomen, his sex against her thighs. She opened her mouth to speak, to protest that she was still upset about the evening, but no words left her mouth, for she met the heated force of his kiss, the savage thrust of his tongue. And as he kissed her, he shifted, entering her slowly with the full force of his arousal, and he moved inside her with a volatile need that instantly swept her into the sheer storm of his passion. She realized how much she had missed him the nights he'd been gone—oh, God, she had wanted him, wanted this . . . and yet she was far to proud ever to admit it. Especially when she was afraid that . . .

She could come to want him too much.

His fingers threaded into her hair. His kisses ravaged her mouth as he moved with his reckless thunder. She writhed, twisted, arched to meet him. Her fingers curled into his shoulders, stroked his back, clenched and stroked, eased and curled and clenched into his muscled bronze flesh again and again.

His mouth left hers, caressed her throat, her breast, her lips again . . . then sucked her nipple. She arched as the world rocked violently, swept fiercely into a hunger that demanded satisfaction regardless of all else. Then it seemed forever and yet too quickly . . . that a climax exploded upon her with a shattering force. She was barely aware of him for long moments, even as his body continued to thunder into her own until he was rocked with the fury of the fruition of their passion.

She lay drenched, and suddenly cold, for he withdrew from her, lifting his weight from her.

He drew her against him then, and his voice was husky as he whispered, "I did miss you."

She didn't reply, but she remained against him. She

realized that she didn't want her marriage annulled, and yet . . .

She was becoming more and more aware of why she had fought Sloan for so long. It was far too easy to want him. Far too easy to admire him, and . . . to fall in love.

And far too easy to be hurt.

She shifted slightly, moving away from him. Caring about Sloan was very frightening indeed. She couldn't help the little tinges of jealousy that clawed at her heart.

Yet she was the one who was with him. As his wife. Marlene Howard was not.

She lay very still, her heart and soul in a strange tempest.

Love itself hurt.

"What is it? What's wrong?" Sloan demanded softly.

She shook her head. She couldn't possibly describe her fears to him.

"Nothing, I just . . . I don't know. I just don't want—"

"What?"

"Nothing. I'm so tired, Sloan, please . . ."

He didn't press her, and exhaustion finally allowed her to sleep.

Sloan didn't sleep. He propped himself up on his elbow and watched his wife as she slept. He felt disturbed, beaten. Each time he touched her, he felt a deeper passion. And each time, she responded as an extraordinary lover. He continually felt as if he were evermore haunted by memories when he was away from her—memories of her voice, her scent, the sound of her laughter, the silken feel of her hair. And yet . . .

Yet she had moved away from him, and her "nothing" was definitely something.

What was it she didn't want?

Children, he thought. His children? Or just children on the frontier?

She hadn't said the word, but it was probably what she had been about to say. He had pressed the point that he

wanted a family, which was true. But it was also a way
to be with her. Damn her, she was throwing everything
away.

But as he lay there that night, he determined that he
wasn't going to force her anymore.

Next time, he determined, she would come to him.

And if she didn't . . . ?

He wouldn't allow the thought. She would come to
him. And if he was dying in an agony of desire . . .

She would still have to come to him.

She knew that she shouldn't . . .

But temptation was too strong.

Sabrina explored his desk.

He had been gone all day; she had cleaned and straightened and mended, and by early evening, she'd been ready
to scream with frustration.

And so she determined to learn more about the man
who was driving her insane.

Most of what she discovered were correspondences regarding his various assignments. They went back quite a
way, and she realized that when she had first arrived, he
had been riding out to whatever Sioux camps he could
find on the unceded lands, bringing with him the government ultimatum about returning to their agencies and reservation lands. He kept a sporadic journal, and one entry
read, "I believe that even Red Cloud is eager to be done
with all that is white, and ride out and join the so-called
'hostiles.' Only the people dependent on him at his agency
keep him from doing so. Since we must speak honestly
to one another and report the written word, it becomes
quite amazing what we are able to say to one another
without speaking words at all. It is ending, and I am heartily sorry, for it will do so with terrible bloodshed."

She gnawed lightly at her lower lip, heard a noise near
her door, and carefully closed the journal. She waited, but
no one came to her door, and she opened the bottom
drawer of the secretary. She found a book and opened it,

and discovered it was an album that contained faded photographs. She perused it quickly, finding the first pages to be mainly from the Civil War. She found photos where Sloan, Hawk, and David stood together, and more. There were photos of houses, of beautiful landscapes. And then . . .

There were photographs taken at an Indian encampment. She saw a bare-chested warrior in breechclout and leggings sitting atop a painted pony, and then realized that it was Sloan. Despite herself, she shivered fiercely. But she kept looking, fascinated. There was Hawk with a beautiful, slender young Indian maiden and infant child. And Sloan again, taken as he stood waist-deep in the water, laughing at a voluptuous Indian woman who cast a spray of water in his direction.

The Cheyenne woman she had heard so much about?

She laid her head down on the secretary, alarmed by the nausea that churned her stomach. Then she sat up in a near panic, hearing the door open.

Sloan had returned.

Sabrina leapt up from the chair in front of the secretary, staring at him. He looked from her to the picture album that still lay open on his desk—to the page of photographs taken at the Indian encampment.

"What were you doing?" he demanded.

"I—just wanted to look at the photographs."

"And you knew just where to find them?"

She wasn't sure if he was angry, or amused.

Her cheeks flooded with color. To her alarm, he strode toward her, taking her by the hand, drawing her back to the desk. "You wanted to see photographs . . . well, come, let me show you what they are."

"Sloan—" she murmured uneasily, trying to draw her arm free.

He wasn't going to allow her.

"Come. It's flattering that you're interested in my past life, my love."

He picked up the book, settled into one of the uphol-

stered chairs, and drew her down on his lap. He opened
the album. "Let's see . . . this is the page you were up to
. . . yes, this must be one of your favorite images of me—I
believe I'm even wearing war paint here. We were heading out for a confrontation with the Crows. Crows and
Sioux are natural enemies—it has a great deal to do with
hunting grounds—just as the Sioux and Cheyenne tend to
be allies. Ah, yes, here's a face you should know. Seriously. He's an important man. Crazy Horse. See the scar?
A Sioux woman is free to divorce her husband, but Crazy
Horse fell in love with a woman who had a very jealous
husband—he shot Crazy Horse in the face. Crazy Horse,
however, survived. A great pity for the whites. He is one
of the most intriguing men I have ever met—white or
Indian. His power lies in the strength of his convictions,
and his dedication to his people. Ah, here—your brother-
in-law's grandfather, two of his cousins, Ice Raven and
Blade. We were quite close until recently. There. Hawk
and his first wife and child."

"Poor Hawk. She was lovely."

"Do you think so?"

"Of course." She pointed to the picture. "The lines of
her face are so beautiful. Her eyes are so exotic."

He was studying her. "You mean that, don't you?"

She frowned. "Of course. Why wouldn't I?"

He shook his head; then it appeared that he decided to
answer. "There are some whites who can't begin to see
anything beautiful in an Indian."

"Sloan, I don't think that you've ever really under-
stood. I do understand that there are different cultures.
And I believe there are many honorable facets to the
Sioux. I'm afraid of the bloodshed and violence."

His dark eyes were upon her, curiously gentle. "Everyone is afraid of the bloodshed and violence. And it's
necessary to be afraid because so many have died—and
will die." He changed his tone, as if he hadn't wanted to
become too somber. "Hawk's wife was lovely. Very gentle. I'm glad Hawk has Skylar now."

He looked at Sabrina again, then pointed to another picture, a slight smile on his lips. "Then there's this one." He paused. It was a full-face shot of the woman with whom he had played in the water. She was incredibly arresting, with strong cheekbones, large, beautiful dark eyes, and a wickedly sensual smile.

"You don't have to show me these."

"Yes, I do. Because you want to know about my past. This is Earth Woman. I'm sure you've heard about her."

"Sloan, please . . ."

He studied her for a long moment. "You said that I didn't tell you about Marlene. I intend to be honest with you."

"All right. Tell me about her."

"Earth Woman and I had a relationship for years, one without commitment. She has lost a number of husbands and doesn't want any more. She understands that I have married."

"I'm glad," Sabrina murmured, but felt incredibly uncomfortable under his scrutiny. "Sloan, please, let me up."

"Indeed, my dear. Of course. Forgive my very bad manners." He set her on her feet, closed the book, and strode to his desk. He opened a drawer from which he drew a pen and paper.

He went to work with his writing.

Sabrina sank back into the chair for several long moments. Then he turned to her suddenly.

"Do you cook anything?" he asked.

She could cook, and she had discovered that Sloan did his shopping through Sergeant Dawson, and that Dawson was an excellent manager of supplies and resources.

"Yes, actually, I can cook," she told him.

He arched a brow, smiled, and returned to his work.

He became very involved with his correspondence and didn't look up again, not even when she began banging pots and pans as she put together a small roast with potatoes and onions.

It suddenly seemed important to her that Sloan find comfort in his home.

She knew that the meal she'd made was a good one, even though they consumed it in silence, except for Sloan's one comment: "Pass the salt, please."

As she cleaned up after their meal, she looked over his shoulder at his work and saw that he was sketching a map of the area west of the Black Hills. It was filled with rivers. The Powder, the Tongue, the Rosebud . . . more.

"What are you doing?" she asked him at last.

As if surprised to hear her speak, he looked up. "These are the 'prongs.' Here's Fort Fetterman, Fort Laramie, Fort Abraham Lincoln. Here's where they imagine they will find the Sioux."

"Will they?"

He hesitated. "They can only go so far."

"The white men or the Sioux?"

He shrugged, an odd smile playing at his lips. "Both, I imagine. The Indians. They're traveling in larger and larger numbers. They can't camp too long in one place; they won't be able to feed themselves or their ponies if they do."

"Who are you drawing this for?" she asked softly.

"Myself." He hesitated. "I haven't received my orders yet, but on my next expedition, I believe I'll be riding from prong to prong with intelligence reports."

"Why don't you ask for another leave?"

He glanced at her sharply, then looked back at the desk. "Because we're entering the end of something. I have to be here." He rose suddenly. "I've tears in a few shirts. Will you fix them?"

She frowned; the tone of his voice was so strange, so very distant.

"Of course."

"Ah."

"Why—wouldn't I?"

"Why not—you are excellent at certain tasks, the perfect cavalry wife."

"If you don't want me to—"

"Oh, but I do want you. To mend my shirts."

He strode into the bedroom and returned with two of the cotton shirts he wore beneath his cavalry jacket. She took them and went for her mending kit, and then sat in the chair where he had taken her on his lap to look at the photograph album.

He continued with his map-making and estimate of troop movements.

She sewed.

Neither of them spoke.

It had grown late by the time she finished with her work. She rose and folded his shirts. He continued to give his attention to his work. She was certain he was aware that she stood near him, but he paid her no heed.

It was puzzling.

"I'm going to bed," she told him after a moment.

He nodded, not looking at her. "Good night."

She hesitated, wanting to talk. "Sloan . . ." she began, and broke off.

He turned to her, his dark eyes sweeping over her. "Good night. Get to sleep."

She turned around, wondering why it felt that she had been so thoroughly dismissed. He would come to bed when he was ready.

She went into the bedroom and changed into her night-gown. She couldn't resist the temptation to walk back to the archway.

He still sat at his desk, his head bowed, busily sketching.

She went back into the bedroom, doused the bedside lamp, and lay down. She turned to her side and tried to sleep, but she lay awake.

It was very late when Sloan came in at long last. He moved about the room, quietly undressing.

Yet when he lay down beside her, he kept a very careful distance from her.

And that night, though they both lay awake for hours, he did not touch her, and she did not move toward him.

Fifteen

$\mathscr{T}$he next few weeks passed in a manner that left Sabrina completely baffled . . . and more and more tormented.

Sloan was polite and courteous to her, but he spent a great deal of time with the other men in the officers' quarters, and worked late every night.

Willow arrived with the rest of Sabrina's clothing and belongings, and she was glad to see him. She felt that Sloan watched her intently as she greeted Willow, but what was on his mind, she didn't know. He hadn't been sharing his thoughts with her.

Willow and Sloan stayed up very late, talking. When she had a chance to speak with Willow herself, she anxiously asked him questions about her sister and Hawk. Once, she caught Sloan watching her, studying her, and she was surprised the next evening when he told her that they could take a few days for a trip to Mayfair to visit Skylar and Hawk.

While they were at Mayfair, Sloan spent the nights talking to Hawk until the wee hours of the morning; she was asleep by the time he came to bed. Sabrina was delighted to be with Skylar, who was growing rounder every day. As Sabrina and Sloan were getting ready to leave, Skylar, who wanted to walk out with them, had difficulty getting into her coat. When Sabrina laughed sympathetically, Hawk teased, ''You'll be in that shape soon enough yourself, I'll warrant, and you'll think twice about laughing then!''

She'd ceased laughing when she noticed that Sloan was looking at her. "Sabrina isn't certain about raising a family on the frontier," Sloan had said lightly; then he had urged her to hurry.

They didn't spend a romantic night in the tipi. Willow accompanied them to the fort because they were bringing back Hawk and Skylar's wedding gift to them—a beautifully carved grandfather clock with the motto "Time Waits for No Man" inscribed on the face.

Custer returned to Washington. The officers and men at the fort worked on the prong that would be leaving from Fort Abraham Lincoln. Sloan was informed that he'd officially receive his promotion to lieutenant colonel in a ceremony scheduled for the end of summer, and winter passed into spring with very little difference. The days could suddenly be warm, and then the temperature would pitch down well below freezing.

Yet it wasn't the weather that left Sabrina so very cold. Sloan had distanced himself from her. She could remember a time when she had been dismayed that he pursued her so relentlessly. Now . . .

He was courteous. He was even charming in the company of others. Yet it seemed that he had tired of her, just when she had realized how much she wanted . . . his warmth.

But just when it seemed that life with Sloan had become a living hell of inner torment, life became worse.

Because hell was better with him than without him.

Sloan was being sent out on an intelligence detail. General Crook was claiming a victory against the Sioux. He believed that he had come upon Crazy Horse's camp, and that his men, under Reynolds, had destroyed the camp. He was hoping for a first and telling victory in the great Sioux war.

Sabrina found out that Sloan would be leaving the fort through Sergeant Dawson, who came to her with a message from Sloan, asking her to pack his belongings for a trip that might last several weeks. Although she usually enjoyed doing domestic tasks for her husband, this one she undertook with a heavy heart.

She was afraid for him to go.

She was folding extra shirts to pack into his bedroll when she felt a prickling down her spine and looked up to discover that he had come back to their quarters. He stood leaning against the archway, watching her with grave, dark eyes as she went about her task. She was unnerved when she saw him there.

"There's—coffee," she told him.

"Thanks." He turned away, going to the Dutch oven and pouring himself coffee.

"They believe that Crazy Horse's camp has been destroyed?" she asked.

Sloan sipped hot black coffee, turned back to her, and shrugged. "No one claims to have killed Crazy Horse, and I'm personally not so certain that Crook attacked any Sioux. The soldiers encountered an encampment and killed Indians. Crook had split his troops, staying behind to guard army supplies with four companies while six companies of men followed an Indian trail. Though Crook is claiming a victory, it sounds as if the attack was a pathetically mismanaged affair. Reynolds's troops were divided into three battalions of two companies each, under three captains: Noyes, Mills, and Moore. It seems that only Mills led the men with any competency, and though they effectively destroyed the camp, they were counterattacked, and as it happened, a number of wounded men were left behind to be scalped alive by the Indians."

"Oh, my God!" Sabrina breathed.

He didn't seem to hear her. "If I'm right, they attacked Cheyenne who were simply living in the unceded lands, causing the government no harm. And now, like the reservation Indians who have been starved out by corrupt contractors, those Indians will travel northward for help from the Oglala or Hunkpapa people, and the 'hostiles' will amass a larger force than any white commander will ever believe.''

"I don't understand; why are you going out?"

"To find out exactly which Indians Crook attacked."

"Oh," Sabrina murmured. With the last of his belongings folded into his bedroll, she stood idly with her arms crossed over her chest. She looked at Sloan, who continued to watch her gravely. "Won't there come a time when you'll no longer be able to straddle a fence?" she asked him. "The whites will want the truth about what you discover. And if the Sioux think that you are going to betray them to the whites, won't they be forced to kill you, regardless of your having been their friend?"

"I don't believe that I'll encounter any Sioux," Sloan told her. He set his cup down. "The coffee was good." He strode past her, picking up the bedroll she had packed for him. "Thank you," he told her briefly; then he turned, striding toward the door once again.

She realized that he was leaving then—right then.

She followed after him. "Sloan?"

He paused, turning back.

"Be careful."

He nodded, the touch of a smile about his lips. "I'm always careful. I'm good at what I do."

"But things are changing."

"Yes, they are. But behave, my love," he said lightly. "I've no intention of conveniently getting killed. I will be coming back."

He stepped outside. The door closed. She stared after it for a long moment, then raced toward it. She flung it open in time to see Sloan talking to Lieutenant Blake as he mounted up on Thomas.

Sloan, who had been listening to Blake, turned. She hesitated on the porch, then hurried down the steps to the two men.

"Ah, Mrs. Trelawny! Excuse me. I'll leave you two alone."

Before he walked away, Blake saluted Sloan, who returned the gesture. Then Sloan looked down at Sabrina.

For a moment, she was tongue-tied. Then she told him quietly, "That was a horrible thing to say."

"What was that?"

"That you will not conveniently get killed."

He smiled suddenly, the wicked, roguish smile that he could somehow cast so compellingly. "Well, I don't intend to get killed."

"Obviously, you didn't mean that it would be convenient for you—but rather for me."

"So it would not be convenient for you?"

"I told you, that's a horrible thing to say!" Sabrina persisted.

"All right, then. I'm sorry. And I'm glad that you're anxious for my return."

"Naturally, I want you to return alive and well."

"Good." He leaned toward her, his hands balanced on the pommel of his saddle. "And naturally, I want you to be alive and well—and *here!*—when I get back."

"Where would I go?" she asked him.

"I don't know. But no excursions, do you understand?"

She saluted, staring at him. She wanted to say something more; she didn't know what. She didn't want him just riding away this way. It seemed so . . . cold. She wished that they'd been angry, that she might have been so irresistible the previous night that he'd swept her into his arms, so she could then carry that memory with her into the days and nights ahead, when she lay awake praying that he was alive.

And not with an Indian mistress.

He pulled on Thomas's reins, moving away from her. "No excursions, Sabrina."

She stood in the yard, watching him ride away. Soldiers saluted him as he passed by; he saluted in return.

He didn't look back.

After a few minutes, she shivered and went back inside. She was suddenly very tired, and she went into the bedroom to lie down. It didn't matter, she realized. Sloan was gone, and it didn't matter if she lay there all night, staring at the ceiling. There was nothing she really wanted to do—until he returned.

The fort was a flurry of activity as wagons were prepared, mules and cattle bought, and men drilled. In the first few days after Sloan left, Sabrina felt entirely listless, as if she had no energy at all.

But the women who were fast becoming her friends wouldn't leave her alone. She was invited to dinner, lunch, coffee, to reading circles and sewing bees. Feeling very lonely, she accepted the invitations. Marlene, often at the same functions, watched her with a secretive smile that Sabrina found annoying. She did her very best to ignore Marlene, reminding herself that Sloan didn't lie, and he had said that Marlene was an ''old'' acquaintance. Marlene was his past. She was careful, any time she was in Marlene's presence, to pine for Sloan's return. It wasn't a difficult act.

Newspapers continued to contain damning political stories about graft and corruption.

Yet, while politics demanded grave attention in print, so did the coming Fourth of July celebrations; it was the centennial year. The United States was nearly a hundred years old—a very young nation compared to those in Europe, but for a nation that had so recently gone through such a desperate test as the Civil War, the centennial was an exceptionally special occasion. Sabrina read avidly about the exposition planned for Philadelphia, the fireworks in Washington, and much more. Everyone everywhere would be celebrating this Fourth of July.

July was still a long way off.

Colonel John Gibbon marched out of Fort Ellis with his prong of the attack in early April; the column leaving Fort Abraham Lincoln should have done so approximately two weeks later.

Custer remained in Washington, in very serious trouble

with President Grant. The soldiers continued to drill and prepare for the expeditions.

They all waited.

"When they leave, the men will probably be gone a very long time," Norah said one day as they worked on a quilt.

Sabrina, who had just received a letter from her sister, paid her little heed. Not that Skylar had any earth-shattering news, but it was always wonderful just to hear from her.

"A very long time!" Norah sighed.

Sabrina glanced her way, offering a wan smile, and read the letter over again.

"Maybe not. Maybe they will find the Indians quickly, and there will be a swift, very heroic campaign!" Libbie suggested.

"And maybe not," Louella agreed glumly with Norah.

"My point," Norah insisted, "is that we should have an outing."

"With everyone so busy?" Sabrina demanded.

Libbie Custer, extremely anxious about her husband's situation, smiled with sudden amusement and told her, "No matter how busy men are, they are often little boys. The general can be like a child, even on campaign, riding off to hunt and shoot—and sometimes . . ." she added softly, "irritate his superior officers nearly to death! My poor Autie! Everyone knows that he must lead his men on this expedition, and Generals Sheridan and Sherman both know that he is the man to get in there and get the job done! If only . . ." She glanced up again, realizing that her speech had turned passionate. She shook her head unhappily. "Grant has ordered that Autie is not to lead the campaign, that he is not even to go on the campaign!"

"Oh, come now, Libbie! Things will work out, you'll see," Louella assured her.

"We need to have a picnic," Norah insisted. "I just know that we can get the men to go along with the idea. We can take a day's ride out and back. The officers are on hold, growing bored and restless. A few of the captains, perhaps . . .''

''We did promise to show Sabrina the countryside,'' Louella said. ''Sabrina, didn't we?''

Sabrina looked up from her letter. ''Of course.''

''Then we must do it,'' Norah said.

Sabrina smiled, thinking that it was just talk, and nothing would come of it. ''I'm sure it's lovely countryside.''

Despite the brutal weather that continued to occur well into April, Sloan, traveling alone, was able to move quickly westward. He followed the trail of Crook's men and saw what had not been emphasized to any of the leaders in Washington; there were any number of travois trails leading southward, toward the agencies. Many Indians had apparently tried to comply with the government mandate that they return to their reservations. No one had allowed them the benefit of any extra time.

The number of ''hostiles'' would surely be soaring.

Two weeks out, he found the remains of the camp that had been attacked by Reynolds's men. Sifting through the rubble, he discovered that rumors were true; this hadn't been Crazy Horse's camp. It had definitely been a Cheyenne camp.

He was bent over a half-burned child's doll when he sensed movement behind him. He flattened, rolling behind a rise of thicket and rock. He quietly drew his gun. He still saw nothing, but he knew that someone was out there, watching him.

He waited.

Time passed, and he heard a flutter of movement. Far in front of him, through a cove of trees, someone was running, bare feet against the earth.

He carefully followed the sound and still discovered nothing. Then he felt the faintest trembling of the earth beneath his own feet. Spinning around, he went dead still, surprised to see not just an acquaintance, but a friend. Hawk's cousin, Ice Raven, had apparently been stalking him for some time, and was now resting on his haunches just ten feet away.

"Ice Raven." Sloan lowered his gun.

Ice Raven recognized him but paused, then lowered his knife slowly.

"You're riding with the soldiers who came here?" Ice Raven asked him.

Sloan shook his head. "No, I am riding alone."

"That's good," Ice Raven told him. "I wouldn't want to have to kill you, Cougar-in-the-Night. But the time is coming when old friendships, even blood, may not matter."

Sloan nodded. "The situation is bitter. But I wasn't with those men. The soldiers who were here believed that they'd found Crazy Horse's camp. I didn't think that they had. I came to find out what had happened."

Ice Raven stayed where he was and studied Sloan's eyes for a long time.

"What are you doing here?" Sloan asked him. "This is a Cheyenne camp."

"You know that we have friends among the Cheyenne. Your soldiers made a mistake. They thought that they attacked Crazy Horse's camp because his good friend, He Dog, who fought with him so many times before, was here. But He Dog had decided to go to the reservation. He was a brave man, but his women and children were starving. He was going to go the government way. And now, well, he has joined with Crazy Horse again. It's a Cheyenne camp, and I was riding with the Cheyenne, too. Tell me—do you want to know if the Sioux camp is nearby, if I will lead you to it, so you can tell the soldiers?"

"No. I asked the question because I am glad to see you, Ice Raven, and yet I am surprised, and I am asking as your friend what you're doing here."

Ice Raven turned, facing the wind. "There was a girl I came to see. A Cheyenne maiden. I was welcomed by her people. I was here when it happened."

"Tell me about it," Sloan said, squatting down.

"Scouts went out from the camp to find the soldiers, but the soldiers came before the scouts could warn the people. They split into groups—and began to quarrel with one another. The men who stole the ponies wouldn't go to the aid of the soldiers fighting in the village. When we rallied after the initial attack, we fired back. Heavy fire. We aimed true. The soldiers burned the tipis—and everything in them. The Cheyenne killed some soldiers and stole their ponies back. The soldiers suffered, because their leaders were fools. The Cheyenne keep suffering, because the whites keep killing. They were left without food, clothing, shelter. They rode to the Crazy Horse people. Crazy Horse welcomed them, but feared he didn't have enough food. Sitting Bull has invited all the tribes to an annual celebration, in the sun. A time for men to dance, to come close again to Wankatanka, the Great Mystery. Crazy Horse leads people to Sitting Bull."

Sloan studied Ice Raven. One of Hawk's cousins, he was no stranger to the white world. His English was excellent; he had often worn denim breeches and cotton shirts, dined in taverns and restaurants. At times, he had lived easily among the whites. No more, Sloan thought. The starvation and killing had changed Ice Raven.

And now, Reynolds and his bumbling men had come along and attacked a tribe of Cheyenne. The Cheyenne would now join with Crazy Horse, and Crazy Horse would join with Sitting Bull. And the white commanders who had learned that each brave was a man unto himself, and each tribe separate, might not accept the fact that the Indians had at last learned from the whites—and would band together to safeguard themselves from annihilation.

"I'm sorry," Sloan said. "I am sorry for what was done, and for what is happening. You said that you came here to be with a girl. Did she survive the attack?"

Ice Raven nodded gravely.

"She survived, and she will remember."

"I'm glad that she lived."

"She is with her people, tending to the wounded." He looked around, shaking his head. "The white commander left many of his wounded. Some were scalped alive and brutally finished. The whites who attacked us will condemn us. They make war, but when we fight, we are the savages."

"I wish there were a way to change it."

"You can't stop the tides," Ice Raven said disparagingly. "Yet I greatly fear the future. They want brave men to become farmers on land that will not grow grass. I have seen the agencies where the once-great warriors drink themselves into oblivion, and the women and children cry for lack of food. I don't see how this will change, though I know that the white men, with their numbers and their guns, will eventually flood the plains. I have seen once-fierce warriors, who are still proud men, bow to the way of the whites. The wind is changing. Some will follow the white wind and survive, and some will fight the last battles. When they are over, there will be nothing but the mercy of a people who call us savages and hate what we are—and must surely know, in their hearts, that they have stolen the land that they claim as their own."

Sloan thought of the eastern tribes—no longer in existance. "The culture will change, but perhaps our ways will always be remembered."

"By drunken men farming dead ground on reservations."

"Some white men are corrupt, but some are good. You know that. It will be a harder fight once the last blood is shed."

"Maybe in that fight, you will be a warrior again," Ice Raven said, and smiled suddenly. "I remember being boys. There were so many buffalo then. They roamed as far as we could see, and we never thought that there might not be enough forever. But there is only one way now. The white way. President Grant told Red Cloud that survival for us would be victory. So some of us will survive. And some of us will fight and die."

"What is your choice?"

"I've not yet made my choice. Where do you go from here, Cougar-in-the-Night?"

Sloan smiled. It was becoming stranger and stranger to hear his Sioux name. It sounded good. Seeing Ice Raven was good.

"I'm going back. I've learned what I came to discover."

"I'll ride with you for a way. I have done my duty to the people here, and now I must do my duty to myself. I want to see my white cousin before I make my decisions. Do you want the company of a full-blooded Sioux? Perhaps your soldier friends will see you and shoot you down, thinking you are one of us."

"If we ride, just the two of us, it's unlikely that we'll be discovered."

Ice Raven smiled. "Then, for just a while, perhaps we can turn back time." He stood suddenly. "Let's hunt a deer. I've not eaten much lately. Too many women and children to feed; too many dead, wounded, and dying warriors."

Sloan rose as well. "Let's hunt a deer," he agreed.

"Well, it's tomorrow," Norah informed Sabrina.

"What?"

Engaged in keeping a journal, which she had begun to do since she'd discovered that Sloan wrote down events upon occasion, Sabrina was startled when Norah walked in without knocking and came to stand behind her chair.

"Tomorrow—our outing. Our picnic."

"Picnic?" she said, frowning.

"Picnic! If the weather holds, it will be lovely. We're just going to ride out to a really beautiful stream that's about five miles away. We'll spend the night with the water and the wildflowers . . . and head back the next day!"

"Spend the night out? Won't that be dangerous?"

Norah shook her head. "Where is your spirit of adventure? We spend the night out when we travel to Mayfair or into some of the surrounding towns. We'll be well protected by the soldiers. Officer's wives often accompany their menfolk on their first night out on a campaign. Camping is quite wonderful.''

Sabrina wasn't so sure she agreed, but that wasn't why she hesitated. "Norah . . . well, I'm not so sure I should go," Sabrina said uneasily.

"Why not? Even Libbie will come."

"Yes, but . . ." She hesitated. Sloan was far away. God alone knew when he would come back.

If.

She gave herself a vehement shake; she would not think in those terms. And yet, in the meantime . . .

She sat here, day after day. Waiting. Growing more and more restless. Even Libbie Custer was going.

"You must come!" Norah insisted. "Please! Please, say that you'll come."

"Well . . ."

"We'll have a wonderful time."

"Sleeping in the woods?" she mused doubtfully. It didn't sound terribly comfortable, and she'd been very tired lately. The harsh winter with its constantly changing temperature was sending numerous cases of influenza around the fort. She wondered if she was coming down with something.

"Sissy!" Norah teased her. "We're adventuresses! We're military women," she reminded her gallantly.

Maybe it would be good to get out, away from the fort for awhile. "Is . . . Marlene coming?" she asked.

"Why, hadn't you heard? Marlene isn't here."

"Oh? Where did she go?"

"I'm not sure. It seems that she received some kind of a wire and left here for Gold Town."

Naturally, for Sabrina, the concept of a picnic sounded a great deal more fun without Marlene. And she only allowed herself a moment's pause, worrying that Marlene might have gone to Gold Town—because Sloan might have sent the wire.

Just because he didn't seem to want her anymore. . . .

Still, she needed to quit spending her days brooding and worrying.

"A picnic sounds wonderful," she told Norah.

Sloan enjoyed spending time riding with Ice Raven.

They hunted deer.

They fished on the way, rode over ice on a few of the rivers, even though the daytime temperatures began to rise to fifty and sixty degrees.

Ice Raven rode with Sloan toward the fort, planning on swinging southward to reach Hawk's property after they had ridden westward. Sloan briefly considered riding the distance with Ice Raven, but he had to report back to Terry, and he considered it very important to authenticate the rumors they'd heard that it had been a Cheyenne camp—and not Crazy Horse's—that had been attacked.

He was also anxious to return to the fort. And Sabrina.

All right, so she was taking her time coming to him.

He was obsessed with his wife, and he was not handling the obsession well. She could, it seemed, quite easily keep her distance. What had he expected? She'd been honest. She didn't want to be married to him, and she didn't want children. She probably viewed his keeping his distance from her as a blessing. In fact, she was probably happy as a damned lark. She'd been charming lately—the very best of wives, cooking, mending, tending to their quarters.

Yet he'd been going crazy, sleeping beside her in such torment that it had been a relief to be sent out on the trail.

Well, now he'd been gone. And he thought that he was ready to go crazy from wanting her. Yet in his very next thought, he reminded himself that he still didn't want to spend his life forcing her to be with him. He wanted her to smile at him the way she smiled at the soldiers she danced with; he wanted her to laugh with him the way she laughed with others. He wanted her to look at him with her blue eyes shimmering the way that they could. He wanted . . .

To be wanted. And yet, he wanted a son as well, and it seemed an ironic jest from the powers that be that she should have conceived so quickly before their marriage, and failed to do so now as the months passed them by. Of course, those nights when he lay in self-imposed celibacy didn't help, but then again, he was determined that she should come to him.

Ice Raven, who knew Sabrina through Hawk and Skylar—and had seen her with Sloan at Mayfair before their trip to Scotland—was amused that the two had married. Though Ice Raven refrained from saying so, Sloan knew his friend had surmised that there had to have been a reason for the marriage, and that would have been a child. Ice Raven apparently realized that the child had been lost, because he spent part of the trip telling Sloan about friends who had suffered a similar loss and gone on to have many children.

Coming westward across the hills, Ice Raven and Sloan reined in together, seeing a cloud of vultures circling high overhead. They glanced at one another, then moved cautiously forward again, over the next rise.

The hill sloped gently downward to a trickling stream. Miners had recently worked the stream.

From a distance, Sloan and Ice Raven could see partially stripped bodies, the naked flesh very pink. There were four of them, shot through with arrows, then formed into a line. Sloan and Ice Raven rode down the hill to the bodies. They dismounted and studied the scene of the carnage. Flies buzzed around the slashed and disfigured bodies of three men.

The fourth body, left unmolested, was that of a woman of perhaps thirty. Her features were attractive, even in death. She had been a clean kill, an arrow through the heart.

Ice Raven wrenched out one of the arrows protruding from the chest of a dead man. "Cheyenne," he said after a moment. "This was done in retaliation. They might not have intended to kill the woman; she would have made a good captive. Perhaps she tried to fight them, which would have made sense. The Indian way is not to mutilate those we respect."

Sloan felt a raw edge of pain and fear circling his heart. They were far too close to the fort and to the trails that led from Gold Town and to Hawk's house. The woman's death deeply disturbed him.

Ice Raven was looking at him. Sloan shook his head in disgust. "An overeager commander butchered peaceful Cheyenne—and these people have paid for it with their lives."

"They shouldn't have been searching for a living in the Black Hills," Ice Raven said grimly.

Sloan didn't argue. He strode to the miners' ramshackle hut and found a spade. Ice Raven watched him dig graves for a moment, then went to the shack, found another spade, and returned to help him.

"Thanks," Sloan said quietly.

Ice Raven dug, then paused, looking at him. "I don't simply hate all that is white. I don't condone murder, my friend. What happened at the camp was murder on a large scale. This is murder as well. Neither is right."

Sloan nodded, and they finished their task quickly. Sloan was anxious to ride again.

Ice Raven said nothing, but Sloan was certain that his friend understood his hurry to return to the fort.

As they neared the fork in the trail where they had intended to part company, they both reined in, aware of conversation, laughter, and commotion ahead of them on the trail. English was the language being spoken.

Ice Raven brought a finger to his lips, indicating to Sloan that he would slip into the foliage. Sloan nodded, frowning, motioning in turn to Ice Raven that he wanted to see what was going on before making himself known as well.

After dismounting, he inched through the foliage and

paused in its thick cover. Ahead, on the banks of the stream, sat a number of soldiers—along with their women. Scanning the area quickly, Sloan decided that there were five soldiers and several women.

His wife among them.

Perhaps it was the length of his ride, the time he'd spent away. Perhaps it was simply that she had chosen to defy him so openly and completely.

Maybe it was the fear that now seemed such a part of him, and the pain that he'd begun to feel when he'd seen the slain woman. Maybe it was all of those factors combined that made his blood boil in a way unlike anything he had ever experienced before. If she had actually been in front of him at that moment . . .

But she wasn't. She was barefoot and being given fishing lessons by Lieutenant Jimmy Blake.

He fought to control his temper, holding his breath and counting until he thought he would expire.

After a while, he walked back to where he had left Ice Raven. He let out a soft birdcall, and his friend reappeared on the road. "It's a group from the fort," he told Ice Raven.

"Your friends?"

"Yes, a number of them. And Sabrina is with them as well."

"You must be pleased."

"Umm, not exactly."

"Ah, yes. The dead woman. Still, I don't think a small war party would venture so close."

"I don't know anymore," Sloan said, and Ice Raven didn't argue.

"Well, you may go on and join your party. I will leave you and be on my way—"

"Actually, I'd like to ask you to stay, just until after dark."

Ice Raven arched an ebony brow.

"What do you have in mind?"

"A lesson in communications," Sloan said dryly.

He outlined to Ice Raven what he wanted to do. Then, as darkness fell, he slipped back through the foliage until he saw Tom Custer and tried to attract Tom's attention. Spinning around, Tom gazed at him with widening eyes at first, and Sloan realized that the man thought at first that he might be facing a hostile attack. Then he recognized Sloan in the shadows. "Major!"

"Shh . . . Tom."

"You're back! What did you discover?"

"It was a Cheyenne camp Reynolds attacked. I've a written report; I'd like you to take it to Sergeant Dawson and have him take it back to Terry immediately."

"We're so close to the fort; surely you will want to report in person—"

"Naturally, but I'd like to surprise my wife. I see that she's with you."

Tom grinned. "Sure. Do I tell her?"

"No, no, don't tell her anything. Tom, I met up with a friend and rode with him for a ways. We found some miners, murdered about ten miles back. I don't think that excursions from the fort are wise at this time."

"Murdered by—Sioux?"

"Cheyenne. They were killed by Cheyenne arrows. I don't want Sabrina venturing out anymore, but it's something I want to discuss with her myself. I'll surprise her myself; please, don't say anything to her at all."

"I won't say anything. I don't want to upset the other women."

"Keep a close watch, Tom."

After all her hesitation, Sabrina was delighted that she had come. Fishing had been fun and exhilarating, and she had been especially excited to catch the biggest fish of the day.

She had spent time helping Jean as well. Pale, pretty, quiet-as-a-mouse Jean, who so rarely said a word and always seemed afraid of her own shadow! Jenkins would have nothing to do with the fun and wasn't glad of the outing at all, but when Jean's friends all tormented him long enough, he barked out an order that Jean could try her hand at fishing. Sabrina, Sarah and David Anderson, and Lieutenant Jimmy Blake had shown Jean how to get the squiggly worms on the hooks, and Jean had, in time, while "oohing" and "aahing," learned to bait her own hook.

They'd ridden in beautiful weather in the morning, talked, chatted, and fished by day, cooked their catches by open fire for supper, watched the sun set and the moon rise. The countryside was beautiful. The day's play had kept Sabrina somewhat occupied, and though she hadn't forgotten to worry about Sloan and wonder where he might be, she had felt the edge taken away from her constant anxiety.

The women had brought canvas military tents, and though a number of men had told her they were all but worthless when the temperatures plummeted, the night was as beautiful as the day had been. There were two women per tent, and she was to share one with Louella.

"I told you that a picnic would be wonderful!" Louella told her smugly.

It was wonderful, but not at all private. They changed into their nightgowns by drawing the cumbersome gowns on top of their heads first, shedding their day clothing beneath, and then pulling the gowns down. They laughed, tripping in the process, falling atop their "bunk," and generally enjoying the situation.

"We're such prudes!" Louella said in dismay.

"Are we?"

Louella cast her a quick glance, then smiled. "Well, you're a married woman, and married to the most charming and—" she hesitated just a moment, then said flatly, "masculine man alive."

"Louella!"

"It's the truth," Louella said. "That's really why we were so cruel, and thought that we had to find something—oh, *something* wrong with you. But you've been outgoing and very strong, and I'm sorry that we were mean, and I wish that—well, I wish that I didn't look like a horse.''

"You don't look like a horse at all," Sabrina lied.

"I'm an old maid."

"You're not so old. And you may not be an old maid forever. Dear Lord, Louella, we lost more than a half a million men in the war! It takes longer to find one these days, that's all."

"Do you think I will ever marry?"

"The right man may very well be out there," Sabrina told her.

Louella seemed more encouraged. She gave Sabrina a quick, tight hug, then retired to her section of bedding in the tent.

Louella promptly fell asleep. She snored, but her snoring was rhythmic.

Sabrina lay awake, realizing that she, too, thought that her husband was the most masculine man alive.

Except that . . .

He was a half-breed cavalryman, dedicated to a peace that seemed impossible to achieve. She was so very afraid for him, and . . .

He didn't seem to want her anymore.

She lay awake for awhile, as she did too many nights. But Louella's snoring definitely had a soft pattern to it. Sabrina found her eyes closing; to her amazement, the sound was lulling.

She drifted to sleep as well.

She didn't know how long she had slept when she was suddenly awakened as a hand clamped tightly over her mouth. She opened her eyes, struggling instinctively against the hold on her.

Then, for a moment, she went dead still in absolute terror.

Oh, God. Oh, dear God!

They were under attack by the Indians!

The warrior atop her wore black paint over half his

face; his chest was dotted with half moons and hailstones. He wore a breechclout and was barelegged except for buckskin boots. She could make out nothing more of him or his features in the shadows, but she felt the absolute power of his strength, and she believed with growing terror that he had certainly come to kill her.

She had to fight.

She would not die so easily.

She tried wildly to strike out, but the warrior was incredibly strong, and she couldn't dislodge the hand he'd clamped over her mouth, even as he picked her up, balancing in a precarious position to escape the tent. She tried desperately to scream, but she couldn't get out so much as a gasp. His hold was suffocating. She could scarcely breathe.

Sioux . . . this close to the fort!

Or Crow?

What difference did it make?

Because she was being taken . . .

Abducted by the hostiles!

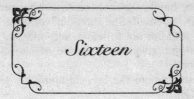

Sixteen

Terror filled her, and she continued to struggle as desperately as she could. What was happening? Where were the soldiers? Had they been murdered in their beds? She had heard no shots, and yet . . .

Perhaps the Indians had slit the throats of the rest of her party as they slept.

The brave carried her, running through the night, and still, she couldn't budge his hold. She had to do something soon, or else she would black out!

The world spun by her in the shadows of the night. She wriggled and twisted wildly, thumping her legs against his body, hoping to hit him in a way that might cripple him, even if only momentarily.

But even as she desperately writhed in her efforts to cause pain, she twisted enough to see the clearing ahead. Another Indian waited there, holding the reins of two horses. Her mouth was suddenly freed from her captor's hold—because she was deposited facedown over the haunches of one of the horses! A second later, the brave who had abducted her was mounted on the animal, and they were racing into the foliage in the darkness.

Her mouth was free, and she used that newly gained freedom to good advantage. She screamed like a banshee. Again and again and again . . .

But perhaps they had come too far away from the camp, and no one could hear her.

267

Her voice quickly grew hoarse, and her sense of terror and despair increased. She should never have left the fort; Sloan had told her not to leave, and now . . .

She couldn't give way to panic. If she did so, she'd have no hope.

She twisted where she lay, clamping her teeth into the brave's thigh.

She heard a stunned grunt—then a hand descended with force upon her rump. The horse's gait caused her jaw to slam shut, and her teeth chattered.

The horse over which she lay was suddenly brought to a halt. She was dizzy; her head was spinning. The brave leapt down. She tried to struggle up, but before she could do so, powerful hands slipped around her waist, and she was hauled from the animal. For a moment, she was set down, and though her legs were wobbly, she started to run . . .

But seconds later she was grabbed and pulled down to the ground. She swore, furious, nearly hysterical. She found herself dragged back to her feet, lifted again . . .

Carried.

Brought into a tipi.

The light from a small fire in the center of the conical dwelling cast strange arcs of orange light against the shadows that lurked upon the buffalo-skin walls. She barely saw the light flickering from the fire before she was cast down upon the skins that composed the flooring. She struggled to her knees, then to her feet. She turned frantically, looking for the brave. He stood by the opening. All she could see was the darkness of his hair, falling almost to his shoulders, and the black paint that covered his upper face. Dressed in nothing but a breechclout, he stood with his arms crossed over his chest.

She was very, very still for a moment, trying desperately not to shake, to find some way out of this terror.

There was no rational way.

Panic filled her again, and she made a wild dash to dive around him and escape into the night.

She had just made it past him when he tackled her. His arms wound around her retreating form, and they plummeted back to the ground together. He straddled her; she fought wildy, trying to gouge his eyes with her nails.

"I'll kill you, you wretched savage, I'll kill you!" she swore.

Her wrists were captured and slammed back against the ground.

"I'll kill you!" she repeated.

The sudden sound of rough, dry laughter from her captor stunned her to silence. The brave was laughing, as if he'd understood her every word . . .

As if . . .

Then he spoke; she heard the brave's voice.

His voice.

Sloan's voice.

"Oh, I think not, my love. I think not."

"Sloan!" She gasped out his name, so astonished that at first, she wasn't even angry.

Then the fury set in.

He had begun to ease back. She attacked him with an energy born from the fear that had shot through her. Her force sent him falling back, and she continued to slam her fists against his bare chest while he swore softly until he recovered from the sheer speed and violence of her assault, wrapping his arms around her and rolling so that she wound up pinned beneath him again.

"Calm down!" he warned her.

"Calm down!" she shrieked. "Calm down, after what you did? You ought to be—scalped. Skinned alive. How could you do such a horrible thing—"

"Why were you in a place where such a horrible thing could happen to you?" he countered furiously.

She fell silent for a moment, startled.

"There's no excuse for this, Sloan. You scared me half to death—"

"I told you not to leave the fort."

"But—I'm not alone."

"I distinctly told you *no excursions!*"

"But you were gone—"

"Dammit, Sabrina, I told you not to leave the fort, and I told you with good reason not to leave the fort! And I think I even warned you that you'd be damned sorry if you did."

She bit her lower lip, searching for the words that would explain to him how much worse his actions had been than her own. She shivered suddenly, aware of the pattern of paint on his shoulders and his face.

He had fooled her.

Naturally, she hadn't had much of a real chance to look at him until now, but he looked all Sioux, and the effect was chilling.

"You're lucky you weren't shot!" she hissed to him.

"And you're damned lucky there weren't any real 'hostiles' in the area. There's a guard posted because I warned Tom it was necessary, and I walked right through the damned guard."

"But there are no hostiles here—"

"There are hostiles too damned close."

"I don't know how you can say that—"

"I can say it because I spent an hour burying three dead men—and a woman—today."

She closed her eyes, unnerved by the fury in his dark eyes—and the paint on his face.

"This was still wickedly cruel!" she charged him. "You could have scared me to death."

"You need to be scared."

"Maybe *you* need to be scared."

"You scare the hell out of me constantly," he assured her, rising to a sitting position at her side. "And I hope you've learned that you need to stay where I damned well tell you to stay!"

A massive shudder ripped through her, a remnant of the pure terror she had been feeling. She gritted her teeth together hard, rose to her knees, and pounded her fists against his chest and shoulders with a new burst of vehemence. She did so with every intention of hurting him, and she knew that she achieved her goal by the grunt that escaped him. "Don't you ever do anything like this again. Ever!"

He caught her wrists. "Don't you leave the fort. And don't hit me again."

"I can't help it! I'd like to rip you into tiny pieces."

"Well, that isn't going to happen."

"Don't be too certain."

She had to be an idiot to be quite so defiant, but then, he had nearly scared her to death. Yet she was caught now, held in the tight vise of his fingers. Despite the paint on his face and his definitely hostile appearance, she was dismayed to realize that her need to pound against him was a need just to touch him as well. She tried to pull away; he didn't let her go. Instead he pulled her closer and closer until her face was just inches from his own.

"Sloan . . . let me go," she murmured.

"So you can hit me again?" he inquired.

"So that we can go back. So that the others don't worry about me. So that you . . . so that you can get that paint off your face. It's war paint, and it's—frightening," she told him.

"What's frightening, Sabrina? The paint—or me?"

"You—don't frighten me," she whispered.

He smiled suddenly. "Then I shouldn't frighten you with or without paint," he told her quietly. She trembled, feeling his closeness, the warmth created between them against the fresh coolness of the night.

Holding her wrists, he drew her still closer. His mouth touched hers, and he pulled her very hard against him, slowly easing her down to the hide-covered ground. His hand cupped her chin as he kissed her, his tongue parting her lips, seeking, searching; his mouth breaking away, then returning.

Her hands were on his naked chest, stroking the sleekness of his flesh, feeling the convulsive ripple of muscle beneath her lightest touch. He caught her fingers, kissed them lightly. She looked into his eyes, reached out and touched the line of the paint on his face, then delicately traced the pattern of one of the half moons drawn on his chest, fascinated despite herself. "How could you?" she murmured again, feeling a renewed stirring of anger.

He captured her hand, drawing it back against his chest. "How could I? Because it's very much a part of my heritage, and I've often seen that the Indian ways are not nearly as savage as the white," he said.

"We should go back—"

"We're spending the night here."

"Here?"

"Don't you recognize where we are?" he asked her.

She shook her head. "I'm in a tipi with a man in war paint."

He smiled. "This is where we took shelter on the trail from Hawk's place."

"Oh," she murmured. "Of course."

She met the darkness of his eyes, and it seemed that rays of heat swept into her. He was right. He was himself, the same man, with or without paint, and she wanted him. She wished that she could reach out. She couldn't quite do it.

But tonight, it didn't matter. He watched her for several long moments, then very slowly leaned toward her, almost as if giving her a chance to escape. . . .

"Come here," he commanded deeply.

"Sloan . . ."

"Come here."

She wasn't sure if she complied or not.

His mouth formed over hers. He ran his tongue over her lips, then plunged between them, sweeping the recesses of her mouth. His kiss was deep . . . then light again. His lips nibbled hers, then seemed to devour with a deep hunger once again. A deep, pleasant langour settled over her. She lay very still, feeling his lips against her own, the deliberate play of his tongue. She forgot the paint and saw only the man.

He drew her up and swept her nightgown over her head. She felt the warm flickering of the firelight over her naked flesh. He took her into his arms as they knelt together. His fingers stroked the length of her spine, his kiss brushed her throat . . . her collarbone. His mouth found her breast, playing with it, caressing it, the rasp of his tongue hardening the nub of her nipple and sending lightning through her. She closed her eyes and felt his touch with each leap and crackle of the flames. His fingers stroked her, within and without. She clung to his shoulders, threaded her fingers through his hair, then fell back . . . and he was with her, running his hand up and down her body, his palm just slightly rough.

Again he played. Slowly, deliberately. His fingers traced patterns around her breasts, and his lips followed where they strayed. He settled over her; she opened her eyes, seeing his face again, half in shadow, half in paint, with the flickering orange glow of firelight upon it. Tremors raked through her as she looked into his dark eyes. She could see the unique strength within him that came from living his dual life, and she wrapped her arms around him, glad to close her eyes and cling to him. Sweet warmth blazed to passion; the color of the night was red. The feel of his flesh was slick and hot, vibrant and powerful. His every touch spread the fire throughout her body. She would always remember the burnt oranges and fiery crimsons of that night, exploding at the end in a rainbow of brilliance that burst and rained upon her like a million tiny slivers of crystal. . . .

They argued no more that night. She lay beside him, glad of the feel of his arms around her.

She wondered if she should mention to him the possibility that had been haunting her for the last week or so. But she hesitated. She wasn't sure yet, not at all sure. And she didn't want to tell him what might not be true. She let her hand close over his.

* * *

She awoke to sunlight filtering into the tipi. She shivered a bit, for the fire had died and the air remained cool. Halfway rising, she reached for her nightgown as she shivered, then discovered that he was seated a slight distance from her, watching her with a gaze of pure amusement as he sipped coffee. His paint was gone; he was back in his uniform again, all the way to his plumed hat.

She paused, holding the nightgown to her chest.

"What's so amusing?" she inquired.

He smiled. "You. You look like a pinto."

She frowned, then looked down the length of her body. His black paint had rubbed off on her—in all the various places he had touched her. She leapt up, swearing beneath her breath, evermore irritated by the easy sound of his laughter. She spun away from him, ready to go striding out, remembering that there was a stream nearby.

"Whoa, hold up! Ice Raven is out there, my love."

She turned back to him, surprised. She knew three of her brother-in-law's cousins: Willow, who lived among the whites, and his brothers, Blade and Ice Raven, who lived among the Sioux on unceded lands.

"Hostile" Indians.

Yet they were all well-educated men, in both white and Indian ways, and all three of them had ridden without regard for personal danger to help her and Skylar when they had been threatened by her stepfather and his hired assassins. She would always be grateful to them; she would always consider them her friends. She felt a tugging about her heart as she realized that Ice Raven would be considered the enemy by most of the people at the fort. The uncomfortable feeling she was experiencing was just a taste, she realized, of what Sloan must feel.

"Ice Raven?" How had she forgotten that Sloan had had an accomplice holding the horses last night? She flushed, furious that he had played such a trick on her in front of others.

He lifted his coffee cup slightly. "He's kept watch. I

told you—miners were recently murdered, not far from here.''

"And whom did he watch for?" she queried. "White men—or Indians?"

A shadow seemed to darken Sloan's eyes. "He watched for danger," he said simply, rising. "Put your nightgown back on. I'll walk you to the stream; I've brought your clothing."

"You brought my clothing?"

"Yes, I brought your clothing," he said, annoyed. "I went back to your camp and got your clothing and your horse."

"So everyone knows that you decided to punish your errant little wife by dragging her into the woods at knife-point."

He stared at her a moment. "I never had a knife, and no one knows what went on between us. Let's get going. I need to report back to General Terry."

She slid into the gown, striding past him and informing him, "I'm sure I can find the stream, and—I'm not in the mood for company."

She walked out.

Ice Raven sat before a fire he had built in the open. The pleasant aroma of fresh-perked coffee filled the air. Ice Raven stood, smiling a welcome as he saw her. No matter how angry she was at Sloan, she wasn't going to betray her feelings to their friend. She wondered how much of their arguments he had heard. "Ice Raven!" she said with pleasure, greeting him with a hug and a kiss on the cheek.

He returned her embrace quickly. "Little Sister," he said, using the "Indian" nickname he had given her. "It's good to see you."

"And you. You're looking well. How did you happen upon Sloan?"

Ice Raven's eyes twinkled slightly. "How did you happen upon Sloan, Little Sister?"

"I believe that I asked the question first."

Ice Raven nodded, his smile fading. "He came to the Cheyenne camp. We met there."

"Oh. I'm sorry."

"I'm on my way to Hawk's."

"I wish that I were going with you. I have gotten to see my sister since I moved to the fort only once." She sighed. "Hawk must be deeply distressed with this situation growing worse and worse all the time. But Ice Raven, you should keep yourself safe; you should stay with Hawk!" she informed him.

He shrugged. "I grow weary of fighting . . . yet I fear that I cannot just walk away." He touched her cheek suddenly, smiling. He drew away his finger, showing the black on it. "War paint," he said innocently.

"Umm. I'm headed for the stream."

Sabrina saw the grin on his face before she turned and walked through a grove of trees to a crystal-clear stream that gurgled and bubbled around dozens of small rapids. She came to the water's edge and hesitated. It was beautiful country, she thought. Exquisite country. Land worth fighting for.

She knelt down to wash. The water was freezing, but she was determined to rid herself of the war paint. She swore softly as she looked nervously about the trees, then drew off her gown and, ignoring the freezing water, used the clean, gritty sand from the water's bed to scrub away the war paint that had indeed given her the appearance of a pinto.

"You missed a spot," she heard.

Swinging around in panic, she saw Sloan at the top of the rise leading down to the water. As she turned, she lost her footing on a slick root and went crashing down into the water. She heard him laughing softly as she surfaced. He stood on the root then, extending a hand to her.

She ignored his hand, seething—despite the fact that her teeth were chattering with the cold.

"Sabrina, I'm trying to help you."

"Indeed. And you were trying to help me last night."

"Actually," he said gravely, "I was. It's dangerous to wander from the fort. Surely, you've come to that realization. Come on, now; take my hand."

She hesitated, then did so.

And she wrenched with all her strength.

To her great pleasure, he came sliding off the slick root. He didn't exactly fall flat, but he did stumble knee-deep into the water, and his handsome plumed hat went flying, landing in the stream.

To her dismay, however, he still had her hand. She tugged on it to free herself, to no avail. He tugged back, drawing her flush against him. "Here's another lesson. If you're going to attack a stronger enemy, be sure that your aim is true, because retaliation can be swift."

"I don't know what you mean—" she began, only to gasp as she found herself swept up—and dropped back into the water. When she came up sputtering that time, he had collected his hat and was walking away—his boots squeaking. "Your clothes are on the bank!" he called to her.

Blue-lipped and shivering, she crawled out of the water, damning him furiously with her every breath.

She dressed very quickly and came back over the rise. Ice Raven was gone. Sloan was seated atop Thomas and leading Ginger. She strode angrily to her horse.

"Need help?" he inquired politely.

"Not from you," she assured him and leapt easily into her saddle.

He didn't reply but led the way back to the riverbank where the others had camped. For the most part, everyone was up and ready to travel back.

Yet, passing a tent as they rode into the center of the camp, they heard a deep angry voice.

"Stupid woman, are you incompetent at everything?"

There was a whisper, then a strange noise and a soft sob. Sabrina glanced sharply at Sloan.

He reined in on Thomas.

"Is everything all right?" Sloan asked as Lloyd Jenkins

stepped out of the tent, adjusting his suspenders.

"Everything is just fine, Major. Sir."

"We just thought you might be having trouble," Sabrina said.

"No. No trouble," Jenkins said, staring at her.

She nudged Ginger forward, feeling very uncomfortable. Poor Jean! No wonder she was so shy and quiet, with Lloyd Jenkins for a husband. The way that he spoke to her was appalling.

Sloan rode next to her.

"That was awful!" she said.

He didn't reply.

"He was awful to her!"

"Yes, and what the hell do you think I can do about it?" Sloan demanded angrily.

She stared at him and saw nothing but his angry dark eyes. Then her gaze slipped to his hands, and she saw that he was holding the reins so tightly that his knuckles were white.

"Perhaps you could talk to him," she suggested coolly.

"Sabrina, the man *is* afraid that I'm going to scalp him in his sleep one night. I hardly think that he would listen to anything I have to say about the proper way to speak to his wife."

"Someone should do something!" she insisted.

Sloan pulled on Ginger's reins, drawing the horse to a halt so that he could come around on Thomas and face Sabrina. "You can't do anything, do you understand? Stay away from Jenkins."

She refrained stubbornly from replying.

"You said that what I did last night was awful," he reminded her.

"Yes, but . . . " her voice trailed away.

"But?"

She shook her head. "There's something—more awful—about this."

"Sabrina, Major Sloan! Good morning!" Louella called to them cheerfully. She was returning from the stream, washed and dressed and with a spring in her step, as if the fresh frontier air agreed with her completely. "Major! Tom said that you were here and that you'd come for Sabrina, but I didn't hear a word! How opportune that you happened to come along."

"Yes—very opportune," Sloan said politely in return.

Sabrina didn't glance Sloan's way, but she realized that he had staged his "attack" well and that he had told her the truth. Apparently, no one knew what he had been doing, and no one, other than Tom, had known he was even among them. Still, Ice Raven had known. And she felt like a fool. She hadn't recognized her own husband.

Others came forward, greeting Sloan. He returned the greetings and when asked, explained patiently again and again that Crook's men had attacked a Cheyenne band and that, no, Crazy Horse and his people had not been among them.

"Then there will still be a major campaign," Libbie Custer murmured knowingly. She offered Sloan a grimace. "Maybe Autie will be needed."

"Maybe," he encouraged her.

When everyone was mounted, the party started back.

When they neared the fort, Sabrina could see that the preparations for the campaign were going forward full force. Sergeants drilled their men; sabers slashed at straw heads as cavalrymen raced down upon them, one by one.

Watching the action as they rode in, Sabrina felt a strange sense of foreboding. Chills assailed her, and she shivered fiercely.

She sensed that Sloan was watching her and she looked at him quickly.

"What is it?" he asked.

She shook her head. "Nothing—except that I was rather rudely dunked in cold water."

"You were already wet," he reminded her.

"Indeed?" she murmured.

"Are you ill?" he asked her.

She shook her head again. "No, I'm fine. Just cold."

She nudged Ginger and went loping on ahead of him.

Although Sloan had just returned from his scouting mission, he was due to report to General Terry in St. Paul.

Sabrina was disappointed that he was already preparing to leave again. When she was left alone in their quarters, she felt as if she were getting ill. She was dizzy; her stomach felt queasy.

She unpacked the small bag she'd taken on the excursion into the wilderness. Then she sat in one of the upholstered armchairs by the stove, her feet tucked beneath her.

It was possible.

Just possible.

She should tell him.

She nibbled pensively at her lower lip. She was still really angry about the trick he had played on her.

But still . . .

She just wasn't certain. And she didn't want to say anything until she was. There would be plenty of time to tell him when she was sure.

Plenty of time.

Seventeen

Autie Custer was returning from the East a deeply embittered and disappointed man.

He had first left Washington on the twentieth of April—two weeks after the column had originally been scheduled to leave Fort Abraham Lincoln—but he was ordered back to answer charges of perjury and character assassination. On May first, he started back to the Dakota Territory again, only to be stopped in Chicago and held on detention—per President Grant's orders.

President Grant remained infuriated with him. Custer had dared to implicate his brother, and Grant, it seemed, was now determined to destroy Custer.

Custer wasn't to lead the Seventh Cavalry in the great campaign of '76. He wasn't even to accompany his troops.

"He says that I am out to crucify him!" Custer complained to Sloan. They had happened to meet in St. Paul, before General Terry arrived at his office.

Sitting in a leather chair by Terry's desk, Sloan watched Custer with a certain amount of sympathy. Now it was time for battle, and Custer, whose greatest glory came from his brave if reckless cavalry charges, was being denied the opportunity to fight.

He turned unhappily toward Sloan.

"Crook definitely didn't destroy Crazy Horse?" he asked anxiously.

"Not yet," Sloan told him.

"You're certain—of course, you're certain. You know a Cheyenne village from a Sioux—hell, you are one—" He broke off, staring at Sloan. "My apologies, Major."

"No apologies needed. I am Sioux."

Custer smiled. He had a look of boyish good nature and charm about him at the moment. The Cheyenne women had said that he was beautiful—even when he was making war against them. At one point, years ago, he was supposed to have had a relationship with a Cheyenne woman, and she was said to have delivered a blond baby, who was accepted as Custer's own child. The little girl had lived only about a year, but Sloan knew that many of the Cheyenne women still considered Custer to be a cousin because of his "marriage" into the Cheyenne tribe.

He had, in fact, smoked a pipe with the Cheyenne—and promised that he would never make war on them again.

Things changed, Sloan thought dryly. Autie, however, would view this particular battle simply as war against "hostiles." Sioux hostiles. And if he were breaking the peace, he would feel justified in doing so. Soldiers, it seemed, could easily find justification for killing, just as governments could easily find justification for making the wars in which the soldiers were obliged to kill.

He nodded at Sloan. "A fact is a fact, my friend. You are Sioux. And a rational man, who can see the great picture of what is happening out here. Grant! What am I to do about Grant? I am the one being crucified. I spoke the truth; I spoke for my fellow officers, I spoke for the enemy we try to befriend—and end up betraying in the process."

Custer started pacing again, his hands locked behind his back, his head bowed. "My God, I tried! I waited and waited to see the president, and he refused, he absolutely refused to see me. He is out to destroy me!"

"He is the head of the armed forces," Sloan reminded him.

"What do I do? My God, help me, if you can, I beg you!"

Sloan exhaled a long breath. "Talk to your immediate superior, General Terry; see if he can't intercede on your behalf. You know that both Sheridan and Sherman will be trying to get you reinstated. Remember, too, that the press has always been incredibly supportive of you—newspapers love a dashing hero. Sherman and Sheridan will speak for you with Grant, and the press will probably hound him on your behalf as well. Get Terry to help you with a letter to the president—and then, write carefully. Don't demand that you be given back command of the campaign; ask for field command of the Seventh. And, Autie . . ."

"Yes?"

Sloan hesitated, wondering why he was trying to help a man hell-bent on war.

But the war was coming, one way or another. Sloan couldn't stop it. "Try a little humility with both Terry and Grant. It might go a long way."

"Humility doesn't win battles."

"That may be true. But, you'll remember, Fetterman boasted that he could clean out the Indians with a force of eighty men. He was slaughtered himself—with exactly eighty men."

Custer listened, lowered his head and nodded. "I'll talk to Terry and beg him to intercede." He was quiet for a minute; then he looked up. "Thank you," he said, and there was humility in his voice. "Thank you for your support."

"Don't count on my support in all your actions!" Sloan warned him.

Custer shrugged. He paced to the door. "Where is Terry?" he murmured impatiently. He glanced at Sloan. "I will be patient; I will be calm. I will be humble; I'll beg on bended knee—I swear it!"

As Custer spoke, General Terry entered the office at last. Both men saluted the general, and he returned the quick gesture. "General, I'll give my report quickly," Sloan said, "as there are other pressing matters here. I can assure you that the camp attacked by Reynolds and his men was not a Sioux camp, but a Cheyenne camp. Where the hostiles are, however, I do not know, for I didn't encounter the Crazy Horse camp as I rode. I did see numerous travois trails, and I assume that a number of Indians are still riding for their reservations. I think we're all aware that the time table given the Indians was scarcely feasible."

Terry arched a brow at him. "Perhaps the deadline was stringent; it came down from the Secretary of War. But you tell me honestly, Major, if you think that Sitting Bull would have complied with any time limit given him. He received notice of the government order, and his reply was that he'd come in at some time, but not then. Since then, the hostiles have been supplying themselves with agency goods—while encouraging Indians who accept government subsidy to run to him and join with his warriors."

"General, as Sitting Bull sees it, he has done nothing but send out invitations to his people to come to him for annual celebrations, for the Sun Dance."

"Sitting Bull is preparing for war, and we both know it, Sloan," Terry reminded him irritably.

"But the war is going to him, isn't it?" Sloan suggested softly.

Behind him, Custer suddenly exploded. "Yes! The war is going to the Indians, and my men are about to ride into battle, and by God, sir! Somehow, I must be with them."

Terry's look of misery was back on his face. He was a man in his mid-fifties, a good soldier—if not an exciting one. He cared about his men, and he was sorry for Custer's torment, but like most men around Custer, he was impatient with the fact that Custer didn't seem to be able to play politics at all.

"Major Reno has requested field command of the Seventh; as you know, I am to lead the campaign."

"Reno!" Custer exclaimed with horror.

Reno and Custer despised one another. Reno was one of the men who had not forgotten Custer's lack of concern regarding Major Elliott and his command after the Battle of the Washita. He was definitely not part of the "Custer Camp."

"My God, Reno cannot command my troops!" Custer breathed.

"Excuse me, General Terry, this is a private matter between the two of you, and I would like to return to Fort Abraham Lincoln as soon as possible. May I be dismissed?" Sloan inquired.

"Yes, Major, you're dismissed. Be advised, however, that you may be ordered to ride out again at any time."

Sloan inclined his head in agreement and left the office. As he did so, Terry took a seat. And Custer went to the general—*literally*—on his knees. Sloan heard Terry sighing and promising that he would do everything in his power to help the man.

Sloan, very anxious to return, wasted no time. He was grateful that the weather had improved, so that his train was unimpeded. It was amazing country, he thought. At times, a man could travel ninety miles in a day. When the weather was bad, the same ninety miles could take him a week.

All in all, reporting to General Terry had taken him three days.

At Fort Abraham Lincoln, he hurried to his own quarters. He was surprised to find that Sabrina was stretched out on the bed, sound asleep on the quilt that covered it, despite the fact that it was the middle of the day.

He decided not to waken her.

Quietly, he left her sleeping.

Troops were drilling on the field. Sloan watched them work, and when they were dismissed, he found himself coerced into a baseball game. Since the Civil War, the game had been becoming ever more popular among military men. This afternoon, different companies were making up the different teams. Sloan, not attached to any company, declined to choose a side, suggesting that he toss a coin. He wound up on Tom Custer's team, playing against the men who served under Captain Benteen, senior captain among the Seventh Cavalry.

By the third inning, both sides had attracted an audience of off-duty men and the fort ladies and children. His fourth turn at bat, Sloan was able to land a ball so far into the outfield that he could walk the bases home. The crowd was in an uproar. Boys ran to him, congratulating him as he came in. He teased the kids in return, sitting back on a bench until the game ended. Tom, a good player, was smugly pleased to claim victory. There was a fair amount of laughter and merriment on the field.

Sloan turned as he felt a tap on his shoulder. Marlene, twirling a parasol prettily despite the fact that the sun had just set, smiled at him. "That was quite a hit, Major. My congratulations on your prowess."

"Thanks."

"May I see you a moment? I've just come back from Gold Town, and I believe I might have something of importance to tell you."

He arched a brow.

"You're seeing me. And you can certainly speak."

She shook her head. "Please, come with me to my brother's house; it will only take a moment."

He hesitated. "Marlene—"

"Why, Sloan, are you afraid of me?" she drawled.

"Marlene, I do admit, I fear the damage you can wreak with your razor-edged tongue as much as I fear bullets, arrows, and knives."

"You jest, and you're being cruel!" she told him. "Please, come have a drink. My brother will protect you. It's important."

"All right, Marlene."

She slipped her arm through his, leading him from the

dusty field of play toward her brother's quarters, where she had kept house for him since her husband's death.

"Charlie?" she called cheerfully as they entered the small, pleasant parlor. "Charlie, Sloan is here!"

There was no reply.

"Well, he'll be right along. What can I get you, Major? Whiskey, brandy—rum?"

"Nothing."

"Come now, Sloan, don't be rude."

"Marlene, what is it you have to tell me that's so important?"

"Sloan, I will not say a single word until you tell me what you're drinking!" she insisted, pouting.

"Whiskey."

"Whiskey, it is," she said with a smile. She poured his drink, then seemed to float across the floor to him, her skirts a whisper of silk. Her sleek dark hair was elegantly swept into a coil at her nape, displaying the perfection of her neck and shoulders, and the classical beauty of her face. She was a completely poised woman, well aware of her position in society, and secure and confident in the extent of her beauty.

And she was still very beautiful. She could be exotic and tempting, and she was a talented lover. At one time, he had found her intriguing. Hell, at one time, he had wanted to marry her. She had taught him a lesson in life that he had never forgotten.

She was absolutely wanton in bed. He wondered curiously at that moment if he might feel the least bit tempted by her.

He paused, feeling her fingers brush his hand as she gave him his drink, watching the fire in her green eyes when they met his with a sultry promise.

Hmm . . .

Amazing. He wasn't tempted in the least. There was a viciousness, a ruthlessness, in her. Marlene hadn't a lick of concern for her fellow man.

"I wonder if you've ever known how very sorry I am!" she breathed to him, standing very close.

"Marlene, you needn't be sorry. I'm not."

She frowned. "How strange . . . life is so ironic. Father was a monster back then. He forced me to marry Clifford Howard."

"Clifford Howard gave you a very nice life."

"He was never you. He was never—" she broke off with a sigh. "Well, you know."

"He was never *Sioux*?" Sloan inquired politely.

"That's not at all what I was saying, and you do know exactly what I mean!"

"No, I don't know."

"Oh, Sloan! We were magnetic together. Once I had been forced into marriage . . . well, I ached for you every night."

"Marlene, how dramatic! But I doubt that's true. If it is, my sympathies lie with our dear departed congressman."

"Dear Sloan! Please, don't be so vindictive!"

"Marlene," he said impatiently, "I'm not vindictive in the least. The past is gone. Things worked out for the best. They have a habit of doing so."

"Oh! How can you say such a thing!" she cried.

He threw up a hand with impatience. "Marlene—"

"Oh, God! Sloan!" she cried suddenly, pitching herself against him with such force that he had to grab her in order to steady them both. As it was, his drink swirled dangerously in his glass. He drank it down and set the glass on the mantel, trying to disentangle himself from her hold upon his upper arms.

"Marlene—"

"Sloan, I had thought, when Clifford died, that I could have a life again, that we could have a life! Oh, Sloan, you'll never know how thrilled I was at the prospect of . . . of picking up where we had left off. I can't tell you my horror when I heard that after so many years, you had married! And yet, I know you, Sloan. I know that there were circumstances that surely forced your marriage—''

"Marlene," he interrupted firmly, managing at last to grasp her arms and free himself from her hold. "Have you taken a good look at my wife?" he inquired.

"She's a child—''

"She's a woman, Marlene, and a very beautiful one."

Marlene gasped, her eyes dazzling with tears. "Oh, my God, she is younger than I am—''

"Marlene, that doesn't have a damned thing to do with this. I have married."

"So you have married! But you can't deny that there were some strange . . . *circumstances*. I know that you loved me once, Sloan, I know—''

"Once, Marlene. Not anymore."

"Sloan, I don't care!" Marlene said quickly. "I don't care that you are married; God knows, I had wanted to be your wife, but I will gladly be your mistress. This doesn't need to matter in the least. Oh, God, Sloan, you have to forgive me the past—''

"Marlene, I do forgive you the past. Completely. But no matter what the circumstances of my marriage, I am in love with my wife. And I need to go home now."

She drew away from him in a sudden fury, striding back toward the liquor cabinet and pouring herself a large brandy. She swung around to look at him.

"Are you still sleeping with that Cheyenne woman? Does your precious wife know about the mistress you've kept for years?"

"I've had mistresses, Marlene. And, yes, I believe my wife is well aware of my past."

She was looking past him, out to the fort grounds. Darkness was falling now, but whatever she saw seemed to please her. She lifted her glass to him. "Cheers, Major! And by the way, I think I know exactly how you and your new lady love met. I did just come from Gold Town."

He crossed his arms over his chest. "Just what exactly is that supposed to mean, Marlene?"

"Well, in truth, I met my father there." She shrugged.

"He gave me a letter from your grandfather. But I do have many friends—especially among the servants at the Miner's Well. It seems that a young lady—or a young whore—slipped into your room there one night and didn't slip back out until morning."

"If you have a letter for me from my grandfather, I'd like to have it, please," Sloan said flatly.

Marlene slipped a letter from her pocket and walked over to Sloan, handing it to him. She smiled again. "You'll get tired of playing the bridegroom, Sloan. Tired of having your pretty little wife nagging you about your every movement. When she becomes too much, I'll be here. I'll be waiting. I know you, Sloan."

"Marlene, I do hope you find a more productive way to spend your time," he told her.

She was still smiling. "Excuse me. You know how to find your way out."

She disappeared up the stairs that led to the bedrooms.

Exasperated, Sloan turned, opening his letter as he left the house.

On her way up the stairs, Marlene Howard hastily ripped at the bodice of her gown. She raced to the window overlooking the grounds, pulled the drapes, and threw open the window. With her gown ripped open, all but completely exposing her breasts, she leaned out slightly, watching Sloan leave.

Sabrina Trelawny stood across the parade grounds, talking with Jean Jenkins. Marlene was quite certain that Sabrina could see her husband coming from the house.

And Marlene herself . . .

Half-naked at the window.

She'd exposed herself just enough, Marlene decided, and she ducked back inside, hastily closing the drapes as if just realizing that she might be seen.

She leaned pensively against the wall for several long moments. It wasn't that she had underestimated her adversary; Sabrina certainly had her assets. But somehow, the marriage had been forced, and a man forced into marriage was seldom happy once he began to feel the constraints. . . .

She walked to her dressing table and quickly studied her assets. She pinched her cheeks, bringing color to them. Her smile faded ever so slightly when she noticed the start of tiny lines around her eyes. Very tiny. Years ago, she'd had her chance with Sloan. She'd gotten distracted when she had seen something shining more brightly, that was all, and she simply hadn't realized that it was fool's gold.

Well, the years had changed her, she thought pragmatically. She wasn't young, and she wasn't innocent. It was a tough old world out there, and she was going to do her damned best to get what she wanted from it. Sabrina was beautiful; she had her youth and innocence.

But Marlene had experience, and staying power.

She could wait.

Sabrina struggled not to gasp out loud.

Not to shriek with fury.

And not to go running across the parade grounds to assault Sloan then and there.

Because he was back. She had known he was back. She'd heard he'd been playing baseball and had made a fabulous hit.

He had come back and played baseball . . .

And gone to see Marlene.

She forced herself to remain still, to focus on Jean. Jean so seldom initiated a conversation, and she had stopped Sabrina. Sabrina pretended to be listening avidly to every word Jean had to say about the proper way to get bread to rise.

There was no denying the fact that Sloan had come from Marlene's house.

And there was no denying that Marlene had been at her window, almost entirely bare-breasted, watching him leave. Sabrina wanted to sink into the ground around her. She carefully and casually looked around, trying to ascertain if others had seen Marlene. She asked herself if it mattered what others thought, or if the knifing deep inside her was all that counted. She was so stunned and hurt that she couldn't think.

Sloan hadn't even seen her yet. He was engrossed in a letter he was reading, walking slowly back toward the wooden dwelling that housed their own quarters. She watched him go.

"Well, I was so delighted that the general wrote and asked especially for *my* bread," Jean was saying, "even though it is so simple a recipe, anyone can follow it."

"Jean, I'm quite sure that no one can make it quite as well as you do."

"Do you really think so?" Jean asked anxiously. She smiled, and her face lit up. She could be so pretty, Sabrina thought, except that she was always ducking her head just slightly, and her smiles were too rare and so hesitant. At that particular moment, Sabrina didn't give a damn about bread. But it was very important to Jean, and so Sabrina tried hard to cool her temper and respond to her friend's question.

"Yes, I think so."

"Lloyd will be pleased. He's always so anxious to make a good impression. And I'm afraid I'm a poor wife for an ambitious military man."

"Don't be silly; you're sweet and charming, and people love you. Don't ever believe anything less of yourself, Jean. Ever," Sabrina said sternly.

Sloan had walked by, across the parade grounds and the field. He'd never looked up; he was so absorbed in whatever he was reading. What was he reading—what had happened?

Jean grabbed her by the arms suddenly, giving her a kiss on the cheek. "Oh, thank you. Thank you so much! You've been so wonderful to me. I'm—I'm going to go make bread!"

Sabrina managed a smile and a wave; then she started home. She opened the door to their quarters. The stew she had been making bubbled on the stove. For a moment, it smelled delicious, then the aroma made her feel just slightly ill, making her more certain than ever that she was expecting a child again. She had wanted it so badly, and now, she just felt numb. It seemed that now she was sure she was going to have a baby, just when she felt the least secure in her marriage and the least sure of her husband, with whom she was falling in love.

She stepped inside. Sloan stood leaning against the mantel. She saw no sign of the letter he had been reading. He sipped a whiskey. She turned around to close the door, keeping her back to him for a moment.

"Where have you been?" he asked her.

She turned around and looked at him.

"I went out for a walk. I'd heard that there had been a baseball game—but that it had ended. I was talking to Libbie for a while, then to Jean. Libbie says that Autie is due back. He's very upset about his problems with Grant—more so because he feels he can't even properly feed his family on his army pay."

"Graft and corruption exist, and they do take their toll," he murmured. "But then, Libbie feeds about seven members of the Custer family nightly."

"The ladies were all quite excited about your baseball game. They said that you made a great hit."

"I did."

"I'm sorry I missed it."

"I came here as soon as I got back, but you were sleeping."

"Ah."

"Supper smells wonderful, by the way. Will it be ready soon?"

"Yes."

She took bowls and silverware from the cupboard and set them, along with the stew, on the table. She felt him watching her as she folded napkins. "Where did you go after the game?"

"After?" he inquired.

"Yes, after your baseball game."

He folded his arms over his chest, his dark eyes simmering. "Why are you asking?"

She set a folded napkin on the table and looked up at him. "Oh. Just because I saw you coming out of Marlene's."

"You were following me?" he inquired politely. "Spying on me?"

It seemed that he lit a match to a fuse deep inside her. "Spying on you?" she hissed.

"Watching my movements."

"I happened to be across the parade grounds."

"Oh. Of course," he murmured coolly. She didn't know if he was being defensive or if he just didn't care.

Sabrina took the pot of stew from the stove and set it down on the table. He took a step toward the table, pulling out his chair to sit.

Sabrina sat as well, in stiff silence.

He sighed, his eyes narrowing at her as he said, "Marlene asked me over to give me a letter. I had a drink with her, that's all."

That was all. And surely, she told herself, it was the truth.

Except that when he'd left, Marlene had been half-naked.

"Oh." She was going to be calm, completely collected. She was not going to cause a scene.

But when she stood to ladle some stew into his bowl from the pot, she dropped his bowl—with the stew in it.

The bowl flipped.

Meat, potatoes, carrots, and gravy traveled across the table. He jumped up just in time to keep the hot food from spilling onto his lap.

He stared at her furiously, and she looked at him in horror. They both knew he'd have been in severe pain if the food had traveled any farther.

She felt a sweep of raw panic filling her at the look in his eyes, but she tried to stand her ground. "I'm sorry; I didn't do that on purpose.'' Despite herself, she backed away slightly.

He strode around the table. She tensed.

But he didn't come near her. He plucked his hat off one of the hooks by the door, setting it on his head and adjusting it over his brow.

''Right,'' he said.

''Sloan, I—''

He walked out the door.

And slammed it behind himself.

Shaking, Sabrina sank into her chair.

How had things gone so badly? She was afraid that she was going to burst into tears of frustration. To prevent herself from doing so, she jumped up, cleaning up the mess she had made of the stew she had so carefully prepared.

The activity was good. It kept her busy for nearly an hour.

But then . . .

The room was completely clean. And she was left with nothing at all to do but pace.

Hours went by. Midnight came and went. She played with the idea of running home to Skylar, but she knew that no one would give her an escort when Sloan was in residence—and besides, she didn't want to be away from him; she wanted to be with him.

She was going to stay.

She disrobed, carefully putting away her clothing, and slipping into a white cotton nightgown. She went to bed and lay there . . .

As more hours passed by.

Finally, she heard him come in. He moved about in the office area for awhile, then came into the bedroom.

She lay on her side of the bed while he shed his clothing. She felt him lie beside her. He was still for so long that she thought he had fallen asleep.

But he wasn't asleep. He reached for her, drawing her back against him. His hand slipped beneath her gown, drawing it up. He was pulling her hips flush against his groin, stroking her buttocks and thighs.

"I keep thinking that you'll come to me," he said softly. "But you don't."

"I didn't spill the stew on purpose," she told him, "but . . ." Her voice trailed away as she felt the seduction of his touch. "Damn you, Sloan!" she cried out softly, dismayed that she could want him so quickly and so desperately that all thought and protest fled her mind.

"Sloan—"

"Sabrina, you're my wife. We're married, and we will have a family."

"Sloan—"

"Damn you, Sabrina, I wasn't with her."

"I saw her, standing in the window."

He pulled her closer. She didn't mean to stiffen, but she did. She felt his fingers brushing aside her hair, felt his lips at the nape of her neck. "I want you, and I want a family."

He wanted a child. She was certain they didn't need to make any further effort to begin a family.

But she kept silent, because she felt the sweet fire of his seduction racing through her, and she was glad that he was there, with her.

He made love passionately, with the fierce hunger that seemed to fill him each time he had been away. She couldn't fight the wild, hot, sweet sensations he evoked, nor deny the pleasure that filled her whenever he touched her.

Yet later, she was aware that he lay awake, staring into the darkness. And she felt as if a great distance lay between them.

Then he rose with a sudden supple movement and dressed in the darkness.

Sabrina realized that he was leaving. She wanted to call him back.

She couldn't allow herself to do so.

He paused briefly in the archway, looking back. "Madam, I don't lie," he informed her.

"I didn't accuse you of lying, Sloan."

"Yes, you did."

"I never said—"

"Not with words, Sabrina. Not with words."

Then he left. The door slamming behind him seemed like a shotgun blast in the darkness.

Eighteen

$\mathscr{G}$eneral Terry helped Custer compose a letter to President Grant. Even though Grant still did not forgive Custer, the newspapers and the people clamored for him because they viewed him as a hero.

Grant finally relented to an extent. Terry was still to head the campaign, but Custer was to have field command of his own troops. He was elated.

Terry and Custer arrived at Fort Abraham Lincoln, and preparations were hurriedly made for the Seventh Cavalry to ride forth from there.

A dance was planned out on the parade grounds. Soldiers cheerfully worked extra hours laying down the flooring for the event.

The days that had passed had done little to ease Sabrina's mind. Sloan all but ignored her, spending a great deal of time with his fellow officers and coming to bed very late.

In turn, Sabrina withdrew. The tension between them became palpable. If he touched her by accident—his hand perhaps brushing her as she reached for a cup—she flinched and quickly moved out of his way.

It seemed that they had a silent agreement, however, not to air their feud in public. They were both polite and courteous to each other in front of others. On the afternoon of the dance, Sloan escorted her out. He promptly found himself engaged in conversation with Terry and his commanders, and Sabrina went on to talk with Louella.

Sabrina was pleased to see that the young captain who had been paying attention to Louella at the earlier social was paying court once again. His name was Adam Adair, Sabrina discovered that afternoon. He was forty years old and had served the Confederacy during the Civil War, and it had been a long hard climb for him to gain his rank in the Union army. He bore no bitterness to the North—the war had been a matter of geography to him, and his soldiers seemed to bear no grudges, either. Sabrina danced with him and frowned when she realized that he was smiling strangely.

"What is it?" she asked him.

"Mrs. Trelawny, you have been asking the questions a father asks!" he told her.

"Well, Louella is a very special young woman, and I wouldn't want you . . ."

"Trifling with her affections?" he inquired.

"Well, I suppose," Sabrina admitted.

"I do intend to marry her," he said solemnly. "In fact, I've asked David Anderson if he'll be kind enough to see that we are married next Saturday, before we soldiers take to the field."

"How wonderful!" Sabrina declared. "Congratulations, Captain! I am delighted."

She kissed him on the cheek and noted that Sloan was watching her, frowning.

But Marlene Howard was in the group where he stood now, and if Sloan was disturbed by her kissing the round little captain, then good.

She ignored her husband, whirling around the dance floor with Captain Adair. "A wedding. How very, very wonderful."

Adam Adair laughed softly. "Thank you, thank you so much. But please, Mrs. Trelawny, have a care! Your husband is a fierce fellow, and I would like to arrive in a timely manner at my own wedding."

"Sloan?" she murmured.

"Cougar-in-the-Night," Captain Adair said, reminding her of Sloan's Indian name.

She smiled sweetly. "He is nothing but a kitten, trust me, sir."

"A kitten?"

To her dismay, Sloan had crossed the floor when she wasn't looking to cut in on Captain Adair.

"Sir!" Adair said quickly.

"Captain, may I?"

"Indeed!"

Adair surrendered her quickly to Sloan and cut in on the corporal who was dancing with Louella. There were far more men than women, and some of the young soldiers made a game of it, wearing scarves on their sleeves and jokingly dancing with one another.

"If you consider me as tame as a kitten, my love, then we've serious problems," he told her.

"He was afraid of you," she told him as she met his eyes. "I was only trying to assure him."

"Assure him of what? Why the kiss for a near stranger?"

"He is going to marry Louella."

Sloan's brow arched high. She was glad to see the smile that crossed his face. "Well, good for Captain Adair. And good for poor, dear Louella!"

"Just because she isn't beautiful—"

"Beauty, my love, perishes through the years. Louella has strength and energy and will probably love the poor man silly, and make him very happy, indeed."

Sabrina was startled to feel a tap on her shoulder. Looking around, she saw that Sarah Anderson was cutting in on her to dance with Sloan.

"May I? If I'm not being too impertinent?" she inquired.

"Not at all!" Sabrina assured her.

Sarah slipped into Sloan's arms. "Sabrina, Jean hasn't come out yet. Captain Jenkins is here, but Jean isn't. He said that she had a headache. It can't be that bad. She is so very fond of you—perhaps you'd be good enough to try to talk her into coming out and joining us."

"I'd be delighted," Sabrina assured Sarah.

The sound of music filled the parade grounds. Walking toward the Jenkins' home, Sabrina looked back briefly. Everyone was on his or her best behavior. Reno—who hated Custer and had tried to take his command—was standing in the same group with him, as was Captain Benteen, who, if rumor was right, didn't particularly care for Reno, but hated Custer as well. It was a pleasant picture, seeing so many men in dress uniform. There were fewer women, but the wives and female relatives who were present were all dressed up as well, dancing and laughing and talking gaily. She was surprised to feel a little shiver of apprehension as she watched them all. She shook off the feeling and hurried on to find Jean, and beg her to come out and join them.

Sabrina reached the Jenkins' home. "Jean!" she called, tapping on the woman's door. There was no answer, and she frowned, hoping Jean wasn't seriously ill. "Jean, it's Sabrina. I've come to talk you into coming out to the dance. The weather is lovely, absolutely lovely—and you know how rare that's been. Even General Terry is out with us."

The door opened, just a crack. "Sabrina?"

"Yes, it's me, Jean."

"Thank you. It's nice of you to come for me, nice of you to care, but . . . I'm really not feeling well," Jean told her.

"Oh, come on out, please. You can't be feeling that poorly. We'll make you feel better," Sabrina promised. "Jean!" she implored, pushing the door open farther and stepping inside the small parlor. "Jean, you're not going to feel well if you don't get some sunshine—"

She broke off, staring at Jean. The young woman had a black eye. A real shiner.

"I'm so clumsy!" Jean said hastily. "I fell. But I feel

ridiculous. I don't want anyone to see me. Please understand.''

Sabrina nodded, looking at Jean—and feeling her temper soar.

She suspected that Jean hadn't fallen at all—Lloyd Jenkins had hit his wife. The bastard had gone too far. Sabrina wished that he were standing right there, right now. She'd give him the tongue-lashing of his life!

"I fell, Sabrina, really.'' But Jean's lashes lowered, and she wouldn't look at Sabrina.

"He hit you,'' Sabrina said.

Jean shook her head; then she suddenly looked at Sabrina. "What difference would it make if he did? He's my husband; I have no recourse. I displeased him—''

"An angel would displease him!'' Sabrina exclaimed.

But Jean's big blue eyes filled with tears. "Don't say anything—you mustn't say anything to the others, please. Oh, Sabrina, please. He is my husband. I have to try not to be so incompetent and annoying—''

"Dear God, Jean!''

"I told you, Sabrina!'' Jean said angrily. "I fell.''

She was going to burst into tears. Sabrina felt that she was making it all the worse for Jean, but she was loath to just leave her. "I'll sit with you—''

"No!'' Jean cried in panic. "Please, go back to the dance. Please, please!''

"All right,'' Sabrina said. "I'll leave, Jean, but you have to take care of that eye—''

"Lloyd gave me a very expensive piece of beef, just for my eye,'' Jean assured her.

Sabrina bit her tongue to keep from telling Jean exactly what she thought of Lloyd's expenditure on meat for his wife's eyes.

"Go back—please, Sabrina? Enjoy the dance. I'm fine, honestly. I just—I just don't want to be seen.''

Sabrina nodded, trying to smile. "I'll come see you tomorrow, all right?''

Jean nodded. Sabrina stepped back outside and started

walking back toward the dance, feeling miserable.

She walked across the grounds toward the dance floor and accepted an invitation from General Terry.

When the dance ended, she walked to the buffet table, anxious to pour herself some punch. She was startled when Sloan came to her side.

"All right, what's the matter? What did I do now?" he demanded.

She shook her head, seeing that Lloyd Jenkins was now dancing with Marlene Howard.

"You're not the guilty one this time," she informed him.

"Will wonders never cease!" he mused.

When she didn't pick up on his taunt, he frowned. "Sabrina, dammit, what's the matter?"

"I think—I'm sure—that Lloyd hit her. He gave Jean a black eye."

Sloan watched her face for a moment, then sighed. "Did she say that he hit her?"

"She more or less admitted it." Sabrina spun around to him. "Oh, Sloan, it's so terrible. So mean. How can he do that to her? Isn't there anything that anyone can do?"

"Sabrina, if I accused him of beating his wife, he'd deny the charge. We'd wind up in a fight, and I'd be accused of provoking it because Jenkins likes to call me a traitor because of my Sioux blood."

"It will be wonderful for her when he rides out of this fort!" Sabrina said passionately.

She felt him watching her. "And tell me, will it be wonderful for you when I ride away, too?"

"I've told you," she said evenly, "that I don't want any harm coming to you."

The music had ended; Lloyd had thanked Marlene for the dance. And for some reason, his eyes fell on Sabrina.

She wasn't sure just how she conveyed her anger and disgust so thoroughly through her eyes, but she must have done so. He stared at her a very long time, then suddenly turned around.

He left the dance floor. Sabrina saw that he was walking toward his quarters.

"Sloan!"

"What?"

"He knows—he knows that I know. He's going to think that Jean told me. He's going to—to hurt her again."

"Sabrina, how could he possibly know?"

"He does!" she insisted.

As she watched, Lloyd reached his own doorway across the parade grounds.

She didn't know what she was going to do; she only knew that Jean Jenkins was defenseless and needed help. She swung on Sloan. "Please, we've got to do something!"

She didn't give Sloan a chance to respond. She started running from the dance floor.

She heard him swearing, then running after her.

Sloan was extremely fast, and he passed her halfway to the Jenkins' door. But even from that point, she could hear Jean's sudden cry of terror.

Sloan slammed a shoulder against the door and swung it open. Sabrina came running up behind him, just in time to see that he had wrenched Lloyd Jenkins off his wife. Jean crouched in a corner, shaking and sobbing while the two men went after one another, exchanging serious punches.

They were really no match for one another. Sloan was lethal, even with his fists. Lloyd Jenkins was screaming for mercy and calling Sloan a bloody savage when Terry, Reno, and Custer burst in on the scene. It was Autie Custer who dared to drag Sloan off Jenkins, and Reno who kept Jenkins from trying to swing back in revenge once he had been rescued from Sloan's wrath.

"What in God's name is going on here?" Terry demanded furiously.

He looked from Sloan to Jenkins, and back again. He stared at the sobbing Jean, and then, very expectantly, at Sabrina.

She opened her mouth to try to explain. Jean suddenly sobbed out her name. "Sabrina!"

She paused.

"All right, then. Reno, get help and escort Major Trelawny to the stockade."

"Wait!" Sabrina began.

But she felt Sloan's dark eyes on her. "I fight my own battles!" he told her.

She fell silent, watching as he was escorted out of the Jenkins' house under guard. "Call a guard for Jenkins," Terry said then.

"Sir! Trelawny burst into my house—"

"Mrs. Trelawny, perhaps you can see to Mrs. Jenkins," Terry said. "Captain Jenkins, sir, you are under arrest as well!"

Jenkins opened his mouth and closed it. Under escort, he, too, left the house.

Sabrina wanted to run after the men. She felt responsible for Sloan's arrest because it was she who had gotten him involved in the Jenkins' dispute. Yet, what choice had she had? Jenkins had been hurting his wife.

Jean was quietly sobbing. Sabrina came to her, drew her to her feet, and hugged her.

"Jean, Jean, it will be all right."

"It will never be all right. But thank you. You—you didn't say anything."

Sabrina smoothed back Jean's hair. She didn't tell Jean she was certain that, despite the fact that Sloan had been taken away under arrest first, she was pretty sure that General Terry had figured out what had been going on.

"Let me get you some sherry," Sabrina told Jean.

She stayed with the other woman until Sarah Anderson came to take her place. She was glad to see Sarah, who was so competent and full of common sense.

"You'd best get home yourself," Sarah told her.

Sabrina nodded.

"Don't worry about Sloan; he'll be all right."

"I made him intervene," Sabrina admitted.

Sarah smiled grimly. "Sloan will be all right. If Jean had really been hurt and he hadn't intervened, he'd have never been able to live with himself. He's a good man," she added lightly.

Sabrina nodded and left Sarah with Jean. As she walked the few steps home, she thought that Sarah was right. Sloan would always stand up for the rights of the downtrodden. When she had first found herself in difficult circumstances, he had determined to marry her. Somehow he maintained his dignity and honesty in the midst of his own emotional turmoil. He was strong and exceptionally noble.

Maybe she had known from the beginning just how deeply she could come to care for him. It was frightening to love this way. She wasn't sure that she could tell him the truth of it yet, but she knew that today, she was in his debt.

Back in the quarters she shared with him, she curled up in one of the upholstered chairs. She was going to wait there until he came home, no matter how long General held Terry held him a prisoner.

Sloan was humiliated at being imprisoned in the stockade.

In all his long years of military service, he had never once been locked up before. There had probably been a few occasions in his wild youth during the Civil War when he might have been locked up for drinking and carousing with his fellow officers, but he'd never had the bad luck to get caught. He looked at his knuckles where he'd split the flesh, hitting Jenkins. The blood had dried.

His fingers hurt.

Surely, though, Jenkins was in worse shape.

Ah, Sabrina. Well, he hoped she was happy. He'd spent years controlling his temper, forcing himself not to get into fights with Lloyd Jenkins, and now . . .

Well, he could readily admit that he didn't regret his actions. Lloyd had one hell of a black eye himself now, and with a prayer, things might change for the better for Jean. She might even come up with the good sense to divorce Lloyd Jenkins.

"Major!"

At Sergeant Dawson's call, he rose from the army cot he sat upon and approached the bars. He heard a key scraping in the lock, and Dawson opened his barred prison door.

"Major, sir, the general wants to see you."

"Thank you, Sergeant," Sloan said, dusting his plumed hat on his thigh and sweeping it back onto his head. He followed Dawson, wondering just what was going to happen now. He prayed strenuously that his wife wasn't going to be involved.

It had grown late, he realized, as they walked across the yard to Terry's headquarters. But Terry was seated at a desk, and Jenkins was already seated in one of the two chairs in front of it.

Sloan saluted; Terry did likewise. "Take a seat, Major," the general told him.

He did as directed, aware that Jenkins was avoiding looking at him.

"We need to fight the hostiles—not one another," Terry said.

Sloan didn't reply.

"The major can be damned hostile," Jenkins muttered.

Sloan shrugged. "I've seen more white men beat their wives than I've seen Indians beat theirs," he said casually.

He thought that Jenkins was going to spring out of his chair and come at him again, but he didn't. Lloyd Jenkins lowered his head slightly, and Sloan saw that he was shaking. He clenched his hands before him on his lap.

"He—Major Trelawny—has been wanting to come at me for a very long time, sir!" Jenkins said. He didn't look at Sloan. "He is an Indian—takes the part of the savages all the time. That's what this was all about. One day, sir, he is going to forget that he's in the U.S. Cavalry, and he's going to join the heathens, running after us all, shooting off arrows and hacking us down with tomahawks!''

Sloan gritted his teeth, remaining perfectly still.

"Was this some kind of a vengeance fight, Major?" Terry asked.

Sloan shook his head. "Sir, Jenkins has been calling me a traitor since we met. If I were going to pick a fight over his calling me a heathen, the battle would have been waged long ago.''

"She's my wife!'' Jenkins exploded.

Terry stared at Jenkins. "Ah.''

"You don't understand, sir—''

"I think I do.''

"Sir, she is my wife—''

"That doesn't give you the right to hurt her, son.''

" 'Wives, obey your husbands'!'' Jenkins quoted. "That's right from the Scriptures, sir.''

"Well, now, I haven't read and reread my Scriptures for quite some time,'' Terry told him, "but I surely don't remember any place where a man is instructed to let his temper fly with his spouse.'' He offered Sloan a severe frown as well. "You should both be in the stockade for a month,'' Terry muttered. "But we haven't time for this nonsense. I'm ordering the two of you to get along.''

"We'll get along fine—'' Sloan began.

"He needs to stay out of my business,'' Jenkins interrupted.

Sloan stared at Terry without saying anything.

Terry looked from him to Jenkins. "Captain Jenkins, if I see your pretty young wife with an injury again, I'll tear you apart myself, do you understand? And not just that— I'll see that you're written up and perhaps drummed right out of this man's army for behavior unbecoming to an officer. Do I make myself clear?''

"Yessir!''

"Now, as to you . . ." Terry stared at Sloan. "Go get some sleep. You're out of here at dawn."

"Pardon, sir?"

"I've briefs for you to deliver to Gibbon in the field. You're to move on out of here quickly, and we'll meet up with you again at the mouth of the Yellowstone. It's important that you reach Gibbon with this information as soon as possible. Also, if you encounter the hostiles along your way, you will be expected to report their position to Gibbon. Is that clear, Major?"

"Yessir."

"You're dismissed, gentlemen. Good evening."

Sloan rose. Ignoring Jenkins, he strode to the door.

He'd leave again, come the dawn. He'd never imagined that he'd be ordered out so many days before the column was due to ride.

He'd wasted so much time.

And now . . .

He had tonight.

And God knew, he wondered enough himself when the Indians would shoot him for being a soldier or when the soldiers would shoot him for being an Indian. Some deep strain of destiny seemed knotted up inside of him. This might be his last night to attempt to conceive a child.

To achieve just a bit of immortality . . .

He assured himself that he was a capable soldier and man. He didn't intend to die.

But still . . .

His feelings didn't really have anything to do with immortality, and everything to do with Sabrina. He was in love with her. He'd told himself for so long that she was an obsession, but it was her pure fire that had attracted him in the beginning, and it was that fire he had fallen in love with as well.

If only . . .

He was leaving again, and that was all that mattered tonight.

He walked to his quarters quickly. When he threw open

the door, he saw that Sabrina sat upon one of the chairs by the Dutch oven. When she saw him, she leapt to her feet and started to rush to him, pausing several feet in front of him.

"You're free!" she breathed.

"No thanks to you," he murmured.

She stared back at him, not contradicting his words. She'd taken her hair down and had been brushing it. In the firelight, it seemed a million shades of sable and deepest red.

He walked into the office, tossing his hat on his secretary, sinking into his own chair. He lifted a foot and an eyebrow. "Want to get my boots?"

She gnawed briefly on her lower lip, then apparently decided that she owed him. She pulled off one boot, then the other, and stood two feet away from him again.

"Sloan, what happened?"

"Well, I just spent a couple of hours in the stockade."

"I know. But other than that—did Terry put you on report? Did he accuse you of attacking Jenkins for the wrong reasons? Will you have to go to any kind of a trial?"

He shrugged, watching her. "Terry is too involved with the coming expedition to create more friction than there already is. I'm not on report. Jenkins accused me of coming after him because he's commented previously on the fact that I'm Sioux. There won't be any trial; the matter is settled."

He stood again, striding toward her. "Excuse me," he said then, passing by her and going to the cupboard for a glass and a bottle of brandy. He poured himself some of the liquor and tossed it down. She stood behind him uncertainly for a moment.

"I'm sorry, of course. I didn't mean to cause this kind of trouble. I—"

"You don't need to be sorry. Jenkins had to be stopped."

She was quiet a moment. "Well, I'm not sorry that you

hit Lloyd, but I really am sorry it caused you trouble.''
She hesitated again. "I'm glad you're back," she said.
Then she added softly, "And I'm grateful for what you
did. Thank you."

She turned around, leaving him there, leaning against
the cupboard. He hesitated, drinking down another glass
of brandy more slowly.

Then he followed her into the bedroom.

She was already in bed, covered to her throat with the
sheets and blankets. He disrobed and lay down beside her,
determined that he didn't give a damn about her mood.
She could curl away; she could stiffen like an oak—it
didn't matter.

It was going to be too long before he saw her again.

To his amazement, before he had even lain down, she
had rolled toward him. And to his further amazement . . .

She was naked.

He lay back, startled, then exhaling on a long breath.
She felt that she owed him. Damn her. For a moment he
was tempted to fling her away.

For a moment . . .

Only a moment . . .

Her hair fell over his flesh in soft waves, teasing his
senses. She placed dozens of light little kisses against his
chest, the tip of her tongue just touching him. She moved
against him, moved down the length of him. Her kisses
fell against his shoulders and chest, and then his abdomen.
Her hair continued to brush against him with each of her
movements. Her fingers held and stroked him as the sensual softness of her body pressed against his.

She went lower.

Lower.

Then her hand was on him, holding, caressing . . .
stroking. Hesitant at first; curious, even, perhaps . . .

Her lips teased his navel. She delved with her tongue.

His fingers wound into the length of her hair. His body
throbbed with desire and in anticipation of what was to
come.

She dipped lower still. Her teasing kisses fell against the pulse that throbbed so wickedly within his sex. Pure, delicious, unbelievable torture. She opened her mouth more fully, and closed it around him. He nearly shot through the roof.

There was only so much he could bear of pleasure that was so exquisitely intense. As the sensation built to a fever pitch, he cried out at last, drawing her up against him and taking her lips, then rolling with a swift, sure movement and pressing her down, down. . . . He kissed her lips and teased and suckled her breasts. He still felt her hands against him, her fingertips lightly drawing patterns on his shoulders, his back, and then suddenly pressing harder into his flesh.

He inched down her body, as she had done with his. His kisses followed a straight line from the valley of her breasts, to her navel, to the triangle of auburn hair at the junction of her thighs. He tormented her wickedly with his tongue, all the while feeling as if the throbbing inside of him was something all but alive, sweetly torturing him beyond reason, and yet . . .

He wanted her to know that same feeling. Desire beyond reason. Hunger that must be sated. Remembered, cherished. He savored her sweetness, felt her tossing, turning, heard her crying out his name.

At last, he felt an urgency so great, it was finish . . .

Or die.

He rose above her, pressed the silk of her thighs far apart, and sank within her, taking her fully, his eyes on hers in the shadows of the night.

Her eyes closed. Her arms wrapped around him. Held him tightly. He slid his hands beneath her buttocks, pressing ever more deeply into her. He tried to move slowly at first; then he jackknifed into a wild, erotic rhythm, each thrust a sweet agony and anguish until he convulsed in a violent climax, sweeping into her again and again and again, until the last of his force was spent, and she shuddered beneath him in a series of tremors that matched his own. . . .

She lay beneath him, imprisoned by his weight. She moved against him, as if burdened by it, and he quickly shifted. The night air was cool now that his body no longer burned with such fire. She shivered, curling slightly away from him.

She had come to him. It was what he had wanted.

But he felt strangely hollow.

He stared at the curve of her back and the spill of her dark hair over the covers. He leaned up on an elbow, watching her, wanting so much more and not knowing how to reach for it.

"Debt all paid?" he queried.

"Debt?" she repeated and spun around, staring at him in the dim light of the fire.

"Debt, of course. You've never initiated the least bit of intimacy before, but tonight . . . well, you felt guilty about my being in the stockade. So you paid your debt. And now you think that's it. I wonder who really owed who?" he demanded, his voice soft, yet husky with an undertone of anger. "Because it seems that I've been paying ever since I married you."

She stared at him, her eyes widening, then narrowing. "If you've paid a price, it's your own fault. I didn't want—"

"You didn't want to be married. But you did go through with it; you stated your vows, made your promises. Well, I warned you what I expected from a wife, and still, I am paying for something, and I'll be damned if I know just what! Am I paying for my heritage, or my past, or is it just me?"

"I haven't made you pay for anything!" she cried, rising on the bed as if she were about to escape it—and him. "I've been a good cavalry wife. I came with you to a frontier that frightened me, I've cooked, I've mended—"

"But I want more!" he informed her, and he caught her arm firmly, dragging her back down beside him.

"Damn you, Sloan!" she whispered. "You just don't understand anything!"

"If you're angry about Marlene—"

"I'm not; I simply don't like her."

"Oh, hell—"

"When you left her house, she came to her window." She hesitated. "Exposed."

His brows shot up; then he scowled darkly. "Fine— she causes trouble, and you think the worst of me."

"No, not really—"

"Well, my love, you know what? Tonight, I just don't give a damn."

She tried to wrench free from his hold, so she could get out of their bed. He cast a leg over her hip, bearing her down with his weight.

"Sloan, you're in a ruthless mood—"

"You bet. And I thought you were so grateful," he taunted.

"I am grateful for what you did, but I've paid my debt."

"You've just begun," he assured her.

"Have I?" she demanded in return, her eyes smoldering in a furious challenge.

He held very still, staring down at her, in a tempest of emotion.

He was cavalry. He was riding away.

He didn't want to argue or explain.

He just wanted his wife.

He caught her lips.

She was angry, wild. Yet . . .

The passion of her anger became the force with which they made love. It was shattering and sweet, exhausting. Yet he remained . . .

Hungry. For more. He was about to leave her. For the first time, he truly felt a sense of his own mortality. Life seemed far more important than duty or honor. He wanted . . .

He didn't know exactly what he wanted. More. More than she could give.

To . . .

To dare to tell her that he was in love with her. He didn't quite know if he could do that or not. He was supposed to have so much courage. But he lacked the courage he needed to bare the truth within his heart.

So he held her.

And held her.

Forced her to want him.

Until the night became the dawn. And she slept.

And he rose . . .

And then rode away.

He was cavalry.

And that was what cavalry did.

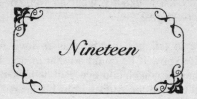

Nineteen

*H*e was gone.

Well, she asked herself, had she really expected him to be there?

Sabrina covered her face with her hands, wondering how it was possible to spend so passionate and intimate a night . . .

And be so very far apart!

How could she have explained to him that she'd been very glad of feeling indebted to him, because it allowed her to have what she wanted—him—and save face with herself. She couldn't simply fall into his arms when Marlene remained in their lives, and yet . . .

She wanted her husband. She was in love with him, and she wanted him.

With a soft groan, she rose. Morning sickness caught her unaware, and she staggered up, seeking the chamber pot. She lay back down then.

If she was going to be ill this often, she hoped that they would have a small family.

Guilt seized her, and she prayed silently and frantically. She'd happily be sick as a dog every day of her life if God just let her keep this baby. . . .

After a moment, she rose, wondering where Sloan had gone. It was late. She had slept late because she'd been up so much of the night.

She was suddenly very anxious to see him. She wished

that their anger hadn't intruded on the night. There had been something especially warm at the beginning.

Maybe because . . .

She had dared to take the first step.

But then . . .

She hesitated a few minutes, then leapt up. She washed and dressed quickly. He had left coffee for her. The aroma that she usually found delicious made her queasy again instead. She determined that wherever he was, she was going to find Sloan. He had a right to know about the baby.

She stepped out onto the porch, looking across the yard. More wagons were being loaded. The Seventh Cavalry was due to leave soon.

She saw General Terry across the parade grounds and hurried over to him.

"General!"

"Good morning, Mrs. Trelawny."

"Good morning, sir. I'm sorry to interrupt, but could you tell me where I might find my husband? I just need a few moments with him. It's important."

Terry arched a bushy gray brow to her. "Well, Mrs. Trelawny, I'm sorry. The major has been gone a good four hours by now."

Her heart skipped a beat. "Gone?"

"Oh, dear, didn't he get a chance to tell you? Perhaps you were sleeping when he came in last night. Actually, he probably didn't need to leave quite so quickly, but after the trouble between him and Jenkins, I thought . . . well, I thought it best if I separated the two of them. Mind you, I don't blame your husband. Jenkins has behaved atrociously, and I imagine that this incident will make a new man of him. He's an ambitious man, and he sees that most of his fellow officers are quite disgusted by his behavior. He'll be on the trail to battle quite soon now as well."

Sabrina stared at Terry, feeling ill all over again. Sloan was gone. She didn't know when he'd come back.

A sudden panic filled her.

She didn't know *if* he'd come back.

"Where did he go?"

"Out into the field, with messages."

"After the soldiers who are looking for Crazy Horse."

"Yes, but don't worry about your husband, Mrs. Trelawny. He knows his business."

She tried to nod.

"Mrs. Trelawny?" General Terry said worriedly.

She shook her head. "It's—I'm all right," she said to him. But she wasn't. She fled back to her quarters. Sloan's quarters. The home she had shared with him. She threw herself down on their bed.

And damned herself for being a fool.

She had to find him, she thought. She had to find him.

He'd be riding into the Black Hills and beyond. Territory beyond the military roads. Seldom seen by white men.

It didn't matter. She had to go to him.

She couldn't go to him. No man in his right mind would help her get where she needed to go.

She lay on her bed, numb with worry. Sloan would be furious with her if she attempted to follow him west into the Black Hills.

It didn't matter. She felt a terrible sense of foreboding, and she felt that she had to see him.

Perhaps Hawk would take her to him?

She quickly dashed that hope. Hawk would never let her ride into hostile territory now.

There was simply no way she could reach Sloan, she tried to tell herself firmly.

But the seed of longing was sown.

On May 17, the column of the prong of soldiers from Fort Abraham Lincoln finally set out, after having been held back for two days by bad weather. At 5:00 A.M., led by the Seventh Cavalry, the party assembled.

It was an awesome sight. Watching from her porch, Sabrina found herself completely awed by the sheer size of the Dakota Column. In addition to the soldiers, there were white civilian employees, servants, newspapermen, and Indian scouts. Since the land was all but barren and it would be difficult at best to forage for food, there was an endless line of wagons carrying supplies. The column stretched for two miles.

Custer was a dashing figure as he rode to the head of his troops. The Seventh Cavalry itself was magnificent in appearance; Custer had long since ordered that Company A ride black horses, while Companies B, D, H, I, and L rode bay horses, Companies C, G, and K rode sorrel animals, and Company E rode grays. Only Company M rode horses of mixed colors.

Libbie Custer and a number of the other women would ride with the column to camp the first night out. Sabrina had been invited to go, but she had refused. Sloan wasn't with the column, and there was no real reason for her to go. She was glad to see the march, however, for it was a sight she would remember all her life. A low fog sat on the ground, and it seemed that the massive column marched off into the clouds . . . and then disappeared.

When the soldiers were gone, she went back home and tried to compose a letter to Sloan. She ripped up several sheets of paper. She couldn't say what she wanted to say on paper.

The next day, Libbie Custer returned in a strange mood. She was usually so bright and confident.

"I watched him ride away," she told Sabrina, coming in for coffee. "I watched him ride away . . . and it seemed that ice congealed in my breast, right around my heart. Oh, Autie does love a call to glory, but . . ."

"The ride must have been fastastic."

"Oh, it was." She finished her coffee and stood. "I'm going to go write Autie a letter," she said cheerfully. "If you write letters to Sloan, I can send them along with my own. There's a steamer that goes up the Yellowstone and will deliver mail to the troops."

"Thanks. I haven't written anything yet." Sabrina hesitated. "I was wishing . . ."

"Wishing what?"

"Well, I was wondering if there were a way to meet up with the troops—with Sloan."

Libbie frowned. "Sabrina, it would be almost impossible to visit the men in hostile territory. And as for Sloan . . . well, you never quite know where he's going to be."

"Yes, but wherever he is, he eventually has to meet up with General Terry, right?"

Libbie nodded. "Yes, of course, but . . . Sabrina, I plan to meet Autie for the Fourth of July. Perhaps we could plan something together. Sabrina, no one will take you out to hostile Indian territory."

"There must be riders who take messages—"

"No one will take you. It's insanity," Libbie told her firmly.

Once Libbie had gone, Sabrina tried to write a letter again. She wrote about watching the expedition leave from the fort, about the way Custer's companies on their different-colored horses looked so splendid. She couldn't say what she wanted to say. The best she could manage was to end with, "I send my love and best wishes for your health and welfare, Sabrina."

She gave her letter to Libbie, who promised to see that it reached Autie, who would hold it for Sloan.

But as she left Libbie's that night, it all became much worse. She had started out when she remembered that she had left her umbrella just inside. When she opened the door, she heard Maggie talking to Libbie.

"Poor, dear Sabrina! I overheard one of the Crow scouts talking with Jimmy Blake today. Sloan is in greater danger than he can imagine. The scout says that he heard from one of the reservation Sioux at the Red Cloud Agency that the hostile warriors no longer trust Sloan. He is in grave danger."

"Whatever you do, don't let Sabrina know!" Libbie warned.

Sabrina quietly let herself out. Her heart was thundering. She closed Libbie's door tightly and leaned against it. Dear God. It was no longer a matter of finding him in order to somehow salvage her own soul.

Now she must find him to save his life.

Sloan moved quickly, finding Colonel Gibbon with little trouble.

He delivered his dispatches and was sent to scout a trail discovered by one of Gibbon's men. He was glad that he had followed the trail alone, for at its end he found a sad Cheyenne family: a very old grandfather, a grandmother— and eight small grandchildren. All three of the man's sons had been killed, along with their wives. The government had beaten them. It didn't matter. The old Cheyenne man was tired; his wife was starving. His grandchildren were young.

They would live in the new world.

Sloan escorted the Indians back to Gibbon and arranged for the family to be allowed safe passage back to their reservation. Gibbon understood what difficulties accrued when nonhostiles were attacked, and rather than simply thinking any dead Indian was a good Indian, he was glad when he could lessen the numbers that were joining with Crazy Horse and Sitting Bull.

Sloan started back with dispatches that night, alone. Lying under the stars with Thomas nearby, he was able to take a certain satisfaction in his work. Some must live, some must die—life was changing. But he was glad that he had been able to help the Cheyenne family. His life hadn't made much sense to him lately. After today, it did.

But he was weary of it as well. Like the Cheyenne, he was weary of the fight. War on the plains would eventually come to an end; how many more must die, he didn't know. War in the future was going to be very different. Learning, rather than fighting, was going to be the key to winning.

He wanted to go home—and stay home. He wanted to

find a way to get close to his wife, and he wanted to find a way to have a future.

He closed his eyes, trying to sleep.

He had barely done so when he sensed movement near him. There was a rustling . . . the slightest rustling in the woods. He opened his eyes without moving, looking around himself. He saw nothing, but he was still certain that someone was near.

He rolled suddenly, seeking the shelter of an outcropping of rocks just above the river's edge. He drew his revolver, reminding himself that he had but six shots. How many men were stalking him?

The movement around him was no longer furtive. He heard the cry of a bird that he knew damned well was no bird; then three young braves stepped out before him. None of them was painted. It was hot, and they were stripped down to breechclouts, leggings, and mocassins. He recognized Hawk's cousin, Blade, before the Sioux warrior spoke to him.

"Cougar-in-the-Night, we're glad to find you alone and not with the soldiers."

He could kill the three, Sloan thought. But then, they knew it. There were other warriors nearby; if he were to kill these men, he might well end up dying very slowly. And he didn't seek to kill. Any more, he thought, than these men wanted to kill him.

He rose from behind the rocks, sliding his gun back into his holster.

"Hello, Blade."

Blade nodded. "Sloan," he said quietly, "you must come with us. You cannot go back to the soldiers. You can tell them too much."

"Actually, I have nothing at all to tell them," Sloan said.

"We can tie you like a fallen deer," Blade said quietly, "or you can ride with us. You may not return to the soldiers; if you try to do so, you will be shot down. It will grieve me tremendously to do so, but I will kill you."

He was right that the first three Indians hadn't been alone. Four more braves emerged quietly from the bushes. One of them was his own cousin, Tall Man.

"Naturally," Sloan said, "I will come with you."

Libbie came to see Sabrina again, extremely excited about the letters she had received from Autie.

"Autie! He is so brilliant, and so naughty! He admits to being reckless at the beginning of the campaign. He and Tom just teased their poor little brother Boston to death, making him think that he was being attacked by Indians just outside the column . . . Autie did make it all something of a lark, but General Terry, it seems, reprimanded him, and he tells me that he realized how very good the general has been to him, and he did, of course, change his ways!"

"Did he tell you anything more about the campaign?" Sabrina asked her.

"Oh, yes! General Crook's men got into quite a fight along the Rosebud—and not terribly successfully, either. The Indians made a stand against him. Terry was not so pleased, either; the army's 'pronged' attack is slow in coming to any useful purpose. Autie says that movement is painfully slow, of course. My husband has chosen the right trails to take—no mean task considering the amount of weaponry and supplies in the expedition. But despite that, General Terry chose Major Reno to command a scouting mission down the Rosebud. Major Reno must have been north on the Rosebud right when General Crook was so desperately fighting, but it seems that Major Reno did not read the signs of Indian movement well. He disobeyed orders, too, and when he was supposed to link up with Autie . . . he didn't. Both Autie and General Terry were fit to be tied, but at least now—" She broke off, flushing happily. "General Terry knows now just what a good leader he has in Autie."

"I'm sure that's true," Sabrina said. "Was there any word from Sloan?" she asked anxiously.

Libbie frowned. "Autie didn't say. Curious. Sloan should have been with General Terry by now. But I'm sure he's fine!" she added quickly.

Libbie seemed to have gotten over her sense of impending disaster.

Sabrina felt it instead. She had to find a way to reach Sloan. She had to!

The Indians, aware of the soldiers' attempts to encircle them, spent long hours in debate.

They celebrated the Sun Dance.

Sloan was stripped of his army jacket and accoutrements; he was a prisoner, and he was told bluntly that he was a prisoner, but he was not treated badly. He was allowed to stay with his cousin, Tall Man, in his cousin's tipi, and was treated kindly by Tall Man's wife.

Earth Woman was among the people, and she came to see him. She didn't mind that he had a white wife, but she understood as well when he explained that he had taken her in the white way—which meant that he must be loyal to one woman. Many of the braves were practicing celibacy because it was the time of the Sun Dance, when men purified themselves and prayed to Wankatanka, the Great Mystery, and received guidance.

He was with Tall Man when Sitting Bull made his sacrifice; sitting in stoic silence while fifty tiny pieces of flesh were cut out of each of his arms.

There were more Indians amassed in one place than Sloan had seen in his entire life.

They camped along the Little Bighorn, in a valley that stretched long in a narrow, grassy pain. To the north, the river angled to the right. Cottonwood trees grew in abundance along the banks. To the east, the banks rose to a series of high, steep ridges, which rolled down again to a series of hills. Jagged ravines were scattered across the plains to the west.

Despite the size of the encampment, each tribe still functioned separately, with the chiefs being summoned to the councils by a rider. Sitting Bull was a Sioux; he did not take the position of the head chief, but he was the host here, and his prestige among the people had grown to heights it had never known before.

June progressed.

The days were explosively hot.

The "hostiles" were ready for war.

"Mrs. Trelawny!"

Sabrina was startled to find herself hailed by Marlene Howard. The woman walked at a leisurely pace across the parade grounds, a parasol keeping the sun from her face.

"I heard that you are harboring a fantasy about traveling out into Indian territory after your husband," Marlene said pleasantly.

"Perhaps," Sabrina told her warily. "Why? Is it a concern to you?"

"I might be able to help you," Marlene said, smoothing back a strand of her beautiful hair. She smiled. "Some old friends of my father's have just arrived. They're going to be traveling up the Yellowstone by steamboat, and they'll accompany you if you want to to meet up with the troops."

"Who are these friends?" Sabrina asked. Marlene was trouble; she might well be hoping to send Sabrina into danger. But Sabrina was growing desperate, and since she'd found no other help, she had little choice but to listen to Marlene.

"Sergeant Lally is a retired army man, solid as a rock and lovable as a stuffed doll. He's traveling with some . . . gentlemen traders. They've actually made quite a fortune trading with the Indians, though at times it's quite difficult to tell. Come with me and meet them." She smiled. "Don't you trust me?"

"No, I don't."

"Now, come, Mrs. Trelawny, not even I can control the wilderness or the Indians!"

Still suspicious of the woman, Sabrina followed Marlene to her home. When Marlene opened the front door, Sabrina heard the gruff laughter of several men. It seemed that they were in the midst of a tale about a not-so-virtuous Indian maiden, but Captain Jones, on seeing his sister and Sabrina, quickly sobered and stood. He didn't look pleased.

"Marlene, I told you that this is a foolish idea—" Jones began.

"Now, hush!" Marlene scolded. "It's a wonderfully romantic idea."

Her brother still appeared tremendously disapproving.

There were four other men in the room, all of them truly rugged-looking individuals, and all somewhere between the ages of forty and fifty, Sabrina surmised.

"Now, Sabrina, this is Sergeant Edmund Lally, late of the Second Cavalry."

"The best in the world!" Lally supplied, rising and doffing his hat.

The other men did likewise. They were dressed in an odd assortment of European clothing and Indian decorations, shirts of rawhide, fringed trousers, and beaded necklaces. Their faces were heavily bearded, and they looked like a group of wild mountain men—which they probably were. The trappers were John, Tom, and Ned, two brothers and a cousin, and they had been traveling the Black Hills long before any white men had actually explored the area. Sabrina figured the men were trustworthy because they were friends of Captain Jones.

"Aren't you afraid of the Sioux?" Sabrina asked them.

"We've become wealthy men because of the Sioux," Ned told her seriously.

Tom nudged him with an elbow, looking at Sabrina gravely. "Of course, to escort a woman safely . . . well, ma'am, we don't like to bring up such things, but . . ."

"I intend to pay you, of course. Please name your price."

"Now, dear, don't go throwing away Sloan's army pay!" Marlene said sweetly.

"I have my own money," Sabrina quietly told the men. "And I am more than willing to pay a fair price."

Sergeant Lally was on his feet, smiling. "And we'll give you a fair price, Mrs. Trelawny. Can you be ready to leave by tomorrow morning? And we like to leave at the very crack of dawn, you know."

"I can be ready," Sabrina assured him. She was anxious to leave at dawn. She didn't want too many people to find out that she was leaving. She was afraid that someone might try to stop her.

She shook hands with the men and said good night to them and Captain Jones, who still looked very unhappy.

Marlene walked her to the door and then outside, looking at the sky as the twilight came.

"Strange weather. It can be icy cold—with snow falling into June!—then hotter than all Hades. Interesting year, isn't it? The centennial year for America—while she expands and decimates the Indians."

Sabrina was somewhat surprised to find Marlene so reflective.

"Why are you helping me?" she asked her bluntly.

Marlene smiled. "Well, he does care for you, you know. Quite deeply."

Sabrina was silent.

"Ah . . . you fell for my little performance at the window, then!"

"Performance?" Sabrina asked.

Marlene's smiled deepened. "My dear child, your husband just couldn't be tempted. Not at this point, at any rate. It seemed far easier to work upon your jealousy than his lust, but then, apparently, I did cause some trouble, or you wouldn't be so anxious to find him. I should warn you, though, that I still believe I shall prevail."

"You won't prevail, and you didn't cause trouble," Sabrina told her. Without feeling a twinge of guilt that she was lying. "I'm anxious to find him because I believe he may be in danger."

"How noble—except that he's often in danger."

"I'm curious, Marlene. If you think you will still prevail, why are you helping me?" Sabrina persisted.

Marlene shrugged. "Well, you may not find Sloan. And you may be killed. And I'm quite certain that Sloan will return. He always does."

"You're planning my death?" Sabrina inquired.

"Oh, don't be silly!" Marlene protested. "I'm putting it all into the hands of God!" Marlene said complacently. "Enjoy your journey, Sabrina!" she said, and, turning, she retired into her house.

Sabrina shivered. She shouldn't go. Marlene was trying to help her just so that she might die.

But Sergeant Lally certainly seemed a sound enough fellow—as did his hairy cohorts. They knew their business and their terrain, and she would be safe with them.

So determined, she hurried home and carefully packed what few belongings she could easily carry.

If she hadn't been so worried, so filled with a sense of dread, and so very anxious to reach Sloan, Sabrina might have enjoyed the trip. The views from the steamboat down the Yellowstone River were exceptional. Summer had come; the sun could be brutal, but it was welcome after the recent bitter cold.

Sergeant Lally was a funny old fellow who liked to entertain her with stories about his boyhood in Ireland. He convinced her that he believed completely in leprechauns, and that the banshees did indeed wail each time they were coming to bring home the soul of an Irish man or woman.

Along the way, she learned from the soldiers they encountered that Major Trelawny was not with Colonel Gibbon's troops, nor had he reported back to General Terry.

With her escort determined to start out over land, moving deeper westward, Sabrina became deeply discouraged. The countryside was huge. Sloan was missing, and she was desperate, but searching for him was like looking for a needle in a haystack.

On June 20, they came upon the remains of an Indian camp. The body of a white soldier lay by the stone-cold ashes of the fire. Lally tried to stop Sabrina from racing toward the corpse, but she escaped him. She had to know.

The body was covered with flies, but she turned it over. The man had been scalped and mutilated—but he wasn't Sloan. She stood up, staggering away from the body, and was violently sick.

Three days later, they followed the trail of a lone horse when an arrow suddenly came flying across the ravine where they traveled.

"Hostiles—three of them, see them yonder! Shooting at us—at traders!" Ned declared.

The Indians had lined up on the plain, perhaps a hundred yards away.

John called out to them in the Sioux language.

One of the braves shouted back.

"What did he say?" Sabrina asked Sergeant Lally anxiously.

"He says . . . ," Lally began.

"What?" Sabrina demanded.

"He says that the traders are no longer friends of the Sioux. He says all white men are the enemy. He says that he will kill all white men on Sioux land."

"They're dead men!" Tom yelled out, suddenly furious. "Lally, take the lady to the ridge yonder. Protect her!"

"Wait!" Sabrina cried out. "Tell him that we're looking for Sloan! Perhaps they won't fight then, perhaps—wait!"

It was too late. The men were already riding out hard, letting out their own brand of battle cries, and shooting their guns.

The hostiles came thundering across the plain. Sabrina watched them come, whooping out their high-pitched war cries in return.

Arrows rose into the sky . . .

And plummeted to the earth, bringing bloodshed and death.

On June 22, 1876, George Armstrong Custer led the Seventh Cavalry out of the military encampment along the Yellowstone River. General Terry had given his orders. Custer had refused an offer of infantry, Gatling guns, and men from the Second Cavalry because the infantry and the Gatling guns would slow down his movements. With only his cavalry, he could move far more easily over the rugged terrain he would have to cover in his search for the Indians.

In the great plan to press the hostiles between armies, Colonel Gibbon would be moving parallel with Custer. His troops were already in motion from the mouth of the Bighorn. Terry believed that Custer could scout out the hostiles and press them between his army and Gibbon's; that failing, he could force the hostiles to where they could be trapped between Gibbon, Custer, and Crook. Custer and Gibbon would be fairly close to each other; when Custer discovered the hostiles, he was to immediately notify Gibbon.

In General Terry's written orders, he stated that he didn't wish to impose precise orders on his commanders, which might impede Custer's progress against the hostiles. However, he wanted his own wishes and views to be clearly understood and followed, unless extreme circumstances changed battle tactics on the field.

Before they rode from camp, Colonel Gibbon cautioned his fellow commander.

"Now, Custer, don't be greedy. Wait for us."

And Custer replied, "No, I will not."

Then he urged his horse, Old Vic, into motion with his customary flair, and galloped forward to lead his troops.

At the officers' call that night, many men were unnerved as Custer, who rarely sought or accepted advice on any matter, asked for suggestions from his officers. He was grave and serious.

Lieutenant Francis Gibson later reported feeling a strange depression that night.

Lieutenant George Wallace stated to friends that he believed Custer was going to be killed.

Lieutenant William Cooke asked Lieutenant Gibson to witness his last will and testament, saying that he had a feeling that his next fight would be his last.

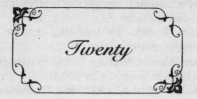

NO OTHER LOVE

The Valley of the Little Bighorn
June 1876

"*C*ougar-in-the-Night, come!" Tall Man commanded.

Sloan had been lying in his cousin's tipi, wondering about his chances for escape. He knew that his family had been ordered to shoot him if he tried to get away.

The massive Sioux and Cheyenne encampment had been moved twice since Sloan had been taken prisoner, and both times, he had helped with the great effort of moving such a tremendous amount of people and belongings. He was careful to do only the work a man, or a warrior, might do. He had a feeling that now it was very important not to lose face with his people. Some tasks, such as the folding of tipis and bedding, were considered women's work, but he was able to care for the animals and help the women who were widowed.

Tall Man told him that soldiers had been seen by a number of the scouts.

The man called Son of the Morning Star or Yellow Hair was among them. Tall Man told him that the Cheyenne considered Custer to be their relative, and that Custer had promised not to make war on them years before, when he had smoked with the chiefs and arranged a treaty.

"The government wants the Indians on the reservations," Sloan had explained to his cousin, "and nothing else matters now. Things have changed."

"We know Yellow Hair is there; we will watch. The soldiers must be suffering; we fought many of them on the Rosebud, and though they attacked, we were victorious," Tall Man told him. And he seemed content; there had never been such a great mass of Indians gathered together before—Cheyenne and Sioux, and among the Sioux, so many tribes: Miniconjou, Brulé, Two Kettles, Santee, Yankton, Sans Arc, Blackfeet, Oglala, Hunkpapa . . . so many people. Under normal circumstances, the tribes would have broken up after the Sun Dance, and in time, they would have to do so. It was too difficult to find enough game for so many in one place, and the grazing for the animals was too quickly destroyed. Such a sight as this would not be seen often.

There were simple things about the Indian way of life that seemed good to Sloan. He observed the way that the Sioux shared, still helping the Cheyenne—who had been devastated in Crook's attack—and caring for the wounded who had been injured in the very recent battle with Crook along the Rosebud. The elderly were respected for their wisdom; the children were loved and raised by extended families. Sloan was allowed to go on an elk hunt, for they had followed a vast herd of elk through the valley of the Little Bighorn. He enjoyed racing the wind bareback. When the hunt was over, he discovered that his own cousin was staring at him, his rifle in his hands—ready to shoot if Sloan sought this as an opportunity to flee.

From what he learned from Tall Man, Sloan deduced that General Crook remained south of them, and that General Terry had kept the columns divided, sending both Custer and Gibbon south along separate trails. Terry would assume that between Gibbon and Custer, he could at last pinch the Indians—and if they escaped, they would ride straight into Crook. But he wondered if anyone in the military could even begin to imagine the size of this encampment. Among all of the troops in the field, Sloan reckoned that there were about two thousand soldiers separated into three main divisions.

But he had never seen so many Indians before. There were more than two thousand Indians altogether, and there were perhaps a thousand warriors among them. If the fighting men in the field were split up when they encountered the hostiles, they could very well be seriously outnumbered.

He knew what the Indians did not yet understand. The soldiers would keep coming. No matter how many they killed, more soldiers would take their place.

It seemed strange to him now that he had known nothing but this way of life when he had been a boy. There were so many things he still loved and admired about the Sioux people and their way of life, but now . . . he needed to escape. There was just somewhere else he longed to be. He had a wife, and for the first time, he had a real home of his own.

"Cougar-in-the-Night! Come!" Tall Man urged, and Sloan realized that he had just been staring blankly at his cousin. He leapt to his feet, feeling a growing sense of urgency.

He followed his cousin out of the tipi and saw a horse awaiting him. To his amazement, Crazy Horse stood by the animal. He wondered if he was supposed to leap atop the horse and ride for his life while the braves sent arrows flying after him. It didn't seem the way of a man like Crazy Horse, but . . .

"Blade saw that some warriors are engaged in a battle with white men. Trappers, he thinks," Crazy Horse told Sloan.

Sloan stared at him, confused, waiting for him to continue.

"Blade knows your white wife. She is sister to his cousin's wife."

"Sabrina?" Sloan said. "Sabrina can't possibly be here."

Crazy Horse shook his head. "Cougar-in-the-Night,

Gray Heron is now attacking the party—and he will gladly take your wife as his own, I imagine, if he is not stopped. If you want your wife, Cougar-in-the-Night, I suggest that you stop him.''

Sloan didn't dare wait any longer. He wasn't being given permission to escape; only to get his wife back.

His wife.

It couldn't be.

What idiotic purpose could Sabrina have in coming out here with a party of fur trappers?

But he leapt atop the mount offered him and rode furiously in the direction shown him.

He could see the fighting going on. The Sioux . . .

The white men.

Sabrina.

Bullets flew. Arrows soared.

The white men were dead. All of them. Sloan rammed his heels hard against his Indian pony, racing to reach the point of battle.

Gray Heron lifted his bow high in his left hand and let out a high, undulating cry of victory, then threw his leg over his horse's haunches to jump to the soft ground of the plain.

He stood very still, all-powerful as he surveyed Sabrina. He raised his bow into the air again, shaking it—claiming victory, claiming Sabrina—letting out his terrible war cry.

Don't fight him, don't fight him, don't let him kill you! Sloan prayed silently. The earth churned up around him. He had to reach her. But he could see Gray Heron, swaggering now, as he approached her.

Sabrina stood still. Tall, proud, still. Don't be too proud, my love! he begged in silence.

''Damn you!'' he swore out loud.

For Gray Heron was playing games, taunting his prisoner. He approached Sabrina, pushing her. She staggered back. Gray Heron persisted. He caught hold of her, wrenched her up in his arms, and threw her down on the ground. But he didn't know the woman he was up against. She leapt up before he could straddle her.

Gray Heron pulled a knife.

Sloan cast back his head and cried out, a cry lost on the wind. Cruelly, he slammed his heels against the pony, needing greater speed. The wind ripped by him. He could feel the setting sun beating at his bare back, and yet he was numb. If he could not reach her . . .

Gray Heron was on top of her again. Sabrina was fighting like a wildcat, struggling, clawing, kicking, swearing . . .

She had hurt Gray Heron—somehow. He staggered back, then slapped her so hard that she went down. And Gray Heron was approaching her again, his knife held out, his face contorted with anger.

At last, Sloan reached the scene. Reining in his pony, he leapt to the ground, flying at Gray Heron. He wrenched the warrior far from his wife, and they struggled together on the ground.

He was vaguely aware that Sabrina was up, coughing, and running. She was trying to reach the pony he had nearly ridden to death in his effort to reach her. She could ride.

But if she tried to escape . . .

She might well die.

He slammed his fist into Gray Heron's jaw. Hard. Gray Heron grunted and went still.

Sloan staggered up. "Sabrina!" he cried, shouting her name.

She went dead still and swung around, staring at him incredulously. He realized he must make quite a sight, shirtless, his chest slicked with sweat and mud.

"Oh, my God!" she breathed. "Sloan!"

She hurled herself at him, throwing her arms around him, trembling. Her hold was tight, the feel of her trembling body in his arms was incredibly sweet. He couldn't believe that it was her. Oh, God, it was her—what was she doing here?

"Sloan—"

He held her away from him, knowing that they faced a difficult situation, and that he had to take grave care. He studied her face. Dusty, but beautiful. Her dark hair was free and wildly swirling about her face in the breeze. Her eyes were huge and beautiful. She was quite a prize . . .

And Gray Heron was definitely going to fight to have her.

"The situation is almost worth the greeting," he murmured dryly, then asked quickly, "are you hurt?"

"No, Sloan, but all these men—"

"Are but a fraction of those who will die," he murmured softly.

"Sloan—" she began, then broke off, looking around them.

They were surrounded by Sioux.

"Sloan!" Sabrina gasped in warning. Gray Heron was coming up behind him.

"I'll—I'll get the horse!" Sabrina cried.

"Sabrina, no!" he commanded before turning around to face Gray Heron. He switched into Sioux. "She is my wife, Gray Heron. My wife."

"Your wife—my captive!" Gray Heron argued back angrily. "You are a captive now, Cougar-in-the-Night. You do not deserve a wife."

"Crazy Horse said that I should ride for her." He stared furiously at Gray Heron. Whatever happened, he didn't dare back down a step.

"Sloan! We have to get out of here!" Sabrina insisted, tugging at him, starting for his Indian pony again.

He didn't dare let her reach the horse. He caught her just before she could leap upon it. He lifted her slightly, holding her in his arms, close against his chest. "Sloan, what are you doing?" she whispered desperately. "We have to get out of here!"

He shook his head.

"Sloan, we can run—"

"Sabrina, there are *thousands* of Sioux and Cheyenne just beyond that hill over there. Thousands upon thousands. More than I have witnessed together in all my life."

"Oh, God, Sloan, the more reason we have to run! Sloan, you've just saved me from that man, taken me from him. Let's escape—"

"Sabrina! I was allowed to save you from him."

"Allowed?" she repeated. Then he saw in her eyes that she was beginning to understand that he was a prisoner himself. "Allowed? Oh, God, Sloan, please, think, do something, dear God . . ." Her voice trailed away as she looked at him, then came back in force. "I can't die now. Damn you, Sloan, put me down, I—"

"Sweet Jesu, Sabrina, don't you dare argue with me now!" he warned her angrily. She had to understand their position, he thought. He didn't dare display his fear; he could only show anger.

"Sloan, set me down, I—"

"Indeed. Madam . . ." He turned in a sudden fury, setting her down.

But she gasped aloud, staggering back against him.

More warriors had arrived on the scene. Dozens of them.

He felt her shivering.

"Just a fraction of my friends and family," he murmured, drawing her close against him so that his chin was just above her forehead and his arms were around her waist in a both defensive and protective gesture.

One of the warriors broke away from the others, riding forward.

"Silver Knife, a lieutenant to Crazy Horse," Sloan informed her softly.

"Oh, God, Sloan, what exactly is going on?" she asked, her voice rising as she nervously tried to pull free from him.

He pulled her back. "Sabrina, stop it!" he warned quietly. "The situation here is critical. I'm terribly sorry to disappoint you, for though I did my best to ride to your rescue like a knight in shining armor, I am, myself, a prisoner at this moment. It's only because one of Hawk's cousins saw that you were the woman in the party Gray Heron rode to attack that I was allowed to ride after him. Of course," he continued with a bitter edge, "what in God's name you're doing out here is far more than I can fathom! If we weren't in such dire trouble, I'd be tempted to take you over my knee for being so foolish and head-strong."

She was silent, trembling in his arms. Dear God, how he wished he could reassure her now.

Silver Knife spoke to him. "This matter must be decided between the two of you. Gray Heron thinks that you have no rights, that you are a traitor to our people. Crazy Horse, says, though, that you have never betrayed us, and that you have always helped our people. So the matter will be between you and Gray Heron, and the Great Mystery. We go back to the camp now, and the matter will be decided."

Sloan nodded to him. He lifted Sabrina up and set her atop the lathered horse he had raced across the plain in order to reach her. He quickly leapt up behind her.

They were instantly flanked by other Indians. "Where are we going?" Sabrina asked Sloan.

"Back to the camp."

They came upon the camp just over the rise. Sloan had yet to see it from this angle. It seemed to stretch forever.

Silver Knife came to a halt in the center of the camp, in front of a small tipi. It was empty, the home of a widower who had recently remarried and gone to his new wife's home.

Sloan leapt down from the horse and reached up for Sabrina. She set her hands on his shoulders and slid down before him. "You have to go in there," he told her.

"Alone?" she queried, her voice trembling.

He couldn't falter, and he couldn't allow her to do so.

Not while he was still breathing. "I'll be with you when the matter has been decided."

"What matter?" she asked.

He had to tell her something of the truth. "Gray Heron is not one of our band. He thinks that I should have been killed instead of taken prisoner, and he insists that because he found you, he has a right to you."

Sabrina gasped. He thought that she was going to fall.

"Stand up straight," he commanded her sharply. "Trust in me for once, my love. Will you do that, please?"

She stiffened; finding strength. She met his eyes and nodded. "Oh, God, how long—"

"Matters will be settled quickly," he assured her. "They know that Custer is out there somewhere, looking for them. They are looking for him as well. I'll be with you soon. Dammit, Sabrina, I've never seen you back down from anything in your life. You've sure as hell never backed down with me. Show those claws of yours. I'm well aware that you have them."

She pushed away from him, her shoulders squared and her head held high. She looked straight ahead as she walked into the tipi.

He longed to follow her; he knew that he could not.

With Silver Knife, Gray Heron, and an escort of warriors, he walked through the camp. They came to Sitting Bull's tipi. Many men entered with Sloan and Gray Heron.

Gray Heron spoke first, saying that he had killed the trappers because it was war, and the soldiers were out to find them. Custer, the Son of the Morning Star, was vowing to put an end to the hostilities. Gray Heron had not just a right but a duty to kill whites, and he had done so, and the woman was his.

Sloan argued simply that he was Sioux, and that Sabrina was his wife. And that she had no desire to go to Gray Heron. He never once let Gray Heron believe that he was fearful of being a soldier among his father's people.

Sitting Bull conferred with other chiefs. Cougar-in-the-Night was Sioux; no one denied that. Perhaps he had been captured before he'd had a chance to betray his people, but it didn't matter—he had never done so. In memory of his father, for his family, he had the same rights as any other man. They both wanted the woman. They would endure purification, and they would fight for her.

Sloan was allowed to go back to her, just briefly. With an escort.

He was amazed to see how late it had become as he walked back to the tipi where she waited under guard. He was guarded himself by two young warriors he didn't know. At least they didn't follow him as he slipped into the tipi.

Sabrina had been sitting. She sprang to her feet, racing the few steps to him. He reached out for her and he drew her to him very hard. He was terrified for her, and he could not let her see it. He was desperate to touch her as well, yet the savagery of his passionate kiss was tempered by a strange, wild sweetness. He couldn't let her go, couldn't have enough of holding her, feeling her in his arms, tasting her.

"Sloan, dear God, what's happening?" she whispered when he released her at last.

He kissed her again, deeply, his fingertips playing over her face, his hands cupping her breasts, sliding down her body.

"Sloan?"

Why had she come? he wondered. He wanted her—wanted her more than he wanted life. She stared at him so anxiously, and he smiled.

"Would you fight me?" he queried softly.

"What? No—"

"Ah, not here, not now! Not with all the Sioux Nation about to go to war."

"No, I would not fight you!"

"Pity, for we have no time!" he murmured dryly.

"No time? Sloan, please!"

He sighed. "This whole matter is an annoyance to the chiefs here, you see. The Sioux have been pushed very hard, and they are making a stand. Your party was attacked because the Sioux do not want their position betrayed before the fighting starts. Anyway, Gray Heron is adamant about having you, so it seems that I have to fight him for the privilege of keeping you as my wife."

"My God, Sloan, no!"

"Such faith!"

"He'll try to kill you—"

"Yes, well, that will be the point."

"Sloan, dear God, please, don't die, please, don't die!"

"I'll do my best," he promised. "Listen to me, Sabrina. Whatever happens now, you're safe for the time being. Warriors don't—" He hesitated, then shrugged his shoulders. "They don't copulate before battle. God knows exactly when this battle will take place, but it will be terrible. Sioux braves believe that being with a woman will make them unpure for the fighting. In the event that something happens to me, you'll have time to get someone to take you to Crazy Horse. He'll be honor-bound to protect you because of our friendship in the past."

"Sloan, stop, dear God, please—" she begged him.

He couldn't bear this. His fingers tightened upon her shoulders. "What the hell are you doing out here anyway?" he demanded furiously. "I told you never to leave the fort without me again. I warned you—"

"I came to find you!" she protested desperately. "I came to find you because a Crow spy told a soldier at the fort that you were no longer safe from the Sioux, that they would kill you if they felt threatened. You weren't trusted going back and forth between two worlds. I had to find you—"

"Why?" he demanded bluntly. "Why?" he repeated raggedly. "We'd both know you were lying if you were to tell me there haven't been a good half-dozen times in the past year when you wouldn't have gladly seen me as a pincushion for Sioux arrows.''

''Sloan, I was trying to tell you—''

He pulled away from her suddenly; his ''escorts'' were coming for him. It was time to fight.

There was no more time to talk. ''It seems that I have to leave, my love. If I do return, I promise, I'll be expecting to hear a great deal from you.''

One of the braves took his arm; he shook off the touch. He drew Sabrina to him one last time; the force of his kiss was wickedly hard, yet he couldn't seem to control himself.

He heard a soft but steady drumbeat, heralding the fight. The chiefs did not want the drummers to alert a band of soldiers to their position.

He had to let her go. He did so, and took her hand, bowed over it, lightly breathed a kiss against her fingers. ''Until we meet again, my love,'' he murmured.

He turned to walk away, by his own willpower, without the restraining arms of those sent to guard him.

''Sloan!''

He was startled when she cried out, racing after him. He turned, frowning as he saw the tears streaming down her cheeks. She flung herself against his chest, and he held her again. ''You can't die!'' she told him quickly. ''Another reason why I came to find you is because I didn't expect you to be gone when I woke up the morning after . . . after . . . when I woke up that morning. I'd waited because I wanted to be really sure. I wanted to be past what the midwife told me was the dangerous time. I didn't want to disappoint you again after everything. I—''

His fingers pushed her hair back from her forehead. He tilted her chin upward.

''What are you saying, Sabrina?''

''You can't die. We're expecting a child again, Sloan.''

A high-pitched, keening war cry suddenly seemed to shatter the night. One of the braves came to Sloan.

''It's time!'' the warrior announced, taking Sloan by

the arm. Sloan didn't protest; he barely noticed.

He'd wanted a family. A family with her. A life together.

If he died, he thought, at least he would die now, knowing this. He would make sure that his family knew, and Sabrina and his child, would be safe.

He stared down at Sabrina, wishing he could tell her what it meant to him. But the second brave came around her, pulling her away from Sloan.

"Let her go! I will come with you," Sloan said.

The Sioux released her. Sloan started out. She started to run after him again, refusing to accept the fact that he would be taken away.

The brave who stopped her didn't hurt her; he just held her.

"Really?" Sloan asked her.

"Yes."

"You're quite certain."

She nodded. "That's why . . . I waited so long to tell you."

"When?"

"The baby will arrive in late November."

"Well," he murmured, trying to sound light and assured. "I should definitely be back by then. Go back to the tipi, Sabrina. For God's sake, keep yourself safe!" Then he walked away quickly. He shook off the brave who held him again, determined that he would walk to engage in his battle with Gray Heron completely on his own.

"Sloan!" she cried out again, her voice sounding strange and anguished.

He paused, then turned slowly. She stood very tall and very beautiful, with firelight glinting in her long, dark hair. She had come out here to find him, to warn him that he was in danger . . . to tell him about their child. And he suddenly realized that he had everything in life that was worth fighting for.

"My love, I will be back," he vowed.

He would be back; by God, he would be back.

He had to survive.

Because there was so much he was going to have to teach his son.

He would teach him about a proud people who had lived and fought and died upon the plain. And who would live, in a legend of bravery and courage, forever.

He would come back.

Because he loved her.

Twenty-one

Sabrina lost all sense of time. Remembering the past merely helped to make her feel more anxious.

She had been a fool to come here. She had realized far too late that she loved her husband.

And now, because of her foolishness, he risked his life.

She wondered how much longer she could bear waiting before she did lose her mind completely and go running out into the night, until a rain of arrows came flying after her or a bullet exploded into her back.

She was nearing that point when she realized that someone was coming to the tipi. She rose to her feet nervously before the fire, watching a woman duck as she entered the tipi and stood before her, staring at her, up and down.

She couldn't determine the woman's age, but her skin was honey-colored and flawless, and her hair was thick and long and beautifully dark in color. Even in her loose-fitting dress of beaded buckskin, the curves of her body were notably lush. Her face was lovely; her form was very sensual. Sabrina realized with a start that she had seen the woman before—in photographs with Sloan.

She felt herself shaking, and for once it wasn't with the jealousy that had so often made her furious with Sloan and caused her to behave foolishly.

Now she was shaking with fear, praying that this woman's sudden appearance didn't mean that Sloan was dead.

346

"So . . . you are his wife," the woman said.

Sabrina nodded, surprised that the woman spoke English so well.

Apparently, the Cheyenne easily read her mind, and smiled. "I learned your language long ago; white soldiers have been killing my people as long as I can remember. It is good to know the people killing you, good to know their ways. You can tell them why, when you kill in return."

Sabrina swallowed hard, wondering if the woman had come to kill her.

"Do you know me?" the woman asked.

"You're Earth Woman," Sabrina said.

The Cheyenne nodded, pleased. "We might have shared a husband," Earth Woman said.

Sabrina chose not to dispute her.

"But I wanted no more husbands; too many of mine had died. Cougar-in-the-Night had one foot in this world, but his other foot was firmly set into the world of the whites. Still, he is like a husband to me. You understand?"

"Yes," Sabrina said. She wondered if Sloan had actually been living with this woman since he had been taken by the Sioux. At that moment, it didn't matter in the least. "I understand. Please, tell me, is he . . . is he . . . ?"

"He is not dead—yet. A lot happens before such a fight commences. I did not come to tell you bad things. I came to see you. I came to see the woman he has taken as such a special wife that he no longer wishes to take warmth from me."

For several seconds, the woman's words left Sabrina somewhat confused. Then she started trembling again, realizing that Earth Woman was telling her that even here, even as a captive, when he might die soon, Sloan had been a loyal husband. To her.

She was going to fall, she thought. To her surprise, the Cheyenne woman came to her side and supported her as she sank down to sit on the ground, her knees suddenly too wobbly to hold her.

"Now, he is my friend, yes?" Earth Woman said to her. "He is like my brother, and you are then my sister. I will come back to you. Don't be afraid."

Earth Woman rose.

"Wait, don't leave!" Sabrina implored her.

Earth Woman paused, smiling. "There are many ceremonies tonight in the different camps of the different tribes. The matter with your husband must be solved. I will come back and see you again."

With that, the woman left. Sabrina found the strength to make it back to her feet again, running after her. When she started out of the tipi, however, she discovered that two warriors guarded her, and they didn't look happy about the task.

She returned to the tipi. Earth Woman had told her that Sloan was still alive. She had to pray that he remained so—and try very hard not to cause more trouble . . .

Even as fear gnawed away at her every sense of reason.

Sloan walked into the night, striding through a vast sea of tipis and people. And he came at last to a clearing before one of the largest tipis, used frequently for councils among the chiefs.

Sitting Bull was there, along with Crazy Horse, He Dog, and many other noble warriors. He saw his cousin, Tall Man, who would watch all the proceedings, to remind them that Sloan was among his people. The Sioux could be hard, as prejudiced as the whites. But they could be just, and far more often than the whites, it often seemed, they could be honorable as well. The fight would be fair, and its outcome would be respected.

A space had been cleared.

And in that space, Gray Heron waited.

He gestured at Sloan.

"Half-breed, for you, it is a good night to die!"

Sloan smiled, rising in a sudden fury to the challenge. He had, after all, been raised Sioux.

"Today is a good day to die," he replied to Gray Heron. It was the Sioux way of saying that he wasn't afraid to fight; he welcomed the battle.

A shaman came up behind each man. Sloan was drawn back into a tipi, where he sat very still, listening as the Indian priest intoned the help of the Great Mystery as he went into battle. He was aware that his family had insisted he be given the same prayers and respect as his enemy.

The rest of his clothing was taken. He washed and was covered with bear grease for the fight, and given a breech-clout to wear for the battle. Finally, the time came.

Gray Heron was a formidable opponent. He was a young warrior with a reputation for having fought soldiers and Sioux, for having counted coup many times in battle. He was muscled like an ox. While some of the Indian people might have suffered hunger, Gray Heron had not. He wasn't as tall as Sloan, but he was heavier, very solidly built. He was cunning and brave. Sloan didn't lack confidence in his own abilities; he just knew that he would have to use everything he had learned in both worlds to best his enemy. He couldn't grow careless.

It was late. Stars dotted the heavens. A fire burned in the center of the clearing as many warriors of the camp watched and waited.

Sloan was given a knife, as was Gray Heron. Before the fight could begin, he asked permission to speak with Crazy Horse.

Crazy Horse agreed, and Sloan was granted a few minutes of privacy with the powerful warrior who had once been his close friend.

"My wife is expecting my son. I believe that Wakan-tanka will fight with me, and that I will win. But if I die, I beg you to intercede and see that she is returned to her sister, Hawk's wife, with my unborn babe."

"Gray Heron will demand her."

"I chose the way of my mother's father when my father

died; I have served the white army. But I have served you
and my father's people honestly at all times. I have never
lied or cringed beneath the anger of the Sioux—or the
whites. If I am killed, I ask that you challenge Gray Heron
in my honor, to win my wife and son for my people.''

Crazy Horse nodded solemnly after a moment. That
was all. It was all Sloan needed.

The chanting began, soft at first, then growing louder.
It was time to fight.

Sitting Bull said that no man needed to die; the matter
could be decided by strength alone.

But the way that Gray Heron was staring at him, Sloan
knew that only death would appease his opponent.

Gray Heron made the first lunge, coming after him.

Sloan veered. Thanks to the bear grease that covered
him, Gray Heron's first angry attack merely brought him
hurtling by. Gray Heron held his knife in his teeth then,
balancing back and forth on his feet, gesturing for Sloan
to come to him.

Sloan circled the man warily. He held his own knife in
his right hand. He baited Gray Heron, waiting.

A warrior cried out, calling him a woman for not leaping forward. Gray Heron seemed pleased, calling out
names himself. Sloan smiled. When Gray Heron became
angry again and leapt for him once more, Sloan stepped
to the side and slashed his opponent's right arm.

Blood gushed from the wound. Gray Heron grabbed his
arm, staring at Sloan, his lips tightening against his bronze
and blue-painted face.

This time when he attacked, he caught Sloan in the ribs
with the blade of his knife, and Sloan felt the warm trickle
of his own blood.

Gray Heron saw that he was weakened. He made a
flying attack that brought them both down to the ground.
He straddled Sloan, trying to slash his throat.

Sloan gritted his teeth, fighting both the bear grease and
his enemy's strength as he tried to keep the sharp blade
from connecting with his jugular. He bucked and managed

to dislodge Gray Heron. He rolled on the ground and then kicked furiously, sending Gray Heron flying across the clearing. Gray Heron fell hard.

Sloan leaped to his feet.

Gray Heron scrambled up. Ducking his head, he ran across the clearing, butting Sloan in the abdomen. Sloan fell back, but Gray Heron grappled with him. Sloan brought his knife against his opponent's neck. Gray Heron slashed his left arm. Deeply. Sloan felt the ooze of blood. Straining for power, Sloan slipped free from his enemy and slammèd both fists down on the back of Gray Heron's head. His opponent staggered to his knees, gasping for breath. He didn't rise. Sloan waited. He started to walk over to Sitting Bull, who had not wanted a warrior killed when they would soon go to war against the soldiers.

But as he walked, Gray Heron came to his feet and dashed after Sloan, his knife raised.

Sloan turned. He couldn't entirely deflect the blow, but the knife slashed across his shoulder instead of stabbing his back. He was growing weaker, he realized.

Loss of blood.

Gray Heron was gasping for breath as well. A few feet from Sloan, he quickly raised his knife, ready to make a flying attack once again. Sloan took the offensive that time, slamming into Gray Heron with such a force that the man was thrown off his feet. Sloan jumped down on him then, straddling him and setting the edge of his blade against Gray Heron's throat.

"It's done!" he cried in Sioux. "Sitting Bull says that you will live to fight another day. My wife is mine!"

It was all he dared say. The world was blurring on him. He was going to pass out soon. He had to be declared the winner.

Gray Heron didn't move.

Sloan staggered to his feet, walking toward Sitting Bull. He sensed sudden motion behind him.

Instinct caused him to spin around and step aside at the same time.

Gray Heron, who had risen to throw himself against Sloan with the force and impetus of his own weight, went flying down to the ground instead.

Sloan heard a strange crackling sound as Gray Heron connected hard with the earth. He winced slightly, despite the fact that Gray Heron had intended to murder him by stabbing him in the back.

He didn't really need to look at the man to know that he had hurled himself forward with such great strength that he had broken his neck when Sloan's body hadn't been there to break his fall. Still, it had been his fight, and he walked to where Gray Heron lay, rolling the Indian over. Gray Heron stared sightlessly into the night, a thin trickle of blood escaping from his lips.

Sloan walked over to Sitting Bull. "I didn't need his death," he told the aging chief.

Sitting Bull, still very weak from his sacrifices in the Sun Dance, nodded. "You may go back to your wife, Cougar-in-the-Night. You may not leave our camp. There are white soldiers very near. Maybe they wish to talk. I believe they want a fight. If they want a fight, we will give them what they want. We have run before the whites many times. Now we will wait."

Sloan wanted to ask him how long they would wait. He wanted to know how long he would be a prisoner of his father's people.

He opened his mouth to talk, but no words came. He could feel the stickiness of his own blood against his skin.

His strength seemed suddenly to leave him.

He fell to his knees, and then to the ground.

Sabrina waited in agony, fingering the delicate locket that carried Sloan's image.

Earth Woman had come, and Earth Woman had gone. She hadn't returned.

And time seemed to go on forever.

Sabrina paced the confines of the tipi. At times, she felt herself shaking again, amazed at what she had learned from the Indian woman—that Sloan apparently thought enough of his marriage to remain loyal to her.

But then she felt again the rising terror that something had happened to him, and she began to pace again, damning Sloan for serving in the cavalry, for being Sioux, for being white—for having been at the Miner's Well the night they met.

But mostly, she damned herself, and the pride that had kept her from realizing from the very beginning that she had hated not him, but what had happened. Because he had attracted and compelled her from the very beginning, from that night when she had first seen him. She had known instinctively that she didn't want to fall in love with him because love with him would be deep, passionate—and frightening. It was very frightening to care too much, and not know what a man felt in return. Sloan was a half-breed in a battle-torn world. Life might have been much easier with a different man, or if she didn't love him. But she did. And none of that mattered now; what mattered was Sloan. Her petty arguments seemed so senseless now. If only he would live, and if only he would come back to her.

She damned herself a thousand times for ever coming after him—he wouldn't be in this situation if it weren't for her.

She spent hours hating the Sioux, and then hating the soldiers for hunting them so mercilessly.

Just when she thought that she would lose her mind completely, a brave stepped into the tipi. He was tall, young—a striking man. He stared at her a long moment, and she stared at him in return, terrified.

Then an Oglala she knew entered behind the tall man; it was Blade, Hawk's cousin. She ran to him in panic.

"Blade . . . please, tell me what's happened, tell me the truth. Oh, God, no, tell me that he's alive . . ." Her voice trailed as two warriors entered behind Blade, carrying a man.

She let out a scream of anguish, falling to her knees

beside the bloodied body of her husband as the warriors laid him down upon the skin bedding. She leaned over him, desperate to find out if he breathed, if a pulse still beat within his veins. She could find no breath at first, but Blade set a hand on her shoulder.

"He's alive, Sabrina. He's alive. His wounds look worse than they are."

She looked up at Blade, trying very hard to control her anguish and fear.

"May I have water, please? For his wounds. And if there is medicine . . . ?"

"A woman is bringing water and medicine."

"Thank you. Blade—"

"You're safe. Gray Heron is dead."

"Dear God, if—"

"There is no one who will seek revenge against Sloan. Gray Heron brought about his own death. He was fairly beaten twice, and would have stabbed your husband in the back. The fight was witnessed by many. You're safe here. For now."

She stared at him, worried about the fact that he had said, "for now."

Earth Woman came in then, bearing water, a small pot, and bandages. She came to her knees by Sloan's side and looked at Sabrina. "He needs two wives now," Earth Woman told her.

"I am grateful for his life," Sabrina said.

Earth Woman smiled. "Then you are a special wife," she said.

Sabrina turned around. Blade and the other warrior had left them. Earth Woman was already working on Sloan, cleaning his wounds. She followed Earth Woman's lead, cleaning his body to ascertain exactly where he was wounded.

"There's so much blood!" she whispered, a little desperately.

"So much blood that you can't see that small rivers may sometimes flood," Earth Woman told her. She smiled, bathing Sloan's chest and showing Sabrina that most of the blood came from a relatively small wound beneath his ribs.

The worst of his wounds was a gaping gash in his arm. "It should be stitched," she murmured.

She was surprised when Earth Woman left her suddenly. Alone with Sloan then, she felt tears form in her eyes. He was so still! She could scarcely see his chest rising and falling. So still, so pale. Stretched out on his back. She touched his face, thinking how deeply she loved his strong features. She loved the darkness of his eyes, which were closed to her now.

And she wondered if he would ever open them again.

She started suddenly, sensing someone and swinging around.

Earth Woman had returned to the tipi.

Sabrina tried to wipe her tears from her face. Earth Woman sank back down beside her.

"There is no shame in grief, fear—or love," Earth Woman told her. She smiled gently. "Don't let any white man tell you differently. Human Beings, as we call ourselves, do cry."

Sabrina nodded, silently thanking her. Earth Woman had gone for the necessary supplies to suture Sloan's arm. Sabrina had never been in a position to have to perform such a task before, but Earth Woman assured her that it was just like sewing—flesh. Earth Woman told her that the sutures she had were from a horse's tail, and that they would work well. Shaking, Sabrina managed to thread the needle Earth Woman gave her. She forced herself to quit trembling. Because she had to, she managed to suture the gash on Sloan's arm.

Earth Woman put a salve on the wounds. She told Sabrina that it was made from river mud and ground roots, and that it had cured many warriors.

Later, a medicine man arrived. Sabrina had far more faith in Earth Woman's help than in the strange ministrations of the medicine man, but the fact that he had come meant that the Sioux wanted Sloan to live, and so she was glad.

Finally, the medicine man left her, and Earth Woman rose, too.

"There is ceremonial dancing in our many camps. I will look among the warriors and see what I can see. There are many boys who will take a suicide oath tonight. They will vow that they will fight to the death when they join the battle against the whites. Listen, and you will hear. Keep Cougar-in-the-Night well. Perhaps they will move camp again in the morning."

"He won't be able to travel," Sabrina protested.

"Our wounded have always traveled," Earth Woman told her. She paused, kneeling down by Sloan again, touching his cheek. "He is stronger—stronger than white, stronger than Sioux. Strong enough to be both. I believe that the Great Mystery will be with him and guard him in this life."

Earth Woman rose again then, and left her as well. Sloan was in her care, and the best she could do for him was to stay by his side through the long hours of darkness that remained, keeping him cool and watching for fever, and praying that morning would find him still alive.

In the Wolf Mountains, there are high ridges known as the Crow's Nest. Some say it's because the Crow Indians found cover there while planning to steal Sioux horses. Others say that the ridges resemble the way that crows build their nests.

In the very early morning, Lieutenant Charles Varnum of the Seventh Cavalry came to the Crow's Nest with his Crow Indian scouts. They rested until daylight, then ascended a very high ridge and found themselves looking down into the vastness of the valley.

Varnum could see nothing himself, but the Crows pointed out a stand of trees and the river, and a clump that they claimed to be a group of ponies. The Crows told him, however, that he shouldn't look for horses; he should

*look for worms, and in so doing, Varnum saw the move-
ment at last and sent for Custer.*

*While Custer decided his next move, it was discovered
that a pack containing several boxes of hardtack had been
lost. When soldiers went to retrieve it, they found an Indian breaking into a box. They chased him but he escaped.*

*In the far distance, two Indian riders also discovered
the troops. Varnum and others chased the riders, but the
Indians managed to elude the soldiers and escape.*

*Custer split his men into three battalions, taking com-
mand of one himself—Companies C, E, F, I, and L—
approximately two hundred and twenty-five men. Major
Reno commanded Companies A, G, and M. Captain Benteen commanded Companies D, H, and K.*

*The troops of Captain Thomas McDougall had not
fallen in line quite as quickly as the others. They were
somewhat in disgrace, so they were assigned the task of
guarding the pack trains.*

*They were dismayed; it was not a noble job to have
been given. And still . . .*

Most of them lived.

*The troops rode, crossing the divide. Benteen was sent
with his companies to the left, across rugged terrain.
Reno's companies were sent across the creek.*

*Reno's men were the first to attack. They rode into the
Hunkpapa camp.*

*They didn't realize that the Indian encampment ex-
tended perhaps another three miles from that first circle
of tipis. They quickly began to discover their mistake . . .*

Twenty-two

*O*nce or twice during the night, Sabrina dozed.

Late in the morning, Earth Woman arrived, telling her that the camp would be moving and that she would return later to show her how to move Sloan.

Earth Woman left, and Sabrina anxiously bathed Sloan's forehead.

His eyes opened. They met hers. He stared at her for several long seconds.

"Sloan! Sloan, oh, God, Sloan, I'm here!" Anxiously, she bathed his head and face again, but his eyes had closed. She laid her head against his chest, trying not to sob. "Please, don't die, Sloan, I love you. Oh, God, please, I love you . . ."

But his eyes didn't flicker open again.

Sabrina was startled then by the heavy sound of gunfire. She leaped to her feet as Earth Woman came charging into the tipi.

"The soldiers have come. The warriors are grouping to fight them. We must get him on a travois and move quickly from this place."

Sabrina's first thought was that if soldiers had come, she was indeed safe. They would rescue her and Sloan.

But looking at Earth Woman, she realized that it was not so simple a matter. Battle was often quick and merciless, and she had never fooled herself into thinking that soldiers weren't capable of killing indiscriminately during a fight. They might not kill her, but they might readily kill Sloan. And if she cried out for help and the whites didn't kill her, the Indians might well do so.

Sloan remained in a deep sleep.

"Tell me what to do," she told Earth Woman.

In a matter of minutes, they had made a travois of tipi poles and skins, and between them, they pulled Sloan's body out of the tipi. Earth Woman directed her along the vast line of tipis and down along the water. "We go downstream, to the Cheyennes!" Earth Woman told her.

They came to a rise.

Looking back, Sabrina saw the soldiers as they came, riding hard into the village.

They shot at anything that moved.

"Come! Come!" Earth Woman urged her.

She watched an old man die; then she watched as Sioux warriors pulled a soldier from his horse and hacked him to pieces with their tomahawks. She was going to be sick or pass out. Women were killed; little children were shot.

Earth Woman tugged at her shoulder. "Come, come now!"

But as she stood watching, Sabrina saw the Indians recover from the initial attack. The warriors were gathering and falling in fury on the whites. As she watched, the soldiers were being forced back, and in her heart, she was deeply afraid. They had dismounted; they mounted again. They raced across the river.

She saw a soldier fall, and another go back for him. The fallen man reached up to take the stirrup of his friend's horse, so that he might be dragged through the water to the other side.

Just as they reached the embankment, an arrow struck the man in the back.

So very close to escaping . . .

He was dead.

Sabrina turned away.

* * *

Custer, working his way to a good crossing on the river, paused, planning to send a message to Captain Benteen, so that the captain could bring supplies and reinforcements as quickly as possible.

He gave the message to John Martin.

John Martin had not been in the country long. He had arrived as Giovanni Martini.

Custer rode into battle with his companies, and as he did so, he began to realize the enormous size and force of the camp he had come up against.

When Benteen received Custer's message, he had some difficulty understanding the words as repeated by John Martin. He wasn't sure where to find Custer, and he didn't know if Custer needed supplies from the pack train.

In his opinion, Custer was a glory hog.

Still, as he viewed the situation, he determined to press forward to Major Reno's position. He just saw Reno's column disappearing, and he followed them. If he reported his command to Major Reno, then Reno would become the commanding officer, responsible for the decisions.

But by now, the bulk of the warriors, Crazy Horse among them, had moved on from their vicious and deadly counterattack against Reno's troops.

They were moving against Custer and his men.

Aware that *people* were dying everywhere—Sioux, Cheyenne, and whites—Sabrina felt as if she were growing numb. She allowed Earth Woman to usher her along, trying to steel herself against the death and mayhem around her.

Warriors rushed around them. She heard them shouting.

"*Hoka hey, hoka hey!*"

"What are they saying?" Sabrina cried.

Earth Woman gazed at her as they struggled up a gully with the travois.

"They say that it's a good day to die," she told Sabrina solemnly.

* * *

Reno's troops were disorganized and shattered. Benteen's numbers gave them greater strength, and at last the pack train arrived. Troopers with no ammunition left for their carbines could fight again. Captain Weir's company was not among the troops, and Benteen asked about them.

Reno remained in a sad state of shock. In forming his lines, he had had his men dismount and mount, dismount and mount. Weir, he said, had moved down from the peak.

Weir and his company were suddenly coming back toward them. They reported that masses of Indians were following behind them. Desperately, the companies grouped together, firing to cover the retreat of Weir's men. They fell back, far back.

The Seventh Cavalry consisted of twelve companies.

The remnants of seven were grouped on the hill, now under the command of Captain Benteen.

They didn't know where Colonel Custer was with the remaining companies of the cavalry.

Reno was scarcely fit to command.

Benteen began to shout orders.

As best as Sabrina could reason, the fighting began sometime in the mid- to late afternoon.

Earth Woman led her far from the fighting, to a ravine where Sitting Bull had taken the women, children, old men, and the injured. The able-bodied among them erected small shelters made of bent willows as they listened to the sounds of shouting and gunfire in the distance.

The fighting seemed to last forever.

Sometime after darkness had fallen, Sloan's eyes opened again.

Sabrina managed to get him to sip some water and a hot gruel Earth Woman had made from jerky and turnips. By then, she was numb, aware only of the sounds of battle—and Sloan's precarious position.

Sloan began to burn with fever, and she ignored everything around them, trying to keep him cool. She heard whoops of victory and pleasure, and she was afraid.

At one point, a youth ran by Earth Woman where they waited in the wickiup. He held a blood-spattered scalp in his hands.

Sabrina was suddenly sick, sicker than she had been in her whole life.

Earth Woman steadied her.

"Men fight battles; women survive," Earth Woman told her. "Surviving is the hardest battle."

Sabrina wondered how many people would survive that day.

George Armstrong Custer had been many things: arrogant, outspoken, a braggart. He had also been a talented commander, brave and hard-working to a fault.

He could behave recklessly and foolishly.

But he had never been a fool.

His greatest mistake had been underestimating his enemies.

He fought to the last.

Separated from greater strength and numbers, he and his men made several courageous stands.

Some of his troops attempted to retreat and were cut down in small pockets.

At the end, his family and close friends were at his side. Tom Custer, Boston, his nephew, Autie Reed, Lieutenant Cooke. They fought valiantly. They came together, and they dug in as soldiers.

They fought together.

They sought glory together.

They died together.

On a distant knoll, Benteen, Reno, and their companies assumed that Custer had seen the great strength of their enemy and had attempted to join with Gibbon or Terry.

They thought themselves deserted. They'd ridden hard;

they'd had no sleep in almost three days, and they were in a desperate situation. They were bitter.

And they were afraid.

Night had come.

But they had no water, and no help was in sight.

And now they knew that thousands of Sioux and Cheyenne warriors were out there, perhaps just waiting for morning.

To kill them.

Sabrina knew that the warriors had been victorious, and that they had won a great battle against the whites.

The Sioux dead were raised on scaffolds. The Cheyenne were buried in crevices in the ravines.

The warriors took their toll upon the soldiers.

The women went out and did far worse.

Many women mourned their dead from the recent battle on the Rosebud. They took their vengeance out on the fallen white men. They hacked them with axes. They cut off their fingers, toes, heads, and feet. They slashed their arms.

Survivors feigning death did not last long, and yet, as quickly as they were dispatched, they died horribly.

Sabrina knew all of this because Earth Woman told her. By then, however, she couldn't even think, she was so numb. Sioux and Cheyenne had been killed, and so the wailing in the camp was loud and terrible. They were moving again, because the Sioux did not stay where their dead had died and been scaffolded. They would move just downriver, though. There were still soldiers out there.

There would be another fight, perhaps, in the morning. And the chiefs would meet. Some of the warriors were convinced that they had defeated Crook's troops. Others insisted that the soldiers were coming from many directions.

Sloan continued to suffer with fever. Earth Woman helped Sabrina to keep him cool through the night.

Sometime in the night, she fell asleep, exhausted from

two full days without any rest. She awoke to discover that she was alone.

She rose quickly, looking out of the wickiup, but she didn't see him. Earth Woman was coming toward the wickiup with coffee. She offered it to Sabrina, but Sabrina already felt tears welling in her eyes.

"Where is—"

"He has gone back to see the scene of the battle."

"Oh, dear God, Earth Woman, how do I get to him?"

"You should not."

"Please, I must."

Earth Woman hesitated. "There is more fighting—not where the carnage lies, but there is more fighting. When it finishes, the chiefs say that we will move again. We have won a great victory, but if more soldiers find us it will become defeat."

"Please, Earth Woman."

The Cheyenne hesitated, then called to a boy going by on a pony. She spoke to the boy, who nodded. He reached out with his hand. Sabrina quickly took his hand and mounted the pony behind him.

They rode for perhaps twenty minutes.

And they came upon a sea of bodies unlike anything Sabrina had ever imagined.

She had heard about the horror of what had been done. And still, oh, God . . .

A lone figure stood in the center of the carnage. The boy let Sabrina slip from his horse. She tried to keep from looking down at the ground as she made her way to Sloan. Tears spilled down her cheeks.

Ten feet behind him, she paused. "Sloan?" she said, whispering his name.

When he didn't turn, she went to him. She was afraid to touch him, and she walked around in front of him, still struggling to keep her eyes from the ground and the blood and gore and death that surrounded them.

For a moment, it seemed as if he still didn't see her. He looked like a Sioux warrior in his breechclout with his wounds, yet his flesh was ashen. His eyes were ebony dark against his pallor; his lips were gray.

"Sloan?" she repeated. Then she was gasping, and her tears were falling like a river. She would have fallen to her knees, except that she would have fallen on a corpse.

He moved at last, catching her by the shoulders, drawing her against him. He led her a few feet away, and they sank down together. He held her very close, trying to dry her tears, but then she realized that his cheeks were damp as well, and that he had been standing there, crying for his friends.

She looked where he looked, and saw a man who had fallen against his horse.

Custer.

The dead around him had been butchered. But he hadn't been. Only his ears were bloodied.

"The Cheyenne . . ." Sloan began. His voice gave. He swallowed and began again. "The Cheyenne counted him a cousin. They did not slash his arms; he will be able to fight in the next life. They poked holes in his ears so that he will hear better in the next life, and remember that he had promised never to make war on the Cheyenne again."

In the distance, they heard the muted sound of gunfire. Sloan staggered to his feet, drawing her up with him. She saw that he was listening to the gunfire. He looked at her face, then drew her against him again, trying to shield her from the scene of such horror, death, and disaster.

"This . . . is ungodly!" he whispered. "But dear God, I wish I could make you understand what has happened to the Sioux as well, to the children, to—"

"I saw women and children killed," she told him.

"So the whites are murderers, and the Sioux are murderers, and I am both," he said bitterly. "And I cannot make peace."

"But there were times when you did make peace. You have saved white lives and Sioux lives," she told him.

He drew away, looking at her. She was afraid, so afraid

of everything that surrounded them. She was so sorry. Sorry for the death.

Sloan inhaled on a shaky breath. "I see how they have fallen, and I try to imagine what they felt at the end. They knew they were fighting to the death, taking their last stand, yet, oh, God—" He broke off, then stared into her eyes. "I can't bear what happened here. I am in agony for these men, my friends. I lived with them, laughed with them, played baseball with them. . . . But still, God, I think that what happened here was the last great battle of the Indian wars, the last stand of the Sioux against the whites. Because there will be little sympathy for the Indians now. Much of the country was sick of the Indian wars and the cost of them, but now those people will want the army to destroy the heathens who have done this. What in God's name do we do?"

Sabrina felt the torment in him, the agony, the terrible anguish. She felt, too, the strength in him as he touched her. He was injured—surely, barely standing. And yet he would shield her still, even while his heart was breaking.

She took his face between her palms and prayed that they could both see one another, and nothing else.

"We survive," she told him. "Earth Woman told me that surviving is the hardest battle. We survive, and we forge a future."

He stared at her, his eyes darker than ebony.

And she was suddenly afraid that he might not care if he survived or not.

"I love you, Sloan!" she whispered. "Please, if there is a war you must wage, don't let that war be against me, or our child. The baby will be white—and Sioux. And he will survive, Sloan, and we will keep it all alive, and remember it, and work so that there is a future, and there is a hope for peace."

"What did you say?" he whispered.

"I said—"

But she didn't need to repeat herself. He drew her hard

against him, and she felt his body shaking, and she was afraid. But he drew away from her then.

"I love you. And I will survive." Touching her cheeks, he said, "Don't look at the bodies anymore; it will live with you forever as it is."

He led her from the scene of such monumental death and disaster. She found that a tall man seated silently and stoically on a paint horse waited for Sloan at the base of a hill. Sloan set her on the horse that stood alongside the man, and mounted behind her.

There was brief fighting that day between the Indians and the troops who remained under the command of Benteen and Reno. But the Indian council had decided that their people must move, and so they did. The survivors in Reno's company, still assuming themselves deserted by Custer, rejoiced. They were able to move to the river then, and after days of hard marching, incredible fighting, no sleep, and precious little food, they made coffee and a meal, and watched the great Indian retreat.

On June 27, General Terry and his troops received a report from their Indian scouts about the terrible battle that Custer had fought. General Terry's troops found the dead, mutilated men.

There would be inquiries and debates, and the debate would become legend, as would "Autie" Custer.

But first came the sad task of burial . . .

And then the most tragic task of all.

Telling the widows and children that their husbands and fathers would come home no more.

Sloan and Sabrina remained with the Sioux for another week; the Indians did not want Sloan to provide the soldiers with any information regarding their whereabouts.

Sloan recuperated slowly from his various wounds, lapsing now and then back into a fever. Sabrina was alternately glad that they hadn't made any attempt to ride back to reach the army, and anxious to have modern medical treatment for Sloan. But after seven days had passed, Tall Man came to tell them that the council had agreed that Cougar-in-the-Night and his woman were free to leave.

A three-day ride brought them to the Yellowstone, and to the steamer.

From friends aboard the steamer, Sabrina learned that Skylar had given birth to her baby, a boy, ten days earlier. She was sorry to have missed the birth, but she knew that Skylar would understand.

The following day, Sloan met with General Terry, and told him what he knew and what he had seen.

When he returned to Sabrina in their stateroom on the steamer, he was solemn.

Sabrina was upset.

"General Terry doesn't think that you were responsible in any way, does he? Oh, God, Sloan, after everything—"

She didn't finish her sentence because he took her face between his hands, and he kissed her. Very slowly, deeply. So slowly and deeply, in fact, that she felt herself stirred by that kiss. More than stirred . . .

Aroused.

They had been close during the past few weeks, but not intimate. Sloan's injuries and the memories of all that they had witnessed had kept them from making love.

But now . . .

Now that some time had passed, a healing of body and spirit had begun. Sloan would always bear the scars from his fight with Gray Heron; both of them would always bear inner scars as well, because no one could forget such a tragedy as what they had witnessed at Little Bighorn.

But now . . .

Oh, God. It seemed like a very long time. What just a kiss was doing to her. Still . . .

"Sloan, tell me—"

"You tell me. You said that you loved me."

"I do," she told him, smiling somewhat ruefully.

"Because I killed Gray Heron?"

She shook her head. "I loved you before you killed Gray Heron."

"When did you decide you loved me?" he challenged.

"I . . ."

"I can answer much better than that," he told her. "I decided I wanted you absolutely and desperately the first time we met. Remember?"

"It's difficult to forget."

"Good. It had better be. And in Scotland—you were so damned brave and determined and independent. I told myself that I had to have my child. That wasn't the whole truth. I had to have you, too."

"Really?" Sabrina breathed.

"Definitely. Then you lost the baby, and I was afraid that you were going to hate me. But it didn't matter. I wanted to try to be your husband, because I couldn't imagine not having you. And then when I saw you at Mayfair that night . . ."

"Yes?"

"Well, you were flirting most outrageously."

"I was not! I hadn't seen you in a very long time. And I had tried to convince myself that I did want an annulment."

"Because of my mixed blood?"

She shook her head. "Because I knew, deep in my heart, that I could fall so in love with you, I'd be desperate for you to love me in return. I knew that you wanted me, but I wanted you to love me. I was afraid, in so many ways."

"I think I knew that night at Mayfair that I was in love with you."

She smiled, and kissed his lips lightly and whispered against them, "I admit, I'm still offended that you thought I was a common whore the first night we met."

"I don't remember ever saying a thing about common."

She arched a brow and hesitated. "And I do admit to a wee bit of jealousy."

"Really?" he asked, pleased.

"It wasn't a nice experience!" she informed him indignantly.

"Well, you had no need to be jealous. I couldn't imagine touching anyone else . . . not since I touched you."

She shook her head. "Sloan, I love you, and I'm so grateful for you!"

He smoothed back her hair. "I adore you, Sabrina, and I promise, I will cherish you until the day I die."

She clung to him hungrily. Their clothing wound up quickly strewn.

He was passionate, urgent . . .

And so painstakingly tender! He kissed the length of her, it seemed, every single inch of flesh—her feet, her thighs, her breasts, and her lips. He was intimate as only he could be, and as the fever soared in her, she desperately sought to caress him as well. She stroked him with her hands, teased him with her tongue, and felt the intimate, wicked thrusts of his arousing touch in return. When they finally came together, they were both wild with desire for each other, and it seemed that a staggering climax seized them all but simultaneously, leaving them drenched but sated, and still, after all else, somewhat awed.

It was good just to lie beside him. And it was a miracle just to realize that they had survived, and that love had survived as well.

Yet Sabrina suddenly stirred against him. "You still didn't tell me about your interview with General Terry."

He hesitated a long while, then told her, "I'm resigning my commission."

"What? But you love—"

"No, I can't remain in the army now. I really believe that we're near the end of the Indian's reign on the plains, and I want—I want to do something else. And I pray that you'll help me."

"What?" she demanded, propped on an elbow.

"I want to build a house first. I own land. Right by Hawk's."

"A house sounds fine."

"Well, of course, we'll have to raise cattle or the like. We've both got money, but we want it to last."

She nodded. "I've nothing against cattle."

He stared at her. "And children. This baby—a dozen more, perhaps."

"I'm not sure about a dozen, but I'm incredibly happy about this baby and perhaps a few others."

He grinned.

"Actually, I want dozens and dozens of children."

"What—?"

"A school, Sabrina. I want to open a school. I want to teach the Sioux about the people who are overwhelming them, and I want to teach the whites about the Sioux. It's going to be an uphill battle . . ."

"The hardest you've ever fought," Sabrina assured him.

"Want to fight it with me?"

She curled happily into his arms. "I'll never let you go again," she promised him.

He kissed her, smiling.

And the vow was made.

Epilogue

Sloan walked up the slope to the great oak. The tree stood in a position of absolute dominance on the ridge that overlooked the valley where they'd built their home.

The house was beautiful and big. It had been designed with plenty of bedrooms upstairs. Their first baby, whom they had kept referring to as "he," was actually "they": twins, a boy and a girl, Zachary and Jill. And now, two years after those babies had been born, Sabrina was expecting again.

Looking down the hill, he could see his wife, and he smiled. She was just beginning to get round again.

She was setting glasses of lemonade on the table they'd set up outside. Skylar was talking with Sabrina as she worked, while Hawk was deeply engaged in conversation with Sloan's grandfather, who had decided to move west after realizing it was where his great-grandchildren were going to grow up.

It was a wonderfully domestic scene. His twins were on the ground, wrestling with their cousins, Joshua—now two and a half—and Kaitlin, who was barely toddling about. They were beautiful children. Exceptionally beautiful. Amazingly, Hawk's daughter was blond. Sloan's son had brilliant blue eyes with dark auburn hair, and his daughter had amber eyes, and her aunt's blond curls. In all of the children, their white blood seemed to predominate, but then . . . they each had a bit of Sioux blood evident in their physical appearances as well. They had strong, well-defined features. They encompassed the best of two worlds, he thought.

Which was what they had tried to give their children.

Today, they were learning new accents. David had come from Scotland with his wife, Shawna, and their family on a long-planned excursion to America, and they added to the mayhem on the lawn.

They had survived.

It hadn't always been easy.

The massacre of Custer and his troops had not been forgiven by the white world. There had been tremendous political upheaval, with everyone blaming everyone else for the fiasco and debating about who had meant what when orders had been given.

In November, after the battle, Colonel Raynald Mackenzie had won a decisive battle against the Plains Indians. More and more, the Indians were retiring to the reservations.

Crazy Horse had surrendered. He had said that he wanted the peace to last forever.

But he had later been arrested, and when he had seen the bars surrounding him, he had run out. He claimed himself worthless to his people because he could fight for them no more.

He was murdered by the Indian police, stabbed to death. He had seen the prophecy as a boy.

It was a sad end to a great warrior. Just as he had mourned Custer's loss, Sloan mourned the death of Crazy Horse as well.

Some Sioux bands had gone to Canada, preferring the White Mother, Queen Victoria, to the white government.

"Civilization" was moving into the Black Hills.

He and Sabrina had opened their school. They now had three new teachers and nearly a hundred students. They taught the children from the reservations, and they taught the children of the white settlers who would allow their children to come. There was a great deal of prejudice against them, and Sloan saw clearly that there still would be, for years to come. They knew that peace was the hardest battle, and they accepted it.

As he looked down at the scene below him, Sabrina suddenly looked up.

A smile lit up her face, and she set down the pitcher of lemonade and excused herself to Skylar.

She started to walk up the hill to Sloan.

It was a long walk, but he watched her come.

When she arrived, he wordlessly wrapped his arms around her. She glanced up at him, her eyes as lustrously blue and dazzling as ever.

''I love you,'' she told him.

He kissed her.

He'd been a warrior and a soldier.

And he had waged dozens of battles.

But it was love that had won him peace. And he would cherish his love, forever.

Unforgettable Romance from

Shannon Drake

"She knows how to tell a story
that captures the imagination"
Romantic Times

NO OTHER LOVE
78137-9/$6.50 US/$8.50 Can

NO OTHER WOMAN
78136-0/$6.50 US/$8.50 Can

NO OTHER MAN
77171-3/$5.99 US/$7.99 Can

BRANDED HEARTS
77170-5/$5.99 US/$6.99 Can

KNIGHT OF FIRE
77169-1/$5.99 US/$6.99 Can

BRIDE OF THE WIND
76353-2/$6.50 US/$8.50 Can

DAMSEL IN DISTRESS
76352-4/$6.50 US/$8.50 Can

Buy these books at your local bookstore or use this coupon for ordering:

Mail to: Avon Books, Dept BP, Box 767, Rte 2, Dresden, TN 38225   G
Please send me the book(s) I have checked above.
❏ My check or money order—no cash or CODs please—for $_____is enclosed (please
add $1.50 per order to cover postage and handling—Canadian residents add 7% GST). U.S.
residents make checks payable to Avon Books; Canada residents make checks payable to
Hearst Book Group of Canada.
❏ Charge my VISA/MC Acct#_____Exp Date_____
Minimum credit card order is two books or $7.50 (please add postage and handling
charge of $1.50 per order—Canadian residents add 7% GST). For faster service, call
1-800-762-0779. Prices and numbers are subject to change without notice. Please allow six to
eight weeks for delivery.
Name_____
Address_____
City_____State/Zip_____
Telephone No._____   SD 0497

America Loves Lindsey!

The Timeless Romances
of #1 Bestselling Author

Johanna Lindsey

KEEPER OF THE HEART	77493-3/$6.99 US/$8.99 Can
THE MAGIC OF YOU	75629-3/$5.99 US/$6.99 Can
ANGEL	75628-5/$6.99 US/$8.99 Can
PRISONER OF MY DESIRE	75627-7/$6.99 US/$8.99 Can
ONCE A PRINCESS	75625-0/$6.99 US/$8.99 Can
WARRIOR'S WOMAN	75301-4/$6.99 US/$8.99 Can
MAN OF MY DREAMS	75626-9/$6.99 US/$8.99 Can
SURRENDER MY LOVE	76256-0/$6.50 US/$7.50 Can
YOU BELONG TO ME	76258-7/$6.99 US/$8.99 Can
UNTIL FOREVER	76259-5/$6.50 US/$8.50 Can
LOVE ME FOREVER	72570-3/$6.99 US/$8.99 Can

And in Hardcover
SAY YOU LOVE ME

Buy these books at your local bookstore or use this coupon for ordering:

Mail to: Avon Books, Dept BP, Box 767, Rte 2, Dresden, TN 38225   F
Please send me the book(s) I have checked above.
❏ My check or money order—no cash or CODs please—for $_____is enclosed (please
add $1.50 per order to cover postage and handling—Canadian residents add 7% GST).
❏ Charge my VISA/MC Acct#_____Exp Date_____
Minimum credit card order is two books or $7.50 (please add postage and handling
charge of $1.50 per order—Canadian residents add 7% GST). For faster service, call
1-800-762-0779. Prices and numbers are subject to change without notice. Please allow six to
eight weeks for delivery.

Name_____
Address_____
City_____State/Zip_____
Telephone No._____   JLA 0197

America Loves Lindsey!

The Timeless Romances
of #1 Bestselling Author

Johanna Lindsey

GENTLE ROGUE	75302-2/$6.99 US/$8.99 Can
DEFY NOT THE HEART	75299-9/$6.99 US/$8.99 Can
SILVER ANGEL	75294-8/$6.50 US/$8.50 Can
TENDER REBEL	75086-4/$5.99 US/$7.99 Can
SECRET FIRE	75087-2/$6.99 US/$8.99 Can
HEARTS AFLAME	89982-5/$6.50 US/$8.50 Can
A HEART SO WILD	75084-8/$6.99 US/$8.99 Can
WHEN LOVE AWAITS	89739-3/$6.99 US/$8.99 Can
LOVE ONLY ONCE	89953-1/$6.50 US/$8.50 Can
BRAVE THE WILD WIND	89284-7/$6.50 US/$8.50 Can
A GENTLE FEUDING	87155-6/$5.99 US/$6.99 Can
HEART OF THUNDER	85118-0/$6.99 US/$8.99 Can
SO SPEAKS THE HEART	81471-4/$6.99 US/$8.99 Can
GLORIOUS ANGEL	84947-X/$6.99 US/$8.99 Can
PARADISE WILD	77651-0/$6.99 US/$8.99 Can
FIRES OF WINTER	75747-8/$6.99 US/$8.99 Can
A PIRATE'S LOVE	40048-0/$6.99 US/$8.99 Can
CAPTIVE BRIDE	01697-4/$6.99 US/$8.99 Can
TENDER IS THE STORM	89693-1/$6.50 US/$8.50 Can
SAVAGE THUNDER	75300-6/$6.99 US/$8.99 Can

Buy these books at your local bookstore or use this coupon for ordering:

....

Mail to: Avon Books, Dept BP, Box 767, Rte 2, Dresden, TN 38225   F
Please send me the book(s) I have checked above.
❏ My check or money order—no cash or CODs please—for $_____is enclosed (please
add $1.50 per order to cover postage and handling—Canadian residents add 7% GST).
❏ Charge my VISA/MC Acct#_____Exp Date_____
Minimum credit card order is two books or $7.50 (please add postage and handling
charge of $1.50 per order—Canadian residents add 7% GST). For faster service, call
1-800-762-0779. Prices and numbers are subject to change without notice. Please allow six to
eight weeks for delivery.

Name_____
Address_____
City_____State/Zip_____
Telephone No._____   JLB 0996

The WONDER of WOODIWISS

continues with the publication of
her newest novel in paperback—

FOREVER IN YOUR EMBRACE

☐ #77246-9
$6.50 U.S. ($7.50 Canada)

THE FLAME AND THE FLOWER

☐ #00525-5
$6.99 U.S. ($8.99 Canada)

THE WOLF AND THE DOVE

☐ #00778-9
$6.99 U.S. ($8.99 Canada)

SHANNA

☐ #38588-0
$6.99 U.S. ($8.99 Canada)

ASHES IN THE WIND

☐ #76984-0
$6.50 U.S. ($8.50 Canada)

A ROSE IN WINTER

☐ #84400-1
$6.99 U.S. ($8.99 Canada)

COME LOVE A STRANGER

☐ #89936-1
$6.99 U.S. ($8.99 Canada)

SO WORTHY MY LOVE

☐ #76148-3
$6.99 U.S. ($8.99 Canada)

Buy these books at your local bookstore or use this coupon for ordering:

Mail to: Avon Books, Dept BP, Box 767, Rte 2, Dresden, TN 38225   F
Please send me the book(s) I have checked above.
☐ My check or money order—no cash or CODs please—for $_____is enclosed (please
add $1.50 per order to cover postage and handling—Canadian residents add 7% GST).
☐ Charge my VISA/MC Acct#_____Exp Date_____
Minimum credit card order is two books or $7.50 (please add postage and handling
charge of $1.50 per order—Canadian residents add 7% GST). For faster service, call
1-800-762-0779. Prices and numbers are subject to change without notice. Please allow six to
eight weeks for delivery.

Name_____
Address_____
City_____State/Zip_____
Telephone No._____   WDW 0297